THE AFTERLIFE OF ALICE WATKINS

BOOK TWO

MATILDA SCOTNEY

The Afterlife of Alice Watkins: Book Two
ISBN: 978-0-6483191-3-9

Cover design by Beehive Book Design

For Wyn Howard
- A truly great lady

CHAPTER ONE _

Several days after Alice's return to Earth, Principal Ryan stood on the Significator's bridge, listening to his new second officer expound the virtues of her new communications array. For the last half-hour, Statesman Junnot had vigorously and enthusiastically presented to the bridge officers her research into enhanced frequency propagation and her early, promising trials with transmissions that exceeded previous velocity limitations.

Principal Ryan appreciated Junnot's zeal and expertise but communicating with anyone without good cause didn't interest him unless they happened to be a newly discovered alien civilisation. That offered a type of challenge in which technology seldom played a part, so he was glad when offered a distraction; a coded message from Principality One, a top priority link from the Office of the World Principal, for his eyes only.

He bowed to Statesman Junnot, promising not to be too long, knowing who called even before he sat in front of the registry to accept the link.

"Aunt Katya."

"Nephew."

"What have I done?" Principal Katya always addressed him as "nephew" when she perceived him in the wrong.

"You are flying about above my head in space dock a whole week, and I have not heard a single word from you. Are you too important for me now?"

"No, Aunt."

"Have you spoken to your mother?"

"Yes."

"Your sisters?"

"Yes, both, and the nieces."

"So, you leave your old auntie to last?"

"Auntie?"

"Yes, it's my new title."

"I called the first day we arrived, but you were in Cloisters, so I couldn't disturb you. I left a message."

"Humph, that was not a message for me. That was an official report on your passenger," Principal Katya snorted. "Very well, I forgive you. Are you coming to the Cotillion Ball?

No-one refused an invitation from the World Principal, no matter how close you were related. She disregarded his look of resignation.

"Yes, Aunt."

He would be there. He wouldn't dare do otherwise.

"Will I see you before then?"

"I'm going home for a couple of weeks, so possibly not until the day before the ball."

"Make sure that is what happens. I will be displeased

if you change those plans. Now, you look pale, Noah. You need proper nourishment—that space junk food is poisoning you."

"It's nutritionally balanced, Aunt. I'm not exactly starving."

"Alice showed us hamburgers," Principal Katya's face broke into a huge grin.

"Hamburgers?"

"Yes, where there is meat—she makes hamburgers, meat that is mashed and squashed flat and called patties. You put them in bread with lettuce and tomatoes and sauce. Far better than anything you can have on your ship."

She didn't paint a particularly appetising picture but eating, like communicating, carried only a nuisance factor for Noah Ryan, something performed from necessity, distracting him from other, more important tasks.

"Doubtless, you are correct, Aunt. I might stick to space junk poison. It would appear you and Dr Langley found much in common?"

"Yes, Noah, we loved having her here. She instructed us in ancient handicraft, even though she was to be on vacation. She gave generously of her time to teach us this crochet and show the chef hamburgers and sauce. She made many friends. Such a breath of fresh air through these musty old halls. I don't think she realised her impact on us all. Did you spend much time with her on the ship?"

"Me?" The question surprised him. "No, far too busy. I realised her scientific significance, of course, but with the ship in preparation for the Gravidarum modifications, the new mission, new second officer and countless other things demanding my attention, I didn't have time."

"Her scientific significance? Noah, she is a human being!"

Principal Katya pursed her lips in annoyance. Her nephew knew that face — time to wheedle himself out of her bad books.

"I only met her a couple of nights before we left Saturn Station, Aunt Katya. I paid little attention. We all got conned into dinner by Abel Hardy, and that was the first time I set eyes on her. Hardy didn't attend the dinner and didn't disclose her identity until later when he assigned her to the Significator for her return to Earth."

"Were you not astonished to learn her identity?"

Principal Katya knew better than to ask her nephew about feelings because he kept his carefully hidden, but even as she dismissed any likelihood of a response, his expression changed. He looked down, frowning, seeking to recapture a moment. She waited. A rare experience to see her no-nonsense nephew distracted and searching for words. When he found them, he didn't look up, just shook his head, his voice soft and reflective.

"I mentioned in my report to you she plays the piano, though I found that out quite by accident. I saw her late one night in the auditorium," then as an afterthought said, "her playing quite puts our resident pianist to shame!" He gave a short, breathy laugh, but his off-the-cuff comment lifted his expression, and Principal Katya smiled. "Then, when I confronted her, she seemed flustered and confused and said she wanted to return to her stateroom. She refused my offer to escort her. I didn't know what to make of it," he concluded, almost to himself, and lifted his shoulders a little as if consigning it to the too hard basket. It seemed to Principal Katya that he was still back in the auditorium, trying to make sense of it all.

"Why would you confront her, Noah?" Principal Katya asked, more sternly than she intended; her nephew was not known for his sensitivity. She didn't like the idea of the gentle, sweet Alice being terrified by him, but she softened her tone to match his unexpected reflection.

"Did she break one of your rules?"

"No!" His reply was too quick, too sharp, and he looked her right in the eye, giving her cause to wonder at his defensiveness. Again, a rare occurrence, her nephew was always measured in his replies.

"No, Aunt, she didn't. I heard her as I was passing and when I spoke to her, got the impression she wasn't sure why she was there. She wore a green dress and no shoes."

He'd added the last sentence without thinking and cursed himself as it left his lips, knowing full well his aunt would latch onto any self-indulgent thought and blow it out of proportion.

Principal Katya nodded sagely. A green dress, eh? He noticed her green dress? So, this girl had captivated not only Patrick but her nephew as well. She'd waited a long, long time for this. She saw the faintest of smiles on his lips before he pulled himself together.

"So, Noah, you paid her little attention then?"

"No, very little," came the rapid and dismissive reply. "But I'm glad you made a new friend."

"We all did. How fortunate are we that it was Alice

who woke and not a cryogenically frozen head onto which we had to graft a body!"

Ryan grinned. Perish the thought.

"I suppose she gave you blue hair too."

"Indeed. In Alice's time, this is what the stylish ladies did," Principal Katya lifted her chin. "It makes me feel distinguished and regal."

"Aunt, you are the most distinguished and regal person on the planet! You are the World Principal! What else would you expect?"

"Alice treated me as a friend and companion. As a contemporary. She is without guile or pretence; I believe we have become good friends."

"That's inevitable Aunt, everyone on Earth adores you."

"Humph," she sniffed, but his words pleased her because she loved the people too. "I am but a figurehead. The mantle of responsibility falls largely to Mellor and Evesham. The local principals generally answer to them now."

"Did Patrick come to see you?" he asked, changing the subject, mindful of the bridge meeting he needed to return to and hoping to avoid any more discussion about Dr Langley. "He went to the surface to see his family, but he only spent a few hours. He's already back on board."

"He came, but more to see Alice, I think. They went down to the waterhole to swim and then shot some arrows. They didn't come back for many hours."

Considering his earlier comment, she watched for a reaction, but there was none. He would not let his guard down again.

"They seem close," she continued, mischievously prodding for a change in expression, but his face remained typically blank. "I wonder if Patrick's days of breaking hearts are over."

"I doubt it," Ryan said, thinking first of Engineer McIntyre and then of Principal Hardy's concerns about Patrick. Perhaps those concerns were not as misplaced as Ryan first thought. He'd dismissed them initially, but maybe that was an error on his part. Patrick's habit of being reckless with female hearts and his romantic pursuits were of no interest to Ryan; they wouldn't be now if not for that tacit directive, the subject and his aunt's apparent fondness. Patrick was still under his command; he might have to ask him about his relationship with Dr Langley, just for neatness sake.

"Well, Noah, I promised Alice she should make her own decisions now. She has gone to her new home, with people to love and protect her; I greatly miss her presence here. Patrick will escort her to the Cotillion Ball, I am sure."

"Quite likely, Aunt Katya, but I must go. I was in a bridge meeting with Statesman Junnot when this top priority call came, demanding an immediate response."

"I can contact you by these methods whenever I choose Noah. As you say, I am World Principal. Who will tell me no?"

CHAPTER TWO _

Alice spent her first morning in her new home getting to know Mary and Jane, their huge slobbery dogs, a cat with half a tail and three beautiful horses who lived in the stables and paddock. The sounds of Australia filled her ears once more, crickets, magpies and even briefly, a kookaburra cackling in one of the tall gum trees.

Mary showed her to the beautiful room she and Jane prepared for her, much smaller than her suite at the Tabernacle but just as comfortably furnished with a large wooden bed, an ancient, triple-mirrored dressing table and a sofa. Mary suggested they go to the city if she wished for anything different or needed other furniture, but to Alice, the room felt cosy and homely, and she didn't want to change a thing. The floor was carpeted, with a soft and luxurious pile that Alice once saw in a shop. She once dreamed of having one for her own home instead of cold linoleum tiles. There were the usual nods to this century; a fancy shower, the never-get-cool bath, a laundry receptacle that made your clothes disappear and later deposited them in a flat pile on a shelf all clean and ready to hang in a closet.

"I love it, Auntie Mary. Thank you," she hugged Mary. "Absolutely no need to go shopping for furniture, and the view…" Alice looked out the window. The sun's rays bounced off the ocean, forming millions of diamond sparkles on the deep blue background, "…the view is spectacular!"

Mary laughed. "Wait till you see it at night, Alice. It's amazing. The moonlight creates a staircase effect across the water."

But one feature in the room, Alice preferred to do without.

"Auntie Mary, do I need to have the registry in here?"

"Well, no," Mary said, not sure why a registry would be a problem. Registries featured in all households in some form. "I know you've made friends along the way, and I thought you might like privacy when they link. This unit is limited; you can use it for local information, weather, city info, and communication. We have the full registry by the parlour. Don't you want it here?"

"You'll think I'm silly, but I don't like that…" she pointed to the blinking command light. "The registry in my room at the Tabernacle was communication only; it didn't have the responder icon."

Mary went to the registry, "I can take it out if you wish, but you can just do this…"

And she switched it off by flicking a beam beside the panel. Of course, a machine would have an off switch. The blinking stopped. This flicking movement hadn't worked previously for Alice; she always needed to wave her hands around as if casting a spell to get a response. Practice, she guessed.

"I didn't think of that. I'm not used to them yet. They couldn't turn off the registry on the principality ship because it was part of the ship's systems."

"That would be the case on the principality ships. We live in an age of technology, Alice; you'll get used to it in time."

Alice decided now might not be the best time to tell Mary why she didn't like the command light and that her first solo encounter with the registry on the principality ship resulted in her seeing her own grave.

Alice recognised few of the variety of dishes served for lunch, only that most were baked and vegetable-based. She tried a little of everything and found them mainly to her liking. Jane, the cook of the family, was happy with Alice's response.

Alice already decided that after Principal Katya's fondness for eating every couple of hours, she would take more care and not eat too many pastries; judging by this meal, the aunties took care with their diet, and she felt much relieved. At the Tabernacle, she always seemed to be sitting down to eat!

The aunties told her about their neighbours, the wildlife and landscape and painted for her a picture of paradise directly opposite Alice's earlier imaginings of the Calamities. Jane placed a portable registry in the centre of the table and displayed stunning areas perfect for walking and horse riding, places to collect wild berries and plants for use in the kitchen and an abundance of birdlife; there was even a sweep over the coastline showing shoals of fish.

Jane spoke quietly, contributing to the conversation in either single words or short, measured sentences. Mary told Alice that Jane suffered chemical gas burns to her throat and mouth many years before while on assignment to Saturn Station. Dr Clere's team saved her life, but at that time, they hadn't yet regrown a larynx, which left her with limited capacity in her speech. Jane and Mary appeared to find macabre humour in being left speechless, and the way they told it, it was funny, although Alice hesitated at laughing at another person's misfortune.

"It seems strange," she said out of the blue, amidst the giggling, "that such a technologically advanced culture would have these accidents. Statesman Patrick, the first officer on the Significator, told me his father was injured in the line of duty." Alice spoke with confidence, and Mary and Jane, not yet familiar with the subtleties of Alice's personality changes and believing her to be Alexis Langley, albeit with amnesia, viewed her comments as nothing out of the ordinary.

"Are there no safety protocols in place?" Alice continued. "How could anyone be placed in an environment in which a chemical fire could be a hazard? At the university, we had vacuous safety packs for that very reason."

Mary responded as if speaking to someone with at least a basic understanding of safety protocols. "The dampening *was* deployed, Alice, but Jane entered the area afterwards. That was the problem."

Meanwhile, Alice retreated to a previously undiscovered corner of her mind, observing and listening to herself speak on subjects of which she knew nothing. For a few moments more, they spoke of chemical burns, combustion, causes and effects and the resulting investigation into the fire before Alice drifted back.

As she reverted to her usual self, Mary saw the difference. Principal Katya told her that Alice was once a biochemist but had regained none of her memories, scientific or otherwise. The Principal also warned that, according to Dr Grossmith, there would be brief intervals when Alice would appear to 'shift' and the scientist within would take over. It seemed to Mary, she'd witnessed one of those intervals, but now, with Jane continuing the conversation about the chemical fire, she saw Alice was out of her depth. She steered them away from the subject, deciding she would explain to Jane later.

"Jane, Alice gave the chef at the Tabernacle cooking lessons."

"Really?" Anything to do with food preparation was close to Jane's heart.

"No, not really," Alice shook her head and waved her hand to dispense with any ideas she was an expert. "I showed him how to make hamburgers and gravy; that's all."

Jane picked up a portable registry and handed it to Mary.

"Registry, hamburgers," Mary said to the responder.

"Well?" Jane looked over Mary's shoulder and grinned at Alice.

"Display," Mary said, and the image sat out above the screen for them all to see.

It was the only entry for hamburgers, describing their

constitution and the method by which they might be cooked and served. The last part floored Alice.

'Entry attributable: Dr Alexis (Alice) Langley,' it read.

"I didn't invent hamburgers!" Alice protested.

"Yes, you did." Mary turned off the registry, still laughing at Alice's surprise. "We hadn't heard of them. Now I want to try them."

"I thought you might be vegetarians."

"We prefer," Jane said, "but meat is okay occasionally."

"You can make hamburgers without meat," Alice said. Michelle had made them a few times. "Hamburgers are the finished product; the meat part is called a pattie."

"But isn't it a meat-only dish? Can it be adapted?" The idea of a vegetarian version interested Mary and Jane.

"Yes, it can. In my time, we called them vegeburgers, and we made them out of chopped-up vegetables and breadcrumbs and an egg. I've never made them myself, but Jane could probably work it out."

Jane had made such dishes but never considered using breadcrumbs as an ingredient. These mixtures are called blindies, she told Alice. Small loaves with a potato base, which sounded exactly like potato cakes.

"Vegeburgers is a great name for them," Mary agreed. "We should try both types tomorrow. We would need to get the Providore, but if he came in the morning, we could take Alice to the city in the afternoon."

A Providore? Principal Katya mentioned a Providore, but she should have asked for more information. A butcher, maybe? Apparently, you didn't do food shopping in the city.

Thinking about it, she didn't see a supermarket or anything like one when she went with Principal Katya. The aunties saw her puzzlement and asked what she didn't understand.

"It's a whole new world," she said. "Providores? I have a lot to learn."

"The Providore is near the city; it's where we get provisions. We grow all our vegetables and fruit Alice, but anything else, we order from the Providore. We place a requirement via the registry, and it's delivered here."

"Can you just go there and select items?"

"No, some people are completely dependent on the Providore. I'm not sure they'd welcome people wandering around."

That night, alone for the first time on her first day, Alice sat at the window in her room. The moon reflected on the ocean exactly how Mary described it, like stepping stones made from moonlight. Millions of stars lit the sky, and a boobook owl called from somewhere in the distance. Contentment spread over her in warm waves, and she sighed, knowing Mary and Jane welcomed her and would share their home and life with her. Often throughout the day, she forgot to call them "Auntie", but other times, when she remembered, they smiled, as if having a unique title was important to them. Today was only her first day here, yet she felt blissfully at home.

Alice woke to the sound of cocks crowing, horses whinnying and birds singing. The blinds weren't automated, so when Alice raised them, the morning burst through in a blaze of glorious sunlight. The aunties were up and about on the verandah that overlooked the smallholding on the other side of the house. Dogs got underfoot, looking for scraps of breakfast.

"Good morning!"

Mary and Jane hugged and kissed her, their delight at her being here thrilling and humbling Alice. Home was never like this; even in her mother's house, she never felt welcome.

"You were right, Mary," Alice said when they were all seated at the table. "The view from my room at night is magical, but the view from here, over the pastures, is pretty special as well."

"Mary says you originally came from Principality 19?" Jane asked.

"We called it Australia, but yes."

"There are maps on the registry with the old names on them."

"There are," Mary nodded, "I think the old names say more about a place than simply a number. I feel we lost something when we denamed the countries."

Jane disagreed. "We gained things too, fewer borders. In your day, Alice, I believe citizens required a document to pass between countries. Is that right?"

"Yes, a passport. I didn't own one. I never travelled."

Jane looked at Alice. "You were born in Principality 19?" she said. "But you weren't found here, were you?"

"No, a country called China," Mary chimed in.

Jane nodded; yes, China, she learned that at school.

"From memory, I lived on the mainland of Australia," Alice explained, "near Brisbane, all my life, I never moved from there. Those are my memories."

"The memories of Alice Watkins?" Mary asked, hoping she wasn't treading in a too-sensitive area.

"You know about that?" Alice was surprised. "I planned to tell you everything. I'd never heard of Alexis Langley until Dr Grossmith told me that was the name found with me in the cave."

"We only know what Principal Katya told us; that you hold the memories of an unschooled, middle-aged grandmother."

Alice nodded, she'd had this conversation before, but it sounded strange to hear it put like that.

"I told Principal Hardy, on Saturn Station, that I don't believe I'm Alexis Langley, regardless of the so-called 'proof' and my appearance. I told him they'd mixed up the labels. I don't know what he did with that information, but as time passes, it seems less and less likely I'm Alice Watkins either. It's just she's the only one I remember."

There was a sudden silence, and they both looked at her wide-eyed, then they laughed and laughed. So much so Alice laughed at their laughter before realising, as they had, what an absurd situation if, after centuries of hope and expectations, that the labels really were mixed up. Instead of a super-duper scientist, they got a real-life, frumpy old housewife!

CHAPTER THREE _

Over the next few days, the two newly christened aunties and their recently acquired niece spent all their time together, chatting and educating Alice about her adopted society. Mary and Jane told her of the implications of choosing a path to the Calamities and tried to help her understand an ideology that eluded her—how a couple can go so far against convention and then get a clifftop house with a farm and gorgeous views?

One afternoon, they asked Alice for details of the society she remembered. Alice reminded them these memories were probably false. Still, they encouraged her, having decided it would not be constructive for her to have no past at all. It was not beyond the bounds of possibility some truths might be mingled in with the false and should not be discounted.

But Alice's world hadn't contained a great deal, and she knew little of anything beyond the four walls of her unit and the local shops. So, she told them about her baking and crochet and jam-making and television, even relating stories about the soap operas she watched. The discussion stretched late into the evening. Mary and Jane stayed wide awake, but Alice became too sleepy to continue the story and went to bed, leaving her aunties to peruse the registry for confirmation of the things she'd told them. They also stored up questions about their favourite soap characters to ask at breakfast the next morning. Alice was happy to oblige. Everything she related, the TV soaps, a coffee shop visit with Michelle or a barbeque at her house, a visit from Eliza and maybe a phone call now and then from Steven, covered the entire reach of her existence. She was surprised that the primitive life she once led was entertaining to others, even if it was a struggle to recall the events accurately.

High above them, nearer to the stars, Patrick flopped down beside Principal Ryan in the Significators officer's lounge.

"I swear, Ryan; I could sleep for a week."

"Problems?"

"Not really."

"So?"

"The core and Substance are in the same position, but having the extra Gravidarum collar seems to affect pitch."

"Pitch?"

"Only single word vocabulary tonight, Ryan? I was counting on something more constructive. Pitch as in sound."

"I know what you mean, Patrick. You have Engineer Oakes. He has A'khet Knowledge. What's his conclusion?"

"He believes it's the fabrication. I'm not so sure. I was specific in the formula, but when I sliced the cylinder's expansion chamber and deconstructed the overhanging flange, the noble metal housing displaced, and Substance didn't light."

Ryan raised one eyebrow at his first officer.

"I didn't attend engineering today because you didn't report any issues."

In return, Patrick cast him a disparaging look.

"I didn't 'attend' the bridge meeting today. Didn't that give you a clue?"

"I'm a planetary scientist, Patrick. I can't make intelligent conversation about Substance."

"You're the principal. Perhaps you should pretend." Patrick leaned back and closed his eyes, covering his face wearily with his hands.

"Patrick, you are a metallurgist and an engineer. You and your family designed most of the generators and housings for all the ships; moreover, you have A'khet knowledge. I can't pretend to know more than you." Principal Ryan paused, "Or are you just venting?"

"Just venting, I think, Ryan," he sighed, sitting up. "But an extra pair of hands would be good—if you and I can do the Albemarle equations for the navigational systems and wave forecasts, Oakes and the others can get into the portage cylinders. The ship's other systems can wait until the magnitude generators are aligned. I don't need your command codes for those. Besides, they aren't giving me grief right now." He rubbed his eyes. "It might just be my neurones that aren't firing."

"We'll get our new statesmen involved too; she's keen to view the nexus for the communications array. We'll both be there first thing. Many hands make light work."

Patrick rose from his seat, then hesitated.

"Is that a joke, Ryan?"

They'd been friends and colleagues for years, and the principal was not distinguished by his sense of humour. Ryan shrugged; he hadn't intended a pun.

Patrick clapped him on the shoulder and left him to his reports but instead, Ryan gazed at the blue Earth through the viewport. He should have asked Patrick about Dr Langley.

The following morning, the usual light-hearted discussions over breakfast on the verandah were interrupted by a link on the primary registry. Mary answered. It was Patrick. After the customary introductions, he asked for Alice.

"It's for you, Alice," Mary said. "Statesman Patrick."

Alice blushed, smiled her thanks, and disappeared inside. Jane drew Mary close to whisper,

"Statesman Patrick?"

Mary nodded, looking towards the door and keeping her voice low.

"He is the most spectacular-looking young man I have ever seen, Jane! And he's contacting Alice! I wonder why!"

"She's certainly very pretty. She mentioned Statesman Patrick before—from the ship."

They talked amongst themselves so they wouldn't overhear her conversation. They wanted Alice to feel truly at home and would afford her as much privacy as she wished.

"It's good to see you, Patrick," Alice said.

"It's good to see you too, Alice. Are you settling into

your new home? Mary Greer seems most agreeable."

"Yes, her wife is Jane, and I call them 'auntie'. I hesitated when Principal Katya suggested it, but she wanted me to make a family connection. I'm okay with it now, though I often forget and just say, Mary or Jane. It's as though I've come home, and I have a family now. I did fear being alone."

"Of course, Principal Katya has done well in finding your 'aunties'!"

"How are the engines?"

"Well, that's why I am contacting you. I may need to remain here on the ship a bit longer, and that would mean I might not get back until the Cotillion Ball."

"Hennessey mentioned a ball, I don't know what a Cotillion is, but he thought I would receive an invitation."

"We call it a Cotillion, a kind of formal dance. There are two each year, one in Spring and one in Autumn. Some people call them the Spring or Autumn Ball. You'll get a formal invitation, but Principal Katya suggested I mention it to you today when I told her I was contacting you. I want to be your escort."

"I'm nervous about going to a ball, Patrick."

"You'll be with me the entire time. Dr Grossmith always attends in Spring, Statesman Mellor, Principal Katya, the Hennessey's will be there this time as well, so there will be people you know."

"Alright, Patrick. Thank you. I'm sorry you can't get away. I would have loved to have shown you my new home."

"I might still, but I don't know when. I'll contact you

as often as I can. I won't have you forgetting me!"

"You're not easy to forget, Patrick."

He blew her a kiss before signing out, and Alice rejoined the aunties on the verandah.

"He seems nice," Mary adopted a conversational tone, trying to hide the fact she was dying to know more.

"Yes, he is nice," Alice agreed but chose not to offer any additional information.

But Mary would not let the matter drop.

"The link was from the principality ship. Did you meet him there?"

"Yes, he was the officer assigned to me."

The aunties exchanged looks; they simply had to have details!

"Oh, do tell, Alice!" Jane declared.

"Actually, there isn't too much *to* tell. Principal Hardy on Saturn Station wanted me to attend a dinner with officers from the Significator."

"And?"

"Principal Hardy couldn't go, and Statesman Patrick collected me from my quarters—I know you noticed his good looks," she added, grinning.

"Well, he *is* handsome," Mary grinned right back.

"I don't think I've ever met a more handsome young man in my life."

"Young man? He must be older than you?"

"Well, to my recollection, Auntie Mary—Alice Watkin's recollection, I'm sixty-five years old."

"Alice, do you honestly believe that? Have you seen yourself? You have glorious red hair, flawless skin, gorgeous green eyes and a stunning figure!"

"I can't explain it."

Alice liked the compliment. In her old life, praise didn't come her way too often.

"Statesman Patrick," Jane couldn't contain her curiosity. "Come on, tell us more."

Alice related most of the story of meeting Principal Ryan and Statesman Hennessey and Statesman Patrick and the concert, leaving out the embarrassing part. She didn't mention playing the piano.

"I remember a Statesman Patrick once assigned to Principal Hallam," Jane said. "This must be his son."

Alice nodded.

"He told me his father was assigned to the Tabernacle a long time ago."

"Why is he contacting you now?"

"There's a dance at the Tabernacle. Patrick wants to take me, but I've never been to a dance."

"A Cotillion!" Jane and Mary cried in unison.

"How lovely!" Jane fetched the portable registry.

"You must have a ball gown," Mary said, barely able to contain her glee. "We can all have a hand in designing it. Will we get to meet Statesman Patrick then?"

"I don't think so, Mary. He's working. I expect I'll meet him at the Tabernacle."

"When is the ball?"

"Soon, I'm not sure exactly. Patrick said Principal Katya would invite me formally."

"Well, we should go to the tailor and get your dress ready and select your accessories."

But the expression on Alice's face set a dampener on Mary's delight.

"You don't seem excited, Alice?"

Alice looked out across the beautiful lawn. The flowers were stunning in their variety of golds and reds. A duck with ducklings waddled around the side of the house, ignoring the barking dog that made pouncing movements at them but not doing any harm. Alice didn't want to go anywhere. She was home now.

"I don't usually socialise, Auntie Mary. I'm awkward in company."

"Alice, you have a young man who is interested in you, the World Principal is your friend, you've dined with senior officers from a principality ship and embraced us and your new life with open arms. You may value privacy, but you are a friendly young girl."

"I'm nervous about being in a room full of people who are principals and councilmen who travel through the stars and run the world. I love that I've learned so much and can retain information, but now and then, I do things which remind me of my lack of education; before all this happened."

"I don't know where this is coming from, Alice," Mary sat next to her, placing her hand on her arm, her voice gentle, motherly. "Saturn Station has at least five hundred people in residence at any one time, not including patients. The principality ship, over three-thousand, eight-hundred crew. The Tabernacle itself is home to more than fifteen-hundred live-in staff. You have called all those places home over the last few months."

Alice understood, but she didn't meet all of those people.

"I was protected somewhat, Mary. I barely spoke to anyone on Saturn Station, only Dr Grossmith and Kelly, my carer, and the library staff. I hardly ever saw Dr Clere. There were conversations and afternoon teas with Principal Hardy and Educator Sebel, with whom I made friends and, of course, Statesman Patrick. I can't think of anyone else except for Principal Katya and Statesman Mellor, and Sarah, who drew the lovely picture you hung in the parlour for me, and the chef and the people who did the crochet group."

"Only and only?" Mary didn't realise Alice had gained so many acquaintances. "All these people, Alice, quite a few to accumulate in such a short time, I might add, would never have judged you as a suitable friend based on your education. I hope we are far more enlightened than that."

"I don't know if they noticed, Mary. They all expected Alexis Langley but forgave me when they realised I wasn't."

"You have succeeded in making many friends on your journey," Mary gently tucked Alice's hair away from her shoulders, just as a mother would a child. "Whoever you are, you are well-loved. Hold your head up. Don't be afraid or ashamed to embrace life."

Alice still expressed misgivings about the ball the following morning, even trying to invent reasons she shouldn't attend. First, because she was sure she was leading Patrick on and secondly, because she couldn't imagine herself at such an event.

The aunties were having none of it. Faced with Alice's

anxieties, they designed a dress themselves and now, after breakfast, placed the portable registry in the centre of the table. They were determined she would go to the ball.

The dress the aunties designed reminded Alice of something her mother would have worn. She politely added her own opinions, modelling her ideas on a design she'd seen in her old life and thought beautiful. The aunties loved it, not noticing Alice had systematically obliterated their concept of elegance. Designing such a beautiful garment helped lessen Alice's anxieties about attending.

Later that morning, Mary and Alice went to collect the goats congregating down in the forest. The two dogs and, oddly, the cat, always accompanied them on outings around the smallholding. Alice thought it hilarious the little cat with no name and half a tail controlled both dogs, cowering them into obedience with just a hiss when they became too boisterous. Watching their antics, a vague thought about Sammy, his wavy tail and his pale ginger tummy wandered unbidden through her mind. She loved Sammy of the one tooth. He was a dear companion. Perhaps that was why she dreamed up ginger hair.

They'd left Auntie Jane where she seemed happiest, in the kitchen. They'd talked so much over the last little while; she'd used up all her voice reserves and was trying to stay quiet and recover. It took effort for her to speak, employing her abdominal muscles to control airflow, and Alice was mightily impressed by the ability. Jane was a natural homemaker. Mary tended the animals, but the two could often be found laughing together, sharing chores, and caring for animals and plants. The goats provided milk, and Alice was shown milking stalls; fully automated and so goat friendly that the goats clamoured to enter, each receiving a scratchy massage along their backs as they were milked. Mary explained the massage relaxed the goats and increased milk production. She showed Alice where they made cheese from the goat's milk and stored it in an outdoor fridge. The fridge had no visible controls or cords, but otherwise, it was just like any walk-in fridge from her own time. Everything stored within was fresh and home produced, cheese, milk, fish…

"Do you like to fish, Alice?" Mary asked as they extricated the last of the happy goats from the stalls.

"You mean you actually go fishing?"

"Well, there's a pretty big ocean over there in case you hadn't noticed." Mary laughed and pointed toward the sea. "Of course, we fish. The salmon is superb, and one fish is enough for a month."

"I wouldn't mind trying," Alice smiled and, without thinking, added, "I've never been. My husband went occasionally, but he never brought anything home."

Mary let it go. Besides recounting her perceived past, Alice occasionally made random observations that she linked to her memories. Mary listened for any that might give her a clue that Alice remembered Alexis, but so far, none had eventuated.

"So, you would like to fish? Can you ride a horse?"

Alice shook her head.

"I have never even been this close to one."

"Later, we'll go to the city to visit the tailor for your

clothing standard. But right now, I'm going to give you a riding lesson!"

Alice wasn't sure. The horses were beautiful, but also very big. The dappled grey horse nudged her with his muzzle on the first day here and whinnied at her each time he saw her since. She liked to stroke his soft face and feed him apples. She pointed to him.

"He looks gentle. It's Jorrocks, isn't it?"

"Yes, I'll bridle him up for you."

Mary slipped a leather harness over Jorrocks's head. She indicated to Alice to stand on the mounting block and demonstrated how Alice should swing her leg across the horse's back to seat herself.

"Aren't we supposed to have saddles?"

"Only in antiquity, Alice. We ride without encumbrances apart from a simple bridle and reins."

Alice stepped up to the block and climbed on to Jorrocks's back. It seemed too high for comfort, and she sat rigid and afraid.

"It's okay, Alice," Mary stroked Jorrocks's neck. "He'll look after you, and I'm not going to let you go. Try to relax. Horses can sense tension in their riders."

"I can't relax," Alice spoke through teeth clenched in fear. "I don't like heights. What will he do if I can't relax?"

"Nothing," Mary soothed. "He's as gentle as a lamb. But he might not be the only horse you ever ride, and I want to ensure you get into good habits and become a confident rider."

Jorrocks stood patiently, merely turning his head when a goat walked by and looking up as the cat jumped up onto the stable door. Alice felt as if he knew she was a novice and allowed herself to relax a little.

Mary took a separate lead and mounted her horse, walking on slowly, Jorrocks following obediently. They walked at a slow, rhythmic pace and Alice's confidence grew.

Mary instructed her in guiding the horse with her knees, proper use of the reins to control and how to stop. Everything Mary told her to do made complete sense to Alice, and the riding lesson was over far too quickly. She felt an odd familiarity about the whole experience, and in turn, it surprised Mary that Alice proved such a capable horsewoman after only the most basic instruction.

At the end of the ride, with no hesitation and as if she'd carried out the movement hundreds of times before, Alice swung her leg over the horse's neck and slid to the ground. She didn't notice she hadn't been instructed in this, only enjoying the fact there wasn't even a twinge of arthritis in her hip. Mary watched her. It would seem Alexis Langley was no stranger to riding, even if Alice Watkins was a beginner.

Jane was on the verandah, waving her arms and pointing to Alice.

"You go ahead," Mary took the bridle from her. "I'll see to the horses. I can teach you how to rub them down and muck them out another time. I bet you can't wait!"

"I've never done it before," Alice called over her shoulder as she jogged to the house. "Every day, there's something new to learn."

At the house, Jane pointed to the registry.

"Principal Katya for you."

29

Alice sat down.

"Principal Katya! How lovely!"

"It is lovely to see you too, my dear. I have deliberately stayed away so you can settle in. Now I can't wait to see you again."

"I love it here, Principal Katya. I feel—I'm not sure…a sense of belonging, I suppose. I just had my first riding lesson!"

"A good place to begin your new life, eh?"

"A wonderful place to begin, with wonderful people."

Principal Katya saw Alice turn to look with affection at someone she herself couldn't see, but the gesture filled her with happiness and confidence she'd done the right thing.

"Now, I trust Patrick mentioned the Cotillion Ball?"

"He did, Principal Katya, but it was Statesman Hennessey who mentioned it first. He told me when he was at the Tabernacle."

"Did he now? Well, I make the formal invitations, and you must consider this as such. I believe Patrick will escort you?"

"Yes, he said he would."

Alice wanted to mention her anxiety about attending but knew it would fall on deaf ears. Principal Katya and the aunties had decided she was going and that—Alice knew with finality—would be that.

"Jane told me this afternoon you are off to the city to be outfitted. I wish I were there to go with you; there is a pasticium at the Calamities which is wonderful, with the most creative chef, I can tell you. You must go to that pasticium and none other. Jane knows it."

"I'll mention it to the aunties."

"So, you are accustomed to saying 'auntie' now?"

"At first, I felt a little awkward. My memories, well, some of my memories, put me roughly in the same age group. To say 'auntie' was a little odd, but it gives me a sense of familiarity, which I love. I still sometimes say Jane and Mary without the auntie, though."

"Your memories? I know of these, but we have never discussed them. Are they getting in the way?"

"Occasionally, Principal Katya, but other times, I simply live in the moment. As I said, I feel comfortable here."

"No-one will ask more of you than you are prepared or able to give, Alice. Of course, we all hope in time, your true memories return, but you are among friends and family. We all have your best interests at heart."

"I know, Principal Katya. And I'm very grateful."

"Well, we will see each other at the ball. I so look forward to seeing you again. Enjoy your visit to the tailor. You will be beautiful!"

Alice smiled. Sleeping Beauty was turning into Cinderella and going to a ball. A fairytale life, she mused.

Jane appeared in the doorway.

"Your formal invitation?"

"Yes, and instructions to go to a particular pasticium this afternoon. A creative chef, Principal Katya says."

"Not the same as homemade," she said and screwed up her face a little, pretending disapproval.

CHAPTER FOUR _

On the Significator, Principal Ryan and Statesman Junnot stood silent and expectant in the engine room. Along with the engineering crew, they'd spent most of the last two days, and in Patrick's and Oakes's case, the nights, working on unforeseen issues with the Gravidarum components. At last, Patrick scrambled his way out of the portage cylinder, followed by Oakes, their faces covered in huge grins.

"Ladies and gentlemen," Patrick announced grandly. "We have seen the light."

Statesman Junnot, still new to Principal Ryan's preference for formality, laughed and applauded but checked her enthusiasm when she found herself at the receiving end of a withering look.

"I don't think we'll have any more problems, Principal Ryan,' Patrick declared. "Thank you for your support. I don't need you further if you have things to do."

Ryan raised an eyebrow. "Thank you, *Principal* Patrick. I will return to my duties."

But Patrick had already turned back to the Gravidarum.

Principal Ryan was glad to get back on the bridge, out of overalls and in uniform. Patrick's skill in engineering was unmatched anywhere in the military, and while the Significator had him on board, Ryan was content to leave all engineering and magnitude issues to him. His only extra support this last couple of days was in attuning gravity contacts as Patrick aligned the Gravidarum, a task easily carried out by a junior engineer. Patrick entrusted the Gravidarum to only a few, so Ryan supposed he should be flattered.

They'd completed the Albemarle equations and wave forecasts, and Statesman Junnot delighted in getting in on the ground floor to see how the Gravidarum/Substance union would drive her communications spreaders. Watching her clambering over the Gravidarum, Ryan could easily see how she came to choose mountain climbing as her favourite pastime.

Patrick and Junnot joined him later on the bridge.

"Are you going to the surface, Principal Ryan?" Statesman Junnot asked.

"Tomorrow or the next day, I'm not sure, Junnot."

"I understand Principal Katya is your aunt?"

"Yes."

Patrick smiled at Junnot's attempts at familiarity. Ryan always resisted any overtures of friendliness. He didn't make small talk with the crew, not even with him, after decades of friendship.

"What about you, Patrick?"

"Me? Oh, I'm not going until the day of the ball. Too much to do in engineering still. I can't leave it all to Oakes."

"Yes, you can, Patrick." Principal Ryan didn't look at him.

"Ryan?"

"You are off duty for the next thirty-six hours. Get some rest."

"I can't, Ryan."

Principal Ryan turned and fixed him with a steely gaze.

"Really? After forty-eight hours on duty? The bottom line is, Statesman Patrick, I'm giving you a direct order."

Ryan's order took Patrick aback. He was pressed to recall a time when Ryan gave *anyone* a direct order. Ryan's strength as a leader stemmed from his confidence in his crew, his belief that a skilled crewmember should be allowed autonomy, and his faith that those abilities be employed to the highest degree that crewmember could offer. In turn, the crew remained loyal and disciplined, seldom giving cause for a reprimand or, as was the case right this moment, be issued a 'direct order', particularly one accompanied by an unyielding glare. And to his first officer of all people!

"Of course, Principal Ryan, I'll consider myself off duty as from now. I might go to the surface and see my mother and Dr Langley," he grinned at Junnot, "I guess you drew the short straw, Junnot, missing the Cotillion."

"Not in my book, Patrick. I'm entirely happy to be here, becoming acquainted with the ship. I can't dance anyway."

"Not much happens in space dock," he warned.

"It's my first command post. Probably best to be stationary. You trust me with your ship, don't you, Principal

Ryan?"

Ryan was deep in thought.

"Principal Ryan?" she repeated.

"I do apologise, Junnot," he turned to her. "What did you say?"

Junnot and Patrick exchanged looks.

"You trust me with your ship, Principal Ryan, at least in dry dock?"

"Yes, of course."

Then he turned and left the bridge, leaving both his officers to contemplate the suddenness of his departure.

The city tailor, far less imaginative than the one Alice met in Principality One, needed considerable direction in recreating her design. Jane wandered off, not much for shopping, and left Mary and Alice to deliberate, or in Alice's case, agonise over what colour would best suit. As usual, and as seemed fashionable, there were primarily the greys and blues and reds offered.

Alice recalled when her granddaughter Eliza attended her school dance. Her dress, a beautiful shade of blue, wouldn't suit Alice's colouring, but the design was exquisite, and it was this design she put to the tailor.

"But not in these colours," she held up the usual suspects and instead provided him with an alternative. "This colour," she said and took the beautiful pearls Patrick gave her from their case.

Mary gasped.

"Alice! These are superb! Where did you get them?"

"Statesman Patrick. He gave them to me before he

left the Tabernacle. A dress in this colour would be lovely."

The tailor imaged the pearls and advised he would produce samples for them to peruse within the hour. Satisfied, they went in search of Jane, waiting in the pasticium Principal Katya recommended.

"Alice chose a non-standard colour for her dress, Jane. The tailor sent us off while he sorts it out. The design looks even lovelier in the colour she selected."

"It was something my…" Alice started to say it was like something her granddaughter Eliza had worn. "…something I saw someone wear once. It wouldn't have suited me then, but it might now."

"Show Jane your pearls, Alice."

Alice opened the case, and Mary laid the pearls reverently over the back of her hand.

"My goodness!" Jane was every bit as astonished as Mary.

"Statesman Patrick gave them to her," Mary nodded her head slowly, her eyes wide and a hint of a knowing grin on her lips. "Did you know Alice, these are not available to everyone? Even in a society such as ours, there are certain, exclusive privileges. If Patrick is the Patrick we think he is, his family would be among the privileged few."

This news came as a surprise to Alice, "I didn't know. I thought everyone was equal."

"We *are* equal, but the source of true pearls no longer exists; the pearls on this necklace are ancient. We believe Statesman Patrick's mother is Elspeth Carmichael; she can trace her family to the monarchies of ancient times. If so, she would have owned the pearls under endowment. Their existence falls outside the Assignment Accord."

Patrick's ancestor's monarchs? It made sense in many ways, he had such a regal air about him, but it made Alice uncomfortable, knowing he'd given her such a rare gift. She didn't want to be beholden to him. She put the pearls back in their box and snapped the lid shut.

"His mother's family name is Carmichael, and you are both altogether too gleeful about him. He really is just a friend," she said lightly to cover her concern.

"Does he know that?" Jane gave her a sideways grin. "Rather a special gift for 'just a friend'."

Alice smiled mysteriously and looked at the registry,

"I will have some coffee and that…" she pointed to a cake, "with cream."

The tailor matched the colour perfectly. He constructed a registry image of the dress on a model with Alice's build and colouring. It looked good on the simulation, but Alice knew that simply putting on something pretty didn't change how you feel about yourself, so now she would have to work on her anxieties about the ball.

But that evening, to her dismay and after a wonderful day of shopping and horse riding, the blood came back. Alice wondered if she should ask Mary or Jane about sanitary towels; they were doctors, after all.

"You must never discuss your pudendals and bodily functions with anyone Alice, do you hear?"- Alice's mother.

Alice had visions of running out of panties again, so she asked Mary about the mechanics of cleaning clothes. She showed Alice a small room she hadn't seen before, with several box-shaped structures.

"Your room has its own washer parrulee, Alice. See here?" Mary pointed out a small oblong structure with a larger structure above, like an inverted 'T'.

"Anything you don't want or need to dispose of in your washer goes into here and on its entry into the parrulee—that's where Substance drives the mechanisms— it's disintegrated instantly. The upper part of the assembly takes anything you wish returned, cleans it and recycles it back to your washer."

"Our things never get mixed up?"

"Never."

Reassured she could get her panties clean and unwilling still to share her secret, Alice stuffed the soft disposable fibrelettes into her panties and prayed her period would be as short-lived as the first one.

Alice's anxiety about the ball grew as it drew closer, despite her best efforts to overcome her fears. Even a long link with Amelia failed to quell her anxiety.

"I bet you'll have a great time Alice. I wish I could see your dress. It sounds beautiful."

"It is lovely. I'm just afraid of making a fool of myself."

"I don't know why you think such things. Relax, you're among friends. If you feel a little overwhelmed, ask Patrick to walk outside with you."

"Where would that lead, I wonder?"

"Don't underestimate him, Alice. You've told him to take it easy. He'll respect your wishes, and I'm sure he just wants to show you off."

"That doesn't help, Amelia."

Amelia grinned.

"I have some good news," she said.

"Do you, what is it?"

"I've been assigned to Principality 19. I'm just across from you on the mainland. It would take me no time to visit."

Alice squealed with delight.

"Come! Now!"

"I'm not there yet. Three days. I wondered why I hadn't received orders, and it was because they wanted me at the school there, and the post was still assigned. It's very exciting."

"I'm happy for you. For me, too!"

"I have something else," Amelia turned uncharacteristically serious.

Alice waited. It wasn't like Amelia to lose buoyancy.

"Dr Clere checked in with me, you know, because of the kidneys. He asked about you."

"Did he? He seemed angry when I last spoke to him. I think I'm a disappointment to him."

"He referred to you as Dr Alexis Langley, but I pointed out you still call yourself Alice. He tut-tutted a bit. I just said you preferred to be known as Alice; then he said that with help, you would recover your memories. When I said, 'what help', he said he'd assembled a team of experts who wanted to study the aftereffects of successful cryo-revival."

Amelia's blonde curls bobbed about as she shook her

head; her expression was thoughtful and concerned.

"Don't doctors keep anything confidential in this century?" Alice said, until now, she'd forgotten her conversation with Principal Hardy back on Saturn Station regarding Clere's intentions. She wasn't overly happy at being reminded, even though she was grateful Amelia didn't keep the truth from her.

"What? No, no, of course not, you've been public domain for so long, they've lost sight of the fact you are now a person."

"They have also forgotten I was never in cryosleep. It was a different method altogether; I was never revived because I wasn't dead, and I was never frozen. Dr Clere is barking up the wrong tree."

"Good point. And one already made. Dr Grossmith and Principal Hardy are opposing him because, amongst other things, Clere is not a cryogenics expert. I know they've both placed objections with the Tabernacle."

"I won't be agreeing to anything anyway," Alice said defiantly, but she felt a flicker of fear, yet another discussion that should have included her.

CHAPTER FIVE _

Alice loved the early mornings. Despite so much being automated, there were still many things to occupy her. Machines didn't collect eggs, feed chickens or herd the goats for milking, nor could they cuddle a friendly dog or exercise a horse. These simple tasks in her daily life brought Alice immeasurable peace and pleasure.

One morning, first out of bed and already preparing breakfast, Alice saw an automatrans with military markings descend at the far end of the lawn. Walking out onto the verandah, she was surprised and delighted to see Patrick, out of regular uniform, hair flying free, shirt open and loose, jogging towards the house. Just like a film star, she thought, realising that had occurred to her before. As soon as he saw her, he waved.

"Alice!"

She waited for him to reach the steps, happy to see him but unprepared for a visit.

"Patrick, I didn't expect you until the ball."

"I'm afraid I was unceremoniously ordered off the ship by Principal Ryan."

"What on earth did you do?"

"Too much!" he laughed. "Ryan insisted I take a break, sensibly to be honest, so I slept for a few hours then came here to take you to meet my mother."

He stayed at the foot of the verandah steps, and she looked down at his hopeful face, silently willing her not to refuse, but given the history of the gift he'd given her, she hesitated.

"I'm not sure about meeting your mother, Patrick. I'm happy you're here but can't you just visit awhile and then go without me?"

"Not on your life, Alice."

He took the verandah steps in one stride, scooping her up in his arms and kissing her quickly on the forehead, depositing her back on her feet before she could protest.

She sighed; some display of affection was inevitable.

"Jane and Mary aren't up yet. They were out at the theatre last night, and I'm making breakfast. Can we at least have breakfast before we go?"

"We most certainly can; it's late at night at my home, so we have to wait a few hours anyway. I'll show you on the registry if you like?"

Alice showed him into the house, finger on her lips to warn him about making a noise and waking the aunties.

He sat in front of the registry and whispered a few coordinates to the responder.

"That's my home," he said and pointed to the image, then he pulled her down onto his knee to show her his 'house'. Seeing it, she forgot to wriggle from his grasp.

"That's not a house, Patrick. That's a castle!"

"A baronial hall, Alice, not too many castles these days. It's been in my mother's family for generations and not as grand as the registry illustrates. It's converted into apartments."

"Your mother is related to royalty, isn't she?"

"My mother is *descended* from royalty, Alice. We don't have royalty now."

Jane came out of the bedroom, and Alice wasn't quick enough in jumping up from Patrick's knee. Jane beamed at the sight of them together.

"Oh, Auntie Jane, this is Statesman Patrick," Alice's cheeks flushed as she got to her feet, pushing Patrick's hands from her waist. She looked on as Patrick reduced Auntie Jane to a quivering mass of girlishness, kissing her hand and bowing and making a fuss about her home and gardens. Alice knew how she felt; she'd experienced it herself the first time she met him. A few minutes later, Mary joined them, his effect on her no less entertaining. Whatever it was that could charm a woman married to another woman, well, Patrick had it in spades.

As expected, Patrick's cheerfulness and anecdotes made breakfast a jolly affair; the aunties were completely won over. Patrick told them of his plans to take Alice to visit his mother.

"Of course, you must go, Alice. Statesman Patrick's homeland is beautiful," Mary urged, not noticing Alice's reticence.

"I mentioned to Statesman Patrick," Alice knew her argument sounded weak, "that I would prefer to stay here today; his visit is a little unexpected."

"Oh, well, of course, whatever you say, I just thought it an opportunity for you to see something of your new world. We would love to know what you think."

For once, Patrick stayed quiet. Mary Greer was doing a better job of manipulating Alice than he could.

Alice knew when she was beaten and agreed. Patrick, unsurprisingly, was delighted.

"You'll love my mother, Alice. She's keen to meet you."

Oh, gosh, Alice thought.

Jane and Mary stood on the verandah as Patrick and Alice headed towards the automatrans.

"Did I speak out of turn, Jane?"

"You might have, I don't know. Alice didn't seem overly keen to go with him, but I'm not sure. She was sitting on his knee when I came out of the bedroom."

"Was she? Then there must be something more than just friendship. I wonder why she hedged about going? Perhaps it's her shyness. In future, I'll stay out of it."

Jane gave her a look that implied complete agreement. Mary huffed a sigh.

"She may not be ready. It's early days."

The automatrans was the swiftest of all vehicles available outside of a spacegoing vessel, and Alice had only travelled in the Tabernacle automatrans. Patrick told her military vehicles moved at hundreds of times the speed of the Tabernacle vehicles, but only out in proximal space and beyond. He explained that for most planet-wide trips, an automatrans reached a very low orbit before engaging limited magnitude. Destination coordinates were programmed. He showed her.

"It's as simple as using any registry, Alice. We are heading for Principality 17, so I select 17 and enter the coordinates, 03.53. If I didn't know the heading precisely, I would enter latitude and longitude and a gridline reference and a name. I did that today to make sure I landed in your garden," he added with a grin.

"It's very clever, Patrick. I came here on an automatrans. It was odd, speeding vertically away from Earth vertically. We left the Tabernacle in the evening and arrived here as the sun rose, but it took less than an hour. Mary said I'd get used to time zones the more I travel."

"You will. It will be early morning at my home, so we'll have two breakfasts today if that makes sense!"

"It's starting to, Patrick," she laughed. "I spend time on the registry, learning new things, but I always end up looking at buildings and history; they're my favourite subjects. The technology lessons aren't so interesting, and absorbing them isn't coming quite so easily."

"Give it time, Alice, have fun learning. If history and architecture are your interests, the registry doesn't offer as much as visiting the sites themselves. Our ability to travel quickly over long distances ensures the heritage of the world is easily available."

"I know, I'm just a bit nervous about exploring."

Despite Patrick's assurances his home was not as grand as the registry displayed, Alice had to disagree. It *was* grand.

Spectacularly grand. Alice thought of the little three bedroomed house where she grew up in Brisbane, dilapidated, old; she would never have taken someone like Patrick to see it. But this? She glanced up at him; he was gauging her reaction. He wanted her to like it. And she did. In fact, she loved it.

"It's *beautiful*, Patrick. I can't believe that something this ancient still exists."

Alice felt her new interest in architecture stirring as she took in the building's grey stone and square lines. Three stories high, the roof of the hall was adorned with small carved battlements. Alice guessed the original defensive battlements were probably damaged at one time in history and replaced with the more decorative but still aesthetically pleasing adornments. Half a dozen chimney stacks were set along the length of the hall, and every window was set back under a hooded arch, typical of Celtic architecture.

"There's been some changes to it through the ages, Patrick?"

"You noticed that?" he smiled. "Yes, this façade is as it would have appeared in the sixteenth century, although the surroundings would have been vastly different. The building's exterior is maintained carefully to preserve its appeal, but the rear of the hall has unfortunately succumbed to time and so has needed repair. Inside, we still have many of the original features, including the limestone fireplaces, which are enormous!"

"I recognise some of these styles from my studies on the registry. What's the history?"

"The entire estate was a bequest," he said. "A

Carmichael was mistress to one of the Stuart kings; she gave birth to a son, John, we believe the estate came into the family after the king declared himself Lord of Ireland. A few old documents suggest John used the surname Carmichael, but he died in his thirties. We don't know a lot about him."

"The hall must have seen so many changes, wars, famines, good times, families. If only it could talk!"

"Well, with my family, I'm not sure that would have been a good thing! But you're right; much has happened in history since it was built. The hall dates from the early sixteenth century at its foundations. The western side, where we live, is part of the original building. As you point out, there's a mix of styles because it's undergone extensive modernisation and renovation over the centuries—some just to stop it collapsing into a pile of rubble. There's a ruin of a castle built in the twelfth century in the grounds," he pointed further up the hill. "The estate was confiscated by the Roundheads in the seventeenth century. They burned and looted the castle, so it's just a few stones sticking out of the ground now. The Halla Barúin, this baronial hall," he inclined his head towards his home, "is all that's left. We don't know why they spared it."

It's beautiful," Alice said, and she meant it, glad now she'd agreed to come, feeling honoured to be invited to this stately home.

Patrick's mother lived in an apartment on one side; a second apartment accommodated his sister, along with her husband and son. The rest of the ancient building acted as halls of residence for aptitude students in agricultural sessions at the school. Considering the number of people residing here, it was surprisingly quiet and peaceful. The gardens were extensive and expertly tended. Besides a few birds, Alice saw no animals, not even a dog.

Elspeth, Patrick's charming and beautiful mother, welcomed her with warm enthusiasm. She'd been intrigued to meet the woman her son held in such high regard; he'd requested some of the Carmichael's legacy jewels to have fashioned into a necklace. And such an urgent request it had been! She'd longed for the day when her son's heart would be so captivated and had responded immediately to his plea, dispatching the precious gems to Principality One's city in all haste, leaving Elspeth curious and excited to learn about the mystery woman.

She insisted Alice use her Christian name and forget all the doctor/statesman nonsense. Patrick's sister, Eileen, as beautiful as her mother, greeted her with a hug. Eileen's husband, Corbin, a statesman to Principality 17, was every bit as welcoming as was their son, Edmund, handsome, confident and outgoing and six months from aptitudes.

Their apartment was only slightly less grand than the hall's exterior if she ignored the oak-panelled walls and chandeliers and the enormous balcony laid out for breakfast. Elspeth insisted Alice sit beside her and tell her "everything" about herself.

It hadn't occurred to Alice to ask Patrick if he'd said anything to his family, and for a moment, she couldn't think of anything to say. Instead, she looked at Patrick, an unspoken plea for help in her eyes.

"As I said, mother," he said, seeing Alice's hesitation,

"Alice and I met when she returned to Earth on the Significator after a considerable time on Saturn Station. She still has long-term amnesia, so 'everything' might be a tall order."

"That's all right, dear," his mother said. "Now Alice, I know you live in the Calamities in Principality 19. How are you finding it?"

Alice told them about the farm and the views and the animals and how the moon made steps across the sea. They asked questions about the aunties, not realising they were a new addition to Alice's life. Patrick's family were lively, engaging, and kind, just like Patrick.

After breakfast, Elspeth, Eileen, and Alice spent several hours looking through family history. They showed her a small portrait gallery that housed paintings of the Carmichael family as far back as Queen Elizabeth II's reign. Alice gazed at the miniature, painted likeness of the Queen she remembered and admired. She'd fashioned her own hairstyle on the Queen's in her old life. Her hand went up to her hair, absently winding a strand of her thick locks around her finger, lost for a moment back in time.

Corbin and Edmund excused themselves to go to work and school, respectively. Patrick's mother continued with a compelling history of both the hall and the Carmichael family, showing her a second, private gallery with earlier family paintings, all in original unrestored condition. There was even one of Cromwell. Eventually, Patrick turned up to lure her away.

"We have some interesting outbuildings as well, Alice. Walk with me?"

She looked at Elspeth.

"Yes, of course, off you go. I'm sure much of this history is invented anyway, dredged up from someone's imagination, I shouldn't wonder!"

"Is it made up, Patrick?" Alice said as he led her away. "It's fascinating."

"No, it's not made up, and Mother doesn't think so either, Alice. She enjoys talking to visitors and rather likes the idea of her ancestor being a loose woman!"

"I'm sure being a mistress to a king was something a woman aspired to, Patrick."

"Yes, but that king had heaps of consorts, although the way mother tells it, her ancestor was his only true love!"

"She's just a romantic."

"Talking of romantic, what do you think of this?"

They rounded the side of the house, and from where they stood, high on a hill, Alice looked down on a village set in rows along the green hillside, a small harbour with bobbing boats stretched out along the harbour wall. The houses were tiny, painted in different colours, and the roofs all made from shingle. It looked like a picture postcard.

Alice gazed on the scene with wonderment. "It's as though time stood still, Patrick," she said, "A glimpse into ancient history."

"I brought you to this spot because of your love of old buildings. In a way, time did stand still. The last wave of plague, the most aggressive wave four hundred years ago, wiped out this entire village and every person within fifty kilometres, every man, woman, and child, including some of my ancestors. The village lay abandoned for a hundred years, then the Seanad Éireann, a token government body at the time, preserved this and other landmarks of ancient Ireland. There was a fair amount of resistance to becoming a principality later on, but I don't believe we lost our individuality."

"Well, certainly, none of your family lost their accents."

He laughed.

"No, all cultures learn the language of their ancestors; you must have noticed Educator Sebel's accent?"

"She's French."

"Not now she's not, but she would speak her native language fluently and use it in conversation with her countrymen."

"Not principalitymen?"

"We still say, 'countrymen'."

"What about people from different principalities who marry and have children? What language would their child speak?"

"It depends on where they live. A child born here would learn Gaelic even if the father was from Principality 14, what you call France. If the roles were reversed, the child would speak French, but as a rule, a child will learn the language of both parents with standard English being the universal tongue."

Alice looked out to sea. The breeze whipped her hair about her face and billowed out her white blouse. She imagined, felt even, the history of this place, stretching back through the ages, full of the ghosts of peasant farmers, fishermen and nobility. Patrick watched her and willed himself not to reach out and encircle her in his arms. He'd already indulged himself enough today; he would not frighten her like he did at the Tabernacle.

"It's beautiful here, Patrick," she turned to him, her eyes shining. "Auntie Mary was right—even if it is a bit breezy!"

"Windswept suits you," he smiled, and she smiled back, not believing him for a moment.

"I've enjoyed this visit, Patrick. I'm glad I came."

"I'm glad too, but I must take you home soon."

He watched her for a moment as if he would say something more, and Alice wondered if he would try to hold her or kiss her, and she made to step back, but he kept a polite distance. When he didn't speak or take his eyes from her, she prompted him.

"Should we be leaving, Patrick?"

"Yes, yes, we should," he took her hand. 'I have to get back to the ship."

It wasn't true, but the nearness of her, seeing her in this setting, he was in danger of forgetting all his resolutions and making a pest of himself.

Back at the apartment, Alice caught sight of a portrait of a dark-haired man with startling blue eyes.

"My father," Patrick said.

"You look just like him."

"So I'm told."

It was easy to see where Patrick got his looks. The picture was under glass, and Alice moved closer to get a better look. As she studied his father's face, she saw a movement and briefly, the reflection of a pale, white-haired young man peering over her shoulder. Suddenly gripped by a sensation of bitter cold, she turned quickly and lost her balance. Patrick caught her as she stumbled. Concerned, he helped her to a seat. Alice thought to tell him about the face, but she'd seen it before, so there was no way it was anything to do with the portrait. Patrick knelt in front of her, holding her hands, rubbing them in his own to warm them.

"I can't believe my father still has that kind of effect on young women!"

Alice smiled weakly, "I'm not sure what happened there, Patrick. I thought I saw someone reflected in the glass, and then I felt faint."

"There's no-one else here, Alice, just us, but you went so pale, and your hands are freezing."

"Maybe best if you take me home."

He nodded, supporting her as she stood, staying close to her as she said goodbye to his mother and sister. The youth unsettled her. She didn't know why he kept appearing, and here of all places. She had no memory of anyone who looked like the youth and wondered if he was someone from Alexis Langley's past. If so, it might be a good thing, and she might remember him in time.

As the automatrans lifted, Elspeth turned to her daughter.

"Bhuel Eileen is é sin cailín álainn amháin," she said with a smile.

"I agree, mother, she is lovely, and it seems my brother has lost his heart."

"Finally!" his mother laughed and raised her eyes and arms to the heavens.

Patrick told the aunties about Alice's fainting spell, and they insisted she sit and take it easy, even though she'd recovered and would have preferred to take Jorrocks out for a ride, but she did as she was told.

"What was it like?" Mary said after Patrick left.

"Impressive, Auntie Mary. There is so much history there, and his family are lovely."

"Good, he's a nice man, Alice. I hope I didn't push you into going. Jane thought you were reluctant."

Alice shook her head; she'd felt easy and comfortable with Patrick today.

CHAPTER SIX _

In the few days before the ball, there were times, Alice knew, to feel brave, you had to act brave. The ball would be one of those times. Principal Katya suggested she arrive the night before and stay for a few days but warned her she might be in Cloisters and unavailable, expecting to have only a little free time in which they might do some exploring of the principality. Alice felt torn, she wanted to spend time with Principal Katya, but now she had a home where she felt safe and loved, she wouldn't want to stay away too long. But she also couldn't refuse Principal Katya, not after all she'd done for her, so Alice accepted the offer to stay, even though she would breathe a sigh of relief when the dreaded ball was over.

A Tabernacle shuttle arrived to collect her, piloted by Sarah's son, Peter, who gave her the welcome news Sarah would act as her steward during her time at the Tabernacle.

Principal Katya waited by the lake for the shuttle to arrive, holding out her arms in welcome to Alice when the exit hatch opened.

"Alice, my dear. I am so happy you are here," she

pulled Alice close to kiss her cheeks. It was good to see Principal Katya, and as they entered the great hall, to accept the warm greetings of Statesman Mellor and Statesman Evesham and the other councilmen she met during her stay here. Seeing them all again made much of her earlier nervousness evaporate, and it occurred to her, with some degree of contentment, she might have more than one home.

"Miss Ling will do your hair for you tomorrow, my dear," Principal Katya informed her. "I have instructed her to make it a little more dramatic for the dance."

"Dramatic?"

Alice wasn't sure if she could carry off dramatic hair. It could mean anything if Principal Katya had a say in it.

"Well, young Alice, you always wear your hair loose, and it is so long and thick. Don't worry; Miss Ling is very creative. Besides, a change from time to time for a special occasion is a good thing."

Alice looked at Principal Katya's blue rinse, intensified to almost purple since she last saw it. Alice smiled to herself; she'd never been so daring.

"You have pretty things to wear?" Principal Katya asked.

"A new dress," Alice answered. "It's lovely. I've never worn anything like it. I always considered myself rather plain and dowdy."

"I cannot believe you would ever see yourself in that light. Consider Patrick's attention to you; he has an eye for a pretty girl. Plain and dowdy would never be on his very sensitive radar. Now tell me, what is dowdy?"

Trust Principal Katya to use a word in context before even knowing its meaning!

Alice laughed and accepted Principal Katya's offer to link arms.

"In all honesty, Principal Katya, I haven't seen anything in this world that even comes close to dowdy."

Unusually, Principal Katya didn't go to dinner that evening and seeing her table empty, Alice decided she too would skip the meal and instead enjoy a walk in the gardens. Later, she engaged in pleasant conversation with Statesman Mellor in the great hall. He told her Principal Ryan arrived in the afternoon and entered Cloisters immediately, along with Principal Katya and various councilmen and statesmen, no doubt to discuss the mission just gone and the one to come.

Politics, Alice thought without interest, not her scene. She enquired if Patrick had arrived, but Statesman Mellor told her no; he detoured to his home principality briefly to see his family and would arrive the next day in time for the ball.

Alice didn't see Principal Katya or Patrick the next morning and sat with Statesman Mellor at breakfast. Patrick hadn't arrived yet, he told her, and Principal Katya was still in her bed. Later, Alice received a very welcome visit later from Dr Grossmith. They walked down to the lake to feed the ducks.

"You look amazing, Alice," Dr Grossmith said, "even better than when you were on Saturn Station. You have a glow about you, and—are those freckles? You must be enjoying the sun!"

"If you want the truth, Dr Grossmith, it's because I'm happy. I expect you know about the relative of Alexis Langley, whom Principal Katya found?"

"I know she found a relative who seemed a close match. She lives in the Calamities, I believe? A bit of a rebel?"

"She has a wife, an indigenous wife. They are a devoted couple, and I love being around them. We have a beautiful home, animals, a vegetable garden; we make cheese! It's like heaven to me."

"It sounds idyllic. You were so concerned about the Calamities," he laughed, reminding Alice of her former fears.

"I was, but now I just feel very blessed."

"I'm glad for you, and I look forward to meeting them. Now, do you feel well, Alice?"

"Why? Are you worried?"

The question came as a surprise because she felt fine, blissfully happy, anxieties about the ball aside.

"I'm not worried," he hastened to reassure her. "Just checking, not so many years ago, you woke from a four-hundred-year sleep, and you've only been aware for a few months!"

"I'm fine, Dr Grossmith. Auntie Jane checks my heart and kidneys regularly. I heard Dr Clere organised a committee to study me."

"Yes, he takes a peculiar view that encouraging you to live your life, to make choices about the direction your life should take, represents an opportunity lost to the scientific world."

"How many people are on this committee?"

"Just he and two others, both part of his team. He can't ask anyone else as you are classified as far as he's concerned. I'm not entirely sure his team agree with him; I believe they feel they cannot refuse. His position is that you are unique, and your biology, which at present is unremarkable, should be studied. We all know what he really wants is to discover the secret behind your extraordinary preservation and how your uncle achieved it. He believes, almost to the point of fanaticism, that you also know the formula and are simply not saying and that your claim of a different identity is subterfuge. He proposes an organised study; tissue samples, brain activity…"

"Why do they wish to study those things?" she cut in, holding up her hands to stop him mid-sentence. "Surely, if someone who, as you say, is four hundred years old and can live amongst humankind once more, that would be worth studying as a social experiment? Not the biology of it all?"

"Clere disagrees. He doesn't want you here. He argues for your return to Saturn Station. I sent a message to Principal Katya regarding the formation of his proposal. She's opposed, and the decision rests with her."

"Not with me?"

Dr Grossmith stopped short. Well, that was unexpected, but on reflection, they should have informed her. He'd been so used to making all the decisions it hadn't occurred to him. So, he asked her now.

"Do you wish to be studied?"

"No, I don't, but Dr Clere should be approaching me about it and not organising a lynch mob! If I knew the answers, what possible reason could I have to keep them secret?"

Dr Grossmith was impressed to see Alice protecting herself, using strong words. Yes, he approved of this progress, independence was to be encouraged, and he should not treat her as a child, making decisions on her behalf. He would mention this progress to Principal Katya.

"Dr Grossmith?"

She was studying him as he considered her new-found confidence.

"Yes?"

"I don't know what all this means and how it will affect me. I just want to be left alone. There are still times when I don't believe this can be real," she looked around her at the ducks, the Tabernacle, the lake, at him. "Alice Watkins could only dream of a life like this. It might just be make-believe with events taking place because I'm asleep in the wrong position or suffered a terrible illness in real life."

Dr Grossmith didn't dismiss what she said; she still clung to the only past she remembered.

"Your knowledge of the twentieth and twenty-first centuries astonished Principal Hardy, leading him to the conclusion you have studied history at some point," he said. "As for this being a dream, I'm not prepared to speculate or confuse you, my dear, but my life is not a dream. I'm real."

He took her hand, covering her fingers with his own to grip his arm, making her smile.

"I dedicated my life to you. To see you awakened and marvelling at your world, even your occasional bewilderment, is a priceless gift. Alice, to me, you and this world are as real and as undreamlike as can be."

"I could dream you up in a dream, though, couldn't I?"

"Yes, anything is possible in a dream world, but this world is the real world. Your experiences up to now are real. We don't know how you managed to survive the centuries and end up here. That is the dream, Alice."

"And a dream for Dr Clere. To have something extraordinary to study. To bring him glory, perhaps?"

"There's truth in that. But Clere will be vetoed. He won't act against the Tabernacle. Now, to lighter things. Are you looking forward to the dance?"

She sighed. "I'm nervous, but Statesman Patrick will be with me, and knowing you are attending as well with Principal Katya and my other friends, I feel much safer."

"Good," he nodded towards the Tabernacle where Miss Ling waved frantically to attract their attention. "Miss Ling appears to need you."

Miss Ling and Sarah spent the late afternoon with Alice, styling her hair and sampling different colour effects in making up her eyes. They didn't let her see herself until they finished, then brought the image definer for her to view their creation. Miss Ling cut Alice's hair into layers without disturbing the overall length, resulting in a cascade of soft waves to frame her face. An effect Alice liked. Miss Ling lifted sections of the hair, weaving the curls to give height to the style and finishing with an alluring single large ringlet that hung down the centre of Alice's back.

Sarah, who adored the creamy pearl colour chosen for the dress, followed the subtlety of the picture she'd drawn for Alice, highlighting the green of her eyes and darkening her lashes. She wanted the natural colour of Alice's complexion to shine through, but Alice wasn't happy about her freckles and took some persuading not to cover them up.

"They're only over the bridge of your nose, Alice," Sarah said, pulling in Miss Ling for solidarity, and in the end, up against such a united front, Alice conceded her skin looked nice even with no cover. Miss Ling performed a manicure, a procedure Alice had never experienced. Wherever Michelle went to have her nails done, Alice was sure three rotating beams of light would not have accomplished it.

While Sarah and Miss Ling put the finishing touches in place, Alice's thoughts wandered to her family. Less and less now, she thought about them as her new life took over. She must try to accept the possibility her memories were false, and those people, those children and grandchildren, were just the wild imaginings of a mind waiting to remember the truth.

CHAPTER SEVEN _

Patrick arrived at Alice's suite with his usual punctuality. Sarah let him in, and smiling, she closed the door behind her, leaving them alone.

Miss Ling creatively arranged tiny pearlised flowers over the lifted hair on Alice's forehead. Around her neck, she placed the magnificent pearl and emerald necklace.

The dress, perfectly matching the pearls' colour, draped in elegant folds away from one shoulder, a slender arm just peeping out from the softly folded sleeve, her other shoulder bare. The bodice tucked into a tiny waistline, showing off Alice's beautiful form before falling away in soft, delicate, and gossamer-like folds. With the pearls and upswept hair, Alice's appearance gave her a softness and maturity she loved, infusing her with much-needed confidence for the evening to come. Fortunately for Alice's modesty, the tailor thoughtfully provided an underskirt to avoid revealing too much through the sheer fabric.

Patrick stood in the doorway, hands behind his back. He didn't move. To him, Alice was a vision. The colouring of her gown, her hair, her eyes matching the emerald green of the jewel in her necklace, to him, she was perfection. He always considered her beautiful, even at their first meeting on Saturn Station, when she greeted him in the too-large shawl, looking frail and bewildered, but now, as they'd become closer, each time he saw her, she took his breath away.

Patrick's usual grey was replaced with a midnight blue dress-coat, two gold bands depicting his rank running over the left shoulder, the collar raised slightly and folded back to reveal a lace shirt. Exquisite embroidery followed the edge of the jacket and extended around to the tail. A frock coat, her mother would have said. Not a stray strand of hair, his ponytail set neatly in place, he presented a handsome and dashing figure, like a hero from one of Alice's much-loved Jane Austen novels. She'd forgotten the significance of the necklace and just felt happy to have him here to guide her through this evening.

"You are stunning, Alice. I am so proud of you," he said, not moving.

"Thank you, Patrick, you look wonderful, my goodness—that jacket! It's beautiful!" Alice looked down at herself. "I'm afraid I'm becoming a farm girl, and Sarah and Miss Ling had to buff and colour it out of me!"

"They've only highlighted what is naturally yours anyway."

He couldn't help himself. He stepped forward and took Alice in his arms, kissing her lightly on the mouth.

"Every time I see you, you are more beautiful."

She studied his dear, handsome face. She hadn't seen him since he took her to his home, where for one day, she didn't have to fight off his advances and found him so easy to be with. He was special to her, but she didn't return his feelings, and it wasn't fair to saddle him with a cold fish.

"Enough of that," she stepped back with a smile. "I'm still nervous about this ball, so it's time we made an entrance while I have the courage."

Alice held onto Patrick's arm as they descended the Great Hall staircase. Her earlier calmness threatened to give way to jangling nerves when she saw how many people were gathering. There seemed to be thousands. She faltered and glanced up at Patrick, so he placed his hand over hers proudly, nestling it protectively in the crook of his arm.

"Don't worry, Alice," he whispered, his voice reassuring. "To most of these people, you are a dear friend to Principal Katya. Few are aware of your origins. Be gracious, smile and don't answer questions if you're uncomfortable. Besides, you're acquainted with many of the councilmen. Just be yourself, and you will floor them!"

Alice took a deep breath. She might not floor anyone, but she also wouldn't let anyone down, least of all herself. She could do this.

Principal Katya and Principal Ryan stood at the foot of the staircase. Principal Ryan, not a fair hair out of place, was dressed in the same style and colour as Patrick but sported three gold braids over his shoulder, reflecting his rank. He looked up as Alice and Patrick descended towards them.

Without realising, he inhaled sharply. He hadn't seen her since the incident in the auditorium. Then, she'd been so pale and waiflike, a little sprite dressed in green who affected him so oddly, and since then had occupied his thoughts more than he would have liked. Now, she was transformed. Her hair reflected copper and gold from the chandeliers, just the hint of a smile on her lovely mouth, a smile she directed to him when she saw he was watching. She's beautiful, he thought, not realising he was staring. When he did, he swallowed and turned away to speak to his aunt. He couldn't look at Alice. Beautiful didn't go far enough; she was dazzling.

Alice saw Principal Ryan's gaze linger a little longer than she would have expected and realised, for the first time, that for sheer beauty and depth, his eyes rivalled even Patrick's. Deep-set, intelligent, expressive, and intensely blue, almost matching the midnight of his jacket. She'd not noticed them before, always too busy either being overawed or intimidated by him. Now, with a sudden boldness, she'd met his gaze and found, in that fleeting instance, a moment passed between them, something not present in any of their past encounters. She knew, somehow, Principal Ryan recognised it too before he turned away. The silent exchange went unnoticed by Patrick and Principal Katya.

When Alice and Patrick reached the foot of the stairs, Principal Ryan, out of respect for protocols, forced himself to look once more at Alice and engage in pleasantries.

"Dr Langley," he inclined his head.

"Principal Ryan." Alice noticed he turned his attention to acknowledge Patrick without waiting for her to respond.

"Dr Langley prefers Alice. It suits her much more, don't you think?" Principal Katya told him, looking from one to the other.

Principal Ryan didn't answer, just glanced unsmiling at his aunt.

"My nephew dedicates himself to protocol, Alice. It is his first love. He uses his given name so seldom these days; he has likely forgotten it. We may have to dream up a pet name, you and I!"

Alice bit her lip to hold back a grin as Principal Ryan's mouth twitched in annoyance at being the subject of his aunt's dry wit. For Patrick, it always amused him to see Ryan brought down a peg by Principal Katya, so he grinned, and was rewarded with a glare from his commanding officer, a glare Patrick chose to ignore. He was off duty tonight.

Principal Katya lifted the sleeve of Alice's dress and praised both the design and colour.

"You really did choose something pretty to wear, Alice child; this gown is delightful. And the shade is perfect. We are all very dull in comparison, not one here with a dress that reveals a bit of flesh!"

Patrick agreed and added a few comments of his own, making Alice blush with all the attention. Principal Ryan deliberately avoided becoming embroiled in the conversation by catching Statesman Evesham's eye, extricating himself as politely as he was capable.

Alice took the opportunity to admire Principal Katya's shawl, crocheted quite unlike any crochet Alice had ever seen.

"Did you make this, Principal Katya?"

"I did not," she admitted, although pleased Alice noticed it. "Remember the statesman who created patterns?

It comes from those. She made it."

The shawl was a stunning blend of coloured gemstones and crochet styles only invented in recent weeks. To say crochet had crossed into another dimension was an understatement. No longer merely a craft for idle fingers—it had blossomed into both a science and an art form.

But Patrick, not at all interested in fashion and being a keen dancer, swept her away as soon as polite. Alas for him, Alice wasn't a dancer. Mary and Jane tried to teach her, but she naturally had two left feet. She might have muddled through with a less accomplished partner, but unsurprisingly, Patrick was a superb dancer. Alice tactfully requested she took a rest.

Stepping away to the sidelines, she scoured the hall for people she recognised. The Hennessey's were there but were standing with a group of people she didn't know, so she decided not to approach them. Several women, seeing Patrick without his partner, vied for his attention. Like flies at a barbecue, Alice grinned to herself.

A few of the Tabernacle staff exchanged pleasantries with her, and one or two senior councilman's wives and husbands spoke politely. Dr Grossmith waved from across the room, indicating he would come across to see her soon. A statesman's daughter glanced her way as she danced past with Patrick, a little smile of triumph in her eyes. Alice was untroubled, and when she was sure no-one was watching, slipped out of the great hall to make her way to the steps to look out over the lake and enjoy the evening air.

Principal Ryan, caught up in what he considered a pointless conversation with Principal Ahmed from the

Accessor, watched her leave.

"So, Ryan, you still have a few months," Ahmed was saying. "Surely you can spare Engineer Oakes for the Accessor's refit? We don't want to have to wait till you get back. We could push out more boundaries if we do it now, particularly with the Significator's new communications spreaders. What do you say?"

Ryan half-listened, distracted by the sight of Alice, disappearing out towards the steps. He raised his hand and moved away.

"I'll give it some thought, Ahmed. Would you excuse me?"

Ahmed bowed and turned to the others in the group; he knew there was little point in trying to detain Ryan when he decided a conversation was at an end.

Having moved up the staircase to watch the proceedings, Principal Katya saw her nephew leave and follow Alice outside. She skimmed her eyes over the crowd and located Patrick, currently diverted by Statesman Evesham's wife, dancing and laughing and no doubt being thoroughly charming. She looked back to where Noah had joined Alice. She would keep her own counsel on this. It was between Alice, Noah, and Patrick. She didn't wish heartbreak for any of them, but Noah was dear to her, and Alice had become the daughter she never had. She turned away. The World Principal could not direct this situation; this she would leave to the universe.

CHAPTER EIGHT _

Alice looked across the lake, facing away from the Great Hall, her long, single ringlet glowing copper in the reflection of the lights. Arms by her sides, she stood still, her gaze towards the fountain. Ryan saw her look up at the night sky as the festivities faded behind them. She gave no indication she heard his approach and responded to his presence without moving, almost as if she expected him.

"Principal Ryan."

"Dr Langley."

Women were never one of Ryan's areas of expertise, and now, he found himself at a loss how to engage Alice in conversation or, the thought occurred to him, even if he should. As he tried to think of something to say, he walked over to the balustrade and half sat, half leaned, facing her and positioning his hands in his lap. Somehow, he imagined he might not be so large and intimidating in this pose, as he was in the auditorium.

"Are you not enjoying the ball?"

It was the best he could come up with, and she gave him a small smile.

"To be blunt, Principal Ryan, dancing isn't my thing. Everyone is lovely, they welcome me, accept me, but I've never had time for social gatherings."

"I understand," he replied, thankful for common ground. "It's the same for me. I overheard Patrick say he would dance every dance with you, so it's a little surprising to see you out here. This is where I typically end up." He looked from her to the lake, "That is, before making my escape as soon as I can."

Alice glanced back into the great hall to where Patrick, unsurprisingly, was charming all the ladies. She laughed a little, and Ryan followed her gaze. Patrick always stood out, even wearing the same dress uniform as all the other officers.

"There would be a lot of disappointed females if I hogged Patrick all evening," she said, turning her attention back to him with a smile.

"You've become good friends?"

He congratulated himself on adopting a friendly, conversational tone, not that he had much practice in friendly, conversational techniques.

"Yes, I suppose we have," Alice nodded. "I value his friendship."

"I know he's visited you here at the Tabernacle and your home."

Half smiling, she widened her eyes and raised her eyebrows, her expression making him feel like excusing himself and returning to the safety of his discussion about refits with Principal Ahmed.

"What is *that* supposed to mean, Principal Ryan?"

Did it sound like prying? He hadn't meant to pry. Well, perhaps he had. He mentally slapped himself. *Ryan, you are a dolt.*

"I apologise, Dr Langley. I wasn't trying to imply anything. Principal Katya told me he came to see you."

He'd never previously envied Patrick's ability to place people at ease, a skill he considered superfluous to a career in the military. Right now, he wished he'd paid more attention. She said nothing at first, then looked sideways at him, tilting her head to one side.

"Principal Ryan, do you think I could do better than Patrick?" her tone was teasing, light, but he didn't have the experience to recognise it.

He stood, considering leaving her to her solitude. This was going badly—he should stick to stellar maps. He'd acted out of character, following her out here, engaging her in conversation, just because he was struck by her beauty.

She laughed at his obvious discomfiture. She'd turned the tables on him! He made her uncomfortable in the auditorium, and now, she was paying him back and enjoying it!

"Don't worry, Principal Ryan," she grinned, "it's not like that. He likes to think we're more than we are. To me, he's a friend, nothing else."

She'd thrown him a lifeline, an opportunity to apologise, "I do beg your pardon, Dr Langley, I didn't intend steering the conversation in the direction of your relationship with Patrick."

"It's okay. I won't say anything," she said, giving him the distinct sense she was still laughing at him. Unlike their last encounter, she didn't seem at all intimidated. "So," her eyes found his. "What about you, Principal Ryan? Are you married?"

No-one asked this of him before, and the question came out of left field. She waited for an answer, her gaze fixed squarely on his face.

"No, I—I'm not. It never featured in my plans. I only ever wanted to be out there," Ryan gestured lamely, idiotically, towards the sky. "In space."

He cursed himself inwardly for the awkwardness of his reply; she'd think him a complete fool.

"You had stars in your eyes as a child?" she teased with a grin, looking up at the night sky. He was grateful she'd made nothing of his simplistic reply. Suddenly, he felt quite comfortable.

"You might say so. I'm the only one in my family who took up a career in space."

"You're an astrophysicist?"

"Yes, but as I work in space and study planetary attributes, geology, weather and so forth, I'm referred to as a planetary scientist."

"Are you excited about your next assignment?" she stepped closer to him as she spoke, so close her perfume reached him, the scent of flowers and spices.

"Excited might not be the word."

No-one could ever describe Ryan as excited about anything.

"Okay, breathless anticipation then!"

"Maybe not that either," he smiled down at her. Everything about her tonight was so unexpected, "But I do look forward to a better outcome than previously." He resumed his half standing, half seated position against the balustrade.

"Ah, do you mean this time, you will avoid stick-wielding natives?"

"Yes, we mishandled it, but we are novices, Dr Langley. Unfortunately, we can't rehearse our first contact skills on unsuspecting civilisations; we have to get the performance right the first time, or we might make ourselves unwelcome."

"You might also make enemies. The A'khet would surely have warned you about hostile species?"

"Not in the sector of space we are heading into this time. A'khet didn't pass through those regions. We're flying blind. We've only mapped proximal space and some sectors of median space. This time we head out further."

"Proximal space? I assume that's charted territory?"

"Yes, we're pushing out the boundaries with the other three starships because, in proximal and median space, they're faster than the Significator. We don't take up magnitude, or capacity until we are into far side median and threshold space."

"Why?"

"When magnitude is activated, faster even than the speed of light, it produces a wake. It's very brief, but the prototype, tested by over-zealous officials I might add, produced a wake that affected weather patterns on several planets. Saturn Station needed extensive repairs. It was unexpected and happened over a hundred years ago. A'khet couldn't offer a solution other than we don't engage magnitude except in open space."

"Such an effect might be viewed as a hostile act by another civilisation."

"Indeed, therefore, we need to discover ways that show we are not hostile."

"Well, the old Earth tribes, when a conqueror..."

"...we're not planning on conquering."

"...that's what the conquerors told all the people they eventually conquered, that they came in peace, gave fancy speeches and made promises they had no intention of keeping, but what I planned to say before you interrupted..."

Ryan shut up. It was a rarity for anyone other than Principal Katya to put him in his place.

"...the tribes welcomed them. An example would be American Indians; they welcomed the conqueror and traded with him. It wasn't until that same conqueror took their lands that hostilities began. Australian aborigines suffered the same fate. And other nations."

"But there were treaties in place, were there not?"

"Supposedly, and broken by the conquerors."

"As I said, we aren't going to conquer anyone. As you so succinctly put it at dinner, we simply want to meet our neighbours."

She nodded. "In my ancestor's time, it was a tradition to bake a cake for a new neighbour. A way of breaking the ice and offering a welcome."

"A *cake*? Are you suggesting we take a cake when we contact the inhabitants of another world?"

She flicked her eyelids up at him, innocently widening

her glorious green eyes and giving him a crooked smile, backed up by a shrug of her beautiful shoulders.

"It's worth a shot. Your last approach wasn't so successful."

"You are very wise, Alice, but…"

"Alice?"

He saw her sudden and fleeting bewilderment as she stumbled forward, and instinctively, he reached out to catch her. Alice felt as if something slapped her between her shoulder blades.

"Principal Ryan?" she gasped, the breath knocked from her lungs. What happened, for him of all people to be supporting her like this? Breathless and confused, she looked down at his hands, steadying her.

"Principal Ryan?" she repeated. He didn't let her go, just kept hold of her arm and placed his other hand on her back to secure her. The night was mild, but as he touched her, her skin felt icy cold.

"I'm sorry, Principal Ryan. I seem to be saying sorry to you quite often," she said, her voice quiet and vague. "Where's Patrick? I've come to rely on him somewhat as my protector, but now I find you saving me from a fall. Thank you."

"Dr Langley, perhaps we should go back inside." Ryan couldn't fathom what caused her to become so confused; she'd seemed fine, "I expect Patrick will wonder where you are."

Alice tried to clear the fog in her mind, "What am I doing out here?" she said, looking up at her saviour. The confident woman Ryan spoke with only moments ago was gone, In her place, a bewildered and anxious girl, clinging to him for support. He had to think on his feet. There had somehow been a shift.

"Just a breath of fresh air, I think," he lied. "I often come out here myself at these functions."

Alice recovered her composure, but she held self-consciously onto his arm even when she could stand without fear of falling. He escorted her into the great hall, carefully watching for signs of unsteadiness. She caught him looking down at her. They stopped walking, recapturing for the briefest of moments what passed between them on the stairs. Again, she noticed the appeal of his eyes, this time mingled with concern. And his face, such a strong face. Alice was bewildered. Had they spoken? Did she have one of her odd episodes, again witnessed by Principal Ryan?

Patrick spotted them and took Alice's arm with a nod to his colleague.

"I'll take it from here, old boy," he said. "Alice, I wondered where you were. I've been looking for you."

"Just be careful, Patrick, Dr Langley is a little…" but Patrick didn't listen as he led Alice away into the crowd.

"… unsteady," Ryan finished, but no-one heard him.

Alice glanced back at him. What just happened?

Ryan, watching as Patrick placed a possessive arm around Alice's waist, wondered the same thing.

CHAPTER NINE _

There were few other opportunities for words between them the rest of the evening. Alice seemed recovered, and though Patrick left Alice with Principal Katya, Dr Grossmith and the Hennessey's once or twice, at other times, he kept her close while he spoke with other officers and principals. Ryan remained distracted by their conversation and her ensuing confusion, almost a rerun of the auditorium incident. In particular, he reflected on her comment about Patrick.

"He thinks there's more…we're just friends."

Did that mean *she* doesn't think there's more?

At the first opportunity, Ryan slipped away unnoticed. He'd put in the requisite appearance, and his aunt wouldn't look for him.

The garden lights cast a soft glow as he entered the courtyard at the side of the Tabernacle, grateful no-one paid him any attention as he left or stopped him for one last pleasantry. He always stayed in the old courtyard quarters away from the residential suites, a concession allowed by Principal Katya, not only because he was family but because she knew he was intensely private.

Once inside his room, he unhooked his coat and sat down heavily in a chair. He pushed off his boots, rested his head against a cushion and closed his eyes.

Dr Langley did little to draw his attention the first time he met her. He'd viewed the evening as a trial, just as he knew his reputation for being a stickler for protocol, but much of it he could do without. The customary dinner with Principal Hardy whenever they passed Saturn Station was farcical; whoever dreamed that up? And these functions where everyone danced and made small talk, with nothing of value accomplished. Patrick took every opportunity to socialise, he loved these occasions, but then, he and Patrick were total opposites.

After the briefing by Principal Hardy, and his ensuing encounter with Dr Langley in the auditorium, Ryan read all the literature on the Sleeping Beauty Phenomenon, like everyone else, he believed, at least fifteen years ago, she was still in suspension at the Bell Institute. The Tabernacle shrouded her removal to Saturn station in secrecy, but she'd been in the textbooks for so long, only dedicated cryonics specialists and anthropologists paid much attention to her. All investigations were exhausted, so there were generations of scientists whose intrigue went unsatisfied. Ryan wasn't one of those scientists. Little more to him than a curiosity at university, his interest lay with the planets and what they offered, rather than an unknown female preserved in an unknown fluid.

But the night he heard her playing the piano, he realised his dismissal of her as an inconvenience, even while acknowledging and admiring Grossmith's achievement, had been a mistake. He gave no weight to the fact Hardy had entrusted him with a real person, with thoughts and feelings. Feelings reflected in her music; at first timid and faltering like the woman he presumed her to be, then strong, passionate, persuasive but also gentle, sweet and tender, ending her performance with a spirited rendition of the Polka.

He should have been more sensitive and left her alone to her music. He knew her memories were scattered and unreliable, but he, arrogant and self-righteous, barged in and made her flee, backing away from him as if confronted by the devil himself.

In those few moments after she turned from him and fled up the steps, out onto the walkway, she'd left an impression on him. He had to admit it, and afterwards, more than once, he'd caught himself thinking of her. Now, this evening, she looked so lovely, he could no longer ignore or dismiss her. Ryan knew he possessed none of Patrick's charm and loquacity, beside him, to the petite and beautiful Dr Langley—Alice, he probably looked like a lumbering oaf.

He sat in the dark for a considerable time, brooding over many things; Principal Hardy's caution about Patrick, the first time he met Alice, about tonight on the terrace, how he'd never seen Patrick so attentive, always having his choice of women. And finally, to McIntyre and all the others. Patrick has no concept of fidelity, he thought with some bitterness.

Still, he could do nothing. Patrick was on official leave, and Alice, well, she never came under his command anyway, but to call Patrick her protector? She was unwittingly laying herself open to all the complications about which Hardy expressed concerns.

Ryan rose wearily from the chair and went to the window. The blinds were still open, so he could view the side garden, where two people, a man, and a woman, stood. The man's arms were around the woman's waist; she, elbows bent and hands against his shoulders, created a subtle and unspoken barrier between them. He watched, feeling no shame at spying on them as Patrick kissed Alice and focusing only on the barrier she created. Patrick would not protect her from himself. Turning away from the window, Ryan woke the registry.

"Principal Ahmed, Tabernacle."

Ahmed's surprised face swam into view.

"Ryan? I only this minute got back to my suite."

"Ahmed, you want Oakes? I'll issue orders tonight."

"Well, thank you, Ryan."

Ahmed was surprised and grateful at this turn of events, so it would be imprudent to question the sudden change of heart or the fact it was well after midnight.

"It will make our lives a hell of a lot easier. Ahmed out."

Ryan knew for certain Patrick would never let Oakes loose on the Gravidarum on the Accessor, nor any of his magnitude modifications, and would almost certainly insist on going to the Accessor with him, leave or no leave. Ryan couldn't order as Hardy suggested, but he did have the authority to influence, and if he did nothing, Hardy would want to know why.

Patrick asked Alice to walk in the gardens towards the end of the evening, and keen to get away from the crowd, she agreed.

Patrick had considerable knowledge about the personal lives of many council members and was more than happy to impart information, but Alice had no interest in gossiping about people she'd come to know and respect.

"I was surprised to meet some female principals tonight, Patrick," she said, steering him away from personal references.

"Were you? Why?"

"I suppose because, in my time, there were far fewer female politicians than male."

"That might still be the case now," he said after a moment's thought. "All the female principals except one were here tonight and around thirty of the male principals. Those not here will attend the Fall or Autumn ball. If you don't come to the Spring Summit and Cotillion Ball, you must come in the Autumn. No ifs or buts."

"A Summit?" Alice heard the word here at the Tabernacle before but didn't know what it meant.

He led her over to a garden seat. She hoped to distract him from romantic notions, but all the time he spoke, he either stroked her hand or played with her hair.

"All principals submit their reports to the Tabernacle yearly. These reports are general but keep the Tabernacle informed of the individual principality's status, needs, wants, etc. Then there are specifics, request for marriages or reassignment. Of course, such things are submitted throughout the year. Individual principals have authority, but some business, a lot of business, ends up here in the Tabernacle, at Summit, in Cloisters."

"We had local government in my time," Alice told him, though she would not have compared it with the government of today. "And state government and federal government."

"Who got the final say?"

"They all thought they had the final say," Alice pulled a face. She found politics confusing. "Local government would say yes, go ahead, then the state would say, paint it yellow, and the federal government would say put orange spots on it. Then, when they'd changed the original idea beyond recognition, they would bicker and argue about who invented it and then put it back in its box, but only after investing millions of taxpayer's money."

"Sounds disorganised."

"We lived with it, and funnily enough, we all managed," the memory of her old world no longer invoked a sense of loss or longing. "We never had one all-powerful government that oversaw all decisions. In many ways, we had more freedoms than you do," she added, not intending to make comparisons.

"At a price, Alice," Patrick reminded her. "You also suffered anarchy and crime and war."

"Yes, I suppose," she conceded. "No-one could say I ever lived in a bland society."

"Do you think that of us?" Patrick was stunned by her comment. "Our world is peaceful and beautiful, and we are safe. That brings an excitement all its own, and we have space exploration. Our society is enlightened and innovative."

He stood suddenly and pulled her to her feet, drawing her close, unaware Ryan observed them from the courtyard residence window. Alice placed her hands against Patrick's shoulders to avoid him pulling her too close, but he still kissed her. And not knowing what else to do, she allowed it without response.

"Why do you reject me?" he asked, and this time, with his voice so earnest, she resolved to be firm. She thought back to the wonderful day at his home where he made no move to touch her or kiss her. That was the relationship she wanted with him.

"Why do *you* have to badger me? I've told you I'm not ready for a relationship," she fiddled with the braids on his coat to avoid looking into his eyes. "I just want to be friends, Patrick; you said you were alright with it."

"I *am*," his response was instant, defensive. Then he made a small movement with his shoulders. "Well, I'm not really. I knew you weren't enjoying the ball, that's why I didn't persuade you to keep dancing. I felt bad when I saw you stuck with dull, old Ryan."

"You thoroughly enjoyed dancing with all those beautiful ladies. Admit it."

"Do you know, Alice? At one time, but not anymore. I felt nothing towards any of those women. What I feel is only for you now."

"Then I will be a disappointment."

He left her no choice. She stepped back, pushing him slightly.

"No," He tried cuddling her back into him, but her arm barrier was in the way, "I won't give up. I have a few months before we leave. You said we'll still be friends, and I will accept that for now, I promise, while making myself irresistible to you. You can evaluate my performance as our departure draws near. I know you'll change your mind," he added, touching the tip of her nose with his finger.

Alice sighed. Patrick's concept of being friends was very different from hers.

"Well, if I don't, I can at least write you a reference."

Patrick saw her back to her suite and, despite his promise of friendship only, kissed her mouth gently once more before leaving her.

She stood inside her room, leaned back against the door, and heaved a heavy sigh. She didn't believe you would kiss a friend of the opposite sex on the mouth, but maybe, she needed to allow it in case she hurt his feelings. She thought about Principal Ryan; how unexpected and disconcerting to find herself outside with him without knowing how she got there. She gained the impression they'd been there for a while, so it would be reasonable to assume they were speaking. If so, what about? She only remembered the slap on the back, not delivered by anyone on the terrace and being propelled forward. Principal Ryan, so concerned and attentive, must have stopped her from falling. Had he not been there, she would have ended up on the ground.

Principal Ryan didn't seem so scary this time. His strong arms held her steady until she regained her balance; his hand had felt so warm against her back. Remembering his kindness and concern reminded her of when their eyes met as she descended the staircase. She'd never studied him, always too overawed or frightened by his towering presence. Everything about him seemed larger than life, his height, his build, his full lips, slightly down-turned at the corners, even his hair, fair with flecks of grey, making him seem unapproachable and dour. But those eyes...

Although Principal Ryan didn't have Patrick's grace and style and certainly not his charm, Alice concluded there was an attractiveness about him. How old would he be? She thought about seeing his face as she descended the stairs. Not so old probably, then found herself surprised she gave the incident any attention at all and that she was still standing, after half an hour, fully dressed, with her back to the door.

CHAPTER TEN _

Officially now on leave, Patrick promised Alice a special trip, insisting she spends as much time as possible with him. She agreed, provided he strictly observed the friends-only rule and that she would also spend time with Principal Katya during her few days at the Tabernacle. Alice answered a tap on her door the next morning before she was ready to greet the day. Patrick stood there, looking miserable and full of apologies.

"Alice, I'm so sorry. I have to leave."

Alice let him in.

"Leave? Why?"

She pushed her hair from her eyes, still not properly awake.

"I'm leaving for the Accessor. Engineer Oakes received orders last night to report there. Principal Ahmed has been pushing Ryan to reassign him until the Significator leaves, and with our refit mostly completed, he'd no reason to block the request. Oakes is an excellent engineer, and he has A'khet Knowledge, but he's still inexperienced with the Gravidarum. The Accessor is a much smaller ship but is due two modifications. I really can't let him do this alone."

"How long will you be gone?"

"A few weeks, possibly all of my leave, the Accessor either waits until I get back from our mission in two years, or it relies solely on Oakes. Neither solution is entirely satisfactory, not if we want to make progress in exploring threshold space."

"Why can't they wait?"

Alice didn't want to say goodbye, even if staying meant fighting him off at frequent intervals.

"We're building a new station at the edge of proximal space. The core is in place and ready for the outer hull, the Accessor is vital to the project, but it's slow. They want to push the station out to the boundary of median space to maximise its reach."

"Don't you have confidence in Oakes?"

"Heaps, but aligning magnitude with Substance and the Gravidarum takes skill and experience; the safety of the ship depends on precision. Two engineers carry out the alignment, one of whom must have Knowledge. At magnitude, Substance ignites a harmonic field that changes the hull structure; if that harmonic isn't present, the ship will yield to the natural forces of space and be incapable of travelling past the speed of light. The A'khet appear not to have had issues with this, but of course, they've never given us information about their ship. Relativity tells us…"

Alice held up her hand.

"A physics lesson, Patrick?"

He laughed.

"Sorry. You understand why it's important I go?"

"I do understand. You're fond of your engines, aren't you?"

"Fond isn't the word, but the Gravidarums are the legacy of my family. I can't just trust them to anyone."

"But you said Oakes has this Knowledge."

"He does, but he's not me!"

"Can't the A'khet simply give it to more people?"

"I can't answer that, and even so, if it goes wrong, I would feel responsible. I've overseen the installation of all the current engines in the military." He looked over to the window. "Alice, I must go. The shuttle is waiting."

"Then go and do what you must. Contact me at home whenever you can. Good luck."

She reached up and kissed him on the cheek. And for once, he didn't pull her close, just smiled and left.

Alice showered and dried her hair in front of the image definer. She looked messy and scrabbled her hands through her hair to make herself look even messier. She pulled a face at her reflection. With Patrick gone, she had no-one to play with. Amelia's new assignment turned out to be very busy, so she didn't want to disturb her, and Principal Katya might likely want to spend time with her nephew. Maybe time to go home. She would suggest it to Principal Katya when she saw her later that day.

Alice didn't get to see her until dinner. An urgent session in Cloisters kept Principal Katya and her nephew occupied the entire day, and that left Alice to her own devices for several hours. Principal Katya sent word to Alice to join her and Principal Ryan for dinner.

"Alice looked delightful last night, did she not, Noah?" Principal Katya asked, hoping for a little information about their exchange on the terrace the evening prior.

"If you say so, Aunt," Noah Ryan was prepared to give away none of his feelings. "I understand little of such things. I suppose she dressed differently from many of the females present."

"Noah, you are so stuffy! Do you never cast your eyes about you? See what is under your nose? Do you never relax? Look at you, all uniform and self-importance. You are not on the bridge of your gigantic starship now. You are here, on Earth with your auntie."

"Auntie? You've mentioned this. What does it mean?"

"That is what Alice calls her aunts—Auntie. Much more informal and affectionate than just 'Aunt', and the way you say it, you may just as well be barking orders at a member of your crew."

"I never bark orders, Aunt and I've always called you 'Aunt'. I'm too old to change."

"Nonsense. Look at you, regulation slacks and jerkin and your hair slicked back, sitting up as if a metal rod was stuffed up the back of your shirt! You are always on duty, nephew."

"You never commented on these things before, Aunt Katya," he sighed. "I'm doing nothing differently."

There was no point in going on the defensive; she spoke her mind both as his aunt and as his principal.

"Humph," she snorted and leaned back in her chair.

"Do you have plans for the rest of the evening?"

Dr Langley instantly came to mind. He still wasn't sure why he gave those orders for Oakes to be transferred but reasoned he was merely following Hardy's suggestions. Patrick contacted him late to say he would accompany Oakes to the Accessor. Ryan made noises about him being sure? What about his leave? And, perhaps Oakes could handle it? But he knew the response. Patrick wouldn't leave those modifications to anyone, just as he knew he was kidding himself. Those orders had nothing to do with Hardy's concerns about Dr Langley, only Ryan himself hadn't planned beyond giving them.

"No, no real plans," he answered.

"Good. You will take Alice to Tibet."

This was unexpected.

"Tibet? You want me to take Dr Langley to Tibet?"

"That's what I said, Noah. Is my English suddenly not so good?"

"Why?"

"A'khet desire it. They came to see her here when she first arrived. She was in their presence centuries ago, but she doesn't remember."

"She couldn't have been in their presence, Aunt," he shook his head. "It's not possible."

"Isn't it? We know so little of her. As you are not possessed of Knowledge, I am unable to speak more of this, only that A'khet requested her presence."

This would be important, possibly imbuing him with information about Alice she might not be ready for him to know. He'd considered perhaps inviting her for a walk in the garden or a trip to the city or theatre, but the A'khet? Tibet?

"I'm not sure, Aunt. I'm not that well acquainted with the A'khet."

He caught sight of Alice as she stepped through the doorway, stopping to speak to Statesman Mellor. She was smiling, wearing buttercup yellow and no less bewitching than the evening before.

Principal Katya, over the rim of her glass, watched him watching Alice. She kept the glass held up to her lips, pretending to sip her drink, but she was hiding the fact she was observing him. He saw her and, knowing most of her tricks, immediately returned his attention to her. The fact he'd caught her out made little difference, and she held his gaze.

"Patrick would be a better choice to take her, I agree—but he's not here—is he, Noah?"

The knowing in her voice flooded him with guilt. Ryan occasionally wondered if having the psychic A'khet as friends made his aunt more sensitive, but in his gut, he knew she knew what he'd done.

Principal Katya smiled as Alice, unsure if she would be intruding, made her way towards them.

"Here she is. Hello, Alice. Sit down."

Ryan stood and held a chair for her. Alice smiled and greeted them both as Principal Katya pushed a plate of little chocolates across the table.

"I might have eaten all these, Alice. Chef brought them out for us to try; they are delicious. Try one. Alice loves chocolate, Noah, don't you, Alice? She eats it all the time."

Alice picked up the smallest rosette of chocolate on the plate.

"I must confess, I do like chocolate, but not all the time, Principal Katya."

She popped the chocolate into her mouth before realising they were both studying her. Although she felt self-conscious at being watched, it was too late, and she flicked her eyes skywards, allowing herself a quiet, "mmmm."

"Doing that with her eyes means it is heavenly," Principal Katya explained with a smile, patting her nephew's hand.

The corners of Ryan's mouth pulled a little. Not a blatant grin, but enough of a response that Alice refused another, citing that it wasn't usual to have chocolate before a meal, knowing full well that such conventions didn't trouble Principal Katya.

"I can forget my manners where chocolate is concerned, Principal Ryan," she said, and this time, Ryan's unsmiling smile made his eyes crinkle up and gave his mouth a little more movement. She imagined he was laughing, just not out loud.

"Do you have plans for this evening, Alice?" Principal Katya asked.

"I thought it might be nice to spend it with you, Principal Katya, as you have been Cloisters. Statesman Mellor tells me you are needed again tomorrow. Perhaps I should go home."

"I am afraid you can't go home, Alice," Principal Katya said in a matter-of-fact tone. "My nephew plans to take you to Tibet."

"Tibet? Tonight?" Alice echoed, trying to remember where she'd seen Tibet on a map and wondering why Principal Ryan wanted to take her there.

"Yes, that's right, isn't it, Noah?"

Principal Katya turned innocent eyes on her nephew.

"I—well, yes, Dr Langley. It seems the A'khet are curious and wish to meet you."

"I met one, Principal Ryan. Here at the Tabernacle."

"Yes, Alice," Principal Katya interrupted with a wave of her hand. "But they have heard about you for so long and followed your journey. Their psychic abilities, though impressive, are diminished greatly when there is only one. A'khet who visited here could not properly get to know you."

"Why do they need to get to know me, Principal Katya?"

"Because you are close to the Tabernacle and to me. If you do not wish to go, my nephew will not make a fuss. Will you, nephew?"

Ryan gave a mute shake of his head. His aunt was a master manipulator, and they would be going wherever she said they would go. He knew it. His aunt knew it. He didn't doubt Dr Langley—Alice, knew it as well.

"Of course, I'll go, Principal Katya..." Alice said. How could she refuse? She never refused, "...if you wish it. I suppose I won't learn anything about my new world if I stay in one place. I've heard of Tibet, but I'm not sure quite where it is!"

"Good, that's settled," Principal Katya's attention turned to the meal placed in front of her. Alice noted that neither she nor Principal Ryan were offered anything. "The shuttle is waiting out the front. Off you go."

Alice looked across at Principal Ryan. Principal Katya had dismissed them, and it was apparent to them both, she'd ordered the shuttle even before this conversation took place.

Minutes later, and alone now with Principal Ryan, Alice realised she still felt a little in awe of him. He was an important man, and even though not officially on duty, he wore almost full uniform. She couldn't help wondering if this truly was his idea or if he was merely acting under Principal Katya's orders. Patrick described him as dull and boring, this might end up a long day if he lived up to that reputation, but he'd been so kind when she stumbled the night before, she decided to make up her own mind about him. She stole a glance as he released the shuttle door, and to her surprise, he looked down and smiled.

CHAPTER ELEVEN _

"Tibet. That's part of China, isn't it? Won't it be dark?"

Principal Ryan stood back to let her enter the shuttle.

"No, it's their morning, Dr Langley. Tibet is separate from China now; the only inhabitants are monks and the A'khet. Few receive invitations. A'khet honour you."

Alice didn't understand. An honour? Why would A'khet want to honour her? Maybe they think she's Alexis Langley. She could ask Principal Ryan, but he mightn't know. Besides, he'd turned his attention to the controls, so she looked out the forward viewport, not sure if he would welcome conversation.

Meanwhile, although he sensed the distinction between the woman he spoke with the previous night and this more reserved version, he considered her the loveliest woman he'd ever met. Since the incident in the auditorium, he admitted to himself he felt a powerful attraction to her. He had no idea what she thought of him, but not speaking would do neither of them any good.

"What are you thinking, Dr Langley?"

"Patrick told me about the different transports," she

smiled, grateful he started the conversation. "This is a Tabernacle shuttle. It can fly at intermediate altitude," she said, echoing Patrick's words, "and can be programmed to fly automatically, but only certain shuttles go into space. All space-going transports need to dock manually with ships in orbit or space dock, except for high altitude automatrans. They're tractored in and fixed to the hull."

Patrick explained it well enough to make perfect sense to her.

"Automatrans are always programmed. They're faster and travel in a low orbit," she finished, surprised at how well she remembered what she learned.

"You're mostly correct, well done. The automatrans is capable of deep space travel, but out there, it's always piloted. When in use in orbit, it's generally automated."

"I expect I got some of it wrong," she laughed. "But I know the panel in front of you is the flight registry, and the smaller one controls internal systems."

"You've learned a lot."

"I seem to remember things a lot better than at first; I think the Eduction chip Dr Grossmith placed in my arm helped. Educator Sebel told me I would get into good learning habits. She may have been right."

Ryan leaned back.

"So, it would appear. Would you like to take the controls?"

She peered out the side viewport. It was evening, and there were houses and schools and buildings to crash into. Ryan saw her hesitation and understood; she turned back to him, her face easily readable with an unspoken, 'no thank you, I don't think so'.

"I've never even ridden a bike, Principal Ryan," she backed up her refusal, emphasising how inept she would be. Her mother believed sitting astride a bike made a girl lose her virginity.

"A bike?"

"Two wheels and a handlebar, from my time."

"It sounds like something Patrick would make. He constructed all manner of wheeled transports as a child."

"You admire him?"

"He's a brilliant engineer and an outstanding first officer. The A'khet welcome him as a friend, and believe me, there are no finer judges of character."

"He told me about his family and his father's accident."

"I've known the family for many years," Principal Ryan told her, "although I'm closer to his sister in age. Eileen is a little older than my sisters and me. The Patrick's lived on Tabernacle land, and we always visited Principal Katya at recess."

"He showed me the house. What was Patrick like?"

"Always inventing things. He made the most amazing go-karts!"

"Go-karts?"

"Yes, something like your bikes, I would imagine. Primitive transports, toys."

"I know what they are. My son..." she quickly corrected herself. "Lots of the boys in our neighbourhood made them."

"Well, Patrick's creations were awe-inspiring! Racing

down the hill from his house towards the river is the stuff of childhood!" The memory made him laugh aloud; his blue eyes sparkled as he looked across at her, and she laughed with him.

"Are you still good friends?"

"More colleagues now, I'm several years older, and our respective paths largely went in different directions until the Significator. As children, my sisters and I only saw him at recess. We felt sorry for him, being there alone."

"How come you are such a young principal? It seems like a job for an older person judging by those I met at the ball."

Now they'd got started, Alice found him far easier to talk to than she'd imagined.

"It's different in the military, Dr Langley. There are only three other ships that travel as far as median space. The others, including civilian ships, stay in proximal. The Significator is the first ship with the capability to explore deep into threshold space. The program was young and innovative, and the Tabernacle decided on a younger principal. Me."

"I'm not clear about proximal and median space, Principal Ryan."

He thought about their conversation the night before when she assumed, correctly, that proximal space was charted space. She seemed to have forgotten. Perhaps the odd spell she took out on the steps triggered her amnesia.

"Proximal space is charted and explored," Dr Langley. "Median space is charted but not fully explored. Threshold space is uncharted and unexplored. I can show you on a registry when we get back to the Tabernacle if you're interested?"

"Thank you, Principal Ryan. I am interested."

Alice became quiet. She should probably ask him about etiquette when meeting the A'khet in their home, he seemed nice, and she didn't want him to think her ignorant, but…

"Principal Ryan, if I say or do something today when we meet with A'khet, something I shouldn't, I hope you'll correct me. Your aunt…"

"You can't say that."

"Can't say what?"

"You can't say 'your aunt'."

"Why not? She calls you her nephew."

"She can call me Rumpelstiltskin if she wishes," and he smiled the funny downturned smile Alice realised she found very attractive, then instantly had to make a supreme effort not to blush at her thoughts.

"When you refer to the World Principal," he continued, oblivious to her suddenly turning her face to the side viewport, "you refer to her always as 'Principal Katya'. She dropped her surname in her address because it's difficult to pronounce, and she wishes to be close to her people, but she's still 'Principal Katya', even in reference to me."

Alice recovered herself and answered as if she'd not been distracted by his smile.

"What is her surname?"

"Szypsikoviak."

Alice raised her eyebrows. "I'm not surprised she dropped it."

"It's a name native to her principality. My mother's maiden name as well."

"And what made you think of Rumpelstiltskin? Like the fairy story?"

"One my aunt liked to recite when we were children."

"You said 'my aunt'," she pointed out, in rapid response to his flouting of the protocols.

"Did I? I'm sorry, I should have said, 'Principal Katya'."

"Being read Rumpelstiltskin by a principal doesn't sound nearly as cosy as it being read by your auntie."

He laughed a little, agreeing. "I suppose not."

As they crossed the coast, Principal Ryan took the shuttle higher, and Alice looked down at the expanse of a dark ocean below. Every day she became more and more embedded in this wonderful reality of fascinating people and technology. Alice Watkins would have had trouble dreaming about such things, Alexis Langley, however...

"You mentioned you have sisters, Principal Ryan."

"I do. And would you believe they are the same age as me?"

"Triplets!"

"No, my mother's biochip was deactivated at the beginning of the second quarter. I came along the following year. The biomechanical component of the chip resets early during lactation, but my mother became pregnant again within two months, with twins, so my sisters were born eleven months after me."

"That's amazing!" And personal, Alice thought, but he showed no hint of embarrassment.

Alice knew about chips. Dr Grossmith found one inside her, but its comprehensive purpose needed more explanation. Principal Ryan wouldn't be the person to ask.

"What do your sisters do, Principal Ryan?"

"They're both veterinary scientists, like my parents and both married to veterinary scientists. Each has a daughter."

"Your parents are vets! Vets are lovely people."

The brief vision of a ginger cat with one tooth drifted through Alice's mind.

"My parent's speciality is mainly equine."

"Equine? Horses!"

"Yes, that's right, and they keep horses now they are retired, but other animals too. A whole menagerie!"

"I like animals," Alice told him. "I feed the ducks on the lake at the Tabernacle."

"So, I heard."

The idea clearly amused him.

"Except now they all swim towards me when I'm on the edge of the lake," she said. "In fact, they swim towards everyone now, expecting a treat. I fear I may have created a demon!"

"Ducks are self-sufficient creatures. It wouldn't hurt if you stopped feeding them."

"It's probably not about them, Principal Ryan."

The ducks represented an almost forgotten familiarity, something she still needed, but she wouldn't say so.

"I get a lot of pleasure from feeding them."

"Then, it sounds mutually beneficial."

"Old habits. Where is your home, Principal Ryan?"

"Principality 5. You called it England."

"I've never been to England. I never left Australia."

"Records say your chamber was discovered in old China. Scientists through the ages assumed Martin Watkins conducted his experiments there."

"Do you know much about me, my history?"

"Some, during our education, we learn something of all the sciences, including cryonics. You came under that heading even though you weren't cryonically suspended. No category existed because you were a living specimen of preservation of an unknown kind."

"I'm glad then I'm not more of a curiosity."

"You should be glad. There were occasional revivals of interest, but Grossmith kept you away from prying eyes as much as he could, and you faded in most people's minds. Anonymity is a good thing."

When she met Ryan on the principality ship, Alice decided that he would be a private man, though she wondered how a principal could ever achieve anonymity.

He spoke to the responder and turned to her, pointing to a triangle that appeared and hovered above the responder.

"It's on auto, that icon—the propinquity alert will sound as we approach. We're not allowed to take the shuttles too close; there is little place for technology in the retreat."

She nodded and waited. He'd put it on autopilot for a reason, and he shifted his position to give her his full attention.

"Principal Hardy briefed me when you came on board the Significator, Dr Langley. None of us was aware you had awakened or heard anything of you since university."

"He told me the story, Principal Ryan, but it must have been a dull forty years for Dr Grossmith. Apparently, I just lay there and did nothing."

"Not dull to him! His instincts about you made a compelling argument. He had sole control over the project in those forty years and kept you away from public and scientific scrutiny. Few had any idea you'd relocated to Saturn, let alone awakened. Have you read much about your time in stasis?"

She shook her head.

"I know I wasn't dead and that scientists weren't able to analyse the fluid or the capsule. It seems I know as little as everyone else. There were a few other parts of people preserved alongside me."

"Those others weren't preserved. They were degraded samples. Our scientists believe they were placed there just to confound anyone who tried to decipher your preservation. The head and tissue treatments were easily explained. The sarcophagus that sheltered you proved impenetrable and impossible to scan, probe or analyse. The first examiners assumed you were dead. As the years passed, they recorded no cellular decay, and as instruments became more accurate, they detected brain activity."

"Dr Grossmith told me, but then…" she hesitated, not sure if she should trust him with her fears. She glanced up; he looked serious but smiled as he waited for her to continue. His scary factor had scaled right down since they left the Tabernacle, so she took a deep breath, "...I saw an image of the sarcophagus, and it terrified me. I hate the word 'sarcophagus'."

He nodded, understanding.

"There was no change to the sarc...capsule over the centuries."

"But I changed, didn't I?"

Alice hoped it was alright to talk about this with him, she'd put a certain distance now between her new life and the subject, and apart from the hated word 'sarcophagus', she didn't give any of it much thought anymore, although she knew others did. And Principal Ryan was proving to be anything but dull.

"Well, I've seen images only," he shook his head. "Your form was indistinct. Analysis of the images from around fifty years ago showed you gaunt, with no hair or teeth."

Alice went pale. The idea of him—of anyone other than Dr Grossmith seeing her like that horrified her. She'd seen her image on the registry when she went investigating but now, to hear it from someone like Principal Ryan was worse than Toby telling her she had chin hairs! Obviously, some of it was still capable of striking a chord.

Principal Ryan swallowed hard. What was he thinking? Why on earth did he start a conversation like this?

"Dr Langley, I do apologise. I didn't mean to be insensitive."

Alice recovered herself; she didn't want him to think her vain, even though they spoke of a time when she had no

105

control over her appearance.

"It's fine, Principal Ryan. I've seen images of myself, but you paint quite a picture. Do go on—if you don't mind, that is."

He hesitated, he was no expert, and now, she was waiting for him to continue. He'd committed himself, so he would make the best of it and choose his words more wisely.

"These features alerted Grossmith to the changes in you. In the literature provided by Principal Hardy when you arrived on the Significator, we learned, around fourteen years ago, a technician noticed a change in your hair and fingernails—they were growing. Dr Grossmith arranged for you to go to Saturn Station, and he never moved from your side. He witnessed the event ten years ago when the preserving liquid and the, er…capsule disappeared instantaneously, leaving no residue. You weren't even wet. No trace of the fluid could be found in your body, as though the liquid was little more than an illusion. You were left lying in a shell-like structure. In the moments following, your life signs failed, and life support measures initiated."

He was glad to have avoided the word 'sarcophagus'.

"Where is the shell now?"

"In the Bell Institute. When your hair began to grow, Dr Grossmith believed the time was close for your awakening. He asked Principal Katya leave to take you to Saturn to protect you from certain pathogens. Moses pathogens. They stop the growth of new tissue. Everyone is immunised, but of course, you weren't, not then anyway. The pathogens can be deadly, and even if you survived the infection, they would certainly have interfered with the growth of your new organs."

"Moses Pathogens? Named after Moses in the Bible?"

"Almost. There are ten pathogens under the umbrella of Moses Pathogens. The scientist who isolated them had Christian leanings and became a Christian when he retired. I can take you to see the shell if you wish. It's a simple polymer dating from the twenty-first century. No mystery at all, much to science's great disappointment, and it gave them no clue as to the constitution of the preserving liquid."

"No," she said quickly. "I don't want to see it. When I saw the image on the registry, it was just like looking at myself in a coffin. I felt physically sick."

Ryan once more felt uncomfortable at having started this discussion. It was difficult to put himself in her place. It could only be unbelievably bewildering.

"Well, I can see why. I hope I haven't distressed you, Dr Langley. An interesting footnote to all this is you didn't age the whole time you were on life support."

"Principal Ryan, you haven't distressed me. I knew many of these things, including the fact I didn't begin to age until a couple of years ago. Dr Grossmith's view is the only one I've heard. I'm glad now I have another perspective, so I thank you for being so frank. I think Dr Grossmith is worried about upsetting me. He's very protective, unlike Dr Clere, who'd like to study me further."

"That won't happen. The Tabernacle will block any attempts to interfere with your life."

"I'm glad to hear it. I wondered in the past if all this might be a dream. I don't want it to become a nightmare."

"You were on Saturn Station a long time. It must

have been hard to leave."

"I don't remember most of it, just those last few months', Principal Ryan," she shook her head. "Before that, I was in some kind of semi-comatose state. They made me walk about to stop me from seizing up!"

Alice laughed at the image that conjured, one of a Frankenstein monster, wandering around a space station covered in bandages, arms outstretched. But it was likely Principal Ryan wouldn't understand, so she didn't share the thought with him. With no warning, the enormity of the changes of these last few months' hit home, and she found herself looking down at her hands, fiddling with the fingers on her left hand as if she were still wearing a wedding ring. It was sobering, and she looked over at him. He was studying her with interest, so she returned her gaze to the viewport and the view.

"My everyday activities were regulated and monitored by my carer and Principal Hardy," she continued, keeping the emotion from her voice. "Mostly, they kept me away from the crew, but I'm not a sociable person, Principal Ryan." She sensed somehow; he would understand that. "But to answer your question, yes, it was hard to leave, I felt safe there," then as if thinking aloud, added, "It was strange, on the station, I didn't give a thought to rain or the breeze, or the smell of grass, but when I came home…I realised how much I missed them."

"Do you feel safe now?"

Alice couldn't help giving him her biggest grin, despite the emotions churning inside her.

"I have everything I could wish for, Principal Ryan.

I'm so blessed."

So blessed. What a beautiful phrase. To have been through so much and to still feel blessed… Noah turned away as the propinquity alarm distracted him.

"We're here."

Alice, so engrossed in her history, hadn't paid attention to the fact that outside, it had turned to bright daylight. The journey passed quickly with their unexpected conversation, but then, with such marvellous technology, nowhere was far from anywhere on this planet.

CHAPTER TWELVE _

From the forward viewport, even after landing, she saw they were closer to the sky than earth. Tree covered mountains slanted in tones of purple and green to the left and the right, set like a tapestry against the azure blue of the sky. What glory! Jumping from the shuttle, oblivious to Principal Ryan's offer of help, Alice breathed deeply of the mountain air and ran towards the scene of sky and trees. She ground to a halt on top of a mountain ledge, a sheer drop stretching below her with no force field to catch any unsuspecting visitor.

She laughed at the danger, then turned her head towards a curious structure that towered above, much of it cleaved into the mountainside. Instead of reaching outwards from the mountain face like the city in Principality One, this edifice descended low to the valley floor, the facade carved in relief from the stone. A maze of terraces tiered down the mountainside, each embellished with elaborate stone fretwork and gleaming white in the sunlight. From where she stood, even this close to the top of the mountain, many, many steps led to the uppermost gallery.

What a magnificent place! A sacred place. The atmosphere seeped through to her bones. Inspired by the view and deeply affected by the atmosphere, she raised her arms to the heavens and closed her eyes, only opening them when she heard Principal Ryan's footsteps behind her. She swung around, wrapping her arms around herself in a hug filled with uncharacteristic freedom of spirit.

"It's *beautiful,*" she laughed, swinging back to the landscape of blue and green and holding out her arms once more to embrace the view. "It makes me wish I could write poetry."

"I know the feeling," he said as he stood beside her. "It makes me wish I could paint. Come along, Dr Langley, we are expected."

"I wish you wouldn't call me Dr Langley. Have you been here often?" she followed him along the path.

"I'll try to remember to call you Alice, but I'm programmed too well and may call you Dr Langley without thinking. Are you aware I should address you formally in company? To answer your question, yes, I have been here before, a long time ago, with Principal Katya."

"I'll forgive a lapse…" she said, then, with a joyful shriek, sprinted towards the steps that led to the uppermost terrace. Ryan stopped, bewildered. What on earth had come over her? She bounded up the steps with the energy of a child, her laughter ringing out and echoing behind her. As she reached the top, she turned, red hair flying in the breeze, hat in one hand and the other stretched out towards him.

"Come on, Martin, you old slowcoach!" she called.

Using her uncle's name sent a chill through Ryan.

What could he be witnessing? A momentary step back in time for her? A shadow from her past? She seemed eerily familiar and at ease in this place.

Alice, still laughing, turned and ran through an archway on the terrace. He spied her above the wall, running up the hill through the grass.

In his confusion, he started up the steps, catching up with her close to a cluster of large rocks, where she lay flat on her back on the grass, in a starfish pose, giggling. Without a word, and with the sense he might be intruding, he sat down beside her.

She swivelled her body to look at him.

"Have I been here before?" she said, her laughter diminishing into breathlessness.

"Honestly? I don't know."

But if his aunt was correct, perhaps she had, centuries before.

Alice jumped to her feet in one swift movement, shaking blades of grass from her hair, and looking around at the view.

"Isn't this beautiful, Principal Ryan?"

He stood, doubting she really needed an answer.

Then, the laughter gone, she stepped close to him, studying his face, her expression sombre.

"Do you think Alexis Langley ever visited here?"

He was about to tell her she'd called him Martin, but at that moment, an orange-robed monk signalled to them from the archway, and the opportunity lost.

The monk escorted them to a stone-walled room. There were no furnishings, save for a table, two chairs and a bench. The window was little more than a narrow slit, permitting only a hazy slant of light to illuminate the room. To Alice, it looked like a prison cell. She hadn't made the connection between the monk who escorted them and the fact this might be a monastery. She asked Principal Ryan for his thoughts.

"It's a sanctuary, Alice, the central structure existed for centuries, but the monks invited A'khet to remain here. They added to the structure and now occupy the lower levels. That way, the monks continue with their devotions undisturbed."

"Were the monks the first people A'khet contacted?"

"We assume so."

Alice would have asked more, but their discussion ended when four A'khet entered the room. As before, the calm and peace she felt at the Tabernacle when the lone A'khet visited descended upon her. Each A'khet touched Principal Ryan's shoulder, smiled and inclined their heads, then continued the same ritual with Alice, only this time, unlike the encounter at the Tabernacle, there was no sudden recoiling of hands.

Alice and Principal Ryan seated themselves at A'khet's silent command; each A'khet took a seat on the bench opposite. A sole A'khet spoke aloud with a thin, smooth, and gentle voice. Alice couldn't tell if it was the same A'khet she first met, as they were all identical in appearance and dress, only with a slight variation in height.

"You honour A'khet, Alice Watkins," the spokesman A'khet said.

"Thank you, A'khet."

"You would like tea?"

Alice felt their attention on her.

"Yes, please, we didn't get to finish dinner."

Principal Ryan smiled to himself as he remembered his aunt ushering them away. A'khet glanced at him; they'd heard him. So easy to forget that here, no thought could be hidden.

A'khet poured the tea into small, hand-held bowls. Strange, brightly coloured petals Alice didn't recognise floated on the surface.

"They are safe, A'khet can assure you," A'khet said, addressing her unspoken concern. "This tea will relieve any hunger or tiredness. It is most refreshing."

Alice sipped it. Sweet and fragrant. Like perfume.

A'khet waited for a moment for her to savour her tea before speaking again.

"You have had adventures, Alice."

"Yes, although it seems I slept through most of them."

"You believe you are sleeping now?"

"At times, yes, but I know you read minds, so I won't try to explain."

Each A'khet watched her with their large gentle eyes holding no expression, the extra eyelid sweeping across in complete and perfect synchronicity. She glanced at Principal Ryan, also watching her. What did they expect from her? Nothing was hidden from A'khet, and even as the thought floated, she heard A'khet's unspoken assurance they would not intrude, and she may think whatever thoughts she chose.

A'khet momentarily turned their attention to Principal

Ryan, speaking aloud once more to allow Alice a moment with her thoughts.

"All is well with the Significator, Principal Ryan? We hear Statesman Patrick has worked his magic once again."

Despite turning their attention away from her, Alice sensed strongly her presence here held more significance than a simple desire to get to know her. She wished she understood why.

"Indeed, A'khet," Principal Ryan responded, "and is aboard the Accessor as we speak, working that same magic to allow us to push out the boundaries of median space..."

"It's not magic."

Principal Ryan turned his attention to Alice, quietly engaged in sipping her tea and delicately pushing the tiny petals floating on top.

"Well, of course, it's not precisely magic..." he started to say, but his tongue stilled, not a paralysis to struggle against, more a tranquil rendering to silence. Unable to say another word, he watched A'khet turn back to Alice. Silence descended in the room, and for some minutes, no-one spoke. A'khet gazed at her, waiting, patient, unhurried—attuned to one another.

"I saw the engines," Alice said dreamily, with just the hint of a smile, her voice soft and low. "Patrick showed me. They chimed and shone, and the harmonies rose above and beyond any sound I ever heard in music, all flowing together into one perfect note. And the light—purple, to blue, to purple." She rocked her head from side to side in rhythm with the words as she summoned the memory, "In here," Alice raised her hand to her chest and her eyes to the

115

A'khet. "The sound, in here," she laid her hand over her breast, below her throat, "and I remember the colours…" then sighing mysteriously, she paused and carried on sipping her tea, the moment as forgotten as that moment which occurred on the monastery steps.

Principal Ryan, stunned into immobility by both A'khet's powers and Alice's response, looked to A'khet for an explanation, but they remained focused on Alice. Manifested on each of their faces, an expression he'd never seen in his few encounters with them, something like—he struggled for a suitable word—recognition? No—not only recognition, more like affection, but more even than the affection they had for his aunt. This expression was love. Undeniably, A'khet *loved* Alice? But he also witnessed a wave of indefinable sadness as they turned their eyes to each other and bowed their heads.

If Ryan was baffled out in the meadow, nothing compared to his feelings now. A succession of how's scrambled through his mind. *How could she know the harmonics of Substance? How could she have Knowledge? How could A'khet know her?*

His aunt was right. There was more to Alice than met the eye, and he was now sure there was more to A'khet than he previously believed.

As if they'd received all they required, A'khet rose. The A'khet who spoke throughout the interview stopped for a moment and placed a hand on Principal Ryan's arm, delivering in silence, just below his throat, in the same place where Alice indicated on her own self a moment ago, an echo of that which is left *after* words are heard.

"Time will be forfeit, dear brother, until then, A'khet entrusts our beloved daughter to you. She is not for Patrick. A'khet always knew you would be drawn to her."

Ryan felt a soft pulsating presence in his chest. Knowledge is drummed into the beneficiary, and this Knowledge was for him alone. But he didn't understand what A'khet meant about time being forfeit. Before he could regain command over his voice to ask, A'khet was gone.

Ryan looked at Alice, puzzled. He *was* drawn to her, in a way he couldn't explain, just as he couldn't explain his conduct in manoeuvring Patrick onto the Accessor. His regard for her began that night in the auditorium, regard neither influenced nor directed by the A'khet. Of that, he was confident.

She smiled up at him; there was a soft glow about her, her eyes held…? He couldn't tell…*something*. Alice realised none of this, still relaxed from the effects of the A'khet and their special tea; it occurred to her she'd forgotten to ask A'khet why they wanted to meet her again.

"The meadow, Principal Ryan," she said, "at the back of the terrace. Would you mind if we walked there for a little while before we go home?"

The incident on the steps and in the meadow from earlier apparently forgotten, he knew instinctively this time, Alice would visit the meadow and see it through new eyes. He didn't answer, just followed her out onto the grass and sat beside her, high on the hill, looking down at the monastery, discussing the scenery and life in space, with him doing most of the talking. The monks brought tea when they realised their visitors had not yet left, and the two continued in amiable conversation for many hours until the sun had almost disappeared, and Ryan reluctantly insisted they return home.

As they descended the hill with Alice still chatting about the views, he half expected her to bound down the steps with the same vigour she'd bound up them, but she stayed by his side. He could only speculate on the two sides of this lovely redheaded girl busily pointing out the monastery's architectural features she thought most beautiful, smiling at him in expectation of his agreement. He wondered why, not once during their encounter today, did the A'khet mention Alexis Langley or address Alice by her real name.

They'd almost reached the shuttle when Ryan stopped walking, overcome by an overwhelming compulsion to turn towards the monastery. Alice continued to the shuttle, not noticing he wasn't at her side. The upper terraces, glowing in the dying sun, threw shadows out towards the mountains, but he could just make out a solitary figure, a silhouette caught at the moment when day moves towards night.

"Our daughter walks with you in earthly form."

Ryan felt the words thrumming against his chest.

"A'khet addresses her as Alice Watkins," he answered from his heart. "Which is she?"

But Noah Ryan felt only stillness as A'khet's form simply melted into the fading evening light.

CHAPTER THIRTEEN _

As the shuttle lifted, and unaware of Principal Ryan's brief encounter, Alice peered through the viewport for one last glimpse of the mountains and monastery, but she could only see a mantle of darkness. A last look would be nice, but she knew in a few minutes, as they travelled, the night would pass into day. Alice was becoming used to this passage of light and time, and as the daylight came through, she smiled across at her companion.

"I loved it there, Principal Ryan. Thank you for taking me. The monks are lovely too and so polite. I have no idea why I was suspicious of meeting the A'khet again."

She settled back in her seat and tucked her hair over one shoulder. Ryan watched her from the corner of his eye, paying him no mind and smiling to herself, looking satisfied and comfortable. Around him, people didn't get that feeling often. Today, he'd seen much to bewilder, not least that she had little memory of the events.

"I loved the tea as well," she continued, "it was gorgeous. Is it something we can get at home?"

"No, I don't think so. I believe the monks make it."

"Oh, what a blow," her disappointed, pouting face caught him off guard, and he laughed, but it gave him an idea, a way of prolonging their time together.

"I could take you somewhere for something I know you do like."

"What is it?"

"I won't tell you yet, but would you be happy to detour to the city before we go back to the Tabernacle? We can have a late breakfast."

"Oh, that would be nice. How thoughtful. Thank you, Principal Ryan."

"You're welcome. Perhaps meanwhile, you would like to tell me about your new home? Principal Katya tells me it's beautiful."

"Oh, yes, it is." Alice sat up, always eager to speak of her new home.

"The house is on a cliff, well, just back from the cliff edge, so there are views of the ocean. On the opposite side of the house, we have lawns and stables with horses, and we have two dogs, which are nearly as big as horses, and a cat with half a tail."

Alice spoke in long sentences and gestured to add emphasis, from broad sweeps of her arms, down to measuring with her hands how much of the cat's tail was missing.

Ryan deliberately slowed the shuttle, he could have returned them in under an hour if he'd a mind, but he was in no hurry for their time together to end. He wanted to stay in her company, enjoy her happy explanations and simple joy, her startlingly green eyes and the freckles across her nose.

He was convinced, occasionally, he'd witnessed a glimpse of Alexis Langley's personality, but he couldn't deny the Alice side possessed a warm and gentle disposition all her own.

She rattled on unfettered for a considerable time, extolling the virtues of her new home, about learning to ride a horse, the fish she caught and cooked, that she was no longer frightened of goats, and the patch of garden she'd cultivated for her own projects. She'd learned modern growing techniques and how to keep plants healthy and free of pests. And she told him in hushed, reverent tones of the view from her room at night when the moon was full. She thought it was heavenly and said so.

"But the loveliest of all are the aunties," she told him. "I confess I still feel odd calling them that sometimes."

"Why? I understood one of them is as close to an aunt as you can get. Principal Katya has assumed the title of auntie for herself."

Alice wasn't sure about confiding in him; He might think her batty for having retained memories no-one believed were hers, so she would give just a little information.

"I know you're aware I have confused memories, Principal Ryan. Some of those memories place me around their age. Whether they're true or not, they still have an impact."

"Perhaps your aunt could help you discover something of your ancestry. It might help things fall into place for you."

"I tried it with Amelia—Educator Sebel, but I found it…well; we only asked about Alexis Langley."

To most people, researching Alexis Langley would make complete sense. Still, after the A'khet's cryptic words on the terrace as they left the sanctuary and that they'd used the name 'Alice Watkins' at the start of the interview, he was at a loss to form any theory. Although not a spiritual man, Ryan had faith events would evolve as they should. To speak of it to her might make matters worse.

Meanwhile, Alice waited for a response to her comment.

"Educator Sebel would be limited as she's not related, and you possibly searched a non-signatured registry. It blocks any information that isn't public. If you use your home registry with your aunt, those barriers aren't there."

"Dr Clere talks about me as if I were public property. Contravening privacy seems not to worry him. He spoke of me to Educator Sebel."

"He shouldn't talk about you to anyone, Alice. He's vaunted his contribution to your recovery in a report to the Tabernacle, and he refuses to see you as an individual. He may take some convincing, but I doubt you need to worry about him."

As she listened, she gazed thoughtfully out the forward viewport. Such a lovely day, and Principal Ryan such unexpected and pleasant company. A day in Tibet and now another day with no night in between. A journey like this would have taken hours in her old life; technology was in for an exciting future—the whole human race was in for an exciting future once they got past the plague.

"I was never imaginative. I don't understand how I would have conjured all this up for myself." Unintentionally,

Alice gave her thoughts a voice.

"Conjured up?" Principal Ryan smiled. "Alice, I don't feel conjured up, and I doubt Principal Katya or the A'khet do either. Conjuring up a completely different species with all their attributes would be a pretty tall order."

"Patrick said something similar, and so did Dr Grossmith. I suppose I feel it was because I don't remember being Alexis Langley, but I'm not the Alice Watkins I think I remember either."

"Perhaps it's a good thing. Paving the way for memories that make complete sense."

"Maybe, but what if the memories of Alice Watkins disappear and no other memories take their place?"

She was expecting an answer, but he had none to offer, so they both retreated into silence. Like Alice, Principal Ryan didn't mind a hiatus in conversation, but this time, he was glad when the city loomed into view.

"We're here. This place we're going—in part, you are indirectly responsible for."

He landed the shuttle on the same platform she and Principal Katya arrived at when Alice first visited the city. Alice kept her intrigue under control until they were inside.

"I don't understand how I'm responsible."

He pointed. "There."

It was a regular, modern eatery, set up with booths and tables, not much different to any eating establishment of this or her own time.

They sat down opposite one another in a booth, and Ryan pulled up the menu on the registry. Without a word, he showed her an entry.

"Hamburgers!" Alice gasped.

"Yes, Chef at the Tabernacle shared your recipe," He flicked the entry to place the order. "It's become quite a local favourite."

"Have you tried them?"

"Not yet, I'm about to," he grinned.

She liked his funny downturned smile; she found she liked everything about him, especially his eyes. And his voice, deep and melodic. He was far kinder than she gave him credit for at their first few encounters and so different away from the Significator. Alice felt comfortable asking him questions about his work and what made him special enough to command a spaceship.

"Spaceship is an old term Alice," he said, clasping his hands loosely in front of him on the table. "I'm a planetary scientist, an astrophysicist and a cosmologist; much of my work on the Significator involves celestial cartography."

He waited for it to dawn on her he'd mentioned this to her the night before, but she showed no signs of recognition.

"I know it's all to do with space," she said, "but I'm not sure what any of it means. My lessons revolved more around Earth's society than space."

"In simple terms, I chart the stars, classify planets and their suitability for exploration by humans or by drones or remotes."

"It sounds important."

He acknowledged her appraisal with a smile. "Now we are exploring..."

At that moment, the food arrived. Alice made a

conscious effort not to let her jaw drop. Crammed full of colourful extras, most of which she didn't recognise, it was clear someone's fancy had run riot and built extravagantly on Alice's original description of a hamburger.

Principal Ryan, beyond impressed, his work forgotten, raised his eyebrows in awe.

"I'm not sure space exploration is as important as inventing hamburgers, Alice. These are magnificent!"

"I didn't invent hamburgers," Alice said in a small voice, not wishing to claim accolades for something she had no part in, certainly not this towering creation, not even recognisable as a hamburger, and possibly a little overwhelming as a breakfast dish. "They're something we had in my time, Principal Ryan. I used to make the meat pattie and put other things with it, but nothing like these monsters. To get one of these, one would have to go to a hamburger restaurant." Even then, she doubted they would have been this formidable.

Alice tackled the concoction by deconstructing it. The chefs still hadn't mastered the bread, but the salad and meat pattie was spot on, and the cheese was excellent. Alice questioned Principal Ryan about the sauces and other additions, which tasted OK, but he didn't seem to know much about food. Alice felt a little self-conscious about the fact the burger kept falling apart and dropping on her, and most of it got applied to her face, requiring lots of fibrelettes to mop herself up with. None of it seemed to bother Principal Ryan, who ate as if he'd taken lessons from Patrick. She spied other people at the eatery with hamburgers and marvelled at how something so simple could catch on. She supposed they wondered about that at first in her time too.

Principal Ryan called for coffee when they finished, but Alice only waded through less than half her meal. In her old life, it would have represented enough for three days' dinner.

"They are amazing, Alice. Well done."

"I didn't invent them," she said once more, with a shrug. What's the use? Hamburgers were hers, it seemed, along with blue rinses and crochet.

"You may as well accept it. After all, there's no-one we can ask."

"But it's not the truth."

She gave up with a sigh, it was pointless to pursue it, and she changed the subject to something she knew he would talk about.

"Principal Ryan, will this registry show us proximal space?"

"Yes, of course, on a small scale, though."

He woke the registry, and on command, it displayed a colourful diorama covering the table. A small Earth and other planets slowly revolved as they made their way around the sun, "in their season", as Principal Ryan poetically referred to them. Other technical commands to the responder resulted in additional components being added, such as asteroids and dust clouds.

"This is proximal space," he ran his finger in a circle around the sun. Alice recognised, with no small measure of satisfaction, all the planets and even Saturn's moons.

"And this area here is median space." He showed her

how median space bounded proximal space.

"Like the brim of a hat," she offered, and he agreed it was an apt metaphor. A small area within median space ran in an arc, directly along a short section of proximal space, containing planets with no names, only numbers. These were for exploration by one of the other ships, he explained. Then he pointed out another section, extending beyond the encircling ring of median space.

"This is Region 931; it's in threshold space, the area we visited on our last mission, which, as you are aware, fell short of success. The area is now quarantined."

She vaguely recalled something about them being chased, but the specifics escaped her, so she pointed to a mark near Saturn, feeling a tiny twinge of nostalgia.

"That's Saturn Station, isn't it? How many stations are there?"

"Three, with a new one under construction. Septimus is set at the edge of proximal space, here…" he opened up an area devoid of anything, just nothing and more nothing besides a structure similar to Saturn Station, "and Hooker Station, here," he pointed to another area, "in the Andromeda Corridor."

She touched her finger on Septimus Station to enlarge the image, but nothing appeared to occupy the surrounding space.

"Principal Hardy told me Saturn Station could move if necessary, can Septimus?"

"Yes, wherever it's needed, it's not as big as Saturn Station. Proximal space is charted and scoured for other life forms, but Earth is the only inhabited planet. Research is carried out on planets within proximal space, and Septimus is moved to the region as required. Its constitution makes it available to median space also, but we haven't got that far yet. Our trajectories always take us past either Saturn or Hooker stations."

"Trajectories?"

"The way we're going or coming."

"What are those curly shapes all over space?"

"Albemarle waves; discovered more than two hundred years ago. The principality ships are too large to engage magnitude in proximal space due to the interaction with A-waves causing atmospheric problems on nearby planets. A small ship, like an automatrans, can negotiate A-waves with no problems if the pilot has enough skill. If we're in threshold, or wherever space is expansive, our sensors advise us when it's safe to engage magnitude."

He showed Alice a region of space closer to the border of threshold space. "This is where the fourth, as yet unnamed station will be located, but it can travel at eighty-per cent S.O.L under its own power, so it will be advantageous."

Her expression told him to explain that acronym.

"Sorry, speed of light."

She nodded, she'd discussed light speed and its peculiarities with Patrick, but much of what he told her went over her head.

"Why is Saturn Station just a hospital? Don't you have hospitals on Earth?"

"It wasn't originally a medical facility. It was just in stationary orbit as a base for exploring Saturn—living quarters for those studying the rings and housing laboratories for scientific analysis. Entirely by accident, they found the Moses pathogens, initially benign and just a nuisance, infiltrated cytobiological studies. Catastrophically, they found their true home and evolved a destructive potential to disrupt new cells. Moses pathogens don't survive in space, so Saturn became a medical facility."

Ryan paused for a moment; it occurred to him he might be bombarding her with information, but rather than showing signs of tiring of the conversation, she seemed wide-eyed with fascination.

"Saturn sounds like an ideal place to get better, but it's a long way to go if you only have a cold."

"There are doctors on Earth too. Like your aunts. They're medical doctors, aren't they?"

"Yes, retired now. Auntie Mary looked after families in the principality, and Auntie Jane looked after people in the Calamities. She worked on a principality ship and Saturn Station for a time, but she wasn't military."

He returned to his explanation on the sectors of space already explored and pointed out the areas where he'd travelled. Alice smiled at him as he explained, his passion for his work evident. At times, he paused and looked to her as he described a discovery or an event, confident she would find space as fascinating a place as he, with something new to learn and discover each day. The way he described it, it seemed to be that way. Eventually, he shut down the registry.

"We might need to leave, Alice. Principal Katya will think we're lost."

"Can we do that? I mean, can anyone get lost?"

"Not really, but we've been at the eatery for three hours."

"Oh, my goodness, I'm so sorry. All those questions. I'm such an idiot."

Her reaction surprised him. "Absolutely not. I seldom discuss what I do. It's refreshing to speak to such an interested inquirer. Nothing idiotic I can assure you and nothing to apologise for."

Alice relaxed. "Thank you, Principal Ryan. You've been very kind and courteous today. You're a credit to Principal Katya."

He grinned to himself. For a second there, she sounded just like his aunt.

CHAPTER FOURTEEN _

Principal Ryan intended returning to the Significator for a few days, thus leaving a respectable interval before contacting Alice again. But after having spent time in her company, he wasn't sure he wanted to wait to see her again. She planned to leave for home early the following morning, and he couldn't think of any reason to ask her to delay her departure. In the end, he elected to stay on at the Tabernacle for a day or two while he gave the matter further thought.

Ryan hoped he might get an opportunity to spend more time with Alice, but she retired to her suite when they got back to the Tabernacle to have a nap. Later, she visited Sarah's home and didn't return until dinner, but even then, her attention was taken by Statesman Mellor and Principal Katya. Ryan barely spoke two words to her all evening.

Well after midnight, he stood at his window, watching the moon, the same moon that Alice told him reflected like little steps across the ocean near her home. He sighed. Earth. Fine for a while, visiting with his parents at their chaotic house, a few days here and there with his aunt, it was pleasant enough, but after a while, he felt trapped, suffocated. Before long, that familiar need, that longing would come over him—the overwhelming desire to be out amongst the stars, his real home. Since childhood, he'd gazed heavenwards, but now...? He ran his hand through his hair. Well, now he wasn't so sure. The heavens and the Earth? He felt torn, and all because of Alice.

Throwing on his shirt and slacks, he left the courtyard and rounded the main building. Music wafted from the direction of the great hall. Sitting alone with his customary late-night bottle of spirits, Statesmen Mellor spotted him and held up a glass in invitation. Ryan silently acknowledged thanks, throwing a questioning glance towards the library.

"It's Alice," he said, "she does this."

"She did the same on the Significator."

"Yes, I know, Principal Katya told me, but she doesn't remember the next day. I spoke to her the first time and enjoyed a rather topical conversation concerning composition—a conversation she denies ever took place."

Ryan took the glass from Statesman Mellor and walked over to the library door. Alice, barefoot and wearing only a nightdress, was seated at the piano. He couldn't see her face, but instinct and prior experience told him he shouldn't interrupt, so he returned to Statesman Mellor.

"She plays well. Chopin."

Mellor nodded. "Yes, she does. She's had tuition. I don't believe she's self-taught."

As they lauded the merits of her ability as a pianist, the playing stopped. A moment later, Alice emerged from the library. Trancelike, she ascended the stairs towards the suites, not pausing or even glancing in their direction.

The two men watched her until she was out of sight, then Ryan swallowed the last of his drink and bade Statesman Mellor goodnight, leaving him to his solitude.

Alice was disappointed not to see Principal Ryan the next morning, but she had Principal Katya to herself at breakfast. Even though she'd given an account the evening before, she happily retold the story of her visit with the A'khet, the scenery and the monumental hamburgers at the eatery.

Principal Katya walked to the shuttle with her to say her goodbyes.

"I hope my nephew wasn't stuffy, Alice. He has no idea how to relax and shed protocols."

"He was lovely, Principal Katya, very nice and polite."

"Lovely, was he? Well, perhaps there is hope for him yet. Embrace me, my dear."

Alice kissed her on both cheeks.

"Do not leave it too long to visit us again, Alice. I am sorry to be so busy."

Principal Katya watched as the shuttle lifted off, then looked for her nephew in Cloisters. His account of the visit to the monastery, typically less enthusiastic than Alice's, and delivered with, as expected, fewer words and more measured responses, left her certain he'd deliberately kept particulars of the encounter to himself.

She'd sensed Alice's disappointment at not seeing Noah, and Principal Katya prepared to give him a telling off. Instead, she encountered Statesman Evesham, who advised her that he detained Principal Ryan on a matter regarding the next mission. At that moment, her nephew emerged from Cloisters.

"Good morning, Noah. You missed breakfast."

"Good morning, Aunt. I went to the kitchen earlier."

"Alice said you were 'lovely' yesterday and 'nice'. You are an imposter. No-one ever describes my nephew in such flowery language."

"Aunt, as I told you last night, the day was pleasant. I did mean to farewell her this morning, but as you can see…" They looked together at the retreating Statesman Evesham.

"And?"

"There is no 'and'."

"I know all about it being a pleasant day, Noah, but what about those things you didn't tell me. About A'khet and Alice. Details."

He hesitated. "I told you almost everything, Aunt."

"Almost, Noah?"

He drew her to a sofa. "I wanted to give further consideration to an event I witnessed," he said, glancing around to be sure they wouldn't be overheard. "I thought I would try to make sense of it myself before speaking to you."

"And have you made sense of it?"

"Not really, Aunt. Alice called me 'Martin'."

"Martin? As in her uncle—Martin?"

"I assume so; it was just the once. She ran up the sanctuary steps—the ones that lead to the uppermost terrace—with the energy of a child. The entire episode seemed so natural," he continued. "It was as if she was recreating a scene from her past. When she reached the top, she turned, held her hat in one hand and her other arm out to me and called, 'Come on, Martin, you old slowcoach'. She didn't comment on it afterwards, only asked if I thought Alexis Langley had ever visited there."

Alice and Alexis Langley. One person? Two personalities? A memory like this surfacing shouldn't be extraordinary, but Principal Katya knew from Dr Grossmith's reports, Alice possessed no memory of Alexis. For Alice to behave as Alexis, this development should be reassuring, particularly as it took place at the sanctuary, but Principal Katya felt oddly unreassured. And she knew those steps; very steep for the uninitiated.

"Then the A'khet are correct."

"It would seem so..." but he hadn't given up all his secrets.

"There is something else, Noah?"

"Yes, Aunt—A'khet didn't...A'khet didn't..." he couldn't form the phrase. A tingling sensation rose in his throat. He wanted to say A'khet didn't address Alice as Alexis Langley at any point during their visit, but more importantly, it appeared Alice was a holder of Knowledge. He played out the words in his head, but they became lost before they ever reached his lips.

Principal Katya watched and waited; she recognised the power that robbed him momentarily of speech.

"I understand, Noah, what you saw, what you heard was for you alone."

She reached over and took his hand. "I find myself fond of her, Noah."

"I can see that, Aunt," his voice now released from the paralysis.

"And you? To go to so much trouble to be alone with her?" Principal Katya fixed him with a wily grin, but he would have none of it, at least none he was prepared to admit.

"What trouble? You sent me."

"Oh, did I?" she said, pretending innocence. "So, I did. You should do it again, and next time I will remember that I sent you."

Alice's disappointment at not seeing Principal Ryan before she left got swept away when she arrived home to hugs and kisses. Mary and Jane sat with her, letting her savour a few mouthfuls of coffee before insisting on hearing all about the ball and her time at the Tabernacle.

But first, Auntie Jane produced a welcome home gift from the parlour. She placed a young lorikeet, grey and yellow, still with baby fluff around his chest on Alice's hand. He cocked his head from side to side and whistled a little, then climbed up Alice's arm and kissed her face.

"He's hand-reared, so you can teach him to speak," Mary told her. "We thought he might be a special friend seeing as your other friends either live in space or have other work to do."

Alice was overwhelmed.

"He's a darling! Thank you so much!"

The little bird picked up pieces of her hair and drew them through his beak, making little pecking sounds as he went. He found her ear and babbled before going again for a strand of hair, accidentally pecking her earlobe and drawing blood.

Alice put him back on her hand and gave him a strawberry while Jane examined the small puncture wound. It hadn't hurt, and the incident gave the small bird his name.

"I think I shall call you Pecky," she told the bird. He looked at her, taking the berry from his beak and squawking as loud as he could. The three women had no idea if he was approving, but it made them laugh.

After introductions to Pecky, now occupied with rocking himself to sleep on Alice's shoulder, attention returned to the ball. The aunties were delighted it hadn't proved so fearsome after all, and Alice showed them registry images of her standing with Patrick at the foot of the stairs.

"You look breathtaking," Mary said. "That dress is perfect. To be honest, it makes all these others…" she pointed to the other women in the background, "…look drab and pointless," then she pulled a mischievous face, a naughty little grin tugging the corners of her mouth.

"Auntie Mary! That's mean. And flattering! Almost all those ladies, including the elderly ones, would have snatched Patrick away in a heartbeat!"

"He is very dashing, though," Jane said. "Look at that uniform!"

"That's a word I use, Jane. It suits him," Alice agreed. "And he is sweet. I understand what all the girls see in him."

Mary and Jane exchanged looks.

"Did you spend much time with him?" Jane asked, making a poor attempt at keeping her tone casual. Alice knew a loaded question when she heard one, just as she knew the aunties harboured high hopes for her and Patrick.

"Only at the ball," Alice said truthfully.

"Oh," Jane said, clearly disappointed. Of the two, she was the worst actor; she'd imagined a romance blossoming in their time at the Tabernacle and hoped a revelation would be forthcoming. Mary was more pragmatic but no less probing.

"Did anything happen?"

"Well, Patrick said he planned to take me somewhere special the day after the ball but was unexpectedly called away to work, even though he was meant to be on leave." Alice shrugged to indicate she didn't understand the workings of the military.

"What a shame. Did he tell you where?"

"No, and I forgot to ask him when he said goodbye. I found out later, though, because Principal Ryan from the Significator took me instead."

"Wasn't he the unfriendly one?" Jane recalled Alice's earlier descriptions about her time on the Significator.

"I thought so at first," Alice admitted, "but yesterday was a whole different story. I can't remember ever having to rethink a first impression to such a degree, and I've had to rethink a few."

"Disappointing about Patrick though," Jane secretly hoped he would be special to Alice. It might be just what she needed, a boyfriend, but for now, her interest transferred to where Alice and Principal Ryan visited. Travel had been a passion of hers.

"Oh, yes, sorry. Tibet," Alice announced calmly, not expecting the chorus of surprise from the aunties.

"Tibet!"

They stared at her, openmouthed.

"Who invited you?" Mary was incredulous. This was a big deal. Ball forgot. Patrick forgot. *Tibet?*

"Don't be silly, Mary," Jane said, recovering from her shock, "A'khet invited her. They're close with Principal Katya."

"Yes, A'khet invited me. Principal Katya said her nephew, Principal Ryan, offered to take me because Patrick had returned to duty."

"Did they mind Principal Ryan escorting you?" The news floored Mary. An invitation from A'khet. Rare indeed.

"I don't know. They seemed happy to see him. Is it important?"

"No," Mary still couldn't believe the A'khet bestowed this honour on Alice. "The Patrick family has a historical connection to the A'khet, so I would expect if anyone were to take you, it would be him. Of course, I have no idea about Principal Ryan's family, apart from the A'khet knowing Principal Katya."

"Principal Ryan didn't give me any information about his relationship with them. We talked about lots of other things, not just the A'khet."

"Well, we've never been there, Alice; few people have. Those admitted to the retreat in later life never leave. We hear it's beautiful."

"Staggeringly beautiful, Auntie Mary, I have never seen or felt anywhere like it apart from here."

"Felt?" Jane echoed.

"I can't explain it; I had…warm feelings. The same as I have here."

"The A'khet can do that."

139

"I loved the scenery..." Alice sensed an echo of something that happened there, something involving Principal Ryan. Surreal and dreamlike, the more she tried to capture the memory, the more it slipped away.

Now accustomed to Alice's occasional descent into vagueness, Jane and Mary also accepted it usually heralded an end to a conversation, so they left the rest of their questions until later. They stood, and Alice, her attention diverted by their movement, shook herself out of her reverie to take a stroll along the clifftop

CHAPTER FIFTEEN _

Several days following her return home, Alice was in her garden, tending the vegetables she'd planted and picking the fruit that grew in record time. The aunties gave her a patch of earth to experiment with the "traditional method". That meant growing fruit and vegetables without the aid of technology, the process preferred by most people of this century.

Alice knelt in the dirt, digging happily, aerating the soil, picking berries and literally, enjoying the fruits of her labour. She felt blissfully happy and at peace, having consigned the day out with Principal Ryan to a one-off, most likely never to be repeated, pleasant experience. Her devoted companion, Pecky, had developed a secondary relationship with her sunhat, so wherever she went on the property, he perched himself on the rim. That morning, Alice popped a poncho over her shirt, tucked her hair into her hat, and tied a sarong around her waist so her clothes wouldn't get too soiled. She looked like an old market gardener, but then—she wasn't expecting visitors.

Principal Ryan arrived, unannounced, on a Tabernacle

automatrans and walked towards the house. Two figures were fishing on the beach, and from the lights, he could tell they were using forcefield lures. Even from this distance, he knew neither of them was Alice. They must be the aunties, he reasoned, which meant Alice would either be in the house or around the gardens.

A noisy and urgent squawking drew his attention. A figure, swathed in a poncho, knelt on the ground, probably the gardener. Perhaps he or she might know where to find Alice. Ryan headed towards the source of the noise, suppressing a smile as he came upon the delightfully pastoral scene.

Alice dug at the ground, mounding up the earth at the base of a small plant, a basket with fruit and vegetables by her side and a large hat on her head. Atop the hat, a young parrot, wings outstretched, tiny beak wide with threats, made noble but ineffective attempts to scare away a hen with her chicks.

So engrossed was Alice in her task, she didn't at first notice his arrival, until his broad frame cast a shadow, causing her to look up, gloved hand lifted to shield her eyes from the sun.

"Principal Ryan, are you lost? Space is that way."

She pointed upwards with her trowel, and he looked up; even though he knew full well the direction of space, he'd lived there most of his adult life.

"Dr Langley, I hope you don't mind me just turning up."

She got to her feet and picked up her basket. The little parrot eyed the visitor but then decided he might make an excellent perch. To Alice's horror, Pecky fluttered across and landed on Principal Ryan's shoulder. He wasn't in uniform, but Pecky hadn't shown himself to be fussy about pulling clothes to pieces. The new perch simply turned his head and spoke to the bird, who kissed him and pulled his hair.

"You've been busy," Ryan said. "What are you growing?"

She held out a handful of fruit. "They're raspberries, Principal Ryan," she said, her voice a mix of wonderment and pride. "Would you believe I grew them? I never grew anything before these."

Alice, always so carefully groomed and attired, to see her now, dirty face and raspberry juice-stained hands, he found her particularly endearing, so at home in these surroundings, unmindful of her appearance.

"They're enormous," he took a raspberry from her hand. It was almost the size of a walnut. Pecky made a lunge for the berry, but Principal Ryan was too quick and put the fruit into the basket, ignoring the scolding he received from the bird in response.

"I'd been worried about them while I was away," she admitted, "but the aunties take such care, I should have trusted them." Alice wiped her hands on her clothes. "Come up to the house, Principal Ryan. They would love to meet you."

He took the basket from her while she retrieved her trowel. But the automatrans had already drawn their interest, and Mary and Jane hurried from the beach to discover who was visiting. They hoped it might be Patrick, come back

143

unexpectedly. Instead, next to Alice stood a large, distinguished, fair-haired and official-looking man. Jane gave Mary a sideways glance. He must be Principal Ryan. Alice had described him well.

"Principal Ryan, Mary and Jane Greer."

He bowed to them both. "Dr Greer and Dr Greer."

Mary offered him a chair. "Principal Ryan, we are just about to have tea." Mary hoped he would overlook the lie, but she had fish scales all over her hands, and she and Jane needed to get inside the house to wash. "We hope you will join us?"

Alice swept Pecky from her visitor's shoulder and put him back on her hat before depositing both hat and bird on a side table.

"Thank you, Dr Greer, most kind."

"We have lamingtons. They are little cakes Alice invented," Jane offered.

"I didn't invent lamingtons," Alice protested pointlessly.

"I've tried another of Dr Langley's inventions," Principal Ryan told them. "Hamburgers."

"Oh yes, we've had them too. They're delicious, aren't they?"

"I didn't invent hamburgers," Alice mumbled, but no-one listened. When tea was ready, and the cakes duly offered around, Alice declined, drawing a look of surprise from Auntie Jane.

"I ate the raspberries as I picked them." She looked at Principal Ryan and pulled a guilty face, "I couldn't resist." She saw the corners of his mouth move with his trademark grinning-but-not-grinning. He inclined his head towards her politely.

"I see you cultivate your garden using traditional methods, Dr Langley."

"I like the feel and smell of the earth, Principal Ryan, and I believe nothing is lost in growing things the old-fashioned way."

"Let's put some on the table." Mary took the basket and placed the berries in a dish. "Alice has done a magnificent job with them, Principal Ryan, she's very diligent, and they grew so quickly. She put Jorrocks's manure on them—would you like to try them?" Mary held the dish towards him.

Oh, my goodness! Alice felt the colour drain from her face. He would think they had poo on them! Why did people in this century make so free with such personal words? She hurried to reassure him.

"It was a while ago, Principal Ryan, and I've eaten them since. They're quite safe. You won't get a mouthful of..." she trailed off, the end of the sentence becoming lost in the realisation she didn't want to explain what it was he wouldn't get a mouthful of.

Principal Ryan grew up around horses and animals and the outdoor life. Unperturbed, he took some raspberries, and Pecky wandered over to stand on the back of his hand to beg for berries. Principal Ryan broke one up for him. This small action and a little bird's trust told all three women a good deal about Principal Ryan.

"So, to what do we owe this pleasure, Principal Ryan? Alice told us you were a most attentive guide to Tibet,"

145

Mary asked after a few minutes. Principal Ryan didn't seem to offer a lot in conversation, and the aunties were a lot less comfortable with silences than Alice.

"We had a most enjoyable day, Dr Greer," he said. "Now, in the absence of Dr Langley's friend, Statesman Patrick, Principal Katya asked..." he smiled politely at Alice, "that with her agreement, I act as a guide to some of Earth's most interesting areas."

"How wonderful. Alice, do you hear that? There are so many fascinating places to see," Mary said, her face alight with enthusiasm.

"I can't imagine anywhere more beautiful than here, Mary, but Tibet came a close second."

"May we suggest the Top of the World, Principal Ryan, or Florence!" Jane mentioned a couple of her favourite places.

"Worthy destinations, Dr Greer, perhaps another time. I was considering Peru if you can spare her, of course. Dr Langley has already taken many days away from you, attending the Cotillion Ball."

"Of course, we can spare her. Alice can choose for herself. Alice?" Mary would tread carefully here, remembering she pushed Alice into going with Statesman Patrick, although, she sensed, Alice seemed far less reluctant this time.

"I don't know where Peru is," Alice admitted.

"A place of history, Dr Langley," Principal Ryan told her. "There's a citadel there, deemed to have been built by the Incas in the fifteenth century. Certain astronomical alignments, which of course, I find fascinating, remain undeciphered. Its original purpose has never properly been defined, possibly a city, possibly a sacred place. Over the centuries, many theories have emerged and subsequently disproved. The site is well preserved and no longer explored for its historical significance, only by a few interested scientists and architects."

"Sounds like me," Alice said without thinking.

They looked at her. Secretly yes, they all supposed—a little like her.

"Machu Picchu, Alice, hidden from the Spanish when they invaded the Americas," Mary smiled a secret smile across at Jane,

"We loved it there," Jane sighed. "It's a special place for us, but we haven't been for years, sadly."

For the first time, Alice saw something approaching regret that Mary and Jane couldn't go to a special place together. Alice had never heard of Machu Picchu.

"The Americas? Not a principality? Is it a long way from the Tabernacle, from here?"

"It isn't so far," Principal Ryan said, "but it is inaccessible by shuttle. Much of the Americas is designated a province, not a principality, I'll explain later. We would have to take an automatrans to get high enough, and there is a lot of trekking, but I don't believe it will present a problem for you."

"Will you stay at the Stable?" Mary asked.

Principal Ryan started to reply, but Alice, in her sudden dismay, interrupted him.

"Stay? We have to stay there?"

"Yes, Alice," Mary answered, "by the time you get

there, it will be morning, and you would need a couple of days to explore. You have to stay."

"The Stable is an experience, Alice," Jane chimed in for support. "You sleep on straw." Alice had never tried anything like it, it sounded intriguing, and with an opportunity to spend time with Principal Ryan now presenting itself, she'd get over her worries about being away from home. She stood and headed to her room to shower and change.

"I'd better go and pack a toothbrush."

"It can get cool at night, Dr Langley," Ryan said as she stood, "you may need some warm clothes, and there are insects that bite, so wear long sleeves."

He loved those off the shoulder blouses she wore, but he would have to forgo that pleasure to save her getting bitten or from freezing to death.

Alice nodded. It was nice of him to come all this way to take her sightseeing when he probably had better things to do.

"I will, Principal Ryan, but I wish you would call me Alice."

She'd asked him that at the monastery, but Doctor, Principal, Statesman, formal titles, last names, came so easily to him. With people he didn't know, it was proper to address her by her title, but…

"Very well—Alice."

Mary watched his expression during the exchange. It was plain to her, the expedition to Tibet made a significant impression on this important man, enough for him to turn up without warning with plans to take Alice to Peru.

"It's Alexis without the 'x', Principal Ryan," Mary said, as Alice disappeared into her room.

"Something like that," they heard Alice call out.

"Toothbrush?" Principal Ryan turned back to Mary and Jane.

"Yes, a device from her time to clean and freshen teeth, before wafers," Mary explained.

"I see." He didn't really; he couldn't even imagine it.

"She has other funny sayings," Mary lowered her voice, just in case Alice overheard, "We understand some of them now."

"That's right," Jane added, "when she tidies up after a meal, she declares everywhere 'spick and span'."

"Yes," Mary looked towards the hallway, "we looked up ancient sayings—it means clean and tidy."

Principal Ryan found this information amusing, his slight smile encouraging the aunties.

"And she also says, 'flying by the seat of her pants'," Jane said with a grin, "that means she's guessing what to do and doesn't know."

"She refers to herself as 'mummy' to Pecky," Mary nodded towards the little parrot now sleeping on Alice's discarded hat.

Alice gave Principal Ryan many reasons to smile, her simplicity, her gentleness, and he loved learning about her from her aunts. He'd vacillated between contacting her and going back to the ship, not wishing to appear too eager. His aunt hadn't sent him to see Alice, he hadn't even confided in her he planned to come here, but he didn't want to admit that to Alice or her aunts. Where Alice was concerned, where any woman was concerned, he could only 'fly by the seat of his pants'.

Alice packed as instructed and kissed Mary, Jane and Pecky goodbye. The trio watched them leave.

"He seems pleasant enough," Mary said. "I wonder how many others there'll be beating a path to our door?"

And they laughed and hugged as the automatrans rose into the air. This must be what it's like to be parents; if so, they loved it.

CHAPTER SIXTEEN _

"It's kind of you to give up your free time to show me around, Principal Ryan," Alice said when the aunties were out of sight. He looked nice today, she thought, not dressed in the same film star style as Patrick, but informal and individual in his way. His hair, minus the regulation oil or whatever officers without ponytails used on their hair to tame wayward locks, was free to flop about his forehead and collar. However, she doubted he dressed with anything other than functionality in mind.

"Alice," he smiled at her as soon as they were inside the automatrans. "As I am to call you by your preferred name, and as we are to spend a few days together and I am at leisure, I think it appropriate for you to use my name. It's Noah. I would prefer not to be referred to as Principal Ryan at Machu Picchu if you don't mind."

"Yes, okay, Noah. Patrick told me your name."

"Did he indeed? I would have thought your conversations would involve more entertaining topics!"

She smiled a little but didn't let on what most of her meetings with Patrick entailed.

"Like Noah from the bible, commanding a big ship," she said.

"Christian mythology. Are you knowledgeable?"

"Me?" she almost spluttered. "Not at all. I just suffered from all the guilt and anxiety my mother, who called herself Christian, instilled in me."

"That surprises me. I'm no expert, but I understood Christianity brought considerable peace to its adherents."

"Not to my mother, fearing God was agony. Do you still have Christians?"

"Yes, we do. Those who choose that way at retirement live a communal life within a realm. Tibet is an example of a realm, but there is no city there as A'khet, and the monks are completely self-sufficient. They have no use for such amenities. Most other realms have no buildings apart from the communal housing and a basic city, but they still have to comply with the statutes of the loyalties."

"What kinds of statutes? You mean laws?"

"Yes, laws. Anyone who wishes to unite with a religious group can only do so after their service to the world is complete—when they retire. If they become unable to serve before then, the World Principal can allow them to enter their chosen realm if there is no hope of them ever returning to service."

"Can they leave the realms?"

"Of course, but the realms are like the Calamities in that there are restrictions on travel. Single travel only is allowed, but their families and friends can visit."

"With a married couple, what if the husband or wife doesn't wish to live in the realm?"

"The partner could go alone and leave the other in the loyalties, I suppose. As I said, I'm no expert. I don't know if it has ever happened. With the system for matching couples, these leanings are considered at the time of marriage application. Not all Christians go to the realms, but if they wish to worship openly and within congregations, fellowship with like-minded individuals would have considerable appeal.

"Do you have Muslims?"

"Yes, we do, and the same applies. And people who embrace Judaism, but all of them gain great joy from serving their world, then gain great joy from retiring into their communities and being with people who understand their beliefs. They don't mind the restrictions. If they did, they wouldn't go."

"People of my time would have accused this society of intolerance."

"That may be so, but those differences and the attempts to integrate them led to wars in the past. We don't have those conflicts now, and I dare say if you spoke to any member of the world's population, they would say our system works."

"In my country, Australia, we proudly proclaimed ourselves multicultural, and we were, provided whoever came there became one of us. We still feared differences, religious, political, colour. My mother wouldn't let me play with aboriginal or Asian kids, and I'm ashamed to say I did the same with mine."

He elected not to react to the last comment, realising she wasn't speaking of Alexis Langley's time. Alice herself hadn't noticed what she'd said, too busy enjoying learning another person's perspective of her new society.

"So, you would say the mixing of culture to such a degree doesn't work?" he asked, not sure which century's society would furnish her answer.

"We made a lot of noise about how our society accepted other cultures, but then made just as much noise about how they must integrate into ours and leave any strange ways behind. I'm only repeating what I heard at the time, Principal Ryan, sorry, Noah, I have little knowledge of my society, but I embraced its prejudices, foolishly and without question. I accept some of your society's methods are far more workable. At first, I didn't, but now, seeing how people treat each other, I've reassessed many of my first impressions." She didn't add that her opinion of him was one.

"I am glad you're feeling more comfortable in our society, Alice. You live in a beautiful area and have good friends. It's something I look forward to in time, a home of my own, perhaps with horses."

"Don't you have a home and friends?"

"While I'm in service, while any of us single people are serving, we're not allocated a permanent home. On leave, we visit parents or family or wherever we choose. For now, my home is the Significator."

"What about friends?"

"Not really, I've never cultivated friendships, Alice," he smiled the funny downturned smile. "People find me 'stuffy' to use Principal Katya's words."

"Yes, I've heard you described like that…"

Such complete agreement was unexpected, but she went on to say,

"...taking me to Tibet and Match...this place today, giving up your time, I don't think you're stuffy—Noah."

Alice stood on the ridge, looking down at the citadel. She'd managed the vertiginous climb without a problem, refusing to use the local transport for fear she may miss the views, and stayed easily ahead of her companion during the ascent.

"Peru is a province? What's the difference between a province and a realm?" she asked as Noah joined her in the view.

"The provinces are areas exempt from the Principality Accord. Areas where the plague's effects were devastating and far-reaching, leaving entire regions depopulated. All of South America was affected, leaving only one region, Principality 32, Argentina in your time, intact."

"All these beautiful places in the world and I didn't know a thing about them," she said wistfully. Noah didn't comment, just stood beside her as she surveyed the glory of the scenery; unable to believe his luck she'd agreed to come with him.

The guide met them to escort them, speaking to Noah in a tongue Alice didn't understand. Noah answered in the same language and indicated she should follow.

Alice tried to look in every direction. Peru. So beautiful here. Breathtaking. As beautiful as Tibet. She returned the smile of an old woman who walked past, shrouded in a colourful blanket and wearing an equally colourful hat, followed by a llama with matted hair who came to investigate as they descended to the citadel. The llama smelled like mouldy cheese, and Noah and the guide laughed when she wrinkled up her face and held her breath.

The mountains rose high in the distance; their tops lost in the clouds. She couldn't see the valley floor from where she stood, and she could almost touch the heavens. Alice Watkins missed out on so much. She would not let these opportunities pass her by now; she no longer lived that small life. Alice paused, turning in a slow circle, viewing every view. Ahead, Noah and the guide realised she wasn't with them and stopped to wait for her to catch up. The guide had seen many people taken with the beauty and ambience, and he gave Noah a knowing grin. Noah knew how she felt; she was more expressive in her appreciation. Had he been a little freer, he may have done the same thing.

There were only two other couples in the group, so they could examine and climb and discuss. Soon enough, the others wandered off to do their own exploring, leaving Alice and Noah alone. He'd visited the area often, and Alice soaked up all his knowledge. The temple area was constructed of dry-stone blocks, and Noah spoke knowledgeably on the life of these enormous bricks, of the terraced fields, the residential levels, and the attempts at restoration over the centuries. Alice couldn't conceal her fascination. Regardless of the subject, she circled the information, considered it, then repeated it back to him to be sure she fully understood. Not once did she appear fatigued or disinterested, and the first they noticed time passing was when the sun turned to orange and lowered in the sky. Noah suggested they go to the Stable and prepare for the night.

The Stable wasn't a stable. Stalls, with straw sure enough, but rather luxurious, definitely artificial straw. A forcefield roof covered the stall to stop its occupants from getting wet if it rained or freezing to death overnight. There were no horses, but a mix of donkeys and mules and llamas wandered around outside.

The "stall" had a washer with a gel-pack shower the same as on the starships, and Alice realised the idea was to give the impression of sleeping rough. In reality, it was all rather comfortable. She wondered what it would be like to sleep out under the stars but wasn't too sure about where the smelly llama spent the night. Besides, she could see all the stars she wanted through the force field above her head.

The guide prepared a fire outside and arranged a circle of stones as seats. Noah waited for Alice while she checked out her accommodation. All day, she'd listened to him and asked questions, responding to this place—one of his favourite places on Earth—with a sense of innocence and wonderment. He didn't want the day to end.

She joined him, sitting beside him close to the fire. The sun was way down in the sky, and she watched the layer of red, sandwiched magnificently between the dark blue of the night and the mountains.

"It's beautiful here, Noah. I love it. I love this," Alice gestured around, and despite wearing a thick hat and her jacket, she shivered. Noah picked up a blanket to drape around her, and she cuddled herself into it. In silence, they watched the evening sky consume the dying sun as it disappeared in colourful layers, leaving behind the brilliance of the stars as a backdrop.

The two couples sat with them and introduced themselves. One, newly married, were both agriculturalists and the other, entertainers. Noah and Alice gave their Christian names, offering no additional information, and none was asked for.

The evening meal offered a mixture of flavours that Alice found spicy and oddly sweet. Interested in sampling the local cuisine and wishing to be polite, she was unsure she liked the taste, but only she hesitated. The others seemed to love it, so she supposed her palate was not as sophisticated. She welcomed the hot chocolate that followed, and afterwards, the guide brought out a guitar and sang to them in the language Alice heard earlier.

The two entertainers collected various instruments from their stable; a guitar, a violin, a drum-like barrel, and a pipe Alice had never seen the like of before. The couple sang beautiful folk songs, encouraging them all to join in. In excellent English, the guide sang along, proving to Alice the use of his native tongue, like the addition of 'straw' to the stable, was merely an effort to make the experience more authentic.

Noah asked if he might take the violin and join in, clearly knowing the songs well and preferring to play rather than sing. Alice was too shy to contribute but loved the music and applauded each song. Noah played the violin as well as he played the oboe, and Alice supposed he hadn't played the violin at the concert on the ship because she remembered he told here there were so many violinists already.

As the night drew on, the others withdrew to their stable, leaving Noah and Alice alone. Alice was fighting sleep. What a wonderful day. Her tired brain conjured up Alice Watkins's not particularly happy memories. She'd learned nothing of the diversity and history of the world, learned nothing to pass onto and inspire her children. Michelle and Steven were limited by their mother's lack of education and vision. What a waste. She shook her head to dispel the thoughts; she didn't want to spoil her mood by overthinking, so she smiled up at Noah.

"I'm tired. I need my bed. Today was magical."

He stood and helped her to her feet; she handed him the blanket.

"You'll be warm enough in the stable, Alice. There are extra blankets next to the bed. I've enjoyed today. Thank you."

She held her hand up in a small wave as she closed her door. Noah stood for a moment before going back to the fire, wrapping the blanket around himself. He caught a faint trace of her perfume. Machu Picchu was one of the few places on Earth he ever felt peaceful, the air always felt so clean out here, and he was close to the stars. He would have liked Alice to stay with him. The fire burned bright still, and he propped himself against the pile of blankets. Sleeping under a forcefield didn't appeal, and as he always did, instead of going to the stables, settled for a night under the stars.

Noah woke Alice in the morning. The sun was high over the mountain, and the guide provided a cold breakfast with a pot of coffee, accepting Noah knew his way around the ruins almost as well as he did. Noah knocked hard on the door, and she opened it in a hurry, her eyes wide with surprise.

"Oh, Principal Ryan, I slept like a log. I'm so sorry."

He smiled at her formality. "It's fine. Get ready and come and have breakfast. We've still got another level to explore."

Alice didn't take long to tidy herself and go out to the fire pit. Noah was digging at the fire, and he grinned as she sat down, offering her the breakfast, but she shook her head and pointed to the coffee. He poured it for her, noting she seemed a little distant.

"Are you alright?"

She nodded. "I suppose so."

He sat next to her, handing her the beaker.

"What happened? You were so cheerful last night."

"Perhaps that's just it," she said. "I've never experienced an evening like yesterday evening. Sleeping out under the stars, even if there was a forcefield above me," she sighed, "even the fact there *was* a forcefield above me. The technology still bewilders and amazes me. And being here in such a historical place and listening to accomplished musicians around a campfire, I guess I realised how small my life was previously, a small life, lived in ignorance and steeped in the ordinary. How little I had to offer."

She shook her head as if dismissing the thoughts, then smiled an apology.

"I shouldn't be saying things like that."

"You aren't ignorant and ordinary. Alice." Noah didn't share this view. "You take a simple and refreshing view of a world many of us are complacent about, and you love learning about your surroundings. Such places were less accessible in your time. I've been here many times, but I'm seeing it now through new eyes, thanks to you. I can't remember watching the sunset here. These sites are a natural part of our education and available to all, perhaps except for Tibet, and in that, you received an honour most definitely not given to everyone."

Alice studied her coffee for a moment and then cast her gaze out over the mountains before looking back at him, a little of her shyness returning as she met his eyes.

"I was frightened of you the first couple of times I met you," she admitted.

"Were you?" Of course, she was. He knew it, but he would pretend ignorance.

She nodded. "Yes," but then took a deep breath and changed the subject. "What do you do when you have leave from the ship apart from visiting here? Hobbies—that type of thing."

Alice wouldn't admit it, but she was as interested in understanding him as she was learning about Peru.

Noah was unused to giving information about his life outside space, mainly because there was little to tell, so he would answer as simply as the question was posed.

"I usually spend some time with my parents and sisters; I like gardening too, flowers especially and roses particularly."

"Flowers?" Not the answer she was expecting.

Noah picked up a blanket. "I weave as well, a little like your crochet. I first became interested in it here when I came with my parents." He showed her the pattern of colours in the hand-woven blankets, "but I mainly weave baskets using patterns like this, although I once wove a rug for my parent's house. It took me ages, years in fact," he laughed, "I did it between assignments."

"I didn't expect flowers and weaving as hobbies," she confessed.

"You consider them strange pastimes?"

"No, but, Noah, you are so educated and important and, well—large," Alice felt foolish making such a personal observation, but she'd expected sport, or body-building, or something—different. "I imagined someone like you, Principal of a starship, explorer, scientist, I don't know…just not flowers and weaving baskets."

"Well, my parents have a rose garden."

He wasn't at all sure what difference the information would make. In her time, male/female roles had greater definition, and his activities might not be considered suitably masculine, perhaps a little on the genteel side. In a rare flash of humour, just to see if his theory was correct, he added, "I also like puppies and kittens. My parents usually have those around the house too." He struggled to keep a straight face in light of Alice's surprise.

"I'm sorry, Noah, amongst the people I knew, flowers and basket-weaving would be unexpected hobbies for a man like you."

"A man like me?" he raised an eyebrow. This was fun.

"Just…ignore me." She went back to her coffee. Trust her to say something stupid. But Noah couldn't ignore it. His theory was correct.

"What did you think? That I bite the heads off chickens?"

But he didn't do a good enough job of hiding his amusement. He was teasing her! And suddenly, she giggled and jabbed him in the arm.

"I am not at all frightening, Alice," he said, smiling at her response, but it reminded him of that night in the auditorium, Engineer McIntyre and myriad others. He had to admit it; he could be intimidating.

"Well, I thought you were scary," she decided not to let him off the hook. "But you're not now," she put her coffee down, stood and grinned down at him.

"Tell me everything about what we are going to see today."

CHAPTER SEVENTEEN _

Alice described herself as ignorant, but with her energy and eagerness to learn, Noah forgot her earlier description, occasionally witnessing sudden flashes of knowledge, as fleeting as they were startling. She appeared oblivious to the episodes, each time delivering this knowledge in the same confident tone and inflexion she used when speaking with him at the Cotillion Ball.

But the Alice who returned from those crossovers, with no memory of the preceding moments, smiled often, listened attentively, asked endless questions, and climbed over walls and rocks, discovered and enquired further. He was coming to recognise these two distinct personalities and concluded, for now, she only fully knew that side which she attributed to Alice. The other, Alexis, must hold all her true memories, those crucial memories her doctors hoped she would recover, and then perhaps the Alice personality would integrate. But her Alice existence seemed valid to him, compelling even, and he perceived a beauty in her that wasn't only physical.

Alice devoured all of Noah's knowledge about the

ruins, and when she'd exhausted everything he knew, tapped into one of the registry terminals to learn more. They laughed about the now long gone Eduction chip, and she told him she wished she'd had one at school. Life might have been quite different.

They returned to the stables late. The entertainers left earlier in the day, so the previous night's jollity wasn't repeated, apart from a few songs from the guide. Alice was again very tired and went to the stable after dinner, leaving Noah outside alone, wrapped in a blanket. Sleep didn't come easily to him, with his mind far too busy trying to unravel the secret of Alice's connection to the A'khet, a connection she clearly didn't recognise. All the data, all the research, pointed to the woman by his side these last two days being Alexis Langley. The observations he made, questions from her and even some of her answers confirmed the fact to some measure. But he couldn't forget that A'khet addressed her as Alice Watkins, the woman whose identity she professed she owned. Alice was no less intelligent than Alexis Langley. She appeared to absorb a considerable amount of information, especially about history and architecture. In her sweet and gentle way, when she spoke, he felt protective of her, close to her.

At some point during his deliberations, the fog of confusion gave way to sleep; he woke to find her standing over him as the sun rose.

"Aren't you freezing?" she asked, holding out a mug of coffee.

He sat up and raked his fingers through his hair. "No, the fire stayed alight for quite a long time. I must have fallen asleep before it died down."

She looked out over the mountains as he took the mug from her. "The sunrise this morning, it's beautiful," she said, then she smiled, "I say that a lot, don't I? Something is beautiful or wonderful?"

He got to his feet and dusted off his clothes and hands; he must be a picture of sloppiness and might need to excuse himself to go and shower.

"Well, it's because they are. They're simply truthful observations."

"Do you ever take it all for granted, Noah?"

"As I said, we can get complacent about our treasures."

"That's just a fancy way of saying you do take it all for granted."

"So it is."

She stood as close to the edge of the ridge as possible, watching the little fingers of dawn heralding the new day. So silent. So still. An eagle screeched as it flew above the trees.

"Tell me about Alice Watkins." The question was unplanned, he might regret asking, but she didn't turn to him to find out why he'd asked. Instead, she laughed—a tiny laugh filled with irony; for once, someone wanted to know about Alice, the person, not her society or her century. She didn't reply immediately but returned to where he stood, seating herself on a large stone opposite him. She considered what she might say and how much. She studied the rocks, the mountains, the remains of the fire. Somehow, she trusted this man. He sat down and waited, uncertain.

"What I tell you might be the ramblings of a crazy

woman."

"Why do you say that?

Alice shrugged, "I told Principal Hardy and Dr Grossmith I believe I'm Alice Watkins, and they tell me, firmly, I'm wrong, I can't be Alice Watkins, it's not possible. I am Alexis Langley, a doctor, no less."

What could she lose, she decided, by telling him everything? He would be on his way back to his ship soon and would probably forget all about her, so with the decision made and the early warmth of the sun on her face, she told him her story.

"I didn't even know other doctors existed who weren't your local doctor, the ones you see for colds and flu and such like." She wanted him to see how difficult it would be for her to accept that anyone should refer to her as "doctor".

"Alexis Langley is a scientist. Scientists are usually titled doctor, Alice."

"This isn't about Alexis Langley. You asked me about Alice Watkins."

He nodded. She was right; he had asked about Alice.

"I had very little education, Noah. I was useless at school, and at one time, they even said I had learning difficulties. I admit it doesn't seem to be a problem now. But a scientist? Not possible."

"So, who *is* Alice Watkins?"

"No-one at all. A person to overlook, insignificant, nothing to contribute." She looked him in the eye, "I'm the girl who was told she would sink, so I never swam."

"I can't believe that."

"Believe it. I lived with my mother; I never knew my father; he died before I was born. My mother was domineering, loud and discouraging. She called herself a Christian, but I feared her more than I feared any god," Alice said, with a slow shake of her head. "Then, at sixteen, I met Ted Watkins, who worked for my mother around the house and garden."

The early sunlight glanced off her hair, long and loose, lifting from her shoulders in the early morning mountain breeze, and he took a moment to be dazzled by her, so lovely, expressive. It made her next comment even more incredible, spoken as if it were irrefutable fact.

"I was not a pretty girl, Noah," she said, looking up. "I was so plain; it was impossible to do anything to improve my looks. All my life, my mother said no-one marries ugly girls, and she would never get me off her hands. So, when Ted paid me attention, unbelievably, my mother quickly agreed to our marriage." Alice laughed without humour, "I used to think she paid him. I didn't like him—Ted Watkins, but I was too afraid of my mother to refuse."

Noah listened with increasing sadness. Why would anyone accept such unhappy memories so willingly?

"I was seventeen when we married. I worked in a bakery, but Ted said I had to stay at home and look after the house, his father's house, we lived there. I looked after them both, and when his father became ill, I nursed him. A teenager with no practical experience of life having to care for a husband and a mean old man. Michelle was born just after I turned twenty-three."

Noah remembered her odd comments, alluding to

children. She believed she was a mother.

"I loved the baby. Ted's father died the same year she was born, leaving us alone in the house. I kept the baby with me all the time; I wouldn't let my mother near her. It was the only control I had over my life. She and Ted governed where I went, with whom and even what I watched on TV or listened to on the radio. They weren't interested in the baby anyway, so she was mine alone."

"How long did this continue?" Noah couldn't imagine such a life or wish it on anyone.

"It was eternal, or so I thought. My lot. How could I escape? I stayed home, accomplished nothing, didn't socialise, got older, did as they told me, and even when my mother died, I wasn't free because I still had Ted. All decisions were made for me. I had no voice at all. Then another baby, Steven, came along in my early thirties. Ted was horrified, and after that, he moved into the spare bedroom. I've never been so thankful." Alice's expression changed, her lovely mouth twisted, and she shook her head. "I despised him. I think I only realised that when I came to this world."

She squinted up at the sky. The sun was brighter; it's light creeping into all the hidden places. "At the time, I believed he was all I was worthy of."

It occurred to Alice then; she'd told Noah about separate bedrooms, she didn't feel embarrassed; there seemed to be a place for it in this story.

"Wasn't she able to leave?"

"And go where?" she gave a harsh laugh. "With two children? I had an uncle, David, but he was sick. So, I was stuck. After Ted died, I was so habitualised at being a victim, at not speaking up for myself, I was every bit as chained as when he was alive."

"And he died when?"

"Seven years ago, now," she answered vaguely, not noticing the outstandingly inaccurate reference to time. "But Michelle took up where he left off. The difference is, Noah," she took a deep breath, "she truly loves me and tries to do the right thing. Michelle's a good girl. She saw how unhappy I was throughout my marriage, but she was a child with no power to change things. Unfortunately, she inherited my mother's and Ted's controlling natures."

"Does she have a family?"

"Yes, she does. Her oldest child, Eliza, is a beautiful girl, tall, sweet, and she adores me. We're very close. We share the closeness I hoped for with Michelle. My son, Steven, has never married. He's thirty now. Michelle was having another baby when all this happened; her sixth would you believe?"

It was all hard to believe. "Are there any other memories, less tragic?"

Her answer saddened him. True or not, she believed all this.

"No, they are *the* memories. But I will say that just before, well, before I woke up on Saturn Station, I'd started to feel comfortable with the world. I sold the house and moved to a little unit. Michelle's other children were growing up, I saw a lot of Eliza, and Steven was working abroad very successfully. Life had taken a turn for the better."

She smiled brightly as if trying to be brave in the face of such overwhelming wretchedness.

"It was the best I could hope for; all the rest had passed me by," Alice gave a little gesture of resignation.

For a moment, he thought she would cry. Tears glistened in her eyes. If she did, what would he do? But she lifted her chin and took a deep breath, and he wondered if the person she believed herself to be was beyond tears.

"I wasted my time not learning. I had no imagination, so I don't understand how I imagined this life for myself; a dream life, with people and things and places I don't understand, people with abilities I've never even read about, machines beyond anything I could comprehend. How can it be?"

Noah didn't know. He could only offer suggestions.

"Isn't it possible, Alice, these people, Ted, Eliza and the others, are the dream? It's only been a few months, a short time to recover memories that have been asleep for centuries."

"I've considered that Noah, but Alice Watkins—I know her story so well, I don't see how I can be anyone else. But things are no longer as clear-cut—this Alice Watkins," she gestured to herself, "may remember all the bad things, but now, I *can* learn, I'm free, I'm no longer disempowered. If this is a dream, I don't want it to end, ever. Although I speak with authority on Alice Watkins, over the months, I'm beginning to doubt she exists anywhere but in my imagination."

He had to mention it. To see what she made of it. See if she remembered.

"Sometimes, Alice, another side of you emerges. You speak with a different inflexion, different confidence, even your body language changes. It's happened on more than one occasion. One moment, I am with you as you are now, but at other times, I believe it may be Alexis Langley's personality."

He decided not to tell her about the incident on the monastery steps, nor remind her A'khet called her Alice Watkins. Somehow, he was sure there was unfinished business there.

"I know, Noah, I've been told this before and sometimes, I have vague recollections, but mostly, I don't remember anything. Listening to you playing the violin reminded me of the time on the Significator when you said I played the piano. I don't remember it at all. I only remember seeing you, being afraid and not knowing why I was there. I've played the piano at the Tabernacle."

"More than once."

"Oh, dear."

"I saw you."

"Oh, my goodness. My steward told me I once went to the library in my nightie."

"Well, I only saw you once, and you were wearing a nightgown and no shoes, but only myself and Statesman Mellor heard you, and we stayed outside the library."

"I need to tie myself to the bed. I can't believe I do it. How can I do such a thing and have no memory?"

"Music is part of a person's soul, a part of their personality. Once it's there, it never leaves. It may not be a part of the Alice Watkins you remember. You can't even be sure you have all her memories."

"You might be right. I led a very gloomy existence, and I have no musical ability whatsoever."

"Then you can't be her. Don't forget, I've heard you play the piano."

"It's how I remember my past," Alice shook her head sadly. "The truth is, Alice Watkins, whether she's a figment of my imagination or not, is in here," she tapped her head, then, moving her hand to her heart, whispered, "and she's in here. Noah, I'm not sure I've got the courage to stand up and say— not yet anyway—that these memories are false, that all I need is time."

"I find it difficult to see the other Alice in you," Noah said, "and I disagree. You have incredible courage. You've come so far."

"Do I seem more like how Alexis Langley would be?"

He had only his instincts; she'd somehow meshed two distinct personalities together, one perceived, the other true. But which of the personalities he'd witnessed belonged to Alexis Langley? The only answer could be that both were her personality, still fragmented from the stasis but separated in Alice's mind until she felt safe and secure in her new world. His thoughts returned to the A'khet, so why would they make a distinction…?

"Alice Watkins seems to be a victim of her circumstances. Was she as bold, as confident, and eager to learn, or as determined? What would her mother's response be to her daughter spending two nights away in a remote area with a man she hardly knows?"

"Horror, but then, I would have been far too shy to

accept anyway. Perhaps Alice Watkins and Alexis Langley are making a new person between them." She hesitated, "Noah, I've never gone into so much detail about my memories, not even with Dr Grossmith."

Then he saw a tear slide down her cheek. She was not beyond the pain. It seemed right for him to go to her, reach down and take her hand and draw her to him. He guided her arm around his waist, and she left it there, curling her fingers into his shirt. Placing his hand ever so gently over the side of her head, he held her to him. Not for one moment did she resist or question, only took the comfort he offered.

She felt small and sweet and soft in his arms, and he closed his eyes. When he spoke, she heard the depth of his voice resonate in his chest against her face.

"I don't know if the memories of Alice Watkins have an explanation," he said gently. "You may need to accept them as part of your new life and make new, happier memories."

"I *am* making new memories, Noah. Wonderful memories," she tilted her head to look up at him, "but Alice Watkins was all I ever was before. I know they aren't happy memories mostly, but they are all I have; without them, I have no past at all. I didn't exist. I'm a ghost."

He smiled down at her, her skin pale against the whiteness of her blouse, her hair still golden in the early sunlight. A little sprite. She rested her head back against his chest, smiling a tiny smile when he momentarily stroked her hair.

They stood for a moment longer, and though he didn't want to be the one to break the spell, high above them was a starship he needed to get back to in a few short hours, he'd already delayed his return far too long. Cursing silently, he took a deep breath and let her go, dropping his arm and finding her hand.

"We have to get back. I am due on the Significator. Thank you," he smiled, wiping a stray tear from her cheek, "for telling me about Alice Watkins."

Alice didn't regret telling him, didn't regret letting him hold her. She felt she could be herself around him, whoever "she" might be, and gave herself a little shake.

"I'm okay now, Noah. I don't want to make you late with my tales of woe."

"My new statesman, Junnot, is in command in my absence. I planned to go back the day after Tibet, but I had to spend time in Cloisters with Statesman Evesham, so I'm very late, and that's not your fault. I'll take you home, if you wish, we can find another place to visit when I come back in a few days. Your aunties suggested the Top of the World. From what we've discussed, you might find it very interesting. It's not too far from here."

Alice felt sad at the thought of him leaving. Sadder than when Patrick left, but he had an important job to do, and she mustn't distract him. Of course, she told herself, he was just being kind when he held her, and she was silly to read more into it than that.

CHAPTER EIGHTEEN _

"Welcome home, Alice," Mary and Jane greeted her as if she'd been away a month. Pecky, riding on the back of a boisterous dog, flew squawking onto her shoulder to nibble her hair in welcome, prepared to forgive her for leaving him now she had returned.

"Good evening, Principal Ryan," Mary greeted Noah. "Alice, how did you find Machu Picchu?"

"Wonderful, Auntie Mary," Alice gushed, "indescribable. Principal Ryan has such knowledge; I'm sure I wrung every last ounce of information out of him!"

"She may be right, Dr Greer," Noah smiled, "and after draining me of knowledge, she turned to the registry terminals and wrung them out too."

"Well, Principal Ryan, we hope you're not in a hurry. We would love you to stay for a while."

Alice saw him hesitate, even sensed his disappointment, but he had responsibilities.

"I have to decline. I am headed..." Noah pointed to the heavens with a sideways smile at Alice, "in that direction."

"Oh, what a shame," Mary wondered at the secret joke between them, "another time, perhaps, you are always welcome."

"Thank you, Dr Greer. Alice, I'll keep in touch."

He made a slight bow to the aunties, but for Alice, his eyes found hers, and he made a tiny movement of his mouth, a small statement, meant for her, and he hoped she understood.

Alice desperately wanted to walk with him to the shuttle, wondering if she did, he might hold her again, but she contented herself with watching him stride away, followed by one of the dogs, who was rewarded by a pat on the head and a kiss on the snout.

The aunties sat her at the table. As always, tea, or coffee, depending on the time of day, was duly served as they settled in to hear all the details. Alice forgot none of her experiences, there were so many special moments, each one memorable, but she didn't tell them about her most unforgettable moment when Noah held her. For now, she would keep it preciously close to her heart.

Noah arrived back at the Tabernacle to find the Significators automatrans waiting. He quickly went in search of his aunt to inform her he would be leaving again directly. She emerged from Cloisters to walk with him out to the automatrans.

"Patrick left a message for you, Noah. He wonders when you are returning to the Significator."

"What did you tell him?"

"The truth. That Principal Ryan escorted Alice to

Machu Picchu and would be back on the ship today."

"How did you know I went to Machu Picchu?"

"I know your favourite place in the world, Noah, and I knew you would never be too long overdue returning to the ship. I guessed the rest."

"Dr Langley likes history. I invited her to come along."

He looked down at her, bending down even further to make sure she knew he could see the tiny, I-know-the-truth smile on her lips. No point in trying to fool his aunt. She would see the heart of the matter just by looking a man in the eye.

"Patrick is envious of you, I think, spending time with Alice."

"Aunt, are you troublemaking?"

"Not at all. Don't worry; I told him I asked you to take her, which isn't strictly true. He asked if you require him on the Significator, as he is arriving here in a few days and plans to see Alice."

"His assignment to the Accessor isn't finished."

Principal Katya took her nephew's arm.

"You know, as well as I do, Noah, he is not on assignment. He can come and go as he pleases. Just as Alice can."

He did not comment, but she saw the change in his expression from the corner of her eye.

"It is you who is jealous now."

"As you say, she can do as she pleases."

"As long as it is with you, eh?"

He ignored that and instead stooped to kiss her,

turning back as he stepped into the automatrans. "I don't need Patrick on the ship right now. I can't make excuses to bring him back when he's on leave. And stop meddling, Aunt, you are World Principal, not Noah Ryan's private life Principal."

"I am everyone's principal, including yours," she smiled. "I just love you the best."

He grinned at her as the door closed, a grin that faded as soon as she was out of sight. He had to go back to the ship, it was outside protocol to leave a new officer in command for any length of time, even in space dock, and he'd already exceeded that protocol by several days. What lousy luck it came just when Patrick was returning. He had to have faith what he and Alice shared meant something to her and that Patrick, for all his charm and looks, still wouldn't turn her head.

Over the following few days, Alice tried not to hope too much that Noah would make contact, but she felt like a teenager with a first crush, something she'd never encountered. Her tummy fluttered, and she watched the skies constantly, becoming distracted when she thought about being close to him. She told herself off for her nonsense, busying herself in the garden or fishing or riding, or showing Auntie Jane new recipes. She spoke to Amelia on the registry and consulted with Dr Grossmith, who examined her heart and insides from a distance. He told her he was back on Earth full-time now, living with his brother, and this would be the last time he would need to check on her medically but would stay in close contact.

Amelia invited Alice to visit, but she felt she'd been away far too often. Mary and Jane were stunned when she admitted to refusing Amelia's invitation.

"You must do the things you wish to do, Alice," Mary said. "We love that you are creating a life for yourself, making friends, experiencing the wonderful things this world has to offer. See Amelia, spend time with her and invite her here for a visit. It will be splendid."

Jane completely agreed, so Alice agreed to visit Amelia the next day on the mainland.

That evening, the registry beeped an incoming link. Alice desperately hoped it was Noah and felt guilty when she saw Patrick's signature, but she smiled brightly to cover her disappointment.

"I hear you have been spending time with dull old Ryan!"

She pursed her lips. Noah was anything but dull.

"His aunt asked him to show me some of the sights," she said tartly, but Patrick was oblivious to her tone. "A little extra education about Earth."

"Principal Katya told me, Alice. I'm coming to the surface early tomorrow, and I really would like to see you. In fact, you are the sole reason I'm coming."

"Aren't you busy?"

She wasn't sure she wanted to see him again so soon after the events of the morning at Machu Picchu.

"I was a little overcautious," he admitted. "Oakes is handling things well, but at present, there is no chief engineer on the Accessor, she left to get married, and the new one doesn't start his assignment until just before the

Significator leaves, so I am 'it' for now."

What could she say? He would be hurt if she refused, and Alice wasn't in the business of hurting people. So she lied.

"Well, it would be lovely to see you, of course, but I made plans to go to the mainland to see my friend Amelia."

"Well, I can come with you. I'm happy to do that if it means I can spend some time with you."

He lowered his voice—a voice Alice suspected he used to seduce. He could try, she thought, but it would never work.

"I miss you," he leaned closer to the registry. "We don't have enough time together."

"Patrick…I."

"I know, just friends," he resumed his familiar, cheery voice and sat back. "At least I can be sure Ryan won't win you over with his charm."

"Don't be unkind, Patrick. He's very nice, and he is very knowledgeable about Machu Picchu. I learned a great deal from him."

"Not surprising, his family love it there. He and his parents and sisters visited there often during family recess. I went with them a few times."

"I liked it, Patrick. I find I like history. My aunties suggested the Top of the World, but it doesn't sound so historic. Noah thought I would like Machu Picchu instead."

She hoped he wouldn't notice her use of Noah's name. He didn't, thankfully.

"That's because he prefers it. The Top of the World isn't historic. It's more a romantic adventure. I planned to take you there myself. If time permits, I would still like to."

"Romantic?"

"Well, Alice, apart from the phenomenon itself and the rainforest, the ambience is artificial, it's not like the historical sights, more a place a man and a woman get close to each other. It's a place of discovery, if you know what I mean?"

How often would she have to tell Patrick romance was out of the question? He was relentless, although she thought she would be happy to go with Noah.

An incoming call signature from the Significator blinked in the corner of the registry. Noah!

"I lost you there for a second, Alice."

"I'm sorry, Patrick, I'm tired. I'll see you in the morning."

"Yes, can't wait," he smiled, blowing her a kiss which she ignored.

Alice waved her hand over the responder, and Noah's face came into view.

"Hello, Alice. How are you?"

"Hello, Noah. I'm fine, thank you. It's nice to hear from you," She tried not to show exactly how nice and wished her heart would slow down. This giddiness was for teenage girls.

"Are your aunts at home?"

"They're in the parlour."

"I understand Patrick is coming to visit?"

"Yes, tomorrow, but I already planned to see Amelia—Educator Sebel.

"That would have disappointed him."

"He didn't say so. He invited himself along, then talked about taking me to the Top of the World before the Significator leaves."

"Did he now? Well, you must do what is right for you."

Noah hated her going with someone other than him.

"He says it's romantic."

"For Patrick, everywhere is romantic."

"You might be right, Noah," she didn't notice his hint of sarcasm, and he was glad. He had no business making such a comment.

"I don't want to go to a romantic place with him," she said, "but he doesn't take no for an answer." Alice was shaking her head, her lips a firm line. It would seem, Noah thought, Alice no longer considered Patrick her protector, but he was bemused, not to mention relieved, that she would probably be the only woman on the planet who didn't want to be romanced by Patrick.

"Do you have a personal registry?" he asked, remembering the registry at her home was communal.

"I have a registry in my room. Auntie Mary turned it off for me when I arrived."

"Why?"

"I don't like the little command thingy. I feel like it's watching me."

He raised an eyebrow at her.

"And you say you don't have an imagination?"

She shrugged.

"It's an interesting description, Alice 'command thingy'. It's designed to listen so it can do your bidding. It's a servant."

"I expect I'll get used to it, Noah. I'm still learning."

"Yes, you are. Now, I'm calling you from my registry in my quarters. I won't be back for a few days. I hope to see you again, but in the meantime, now I've caught up with what was waiting for me, I'd like to call you. If you prefer your aunt's registry..."

She was already standing. No, she wanted Noah to herself.

"Shall I wake the one in my room?"

He looked down and away from her as if checking something out of frame.

"Yes, I've found the signature, but as you say, it's inactive, so I would need to place another link. Do you know how to reactivate?"

"Do the opposite of what Auntie Mary did when she turned it off?"

"Yes, it'll come up with a grid of red lines and take a moment to connect. Do you want me to wait while you do it?"

"Yes, please."

She glanced at the aunties pretending to be engrossed in the entertainment registry in the parlour, then hurried to her room. She ran her hand over the back of the registry. Nothing happened. She tried the flicking movement, which worked on the second attempt. The red grid came up, as Noah said. In a moment, it connected, and the feared command icon blinked at her.

At the other registry, Noah waited.

"It looks active now, Alice."

"Yes, I think it is."

"Okay, I'll place another link. Your personal registry will record my call signature; then, you can also call me. If you wish to, of course."

She nodded. "Yes, but I probably won't. I'm almost certain to call when you are busy. My life is more predictable. Better you contact me when you are available."

She thought he was about to say something, protest maybe, but instead, he told her to go to the other registry and wait for the link.

It came through immediately, and Alice closed her door.

In the parlour, the aunties grinned at one another.

"Patrick *and* Ryan," Jane said.

"Yes, but it's Ryan she's speaking to privately. I think she likes him, really likes him."

"He's a principal; possibly it's private."

"Maybe, but she's seeing Patrick tomorrow, and if he is here and Ryan is there…well, who knows?"

"I knew you were the one for me right away," Mary slipped her arm around Jane's shoulder

"I knew too."

Red lines and lights swathed Alice and her entire room.

"What did you do?" Noah laughed as she appeared on the registry.

"I don't know," she swivelled her head around to look at the kaleidoscope surrounding her.

"Did you make a command to the responder?"

"It doesn't have a responder; it's just the panel."

"From the signature, it looks like an old-style registry, used for games and communication only, usually for children. They do odd things sometimes. Can you see a small curve, like a half-moon on the panel?

She nodded.

"Touch it."

She touched it, and all the lines disappeared. "Like I said. I'm learning."

He grinned. "Well, you looked very nice in red, Alice."

They talked about every subject from sport to food to space to planets. A large part of the scientific topics went over Alice's head, but to hear Noah speak of the things he'd seen made her long to know more. She wished she'd paid more attention to the journey back from Saturn, that she'd tried harder at school, and not listened to her mother when she told Alice she was stupid.

But Noah recognised some of these things were new to her and answered her questions patiently, even though she knew some were simplistic. He told her about the holographic interface navigational system on the ship and an amusing, fascinating tale about how technology was scaled back to limit the population's reliance on household and personal gadgets. It painted a hilarious picture in her head that made her laugh. They viewed images together of remarkable inventions that were in use for a while before being discarded. He laughed along with her, but never once in their conversation did he offer any endearments or make remarks that might make her uncomfortable. They were just happy to chat easily and enjoy each other's company, even though he was orbiting the world in a magnificent ship, and she was tethered here on Earth.

Hours later, after he said goodnight, she sat staring at the blank registry. The command now having lost its menace. She thought of her earlier conversation with Patrick, always about what he might gain from a situation. He wasn't unkind; he was dear to her in many ways, but her lack of romantic interest in him had intensified since she spent time with Noah. Patrick would never accept that she wasn't remotely attracted to him, and she found it difficult to think of Patrick without comparing him to Noah Ryan.

CHAPTER NINETEEN _

Mary and Jane insisted on tidying up and tending the animals and garden after breakfast the next morning, leaving Alice to prepare for her visit to the mainland. They watched from the window as Alice waited on the lawn for the shuttle to land. Patrick greeted her with a hug, lifting her feet from the ground.

"You are more beautiful each time I see you," he said as he put her down.

"It's not been that long, Patrick."

"Feels like an eternity," he whispered, lifting a strand of hair from her shoulder. She'd deliberately dressed modestly, passing over her favourite off-the-shoulder blouses in favour of something more sedate. Her change in style did not affect Patrick.

The aunties waited a respectable few minutes, then came out onto the verandah, the distraction allowing Alice to wriggle from Patrick's embrace.

"Ladies," he bowed, kissing a hand in turn. Jane couldn't stop beaming. As far as she was concerned, between Ryan and Patrick, Patrick was a clear winner.

"You're quite the charmer, Statesman Patrick," she giggled.

"I beg to differ, Dr Greer, or else I'm out of practice. Alice here spurns me, and I cannot muster anywhere near enough charm or cajoling to make her fall into my arms."

Alice sighed, casting a wearied look to Mary, who sent her a small, private smile in return, remembering the evening before, when Alice spoke to Principal Ryan behind closed doors.

The aunties saw them to the shuttle, telling them to enjoy their day and that they looked forward to entertaining Statesman Patrick to dinner, an invitation he accepted with unconcealed pleasure. They watched as the shuttle headed towards the mainland.

"He is one spectacular looking young man," Jane declared. "And his manners—I think he is perfect for Alice, I thought so before, I still think so."

"If it was just a matter of looks, Jane," Mary countered, "perhaps there would be no contest, but I suspect Alice doesn't bother about such things. Besides, Principal Ryan is quite handsome, and his manners no less precise."

"Come on, Mary. He's nothing like Patrick—and you can't tell me Principal Ryan has an engaging personality, plus he's huge! He makes Alice look like a doll."

"Yes, but which of them did she speak to for hours last night?"

"Good point. It'll be interesting to see what she does."

"She might meet someone different altogether."

"That's not beyond the bounds of possibility."

———

Spending time with Alice put Patrick in a gleeful mood. "Your aunts are fabulous. I meant to ask before, what happened to Jane's voice?"

"A disaster on Saturn Station, years ago, chemical burns. She does well, considering she needs to coordinate her abdominal and throat muscles to speak. Auntie Mary says she has far more to say since I arrived."

"What was her name before she married?"

"Scott, I think, I'm not sure."

"I remember the incident on Saturn Station. It was when the station still served the geological teams in Saturn's rings. I was still at school, long before they transferred you there."

Patrick spoke to the registry. It displayed a text, along with images. Alice sat forward as a younger version of Auntie Jane appeared.

"Dr Jane Scott," Alice read, "I've never seen this before, Patrick."

"We don't have time to read the full text, but as I remember, three doctors entered a control field after an explosion, to save the crew inside. No lives lost thanks to them, but each one suffered injuries to varying degrees. Jane Scott was the last to leave; she gave her life support helmet to someone else; that's why her voice is damaged. Your auntie is a hero!"

"I didn't know the whole story. The aunties told me the station deployed safety precautions."

"The control field stops fires and the spread of gases,

but if you're caught within it and not properly protected, you're on your own until someone rescues you. One person on the research team got complacent, Alice, using chemicals and minerals he believed to be predictable. The team only wore their contamination suits, which wouldn't filter fall-out from chemicals. It hasn't happened since, though, and I doubt it could now. Safety protocols are paramount."

"Poor Auntie Jane."

"I wouldn't say so, Alice. She has Mary, and now, she has you."

Alice smiled. "I'm lucky to have them both in my life."

"I wish you would make room in it for me," he laughed, but she picked up a serious note.

"It was you who decided to poke your nose into the engines on the Accessor. I didn't send you," she pointed out.

"Poked my nose? Alice, what an odd saying, but that's exactly what I did, if you mean I supervised the work of someone else. Are you scolding me?" he grinned. "I promise I'll try to get more time away to be with you."

She wasn't scolding, and her comment backfired. She didn't mean he needed to spend more time. She turned her attention to the side viewport and supposed any other woman would be flattered by his attention.

"I'm sorry," he said, "I've made you quiet. We only have a few weeks before the Significator leaves, and I thought, well, you know what I thought."

"It's okay, Patrick. I do like to see you, but...you *are* pushy."

"Sorry, I'm used to getting my own way."

Alice didn't try to conceal her sigh. "More like you don't know how to take no for an answer."

He nodded, yielding without defence to the excellent point she made.

Amelia waited on the university landing pad. Alice sent her a message earlier to say Patrick would be accompanying her. He greeted Amelia formally, turned on the charm, and promised to spoil them both for the day.

"Have you ever been here before, Statesman?" Amelia asked.

"I have, Educator Sebel. I spent time at the university. My mother lectured in geology here for a while during my education, so I know the harbour area well. And all the best pasticiums and eateries for miles."

"They may have changed since you were here, Statesman, thirteen, fourteen, or so years ago? Maybe more?"

"You wound me, Educator Sebel," he said, pretending hurt. "I'm sure even at my advanced age, I am not too feeble to recognise important landmarks. I doubt things have changed too much—what do you think, Alice?"

He placed his arm around Alice's shoulders and kissed her on the top of her head, throwing all formality out the window.

"Here we go," she groaned inwardly, smiling awkwardly at Amelia's wide-eyed delight.

Throughout the day, observing Patrick's easy manner with Amelia, Alice couldn't help but notice how much more suited they were than she and Patrick. Amelia, beautiful, funny, bubbly, bright, curvy and, Alice conjectured, doubtless very sexy and in possession of all the attributes that would attract a man like Patrick. Alice had no idea what Patrick saw in her, maybe because she stubbornly refused him, and rejection was not something he was prepared to accept.

Apart from when they stopped to eat or admire a view, Alice barely had time to catch her breath. She'd never been to Sydney—though no-one called it that anymore. No iconic landmarks from her time existed, no opera house, no bridge, even though a monument stood at both sites. The schools and universities sprawled for miles, but the countryside along the river was pristine. Patrick took them to the mountains in the shuttle, following the river before turning inland to view landscapes she'd read about hundreds of years before but never seen. She walked miles, but each mile was worth every step. Another wonderful step in a series of wonderful steps. It would have been perfect had Noah been there. She checked herself; not the first time she thought of him today.

Later, Patrick waited inside the shuttle while Alice and Amelia hugged each other goodbye, Amelia whispered, making sure Patrick didn't hear.

"I'll call you in the morning. Something exciting to tell you."

"I can't wait. Give me a hint?"

"No, not with Statesman Patrick here. It's private. I'll tell you tomorrow."

Patrick stayed for dinner, entertaining Alice and the aunties with stories of space anomalies, engineering feats and alien worlds, all of which, he assured them, hand on heart, were entirely true. He ignored the glaring conflicts in distances and time, which were obvious even to the uneducated Alice, but Jane and Mary enjoyed the evening so much, they extracted a promise he would visit again soon. A promise he was more than happy to make.

Alice walked with him to the shuttle. Once they were out of sight of the house, he drew her to him. She put her hand on his waist and didn't return the embrace. Resting his chin on the top of her head, he sighed.

"I love you, Alice."

She didn't move, wondering if this was prompted because of the time she spent with Noah.

"Don't you love me even a little?" he said when she didn't respond.

She stepped away, reaching around to remove his hands from her back, but keeping hold of them as she looked up into his face.

"I love you dearly, Patrick," she said, giving his hands a little shake, "as a friend. What you feel for me, I can't return. It's just not happening. I don't know what else to say."

He closed his eyes as he pressed her fingers to his lips.

"I was going to contact Principal Ryan to advise him of my application to withdraw from the military, to stay here, with you."

Alice's jaw dropped, and she pulled her hand away,

mortified. This time she didn't spare his feelings. Raising her voice, Patrick got treated to a sudden outburst of fiery anger.

"And do what, Patrick? Woo me? Bamboozle me into accepting you? If you can't accept friendship, then I have nothing to offer!" She would have turned on her heel and stalked up to the house, but she was too busy exploding. How dare he? How could she get through to him the truth of the situation?

The shock on his face slowed her temper.

"It seemed like a good idea at the time. Don't worry, Alice," he sighed. "I didn't follow through with it. I knew you would disagree."

"Thank goodness for that!" she took a deep breath to regain her composure. "Patrick, I'm sorry for reacting, but you must understand how I feel. Besides," she added, her anger subsiding, "those engines are your babies. You can't leave them. Look what happened the moment you learned Engineer Oakes was assigned to the Accessor, you dropped everything, including me, practically to get there ahead of him."

He thought for a moment, then grinned. "I did, didn't I?"

"Why would you give up everything you've worked for on a whim?"

"Not a whim, Alice," he shook his head. "You're not being fair. I mean what I say."

"Perhaps, Patrick, but I know you would hate being stuck here just in case I changed my mind. What about the Knowledge A'khet gave you? Patrick, it's a tremendous gift."

Her unexpected anger caught him off balance, but to

leave here with no hope didn't bear thinking about, even though she was wise to remind him of his responsibilities.

"I won't give up on us, Alice. I believe with all my heart we are meant to be together."

"Purely as friends, Patrick, I'm sorry."

"As I said, I'm not giving up. I won't lose hope, Alice, and though I find it impossible not to touch you, desire you, I do respect your feelings. I know if we spent more time together..." He moved towards her again, but she put up her hands and turned her face away in defiance, refusing to look at him.

"...it would make no difference," she insisted, her tone lending weight to the language of her body. Patrick's arms dropped to his sides.

"As you wish, Alice. Like I say, I'm used to having my way."

"Something to do with women falling at your feet probably," she said, softening her voice.

"I've led a fortunate and blessed existence, Alice. Everything came easily to me. I excelled at school, graduated with the highest distinctions in engineering even before A'khet bestowed Knowledge. The military requested me before my graduation, and not on the strength of my family name. And women? Well, I guess I've had my pick, but now, for the first time, I'm being refused something I have an indescribable love and longing for."

"I still say you scarcely know me, Patrick. I scarcely even know myself."

He wouldn't be able to persuade her, at least not yet, he needed more time, and time was fast running out.

"I'll try to be patient. I'll call you soon."

As the shuttle lifted above her and sped away, Alice hoped her response didn't hurt Patrick too much. She didn't want to make him sad, but he wouldn't listen, and how could she even consider loving him when her thoughts were with someone else?

CHAPTER TWENTY _

Mary and Jane stayed on the verandah while Alice said goodbye to Patrick, she was gone a long time, and they speculated privately about the farewell.

"He's a lovely young man, Alice," Jane said when Alice returned.

"He's a pushy young man, Auntie Jane."

"Accustomed to having his way, I imagine?"

"Exactly," Alice smiled and kissed them both before excusing herself to go to her room. She checked her registry, disappointed at not finding a message from Noah and chiding herself for her behaviour, but she had no control over the butterflies in her tummy when she thought of him. She remembered Michelle, at fourteen, and her massive crush on Gavin McGee. He played football, and Michelle swooned and moaned about the house for weeks, desperate for him to notice her. But he never did, and Alice told her to stop her foolishness. She understood now, and it was her turn to feel foolish because she wasn't fourteen and should know better.

Alice stood in front of the mirror to brush her hair.

Over recent weeks, it had become thicker, longer, and wavier, and the sunshine had bleached streaks of gold into its carrotiness. The layers Miss Ling cut through it before the ball still sat nicely, and her smattering of freckles had found their way out onto her cheeks.

Alice placed her hairbrush on the table. It had been a long day, and the argument with Patrick upset her. Perhaps a shower and bed. Hopefully, she'd feel better in the morning. Unfastening her blouse, she let it fall from her shoulders, stopping as she caught her reflection in the mirror. Her breasts were saggy in her old life; once, Ted described them as golf balls in the toe of a sock when he came upon her unawares. She'd cringed with humiliation at his sneering, and after that, took great care he should not see them again. But these breasts, the new ones, sat up nice and even, cheerfully looking back at her like two cherry-topped ice cream cones. She tilted her head from side to side, admiring, evaluating.

The registry beeped, and Noah's private signature linked through. Hurriedly, she pulled her blouse back on before she answered. To her surprise, he was also shirtless, even though she could only see from his chest up. His upper arms and shoulders had muscles on muscles.

A surge of something that had never surged before in Alice gave her a need to restrain her eyes from popping out of her head. My god, she thought, I'm turning into a hussy!

Noah just smiled and greeted her, seemingly unaware of the effect her limited view of his naked torso had on her.

"Well, how did your day go?" he said, his tone conversational.

"Lovely, thank you, Noah." Alice made a concerted

effort to only look at his face, "We spent time walking and visiting the countryside. We went to the zoo…"

"The zoo? Like the ancient enclosures for animals?"

"Kind of, there were breeds of dogs and cats I'd never seen before."

"Did you go out on the harbour?"

"Yes, on a real boat, and we had lunch. Patrick took us to the mountains as well—they were magnificent; the scenery was stunning in every direction. Amelia and Patrick got along well."

"Matchmaking, Alice?"

"Maybe."

As in their previous discussions, they discovered endless subjects of interest. Once or twice, Noah found her moving away from herself and speaking on topics which, as a scientist, he understood, but he knew Alice Watkins would not. In response to a comment he made about molecular density, she launched into a sequence about cellular longevity and neural energy patterns. She told him about her "team" research, which to Noah, sounded like KELA procedures, such as the ones medical technicians underwent when caring for a long-term patient. He knew if he reminded her of this conversation, she would remember none of it, or at best, snippets which she would deny understanding. She didn't volunteer information on how she knew the procedures or her involvement in the development, and when he asked, she slipped back into Alice.

Noah found himself particularly drawn to the side of her personality he considered "Alice", the simple, refreshing and gentle girl who made him laugh with old-fashioned references, while displaying an impressive ability to remember and recount things she'd learned. Alice loved that she found him so easy to talk to, and that conversation never dried up or became uncomfortable.

It was late when he said goodbye, and almost immediately, Principal Katya's signature linked through to his quarters.

"Noah."

"Hello, Aunt."

"I hope you intend remaining on the Significator for a few more days. Statesman Evesham is arriving to discuss your trajectory proposals for the hundredth time. He must decide your final briefing. It's getting close."

Principal Katya noticed he paused before replying.

"Of course, Aunt, when is he arriving?"

She disregarded the question.

"You have other plans?"

"Not really. I'm coming to the surface."

"To see your parents? Or do you have another destination in mind?

"My parents." It was partly true, though he didn't know why he bothered trying to throw his aunt off the scent. "It'll be the last time for two years or so."

"After the trouble you took to eliminate the competition, I should hope you will be seeing Alice."

"Dr Langley and I are both interested in history, Aunt. I thought she might like to visit a few of our historical sites, and regarding your comment about 'competition', I only agreed to let Engineer Oakes go to the Accessor. I didn't send Patrick."

"Humph, semantics," she snorted. "Well, make sure you stay put for the next few nights. That will give Statesman Evesham the time he needs. Then you can go and show Alice the sights."

"I'll remain here for as long as I'm needed, Aunt. The Significator is my priority."

"Is it? I worry it is your prison. You have barely spent any time on the surface in the last four years. I am glad you now have interests here on Earth."

Although she liked to pretend, she never felt truly stern towards him. She loved him far too much for that.

"Have you seen Patrick since the Cotillion? I hear he is going out with the Accessor to oversee the new Gravidarum in median space."

"I haven't seen him, Aunt. I know he's going out to median, but it's a short trip; he'll be back on board here in plenty of time. Statesman Junnot is attending the final briefing, so Patrick will remain here on the ship."

"I see. Well, I might see Alice before you do. I am going to call her and invite her for a visit."

"Yes, Aunt."

"And Noah, please don't answer the registry to me again when you are naked."

The registry blanked before he could react.

He looked down at himself, he was wearing pants, and she could only see his shoulders. He seldom put his shirt back on when he'd showered and was retiring for the night. He's the principal of a starship goddamit! Just about as grown up as you could get, but faced with his Aunt Katya, well, he was just a little boy. Sighing, he reached for his shirt.

Amelia called early the next morning and Alice crawled out of bed to answer the link.

"Can't you sleep, Amelia?"

"Well, I could have," Amelia whispered, "but…" she gave a sneaky glance over her shoulder, "I had company."

Alice waited as Amelia's registry displayed, giving Alice a view of Amelia's bed. It contained a male, apparently asleep and thankfully, covered by a sheet.

"Amelia, a boyfriend! When did this happen? And in your bed!"

Amelia shushed her. "Well, where should he be? Yes, his name is John. We met the first day I arrived and hit it off straight away. I couldn't tell you yesterday with Statesman Patrick hanging around."

"Of course not, how wonderful, but you haven't been there that long, and you're in bed with him?"

"I'm not sure what it was like in your time, Alice, but we get physical early in a relationship." Again, her voice dropped to a whisper, emphasising each syllable. "And he is the best!"

Amelia told her before, sex was recreational, but sex was never fun for Alice. She shuddered involuntarily at an unwelcome and unbidden thought of Ted and his rough hands. Amelia's face fell.

"What's wrong, Alice? Aren't you happy for me?"

"Amelia, I'm just so surprised, but I'm thrilled for you. I can't wait to meet him."

"I think this is the one, you know, Alice, I really do.

And for what it's worth, Patrick is totally smitten with you."

"So, he says."

"You are playing cautious, aren't you?

"Well, I'm new to this life. I'm not ready to incorporate another person into it romantically." Even as she said it, Alice knew it wasn't strictly true.

"Very sensible. He'll wait. He'd be crazy not to."

"But this is about you, Amelia," Alice didn't want to mention her feelings about Noah, not yet, Amelia knew about Tibet and Machu Picchu, but she dismissed those as him doing his duty by Principal Katya.

A sleepy face appeared behind Amelia. Amelia saw Alice's face light up with a smile, and she looked around.

"Hello, Alice," the man said. John was tall and thin, with a goatee beard and messy brown hair.

"Hello John, how do you know I'm Alice?"

"Because dear sweet Amelia talks of no-one else!"

He pushed Amelia's blonde hair to one side and placed his head against her neck, one arm loosely over the other shoulder, facing the registry. They seemed so at ease. So happy.

"I wanted to tell Alice about you yesterday," she said, bringing him into the conversation, "but I couldn't while her boyfriend was with her. Girl talk."

John nodded. "I know all about girl talk."

"No, you don't," Amelia pulled both his arms over her shoulders and held them there.

John was chatty and friendly. He smiled often and kissed Amelia's ear as they spoke. Very likeable. Amelia had done well, and Alice was pleased—pleased with just a twinge of envy.

Later, she told Auntie Mary about Amelia's new love.

"Amelia is my first real friend; I'm so happy she met John."

"That's a sign you are genuinely fond of her."

"What is?"

"That you're happy for her, even though it means she'll be distracted, and you might see her less."

Alice hadn't considered the implications of her friend's new romance; she paused to give it thought.

"No, I'm still glad for her. She deserves to be happy."

"And what about you, Alice? Are you happy?" Mary patted Alice's cheek. In return, Alice hugged her.

"Ecstatic, Auntie Mary. I'm happy from the tips of my toes to the moon and back!"

"That's a lot of happy!" Mary laughed.

"All thanks to you and Auntie Jane."

"And does Statesman Patrick have anything to do with it? Principal Ryan?"

Alice looked up as Jane came in with Pecky on her shoulder. He fluttered onto Alice's head and chattered into her hair. Alice just gave a slight, inward, and mysterious smile.

"Like I said, all thanks to you and Auntie Jane."

CHAPTER TWENTY-ONE _

Noah stayed on the ship for a further six nights, dealing with the pedantic Statesman Evesham, poring over star charts, predicting temperatures, checking trajectories, checking, checking, then endless rehashing. He longed to get away, having to content himself with two or three quick links with Alice. On one of those links, he found himself rattled to see two dozen passionfruit roses behind her. He already knew the answer, but still, he asked.

"Patrick sent them," Alice glanced over her shoulder, "and red ones yesterday. Those are in the parlour. I think he arranged to have them sent every day for the last few days. Yellow ones arrived today, and we put them in a box we use for smoking fish because we had no more containers. It's kind of him, but I hope he doesn't send any more."

Noah cursed himself. Sending flowers, what a great idea. As an authority on roses, he understood their language, although he might have chosen something a little less suggestive than passionfruit blooms. Trust Patrick to make a blatant statement.

"Do you understand the language of a passionfruit

rose?" he asked, doubting she did.

Each bloom was cream-coloured with purple fringes. Long-stemmed and plushly elegant, Alice had never seen any flower so exquisite, nor with such a divine fragrance.

To his surprise, she nodded. "Auntie Mary told me. They're long-lasting, to signify a long-term relationship."

"One rose does, Alice. Two dozen? That's optimistic."

Alice looked at the roses again, unmoved. Noah imagined indifference or disinterest in her expression.

"Well, he's an optimistic person. He's aware of my feelings, Noah; perhaps he's just being pleasant. I didn't read anything but that into them."

She didn't tell Noah that Auntie Mary also explained to her the sexual nature of the rose, their form and meaning. Alice felt embarrassed by the revelation, particularly in the light of her recent awakenings, but she couldn't say so to Noah. As a rose grower, he'd know their significance and hoped he would change the subject, but he didn't want to dwell on the roses either.

"Principal Katya is hoping you'll visit her. She'll call you. Soon."

"That would be nice. Are you still coming back?" Alice felt forward in asking him, but he only smiled.

"I am, Statesman Evesham's examinations here conclude tomorrow. I'll be free then. I would like to stop by and see my family, and then I thought it would be nice to engage in more of your 'sightseeing'."

"I'd like that. It's only a few days now before you leave, isn't it?"

"Yes, Alice," he didn't want to speak of leaving. "I should be able to get away within the next forty-eight hours."

Later, Alice gazed at the passionfruit roses. Then at the red ones, then the yellow ones in the fish box. Patrick was a sweetheart. She hadn't wanted to hurt him but couldn't fathom why he wouldn't take no for an answer. Did he really believe flowers would turn her head? Alice Watkins never received flowers in her life. She wondered whether Alexis Langley had.

The next afternoon, Noah put in a call to his Aunt.

"Good afternoon, Noah."

"Aunt. Statesman Evesham is just about to leave. I'll come by the Tabernacle in the morning before going home."

"Alice is here."

"Oh? Since when?"

"She arrived yesterday afternoon. Her aunties would not let her refuse an invitation from the World Principal, even though Alice says she spends too much time away from them. They bundled her up into the shuttle and sent her on her way."

"You did well in finding her such lovely people."

"I did. And they have Alice's best interests at heart. When I invited her, I intended to be free for a few days, but as you know, life in the Tabernacle is unpredictable, and now, I am presented with issues that may demand my full attention. If so, and as you are coming here, you won't mind entertaining Alice until you depart for your parent's home?"

"We discussed visiting one or two historical sites."

"That would be good, Noah. I believe Alice is not looking forward to your departure. Now, I will expect you before breakfast."

"Yes, Aunt."

The next morning found Alice and Principal Katya in the garden. Principal Katya purposely didn't tell Alice, Noah was arriving. She mischievously wanted to gauge Alice's reaction and interest. Fortunately, Principal Katya was unaware Noah and Alice were in such regular contact and that he'd already informed her when he would be free, nor did she know Alice spied Statesman Evesham arrive late the night before.

Alice dressed for the occasion. She loved her yellow slacks, but today she teamed white shorts with her favourite off-the-shoulder floral blouse. Auntie Mary gave her a pair of sparkly sandals, which she loved.

Her heart leapt when she saw Noah walking from the direction of the courtyard. He'd abandoned any semblance of uniform, instead wore casual grey slacks and a white shirt. Alice guessed her reactions were on display but maintained composure in front of the eagle-eyed Principal Katya.

Noah bent and kissed his aunt, then turned and bowed to Alice.

"Aunt. Dr Langley."

"Sit down, Noah, and have tea. Have you eaten?"

He hesitated. His aunt had instructed him to arrive before breakfast.

"Yes, thank you, Aunt. I brought it with me on the shuttle."

"You shouldn't eat while you are moving around, should he, Alice? For one so stuffy and steeped in protocol, Noah, you do some odd things."

"Well, we used to have 'take away'," Alice ventured, defending the concept of eating on the run. "Dishes designed for us to have while we're on the move, as well as for convenience."

"Take away?" Principal Katya's face lit up with interest. In an instant, another old Earth tradition surfaced for Principal Katya to examine and possibly, implement.

"Hamburgers came in little boxes or containers so you could eat them walking around or driving. You got them from places called fast-food restaurants."

"Didn't anyone choke?" Principal Katya would consider such a project if it could be proved safe. She had no idea the concept was already unofficially implemented in starship engine rooms and had been for some years.

"Probably, but it was an accepted way of eating."

"Did you do this takeaway?"

"Seldom, only once or twice."

A councilman interrupted the conversation; he bowed low to whisper urgently to Principal Katya before formally acknowledging Noah and Alice. Principal Katya stood to leave.

"I am afraid this is important. I am needed in Cloisters. I planned for us to have at least this morning, we three, but it seems that will not happen, as I suspect this will take many hours. Noah, it is unlikely I will see you before you leave to see your parents. Give my love to my sister and your father. Alice, you are welcome to stay as long as you wish, but I would understand if you chose to go home. I am sorry I brought you here under false pretences, but I know you understand my position."

"No need to apologise, Principal Katya, our time together yesterday was delightful, and of course, I can come back whenever you wish. I enjoy my time here. It's like my second home!"

"Give your aunties my best wishes, won't you? Come and embrace me, sweet girl."

Alice stood and kissed Principal Katya. Noah did the same. Alice felt disappointed not to spend more time with her; her gratitude toward this amazing woman often overwhelmed her, and she felt privileged Principal Katya welcomed her as a friend. She watched until Principal Katya, and the councilman were out of sight.

Noah sat down as soon as his aunt left, pushed back his chair and leaned back, placing his left ankle over his right knee, one hand resting on his boot. He leaned his elbow on the armrest and curled his fingers on the side of his mouth. She sensed his eyes on her.

Her whole body felt warm, a warmth not due to the morning sun. She turned her head to meet his gaze; she didn't smile, simply stood, looking into his eyes, and even when the trembling in the pit of her stomach shifted into her thighs and up through her spine, she didn't move. This feeling, she knew, though she'd never experienced it before, was the feeling her mother warned her of so many times.

Even in informal dress, Noah was still too big not to be a presence, maybe 6 feet 5 inches in old money, she guessed, with a large collar size in a shirt. His hair was thick, soft and fair, and the silver highlights glinted in the sun. He was a sweet and kind giant of a man, watching her with those deep blue eyes, and she, watching him right back, desperately tried to hide her trembling.

Noah didn't try to read her. He possessed none of his aunt's intuition; he wanted only to take in Alice's loveliness. The soft paleness of her shoulders, her hair loosened and shining in the sunlight, her green eyes sparkling, singularly sweet and feminine today.

"I got your message," he said, his voice deep and soft, keeping his eyes on her face.

She sat down, a blush stealing across her cheeks.

"I appreciate you keeping in contact, Noah," she babbled. "I didn't want you to think I was ignoring you. I hope it was okay, putting the message on your private signature, but I left quite suddenly, just after you and I spoke. My aunts said I should not refuse Principal Katya, but..." Alice stopped when he smiled.

"And you shouldn't refuse her, Alice. She's fond of you and delighted you said the Tabernacle is like a second home."

"I meant it," she said, her nervousness subsiding.

"My aunt is dear to me, Alice, but she likes to govern. I told her we might look at a few historical sites, but now, she thinks you may go home."

"Historical sites sound nice," she smiled, wanting to spend time with him, even it was just one day.

Noah paused. An idea presented itself, an idea that would keep Alice with him for as long as possible before he had to leave.

"There's no reason you can't come with me to my parent's home. I'd like to take you. It's a historic site itself."

"Wouldn't your parents mind?"

"They're not there. They're not expecting me."

"And they wouldn't mind a total stranger in their home?"

"Believe me, Alice, my mother prefers total strangers. Blank canvasses to her. If she were home, you would be organised and sorted. She's Principal Katya's twin. They are identical. My mother's friends are acquainted with her organising ways, but this time, you're safe. They're away on respite. I planned to surprise them; they didn't say they were going away."

"I'm sure your mother means well."

"Yes, she not only means well, but anyone who plans a visit can expect only the best of everything. She is a master at planning. I know you're fond of Principal Katya; my mother has all her best traits, plus some of her own. You'd get on well with her, but even without them there, I think you'll enjoy it. And there are horses."

"I love horses."

"I know. When do your aunts expect you back?"

"Not for days. They won't worry."

"I only have a few days before I need to be back here for the final briefing. Meanwhile, would you indulge me in something? Trust my judgement?"

"Of course."

"Can we keep this to ourselves? My aunt will assume we may make one or two visits to ancient sites today, but I won't advise her I'm taking you to my parent's home. I didn't get as far as telling her they're away. I have my reasons for privacy."

"If you say so, but not even tell our aunts?"

"Especially not our aunts. Meet me in the courtyard." Then he grinned, "Pack a toothbrush."

CHAPTER TWENTY-TWO _

Alice hurriedly gathered her belongings and joined Noah in the courtyard, elated to be spending this time with him but wishing the butterflies in her tummy would settle.

Although she trusted him, she wondered about the secrecy because Principal Katya seemed to realise they'd become friends. He smiled when he saw her watching him.

"Am I allowed to ask why this is such a big secret?" she asked.

"Maybe later, but in part, I'm well-known at the Tabernacle for not socialising, and I don't care for our friendship becoming a subject of speculation or gossip."

"I didn't realise they indulged in gossip in the Tabernacle."

"It happens," he grinned, then changed the subject. He would tell her, but not right now; he wanted to wait and see what developed over the next few days. Reading signals was not his strong suit, and there may yet be no need for secrecy.

"You'll like my home, Alice," he said, "besides horses, we have ducks and geese and dogs; mother acquired a goat with a leg missing a few weeks ago, I expect she kept it. Incidentally, we also have a piano. My father plays."

"You're so lucky playing musical instruments—and remembering you played them," she added drily.

"My father plays piano and cello, and both my sisters play the cello. Zoe plays the saxophone as well. She likes twentieth-century music—jazz, that style didn't last much past the twenty-second century."

"I don't like jazz," Alice shook her head. "Too noisy."

He laughed. "I agree. I've always leaned towards the classics, and there are many excellent composers from the last four hundred years. Speaking of classics, I know for you, history is up until the twenty-first and twenty-second centuries, but now, there's more history to explore."

"What sort of history?"

"In all its forms. Inventions, architecture, medicine, but I know you have a particular interest in architecture, so I'm going to show you something from our history, but what you would have said was your future."

Alice and Noah settled into their easy discussions, just as they did on the registry. He even gave her instruction in flying the shuttle. Seeing Noah and Patrick piloting had seemed impressive, but now she realised it was only a matter of coordination with fingertip interaction to the console, mainly to correct altitude and speed. Even with those, the shuttle could mostly be automated and set to sense changing requirements. But it was such fun! And his confidence in her abilities, in turn, gave her confidence. At the end of an hour, she felt entirely at ease at the controls, but she needed his help to make a manual landing in a clearing, where a structure towered above the trees.

"Is this what you wanted to show me?" she said as she jumped down onto the grass.

"Yes, I'm interested to know what you think of it."

It looked like an enormous glass rectangle, well, almost a rectangle, because one corner lacked symmetry, bulging out like a swollen eye. The entire central glass section was topped off with a wooden roof. Supporting the glass from below, similarly asymmetrical, another wooden rectangle, somewhat wider than the roof, acted as a balcony or terrace. The whole structure, supported by four slender columns, reminded Alice of a 1960's coffee table, or possibly, an artist's rendition of an oversized glass sandwich. It rose from the earth beneath and the sun reflected like fire in the glass, imposing itself on the landscape, higher than all the trees crowding in on one side.

"What do you think?" Noah smiled down at her, quietly eager for a response.

"It's very modern, Noah, futuristic even," she said, trying to make an honest appraisal. Older buildings like the Tabernacle piqued her interest in architecture, along with the Colleges and Universities, but this was a monstrosity.

"It looks like it just landed or recently returned from stalking the countryside."

He frowned. Clearly, his opinion differed from hers. Alice hadn't meant to be disparaging.

"Landed from where?" he asked.

"Outer space."

He looked back at the house, trying to gain her

perspective. "I've never seen a ship in space that looks like this, Alice. Although to you it might seem futuristic, to us, it's history. It's two hundred and fifty years old."

"Two hundred and fifty years old? I can't believe it!" she gasped. Learning the building's age influenced her attitude, but possibly not as much as his next announcement.

"Welcome to my home!" he laughed, and stretched his arms towards the house.

"Your home." Alice surprise was genuine. "Well, in that case—show me around!"

Walking through the gardens, listening to his voice, Alice could hear Noah's love and enthusiasm for his home. Personally, she failed to find any real beauty in its exterior but appreciated its historical appeal. Before he showed her the inside, he wanted her to see the rose garden at the rear of the house.

A broad paved area skirted the building, and judging by the outdoor furniture, appeared to be used in much the same way as the verandah at the aunties house.

A gangly dog lay inelegantly in a hammock on the paved area, just moving his head to watch the visitors. Two other elderly canines, languishing on blankets, thumped their tails against the ground in welcome but didn't trouble themselves to get up to greet them.

"Those are Dogs," Noah waved his hand towards the patio.

"I can see they're dogs, Noah."

"Yes, of course, sorry. They're all called Dog unless they're puppies, then they're called Puppy until they grow up. Only the horses have names." He pointed to several horses grazing a distance from the house, then took her hand and led her to the rose garden.

Alice imagined the garden might be small and manageable, for the times when he was on leave. But this rose garden, walled and gated with an old-fashioned wrought iron gate (to keep out the animals, he told her, and aesthetically more pleasing than a force field), had an abundance of well-trained, shiny green ivy lining the wall. And mingling deliciously with the perfume from the roses, the heavenly scent of honeysuckle wafted through the air. Archways bearing the glorious vines dotted the pathway. As they meandered through the rose beds, each growing many varieties of rose, she saw no sign of blemish or damage to any bloom, each bud, each flower, a perfect creation. She wanted to linger here, her hand in his.

"Did you grow all these?"

Alice reached out to touch a magnificent bloom, its petals velvety soft and deep red.

"Mostly. I created the garden when I was about eight, so the roses are well-established. The honeysuckle is my mother's idea. She spends time out here now, so I can't take all the credit."

"You are too modest, Noah. I don't know what to say; it's just beautiful."

"I knew you'd love it. Shall I show you the inside of the house now?"

As they closed the gate behind them, a camel rounded the corner, casting a mere blink of a disinterested glance their way as it strolled past.

Alice looked at Noah.

"Don't tell me—that's Camel," she smiled.

"Yes, Dad hand-reared her from a baby, but she fell in love with Carl, our neighbour, and she lives with him now, but she still visits us."

Noah took the camel visit in his stride; for a moment, Alice watched the retreating rear end of the animal. This was an extraordinary place, and Noah, an extraordinary man, full of surprises.

"This must have been an amazing place to grow up," Alice said, stopping to look at the trees and endless fields, as far as the eye could see.

"Absolutely, great for us kids. The school is near the city precinct, so everything we needed was always within a short distance from home."

"Yet, you left it all and went to the stars."

"It's still here, Alice, and no child remains at home forever. Life beckons. I never considered any vocation other than one that would take me into space. Even when I created the rose garden, viewed from above, each section is set out like a constellation. I was too young to go into space, so I made my heaven on Earth."

He felt slightly foolish telling her this, he'd only been a child, but her eyes became distant, lost somewhere, and it seemed she no longer heard him. She spoke, her voice dreamy, barely above a whisper.

"*Silently, one by one, in the infinite meadows of heaven, Blossomed the lovely stars, the forget-me-nots of the angels.*"

Noah knew the poem, reading it as a child many years ago, inspired him to lay out his new garden, copying his favourite stars in the sky. She couldn't know how much that passage meant to him.

"Do your parents usually go away and leave the animals?" her voice, suddenly bright, startled him from his reflection.

"Yes, yes, of course. There are food and water dispensers, but if the fancy takes them or they want human company, the dogs wander over to Carl's house. If my parents are away for a long time, a steward comes from the city to look after them. Otherwise, Carl comes over."

"Are you sure your parents won't mind me wandering around when they aren't here?

"No, why? This is my home, too. I'm welcome here regardless if my parents are here or not. Weren't you welcomed at all times in your family home?"

"I didn't even have a key, Noah, not that going to my mother's house after I married held any appeal."

"Well, it's not like that here. We're welcome, I assure you."

Noah knew his parents best, so Alice accepted his reassurance. They walked back to the paved area where the dogs still lay unmoved, and he waved open a door that led to an elevator. The elevator opened directly into a large room. Blankets and veterinary equipment was piled high against one wall. The furniture looked vintage, with a slightly dilapidated air. A cat sat in a particularly saggy chair and meowed when it spied Noah, standing up and stretching in greeting. He picked up the cat and kissed its head. Alice went to the edge of the glass rectangle, less of a window and more of a wall, but with a beautiful outlook above the trees.

A stream and a forest lay to one side, and in the other direction, the spires of a city. A huge city.

She turned to Noah, "Why so many trees? I can't see other houses."

"There were others here before," he told her, "built before the last wave of plague, but they didn't survive the aftermath. They built this one later. Our nearest neighbour, Carl, is a couple of miles in that direction," Noah pointed towards the back of the house, "This house came into my family after one of my ancestors purchased it from the designer."

"I understood people were only assigned homes when they retired or started families?"

"Largely. If they wish, a married couple can be assigned a home but usually live wherever their assignment takes them. If possible, they'll be assigned together. If they have a child, they're assigned a home automatically, and that home remains theirs until they no longer want it or ask for somewhere else."

"What about individuals, people like you? My friend Amelia lives on a school campus."

"Accommodation is provided on assignment, and at leisure, there's always somewhere to stay. Otherwise, single people are only assigned upon retirement. For military personnel, it's their ship."

"What about personal items? What if someone likes ornaments or books?"

He shook his head. "Only in their assigned quarters."

"So how come this house stayed in your family?"

"Because it's an historical site. Like your aunt's house,

most houses are much more recent builds and part of the Assignation Charter. This one was already under ownership by the Ryan family when the Charter was passed. If a house has a family history, it's assigned in perpetuity—meaning it stays in the family until the family is no more."

"Like Patrick's home?"

"Yes, the same. Did he take you there?"

"A few weeks ago." Alice stayed at the window, her back to him, looking out over the trees, so she didn't see the sudden tightening of his jaw. "He took me to meet his mother and sister. They told me all about their family; they have a real history."

"Did you go to the old village?"

"We didn't have time. It would have been interesting; I'm particularly fascinated by those old buildings. Who decides who inherits the family home?"

"The family."

"But you have two sisters. How does that work?"

"We're all eligible under Assignation. It doesn't matter who lives here; it will always belong to our family."

Alice loved this about her new society, so giving and accepting, competition and family problems seemed a thing of the past. In some things, although not all, these people had learned a better way.

Noah watched Alice wander around the room. He wanted her to love his home as much as he did, many of his best memories lived here, and he wanted to share those things of most importance to him before parting from her. He knew this house was not as impressive as Patrick's baronial hall—and it smelled faintly of dog. Few surfaces didn't have something to do with animals deposited upon them; somehow, it hadn't bothered him before.

"You're quiet, Alice. Is it not what you expected?"

She turned to face him and grinned.

"Not what I expected at all," she said with honesty. "You are so precise and neat and well—I've said it before—grand and this house is amazing and old and unique, it looks so lived in and..." she struggled to find a word to sum it up, but he read her reaction wrong and thought she was about to comment on the smell.

"...and it smells of dog. I'm so sorry. I guess I don't see the untidiness. It's never been any different, and I've always been so happy here. My parents nursed a lot of orphaned animals and needed to keep them close. They set up the house to accommodate that. You should have seen it at the height of their careers when we had horses! We loved it, growing up, and Alice—my mother would disagree that I'm neat and precise. She would laugh out loud at 'grand'."

She smiled. Mothers see different things in their children.

"I was going to say comfortable and homely. I would have loved growing up somewhere like this. When I first saw the house, it looked to me like a giant glass sandwich," she wagged a finger at the glass wall, "but my aunties house has a doggy smell too. I can't believe you didn't notice. I feel quite at home."

He relaxed.

"I hoped you would like it. Shall we have coffee?"

She didn't even have to answer. She never said no to coffee.

While he was busy, Alice inspected several accolades lined up along a shelf, trophies she decided, even though they were little more than flat circles of plastic-like material, on each one, she made out a name, Noah Ryan. He handed her a mug and picked up one of the awards.

"You were surprised when I said I grew flowers and liked weaving."

"Yes, sorry, preconceived ideas surfacing."

"No, that's okay, you probably expected something more active. These accolades are for archery. I took part in several championships. I won all of them after practising for hours at the Tabernacle range when my aunt was a statesman there. She's quite a marksman herself."

He didn't seem proud, but Alice thought it remarkable, remembering her futile efforts at archery, and said so, but he waved away her praise.

"It was a long time ago. There's a range on the Significator, and the new statesman is a champion, so I'm looking forward to a challenge. Meanwhile, Alice, I can't offer you much to eat. My parents don't cook, so they have no provisions. The Providore delivers meals for them as they need."

"That's okay. I'm fine for now. What about you? Did you need to order from the Providore?"

"Let me finish showing you around first. We can visit the city later."

"Noah, there's no real need to visit the city." Alice didn't want to spend time in any other company. "I can cook. I'm quite good, that is if your mother wouldn't mind me using the kitchen."

"I doubt she knows we have one."

Alice pointed down. "We're standing in it."

"It doesn't exist to my mother."

"What did you eat growing up?"

"Weaned onto the Providore, my sisters and I."

"Then you don't cook?"

"Coffee from a dispenser is my limit."

She cast a practised eye around the kitchen area.

"Cooking is a pleasure, Noah. You don't know what you're missing."

"I would be a willing student, Alice. It simply has never been suggested before. I'll contact the Providore. What will I ask for?"

The kitchen appeared well-equipped, and the cooking lights and plates were of a similar design to the ones at home, and responded rapidly to Alice's voice and commands. She could probably do something here.

Alice made a list on the registry, it had only been a matter of hours since breakfast at the Tabernacle, and because of the time difference, they would be planning dinner later, so she chose appropriately.

Noah linked through and spoke to the Providore for a few minutes; obviously, people he knew well.

"They'll be here in an hour or so. They know my parents are on retreat, so they were a bit surprised to hear from us. My father has been ill and taking his rehabilitation slowly."

"I'm sorry to hear that, Noah. You have seen them since you got back?"

"I spent time here before the ball, and they'll come up

to the ship before I leave. They always do."

Noah showed Alice the rest of the house and the guest room, which afforded a view of the stream and forest. In contrast to the living area, the room was spotlessly clean and smelled of the honeysuckle growing below the window.

He also showed her how the house 'worked'. Every system drew power from panels powered by the sun. Alice wasn't sure this was such a novel idea. Michelle had solar panels on her roof for hot water, and Alice had heard of people who got electricity the same way; but as Noah proudly told her how his parents preferred 'old-fashioned' power sources, she kept her opinions to herself. Later, it came as no surprise to see a small parrulee alcove and Substance energy chamber, standard in most buildings.

They walked down to the edge of the stream and sat on the grass, chatting about the differences in buildings from her time and the diversity of styles she saw now. The house rose above them on its legs, looking less and less like a spaceship and more like the happy family home Alice knew it once was, her earlier critical view of the house transformed.

"You like the house?" Noah half lay, half propped on his elbow, watching her.

She nodded and looked around. "The setting is gorgeous. Where does the stream run to?"

"Through those woods."

He sat up and placed his hand on her shoulder, leaning close to point further down the stream.

"My favourite place as a kid," he laughed. "I'll show you tomorrow if you like. I still like to ride through it."

His hand felt warm on her skin, and she closed her eyes. This would be a torturous few days if he kept touching her.

CHAPTER TWENTY-THREE _

Alice loved cooking for them both. She showed Noah how to prepare a salad, but mostly he just got in her way. He'd never considered preparing food and displayed no flare, so she ordered him from the kitchen.

The evening couldn't have been more perfect. They took dinner out to the lower patio, surrounded by the dogs and the cat, which had somehow found a spot on the hammock with the larger dog, who it appeared, hadn't moved all day. The lights of the city twinkled in the distance, but here all was quiet, save the music of night birds and insects.

"It's summer here now, isn't it, Noah?"

"Yes, though my favourite time of year is at the end of summer, just turning to Autumn."

"It's winter at home now in Principality 19, even though it's not cold, we called it July, I arrived on Earth in April. I miss saying the months of the year."

"Then my favourite month is September."

"You know the months?"

"I do, I read a lot, early literature speaks only of

months. Quarters and numbers possess little poetry."

"How do modern novelists manage if there is less romance in words?"

"They manage well; a creative mind can summon poetry from just about anything."

"Mary and Jane don't have real books, only the registry readers, and I've never seen a bookstore."

"I assume that's a place to obtain books?"

"Yes, and we had libraries, to borrow books for a few weeks, then we exchanged them for different ones."

"I see," but he didn't see, the concept of using money escaped him, and he wondered at the wisdom, given what he knew of her society, of trusting property to unknowns.

"Principal Hardy has a lot of books, and the Tabernacle library, so they are available, aren't they?" she asked.

"Yes, the author supplies bound copies upon request, but it's not very common."

"Not the same as browsing a bookshelf for a title that takes your fancy," she grinned, and her expression suggested he was missing out on a long-lost pastime.

"I can browse a registry for books, if I wish, Alice, but for a true escape from work and everyday issues, I come here. I feel at peace, even when mother and dad are home with all the dogs and animals, and it's just one big noise."

"Isn't space quiet?"

"Not for me. It's a workplace. I don't have any set hours of work, and I can be called at any time. Patrick and I share command duties, but I'm in command if I'm on the bridge. If I want time off, I can delegate to him or, in the case of our next mission, Statesman Junnot."

"Is he in the military?"

"Military, yes, but he is a she. She was due to come with us last time but suffered a serious injury while mountaineering. That's why Hennessey came on board."

"It didn't occur to me you would have a female second officer," she admitted, although there was no reason it should have surprised her. "I rather warmed to Hennessey the second time I met him."

"He just wanted to get home. Once word came through he'd become a father; all thoughts were on returning to his family."

"That's understandable."

"Yes, it is. He spent time on Septimus Station and the Inquisitor but never chose a military career. He only ever wanted to raise a family and then found himself in space when it happened."

"Couldn't you have chosen someone else?"

"Yes, plenty of people, but not with his background in linguistics. We were contacting a new species. Junnot has the skills, but of course, she wasn't available, so Hennessey got pressganged."

"Didn't he want to go?"

"Under other circumstances, yes, but he and his wife were preparing for a pregnancy, so not a good time. Junnot's accident happened only a few days before we departed, but I think, despite the situation, Hennessey was rather intrigued at meeting a new civilisation."

"It's a shame it went pear-shaped."

"Pear-shaped?"

"Didn't work out."

"Yes, but we couldn't predict the outcome. I'm sure we'll do better next time."

"Take a cake," Alice suggested.

He leaned forward, instantly reminded of their conversation on the Tabernacle terrace.

"What did you say?"

"Take a cake. That's what my mother did when she wanted to meet new neighbours."

Alice was distracted by a horse walking over to the dog in the hammock. It nudged it none-too-gently with its nose, and as the hammock swung, the dog fell out. Unhurt, it stretched and flopped down on the paving.

"The horses here—they're enormous," Alice said. "I thought Jorrocks was big at first. But these horses…"

"We need large horses," he pointed to himself. He was right, she agreed, pity a little horse with short legs carrying him around.

"What about your mother? If she's Principal Katya's twin, does she have a pony?"

He laughed. "No. She rides these horses, and she controls them. No nonsense there. Don't worry; you'll have no trouble."

"Oh, are we going riding?" Alice didn't hide her dismay; these horses were for giants. Jorrocks was for midgets like her.

"Tomorrow. We'll take the horses down to the woods. They love the exercise, and I can show you the countryside."

The rest of the evening passed in pleasant

conversation until Alice stifled a yawn. She felt tired, even though she didn't want the evening to end. Noah stood, offering his hand to help as she wriggled out of the oversize chair, but instead of letting go, he kept her hand in his, and she looked up at him, her heart beating wildly. Was he going to kiss her? Touch her? But he only smiled.

"Goodnight, Alice. Another wonderful day in your company."

"Goodnight, Noah. Thank you."

He watched her leave. He wanted to kiss her, to touch her, but he couldn't find the right moment. He waited for the sound of her door closing before he sat down again, contemplating the lights of the city and his ineptness. More than once, he'd considered creating an elaborate seduction scene, even though he'd never tried such a thing before, and the only person to go to for advice just happened to be the other person in love with Alice.

He thought about her standing in the Tabernacle garden before he asked her to come here with him. He couldn't take his eyes off her. God, she was beautiful. Her shoulders—so pale, and that blouse with lace and flowers that sat just above her breasts. She'd held his gaze. She felt something too.

Sweat trickled down his face; he wiped it away with the heel of his hand. He walked out onto the lawn, whistling to the dogs to accompany him, an offer taken up by only one. The night brought on a breeze, but it didn't cool him, so he wandered down towards the stream with the old dog ambling behind.

Noah looked up at the star-filled sky. They all seemed

so far away, and he took no comfort in the fact he would soon return to them, not while she was here. He wanted her with him tonight, to wake beside her tomorrow morning.

Loosening his shirt, Noah walked off into the night, not noticing the old dog no longer followed him, preferring the comfort of his blanket rather than trying to keep up with the long strides of his master.

Noah was up and dressed when Alice emerged from her room early the next morning. The early morning mist shrouded the trees, and the first rays of the sun, pushing through the haze, brought the promise of a beautiful summer's day. Alice, looking fresh and dainty in white, joined him out on the terrace. He'd had a dreadful night—or maybe a wonderful night—filled with thoughts of how it would be to hold her in his arms, thoughts that kept him awake and restless.

She caught his expression. "What's amusing?"

"Nothing," he assured her. "Do you want breakfast before we go out? I've poured coffee for you, and the Providore brought chocolate pastries. We can eat out here where the animals won't disturb us."

Alice's green eyes widened, thinking about chocolate pastries; she didn't even need to say, "thank you", her look said it all. She took a pastry in one hand, held her coffee in the other, and, turning to him, smiled as she sat down, one leg tucked under her.

"You've heard of Stonehenge?" he asked, pulling up a portable registry and sitting beside her.

"It's a formation of stones," she said, quickly

swallowing a mouthful of pastry and pointing a finger at the registry. "Lots of theories about how it came about. A bit like the pyramids, lots of theories there too," she said thoughtfully, putting her breakfast on her knee and in a very un-Alice like way, dusted her hands. "Some say the pillars at Stonehenge are a burial ground. Have you heard that? And no less than sixty individual skeletons found there? Some bones date back around three thousand years, lending weight to the evidence it may have been a burial site. Archaeologists also found bronze age tools and remains of an ancient village. In 2080, they found some metallic implements they couldn't analyse or determine a purpose for. I don't know much about it, but it would be interesting to visit. Have you been there, Principal Ryan?"

She picked up her coffee and sipped, eyes on him, waiting for an answer.

This girl before him, who looked like Alice, but direct in her speech, with no signs of shyness, rather sure of herself, unmistakably, was not Alice. This had to be Alexis Langley.

In the few seconds it took for him to ponder the shift, she changed.

"Did you say something about Stonehenge, Noah?"

He looked for any sign of Alexis Langley, but everything about Alice reverted to her usual self, demeanour, and voice.

"Yes, would you like to visit there?"

Alice knew little of Stonehenge. She hadn't got as far as ancient history in her studies and heard it was just a pile of rocks in a field somewhere in England. Possibly not too exciting, but if he wanted to show her, then she would go. She followed him outside, taking a moment to linger at the rose garden while Noah fetched the horses. Alice, still dismayed by their height, sighed, not at all sure she was experienced enough to ride such robust animals.

"They're awfully big, Noah."

He wouldn't be dissuaded, "You can take this one; she looks like the one you ride at home. Come on."

He lifted Alice onto the horse's back. It was a long way down.

"She's called Fleet. We call her that…" Noah began,

"…because she runs very fast?" Alice chimed in, any semblance of courage deserting her as she clung to Fleet's mane.

"No, it's a misnomer. It's the opposite of what she is. And this is Bay, my father's favourite."

They headed off toward the hills. As Noah promised, Fleet was remarkably calm, and Alice soon felt more comfortable. Noah told her the history of the area, its old name, Wiltshire, and how, in ancient times, it was considered an area of paranormal activity.

"Paranormal as in ghosts?" she asked.

"UFOs more. Unidentified Flying Objects, crop circles, lights in the sky. They all perpetuated the myth that Stonehenge wasn't man-made but built by aliens as a kind of homing beacon."

"And it wasn't?" It wouldn't have surprised her if it had.

"No, of course not."

"You said no-one knew how it got there."

"That's right."

"But it wasn't aliens."

"No, not aliens."

"How do you know?"

"I suppose we don't know for sure."

"Oh, okay. What are crop circles?"

"Elaborate designs which appear in crops during Spring and Summer, it's said they're created by extraterrestrials too. Local people have reported strange lights out in the fields at night, but none of those stories has been corroborated. A field can be clear at sundown and a circle there in the morning. They've appeared for hundreds of years, common in the twentieth and twenty-first centuries, but less frequently now, some say since the arrival of the A'khet."

"I see. How elaborate are the designs?"

"Very elaborate. I'll show you on a registry when we get to Stonehenge. If there are any around, we can bring the shuttle for you to get a better look."

"If it's not aliens who create them, who does?"

"That hasn't been established, but each one is investigated."

"Why can't it be aliens?"

"I believe, with our technology, we would detect any activity by an extraterrestrial race."

"They investigated Stonehenge too, didn't they?"

He conceded that to date, no-one had ever proven who or what built Stonehenge or who or what made crop circles. The stones made a talking point for sceptics, some of whom still questioned the possibility of life on other planets, despite the presence of the A'khet, and with full knowledge the military had contacted other civilisations.

As they reached the top of the hill, Stonehenge, standing like a cathedral, stately and majestic, rose from the remnants of the early morning mist. Alice felt its timelessness. A guardian of the ages, it had witnessed centuries of humankind; their successes, innovations, wars, plague, and yet, there it stood, unmoving.

"Noah, it's amazing. Can we get closer?"

"Yes, as close as you like."

She cantered off, glancing behind once to make sure he was following, but after an initial burst of energy, Fleet slowed, and Noah overtook her easily. He arrived a good few minutes before her, and he helped her down from Fleet's back. As soon as Alice planted her feet on the ground, she was off, running her hands over the stones, leaning against them, and closing her eyes, not minding their dampness, absorbing their history.

Despite the early hour, a few other people also visited the stones, but Alice was too enchanted to notice them. Once again, she asked herself how she'd missed the magic of history? It could have been an all-consuming passion, a light in her previously deadly dull world.

"They're remarkable, aren't they?" Noah looked up at the stones, they'd been part of his childhood, but they still filled him with awe.

"Noah, I can't believe this is in your backyard!"

"I assume you mean garden. We used to come over here as children, but we always respected the stones. To us, they're a monument, to what, or to whom, we're not sure, too many theories to choose from, but they've stood for thousands of years, so they're of significant historical importance. I respect that. All of us respect them."

"Tell me more about the stones and your crop circles."

"Well, come over to the pavilion, and we'll check out the registry. It's pretty comprehensive, and certainly, research has been added since your time."

The pavilion and registry were devoted to the plains area. Alice didn't know what information was added, and none of the research dated. It didn't matter, she'd no prior knowledge to compare anyway, but the whole idea of the stones fascinated her.

Noah also showed her images of crop formations, flicking through several jaw-dropping pictures until, eventually, she looked up at him.

"I don't believe any human can carry out such a feat, during the night, in the dark, even with all the advanced technology of today, and not make mistakes." She shook her head, "Got to be aliens."

"Over the years," he grinned at her straightforward appraisal, "people imitated the circles, but as they did, the designs became more complex, almost as if the original designer was aware, and made it harder for them to be reproduced—rather a fanciful theory."

"Someone intelligent then?" Alice was prepared to believe it. "More intelligent than the counterfeiters?"

"Perhaps. Or a hoax."

Alice pointed to the registry, calling out a display of part of one formation. "That's not it. See here? In crop circles, the wheat structure is altered, but at some point, scientists discovered how to duplicate that change. After this discovery, the molecular framework of the wheat exhibited a new change, one that confounded science again." She sat back and wagged a finger at him, "Whoever is doing it always stays a step ahead of the hoaxers. What's your answer to that, Mr Astrophysicist?"

For the second time this morning, he witnessed a shift in her personality, and now, arms folded, a small smile playing on her lips, her head tilted to one side, she waited for him to comment.

"Where did you learn this?" Noah didn't have a response, he was too busy being perplexed by the sudden change, so it was all he could think of to say. Her information was hopelessly out of date, even though she appeared to believe it current, and science had long moved past looking for answers in the crop itself.

"I read it," she said. "There are several dissertations and treatises on the matter of crop circles. Investigations like phototropism, germination, and innumerable others I can't think of right now were carried out. I haven't read too much, but research indicates each stalk stopped growing at the point the circle was created. Did you know not one crop event was documented during the plague years? That's nearly eighty years without a formation, the first new one, when I was at school in Sydney, caused quite a stir, but I think that one was in Chile, not here in England. I've never personally seen one, and I must admit, I would be intrigued. That computer would have records—" she pointed casually to the registry, then suddenly raised her arms and grabbed her hair, twisting it into a knot, looking around as she did so.

Computer? Noah frowned, watching her.

"What are you looking for?"

"A hairband, I was going to tie my hair out of the way. It's way too long. Never mind."

She released her hair, allowing it to fall in a messy glob of red and gold around her neck. The movement struck him as natural and familiar, but it heralded a shift, and Alice again returned to questions about Stonehenge, her old-fashioned discourse on crop formations forgotten. This time, he made sure not to be caught out and negotiated her personality change more easily.

When the registry finished its summary of Stonehenge, they found the location of two crop circles. He promised they would fly over before they left. She seemed preoccupied with the idea and talked about them all the way back to the house, convinced they were from what she called "outer space" and not using any of her earlier, more sophisticated language.

If A'khet exists, she argued reasonably, and the other aliens he'd seen for himself, then surely there must be others? But why draw pictures in fields? Why not make proper contact? Maybe it's their way of bringing a cake? She dreamed up a whole list of ideas.

Yes, he agreed, when she posed the question, besides the A'khet, he'd met other beings. No, he didn't understand why other species might draw pictures and not present themselves in person as humans did, reminding Alice of how their attempt at first contact turned out. It amused him, listening to her try and gain some sense of Stonehenge's origins and of crop formations. These questions, asked countless times, rehashed, discounted, put away and brought out again for further discussion, were all new to Alice, and she treated each concept with astonished reverence. The registry at her home, Noah thought, was in for a workout.

CHAPTER TWENTY-FOUR _

When they reached the hill above the house, Alice pointed to the stream.

"I'd like to see the woods. Are you still happy to take me there?"

"Yes, of course. I'll race you!"

He took off at speed, Bay's tail flying in the wind. Alice tried to push Fleet onwards, but the horse missed the fact she was supposed to be racing, ambling along after her stablemate at a leisurely pace. Alice lost sight of them, but Fleet seemed to know where to go, following the stream and taking Alice into a clearing. Narrow shafts of sunlight slanted through the broad canopy of trees. Dragonflies darted in and out of the sunbeams, their wings lighting like jewels. Noah had dismounted and had already led Bay down to the stream to drink.

He grinned when she arrived.

"I thought I'd lost you. I told you Fleet is a misnomer. I took advantage, I'm afraid."

Alice swung her leg over Fleet's neck but stayed seated, as if in sidesaddle, her back straight, breathing in the earthiness of forest, fragrant with loam and leaves and grass. The stream flowed crystal clear.

"Noah, it's beautiful here," she breathed.

She tilted her head back, sighing with pleasure, and closed her eyes. He watched as the soft sunlight rested on her face and hair; no-one, no *thing* he had seen on Earth or in space ever affected him this deeply. He felt changed by her.

"*You* are beautiful."

Alice opened her eyes. Noah had moved from the stream without her realising it and was standing beside Fleet, looking up at her. He lifted his arms and silently, she slipped from Fleet's back. Time slowed, the sounds of the forest became distant; she thought she heard Fleet whinny a greeting to Bay at the stream. Alice slid her arms around Noah's neck and curled her legs around his body as he lifted her down, moving his hands to her thighs, gripping her, and pulling her close. Slightly above him still, she dropped her mouth gently on his, and even when he laid her down on the soft ground, he didn't let her go, not once breaking their embrace, only moving his mouth from hers to lightly kiss her neck and shoulders. He loosened her blouse, pulling it from the constraints of her slacks, and from somewhere deep inside, Alice felt herself sigh, but whether it ever escaped her lips, she neither knew nor cared. This was more than she'd ever hoped for; the feel of his skin against hers, the strength of his arms around her, the softness of his mouth. The sensations she'd felt as he watched her at the Tabernacle spread over her again, but this time, instead of concealing them, she welcomed them. Noah felt her trembling and hesitated, but she smiled and reached up to touch his face, reassuring him she trembled not from fear, only from longing.

Alice's skin tingled as his mouth traced a path along her breasts, and she closed her eyes as her body came alive at his touch. Every part of her responded to him, each caress prompting a gasp of delight, as never-before-felt sensations took her breath away. And then it was her turn to discover the deep sensuality of exploring his body with teasing kisses, enjoying the deep groans each kiss, each touch, dragged from his throat.

They held nothing back, and there, in the forest, under the trees, they gave in to their desire for one another, and as their bodies intertwined, she held him close, wanting him. With every movement they made together, she felt a blissful tension building until her head filled with stars, and her mouth relaxed and she sighed a soft, "Ah!".

She opened her eyes, still gasping. Noah was smiling at her pleasure, but only for a moment. He buried his face against her neck and crushed her against him, and with it came that delicious tension and a new shower of stars before her eyes. She gasped against his chest, allowing her back to arch naturally against him, her hands gripping his shoulders.

Later, wrapped in each other's arms, Alice gave a quiet grin as she saw their clothes strewn on the forest floor. She was here, naked, and she felt safe. The clothes could stay where they were. Her breathing hadn't yet returned to normal, and her cheek and hair were damp against his shoulder. She moved slightly and heard a low chuckle in his throat.

"You are so sexy!"

Alice, still in wonderment at what she'd experienced, what she'd felt, smiled. She remembered every delicious moment. "Trust me," she murmured against him, "I'm just as surprised as you."

As her breathing settled and not yet willing to let the moment pass, she gently tightened her embrace. Noah, understanding, did the same, stroking her hair and kissing the top of her head. All these years, she thought. All those damned wasted years, settling for what, *Ted?* When love, deep love, brought *this?*

She didn't feel like a hussy. She felt beautiful, desirable, and natural. He wanted her, wanted this, as much as she wanted him.

He brushed her hair back from her face so that he could gaze at her. All his life, he felt sure nothing was missing, but now, a massive space in his heart opened, one only she could fill. There were no new worlds, no star systems, no alien civilisations, nothing out there in the expanse of the cosmos that would ever inspire him more than discovering this truth.

"You're so lovely and so delicate, Alice. I was afraid I might hurt you," he said gently. "It's been a long time, and I wanted you so much."

"You didn't hurt me, Noah," she tilted her head to look at him. "Besides," she grinned, "it's been longer for me. Centuries."

"Of course, I didn't give it a thought," he grinned back. "As soon as I held you, I didn't give much of anything a thought. Alice, I can't believe we're here together. The last few weeks have been torture."

"I've never done anything like this, Noah."

"Never?"

"Well, apart from what I told you before, I don't know what Alexis Langley did."

"I was worried you might think me a clumsy oaf."

"And I was worried you would think me a hussy."

"A hussy?" He shifted his weight and propped on his elbow. "A hussy?"

"Do you know what a hussy is?"

"Yes, I do. I liked you being a hussy."

"My mother wouldn't agree."

"Well, she's not here," he grinned, sliding his arms over her back, and tucking her legs between his. "But you are."

Much later, they rode back to the house on Bay. Fleet had left for home, a habit she had if left to her own devices. Alice's arms were around Noah's waist as they rode, her face nuzzled against his back. That night, in her bed, after losing themselves in each other, she lay nestled against Noah's chest, his arms around her, keeping her close. Alice was incredibly happy, too happy to sleep, to let these special moments pass by without her being fully in them. In this world, events developed over such a short time. Only twenty-four hours ago, she came to this bed alone, convinced he only wanted friendship. Now, she lay in his arms, close to him, free to love him. The hairs on his chest were soft against her face, and she smiled, listening to the soft rhythm of his breathing, sleeping beside her. Once more, she wondered at the magic which brought her here, to this.

The next morning, Alice and Noah explored the countryside on horseback. In his best tour guide voice, Noah pointed out landmarks and places of interest that were, as Alice liked to say, in his backyard. Late in the afternoon, they approached the house from the direction of the city. A second shuttle with city markings was just leaving.

"My parents must have come home early," Noah said as it flew over their heads.

"Are you sure they won't mind me being here?" Alice suddenly felt out of place.

"Not at all. Mother will be delighted, even though I hoped to have you all to myself."

Noah steered them around through the trees at the side of the house to avoid being seen.

"Alice," Noah held onto Fleet's harness to stop her walking away. "I have to introduce you formally, as Dr Langley, to my parents. My mother will ask all sorts of questions—trying to throw her off the scent by telling her you had a brain injury and have been on Saturn Station for ten years won't be enough. She will want to know what happened before. She'll tie you in knots, Alice. Tell me what you want me to do. Shall I be honest and tell them you are Alexis Langley or wait to see if she makes the connection? It has to be your decision."

But Alice had no doubt the course of action they must take. "I assume your parents would know about me—about Alexis Langley?"

He nodded. "Yes, almost certainly."

"Then we'll tell them who I am and about the amnesia because that's all we know ourselves. There's little else of anything else factual to tell."

Noah's parents were sitting in the room with the big window. They looked up as Noah and Alice entered. His mother, a facsimile of Principal Katya, sent a surprised and welcoming smile towards Alice as she hurried to greet her son with an embrace that saw her lifted off the ground as he caught her.

"Noah, why did you not tell us you were coming," she spoke with Principal Katya's accent and inflexion. "We would not have gone away. When did you arrive?"

"The day before yesterday. Mother, this is Dr Langley. Alice, my mother, Dr Selina Ryan and," he introduced the older version of himself, "my father, Dr Benjamin Ryan."

Ben Ryan bowed to Alice. His hair was grey and slightly thinning, but he was possessed of the same vivid blue eyes as his son and built every bit as powerfully, despite his recent illness.

Selina Ryan took Alice's hands and drew her to one of the antiquated sofas. Alice glanced at Noah, who smiled to reassure her, he was there, close by, if his mother, like her sister Katya, became overwhelming.

"Come and sit down, Dr Langley. I am so excited to meet you. Noah never brings friends home." She shot an accusing but affectionate glance to her son, who smiled in return. Selina kept hold of Alice's hands, exactly as Principal Katya did when seated together.

"Where did you meet Noah, Dr Langley?"

"We met on Saturn Station, mother," Noah cut in before Alice responded. "Dr Langley was recuperating."

"Oh, nothing too serious, we hope?" Selina Ryan considered Alice's face as if there, she might find a clue to whatever ailed her.

Alice looked at Noah. Perhaps now might be the time. Sooner rather than later. She could always leave if it made anyone uncomfortable. Alice thought of Sarah, who received the news well and in her stride. If these people were anything like their son, they would too.

Alice looked down to where Selina held her hands, then back up to Noah. Her courage failed her. Perhaps some help? Noah understood.

"Mother, Dr Langley is Dr *Alexis* Langley. She was on Saturn Station for ten years." It felt odd to say, to announce the presence of history, to open up an age-old mystery and present her in this way. Alice is a miracle; he thought it as he spoke, strange that he would be part of her story, a story that continued here, now, in the privacy of his family home.

Selina Ryan smiled in puzzlement at her son, not comprehending why the use of this name might constitute an explanation. It was his father who made the connection, putting a hand to his head and making a small gesture, like pointing, as if the truth were too staggering to consider, or as if his son was playing a joke, an event he didn't believe he'd live to see.

"Alexis Langley? Bell Institute Alexis Langley?

He stepped forward, then stopped, finding a seat opposite, plainly bewildered, but Noah's mother still didn't grasp the situation.

"I do not understand any of this," she said, looking from Noah to her husband.

"We saw you," Ben Ryan said to Alice, his voice faltering, "About forty years ago, when Jim Grossmith first joined the team. He and I had a semester at university. Selina," he drew his wife's attention, "Dr Alexis Langley. Sleeping Beauty."

Selina Ryan turned her puzzled gaze to Alice. "It is not possible."

Alice remained quiet; now they knew, Selina's hands still held hers.

"Alexis Langley?" she studied Alice's face. *"Alexis Langley?"*

In the silence that followed, Alice felt perhaps she should probably leave, but then Selina's face broke into a smile of delight and amazement, mingled perhaps with a touch of incredulity.

"Ben! Alexis Langley! Did you hear that? Oh, my dear," Selina Ryan was quite overcome. "Grossmith believed with all his heart you would wake up. And you have, and you are…" she made a sweeping gesture with her hand and caught Alice by the shoulders *"…real!"* She practically shouted the last word in her excitement. So like Principal Katya.

Alice thought this must be what it would be like to be a famous actor when confronted by a fan. Not an entirely comfortable experience. She was so glad Noah was here.

"Dr Grossmith continued to care for me after I woke, Dr Ryan, he has been very kind."

"Selina," Noah's mother said absently, still marvelling

251

at the news, and still holding Alice's shoulders.

Ben Ryan couldn't stand. A sense of disbelief had overtaken him. Where he had a brief fascination, those who saw the Sleeping Beauty often did, Jim Grossmith was preoccupied with her. He recalled joking with Jim about his so-called sixth sense where she was concerned, but it appeared he'd been prophetic, Jim's dedication, devotion and sacrifice paid off, she was here, living, breathing, speaking, and what's more, in the company of his son.

"When we saw you, all those years ago," he said, his voice low and deeply respectful, "not for a moment did we believe you could be revived. You've been part of our history, our folklore, for so long. It seems impossible you're here, and you are a lovely, normal young girl. A girl like any other."

Selina felt the same awe, "Forgive us, Dr Langley. We are at a loss."

"Please call me, Alice."

"Alice?"

"Her name is pronounced 'Alice', mother," Noah explained, "Alexis, without sounding the 'x'."

"Oh, of course, we will. Alice, we are thrilled, honoured, to have you here. Do you have memories of your previous life? How were you awakened?"

Alice shook her head. Selina meant Alexis's memories, so Alice could answer truthfully.

"No memories at all, and I woke naturally."

"Alice has amnesia, mother," Noah added, "so she has taken to learning as much of our world as she can. She is quite the student of history."

A little face peeped out of a pouch suspended around Ben's chest, and Alice seized the opportunity to divert attention away from her.

"Who is this?"

Benjamin lifted a small puppy from the pouch.

"This is Puppy," he said. "He's been abandoned by his mother. See his leg?"

He brought the puppy over and crouched beside Alice to show her, taking a moment to study her face as he got closer, as if expecting her to show some sign of great age or effects of her preservation. Alice understood he hadn't quite got over his surprise. She examined the puppy's leg, which appeared to be twisted.

"Poor thing. Can it be fixed?"

"It can, and we will, but he is too little and weak." Ben stood. "Noah, Puppy needs a feed. Would you grab a feeder?"

"Is there one prepared?"

"Yes, it's in the case."

Noah got the feeder, took the puppy, and settled it against the crook of his knee to give it the formula. Alice could see he'd performed this same task many, many times before.

Ben went back to his seat, leaving the puppy in Noah's care. He and his wife looked at each other often, and Selina seemed unwilling to let go of Alice, although thankfully, she'd moved from her shoulders to her hands. Alice decided she needed to prove how ordinary and unremarkable she had become since re-entering the world.

"Your son has been kind enough to show me a few

historical sites. He's been very generous with his time."

"Well, that makes sense. Noah likes history," his father said. "How long will you be staying, son?"

"I have briefings in a couple of days; then I'm due back on the Significator. We have tomorrow all day and tomorrow night here, then I promised Alice I'd show her a few other places."

"Oh, how wonderful!" Selina exclaimed. "There is plenty of history around here. So—" lifting a finger, his mother counted off the hours she needed to occupy, "—we have tonight, all day tomorrow and tomorrow night? Well, what I propose is…"

And precisely as Noah predicted, his mother organised their entire day for them.

How could she not help but warm to Noah's parents? His mother, bubbly, witty and cheerful, was just like Principal Katya. His father, quieter and more serious, like Noah. And they accepted her.

Still seated beside Selina Ryan and listening to her plans, Alice allowed herself a small glance at Noah. He saw her and winked. Father and son sat alike, left ankle resting on right knee, right elbow on the chair arm and cheek resting on the back of the hand, the little puppy asleep on Noah's knee. Both men listened to Selina, not offering any input, knowing to do so would be a futile exercise anyway.

"Alice, has Noah taken you to Stonehenge?" Selina asked as she decided on her schedule.

"Yes, and Tibet and Machu Picchu. Principal Katya asked him to show me some of these places. I know he only has limited opportunity to visit Earth, but we've done a lot of exploring."

Alice avoided Noah's gaze, but in her peripheral vision, she saw his mouth twitch. She bit her lip against a grin; he saw it and wondered when they would get another opportunity to explore. They would have to make an opportunity.

CHAPTER TWENTY-FIVE _

The knowledge her sister had orchestrated her son's friendship disappointed Selina. When she saw he'd brought a woman to the house—a first for him—she hoped this might be a romance, even after the astonishing revelation and the fact Alexis Langley was a person of note. Noah hated the spotlight, but Alexis, or rather Alice, turned out to be sweet and pleasant, not to mention gorgeous, so maybe? Something? She allowed herself a glimmer of resurrected hope, a hope she'd abandoned years ago—the possibility of Noah ever marrying.

"Noah should take you to the Top of the World, Alice. It is an amazing experience!" Selina's enthusiasm for life rivalled her sister's.

"I hear it's not an historical site, Selina, like Stonehenge, but a place for couples."

"Who told you that?" Selina said.

"Statesman Patrick."

"I doubt there's a single romantic destination Statesman Patrick hasn't visited," Ben laughed. "And it has romance. The Top of the World is a natural habitat for native animals and plants. From there, it's possible to access a phenomenon in the exosphere, discovered after the A'khet gave certain of us Knowledge to enhance our speed capabilities in space. This phenomenon exists on other worlds, harmless, fascinating, but the effect can only be experienced at near light speed."

That was intriguing, and Alice wished to learn more, but Selina had other ideas.

"Of course, there is romance to be found wherever you go," she added, focusing on the romance and not the phenomenon, "there is a wonderful lodge, built behind the waterfall, a beautiful structure, and the rainforest is stunning. Perfect for long walks together, and the wildlife is varied and mostly quite tame. Have you ever been behind a waterfall, Alice?"

"Yes, I have," Alice said, remembering the day she spent with Patrick at the Tabernacle, it seemed so long ago.

"I'll take you there, Alice," Noah smiled, deciding it might be wise to steer his mother away from concentrating on romance. "Mother, Alice can cook."

This second revelation about Alice drew more admiring looks from both his parents.

"Really?" Selina appeared not to believe her ears.

Alice nodded.

"She invented a dish called hamburgers," Noah continued, dragging a silent groan from Alice, "so popular, they serve them now at one of the Tabernacle city eateries."

"I didn't invent hamburgers," she protested in a small voice, which as usual, went unheard.

"Alice, would it be an imposition?" Selina asked.

Faced with such earnest expectancy from both Selina and Ben, she couldn't refuse. Besides, Noah was already ordering from the Providore.

They spent the evening on the terrace, the night was clear and mild, and Noah sat beside Alice, his arm draped casually over the back of the seat. Now and then, she felt his fingertips brush her arm. Selina, as eagle-eyed as Principal Katya, saw it, saw the momentary flutter of Alice's eyelashes, and it only increased her speculation about what this young woman meant to her son.

Selina and Ben made polite enquiries about Alice's past and her time on Saturn Station. Noah reminded them about Alice's amnesia, but she was happy to share with them everything she knew and about how difficult it was to say goodbye to Dr Grossmith when she left. She told them of Principal Hardy's belief that she'd studied the history of the twentieth and twenty-first centuries and carried on an interesting discussion with them about life and society in that time. Selina and Ben were eager to hear the stories, and Alice took care not to place herself in any of the accounts. Even Noah had questions for her, which she answered with confidence. On Saturn Station, in a moment of sadness, she'd asked Kelly to search the registry for images, desperate to see something familiar, a place or landmark she could recognise to soothe her homesickness. Instead, she learned many hard and shocking facts about the society she thought she knew. The truth was, she'd been in total ignorance, but she found she could now speak of those times with a sense of detachment.

Later, Selina picked up the puppy. "I am going to

bed, Alice, Noah," She hugged them both, "I am so looking forward to tomorrow, Alice, meeting you…is astonishing! I am still in shock! Ben, I will pop Puppy in between us, so I will know when to feed him."

The puppy got wrapped in a blanket and carted away in Selina's arms. A poorly little dog in bed didn't even cause a ripple with Noah and Ben, and though she hated leaving him, Alice thought it might be good for Noah to have time with his father, so Alice suggested that she, too, might bid them goodnight.

Noah saw Alice to her room, with a glance behind to make sure they were alone, pulled her close, kissing her deeply and fiercely. Alice's body responded urgently, sparks of desire flashing up her spine.

"Oh, Noah," she could scarcely breathe.

"I won't be too long…"

Alice shushed him. "I'm not sure I would be comfortable, not with your parents at home."

"They would be more surprised if I stayed in my own room," he said as he carried on kissing her neck and mouth so she couldn't speak. "I love those panties," he murmured, his voice low and husky against her throat.

She stifled a giggle and stroked the front of his shirt. "You still haven't told me why all this is so secret," she whispered.

"I will tell you, but," he released her, "for now, you go to bed. We'll let my mother direct our day tomorrow."

"She's lovely. They both are. I'm glad we told them the truth. Keeping it a secret makes my life a lie."

He kissed her again and opened the door, giving her a

wicked grin as he filled up the doorway, making sure she had to squeeze her body past him.

In her room, Alice went to the window. The scent of the honeysuckle filled the night air, and she breathed in its perfume. This was beyond her wildest dreams—just the thought of Noah, the pressure of his mouth against her lips and throat…

The moon was high above the trees, so bright she couldn't see the stars. She was glad. The stars would soon take him from her.

Noah went back into the parlour. His father was playing the piano—as an accomplished musician, he continued to play as he acknowledged his son's presence.

"Your mother won't wake up when Puppy needs feeding. I thought to stay up until the first feed, probably the second as well if I can't wake her." He smiled, "So, how are you, son?"

Noah nodded that he was good. Very good.

"And Dr Langley, Alice?" Ben stopped playing when Noah hesitated and took a deep breath. He gave his son his full attention.

"Alice has a lot to do with how I feel, Dad."

"I suspected."

"Did Mother?"

Ben raised his eyebrows and grinned.

"What do you think? Until today, she believed you were married to the Significator."

"She's right, at least until I met Alice. I encountered her a few times before I realised…well, what I realised."

"How drawn to her you are?"

"Yes. I can't recall ever being happier than when I'm in her company."

"And Alice, does she like spending time with you?"

"Yes, she does. We've become…close."

"Then why do I sense a dilemma."

"Patrick's in love with her. He's very persistent, Dad, you know him. I thought she was maybe a passing interest, but now I'm not so sure. He's on the Accessor right now."

"The Accessor? Why? Don't you need him?"

Noah shook his head as he remembered the part he played in Patrick taking off to supervise Engineer Oakes.

"Ahmed asked me for Engineer Oakes," he admitted, "who also has A'khet knowledge, to oversee the establishment of Patrick's upgraded Gravidarum. I was inclined to refuse, so close to us leaving, but it would mean the Accessor waiting until we got back from our assignment. Ahmed didn't want that. Oakes could have handled it; the systems on the Accessor are far less complex than the Significators. I knew Patrick wouldn't let Oakes go without him, so I signed the order. Patrick followed the next day."

"Leaving Alice without a friend?" his father nodded in understanding. "A role into which you gladly stepped?"

"Yes, with a little help from Aunt Katya."

"And now you've fallen in love, replaced Patrick in Alice's affections, and you have to keep this a secret from him for the next two years?"

"In a nutshell. But I haven't replaced Patrick, she considers him a friend and only a friend, and yes, it is a secret at the moment. Principal Hardy asked me to keep an eye on the situation with Patrick, concerned that Alice is fragile and might get hurt. I'm ashamed to say I gave him the impression I didn't care. Part of me thought he was being precious because of who she is, and you know, I never make other people's problems my own."

"Alice isn't a problem, Noah. For centuries she has belonged to us all; now, she's on a journey to belong only to herself. Hardy's concern for her wasn't misplaced; he asked little of you."

"I know, but Patrick, as you would expect, continued doing what he always does, with several female crew members."

Noah sat down heavily on the saggy armchair favoured by the cat. His father stayed at the piano but turned to face his son, leaning forward, his hands clasped loosely over his knees.

"What Patrick does at leisure is not your business, Noah, even aboard ship."

"Dad, interpersonal relationships on a principality ship and sex as recreation are a normal facet of life. Patrick isn't doing anything different to what most others do, I accept that, but it isn't how Alice conducts herself."

"It's not how you conduct yourself either, Noah."

"I have no power to rule on relationships unless protocols get breached, but then I saw a female crewman leaving Patrick's quarters after I—well, noticed Alice."

"You judged him?"

"I guess I did."

"And you wanted Alice?"

"Not consciously at that point, then later, I couldn't stop thinking about her, after the Cotillion Ball, I used

Hardy's concerns as justification for encouraging Patrick to the Accessor. I conveniently disregarded the fact Alice turned my ordered life on its head. Dad, Patrick loves easily and then discards. I thought he would do the same to Alice, then Aunt Katya, with her sixth sense, realised what I'd done and sent me to Tibet with her. A few days later, I took her to Machu Picchu. After I returned to the ship, we spoke over the registry,then later, I asked her to come here."

"And Alice has told you she doesn't return Patrick's affection?"

"I know for sure she doesn't."

"He knows nothing about this?"

"Nothing at all. He knows about Tibet and Machu Picchu but believes they were at Aunt Katya's behest. Patrick is convinced I'm so dull; spending time with me must have been an ordeal for Alice."

"You are a very solitary man, Noah; few truly know you. I haven't heard you say this much in years, and I'm your father! I assume A'khet requested you visit them? Why?"

"They requested Alice. Aunt Katya said they were curious, I accompanied her, but the darndest thing, I swear they were expecting me."

"I can see why they would be curious about Alice, but now you have a situation with your oldest friend."

"I don't know what to do, Dad. I can't say, 'Patrick old boy, guess what, we're in love with the same woman, but she chooses me'. From what Alice has told me, he's convinced he'll win her over when we get back."

"Does she choose you?"

Noah didn't speak, the silence giving his father the answer he'd anticipated anyway.

"You believe telling Patrick would be a risk?"

"I believe so. He would see this as a betrayal."

"And now you have two years apart from Alice to dream up a suitable story for when you return, and he finds he didn't win her over because she's been involved with you since before you left?"

"It sounds underhand put like that." Noah rubbed his eyes, suddenly feeling very weary, "I did consider telling him but then realised if he's genuine, he might withdraw from the mission and ask for local reassignment, then he would be here, and I would be out there." He gestured towards the window, "And Alice would be here as well."

"I imagine the Tabernacle wouldn't find his reasons for withdrawing at such late notice valid, Noah, not without extenuating circumstances. And you don't give her credit. She's not a child. You need to have some faith."

"That's the whole point; she *is* a child. Everything is new to her."

"If you are so certain of her feelings, have you thought about asking her to marry you? You could take her with you."

"She's only just returned to the world, Dad, to living, breathing, learning, and discovering. I can't bundle her off to space, not now when she needs time to learn and grow, and can you imagine me taking her on board as my wife without telling Patrick first?"

"There would be some fallout, but I suspect he'd get over it. Noah, starting a relationship with a lie may be a mistake. You are a principal, not a teenager in a first crush. I have never seen you blur the edges of your decisions like this; that is why the most important ship in the fleet is under your command and not in the hands of another, less singular commander."

Ben watched his capable, strong-willed son struggle, for the first time in his life, with emotions he'd denied himself in favour of a career. He waited.

"Alice plays the piano," Noah said at last.

"Splendid, perhaps she will give us a recital."

"She never remembers playing. Sometimes, random memories surface, revealing her education, intelligence, brilliance, and at those times, she is outgoing, confident, and larger than life, completely sure of herself. Other times, she is shy, quick to learn, humble, sweet."

"And you love both ascensions?"

"I find now I can't separate them; there appears to be two distinct elements, the one you met tonight and another, the scientist who emerges when I least expect it. Together, they make a third person, contrary, wise, gentle, educated, all the things I described."

"Is it wise then to take her to the Top of the World?"

"Why not?"

"If she elects to visit the wave, it might confuse her."

"It might give her clarity."

Noah's father smiled sagely and returned to the piano. Noah bowed a goodnight and turned towards his room. His father looked up as his son stopped in the doorway.

"You and mother were unbelievably restrained when I introduced Alice. Thank you."

"Believe me, Noah," Ben grinned, "when the information sinks in, I suspect I will experience another episode of disbelief. Alice is a member of our society now, and we will afford her all the privacy she requires. I promise we will tell no one."

"I didn't tell Aunt Katya I brought her here," Noah admitted, giving his father another reason to sigh.

"I'll tell your mother about Patrick's involvement with Alice and the part you played in his reassignment. She'll understand the implications and won't tell her sister. Not if I ask her not to, but Noah, you need to sort this out."

"I know, Dad. Thank you."

Noah passed Alice's room and, for a moment, stood, wishing he could just open the door, climb into bed beside her and let her convince him he should stay with her. He bit his lip, trying to adjust to the fact in a few days, he would have to leave her. So little time, so few opportunities and now, he'd involved his family in a secret, a secret he hoped he wouldn't come to regret.

Closing the door to his room, he peeled off his clothes and stepped into the shower, allowing the warm water cascade over his face, closing his eyes, he reflected on his conversation with his father. A movement behind distracted him, and his lips curled into a soft smile as he felt Alice's hands lightly touch his back, encircle his waist, and slip slowly upwards over his chest.

CHAPTER TWENTY-SIX _

An unexpected scene greeted Alice on the patio the next morning. The Providore had laid out breakfast, and it seemed as if every animal in the neighbourhood received an invitation. Selina was busy feeding titbits to the three dogs and the goat with the missing leg. Ben perused world affairs on the registry, and Noah hand-fed the puppy on his lap from a bottle, all the while brushing away a few wild and not so wild birds that came in search of food, eventually finding their way to a crumb tray on the table. Noah and his parents looked up as she joined them.

"Good morning Alice," Selina smiled. "Please excuse us; we tend to spoil the animals a little."

Noah grinned as she sat down. He'd reluctantly dragged himself from her embrace much earlier to help his parents with the animals. Ben acknowledged their guest with a quick bow of his head, then went back to the registry but couldn't concentrate. He'd spent a good part of the night reading up on her, though almost all information stopped at fifteen years since. This morning, he wanted to stare at Alice, finding it hard to believe one of the most remarkable puzzles ever presented to science stood here, with his family, on his patio.

Noah placed the puppy in Alice's lap and gave her the bottle to continue feeding him.

"I'll get you some coffee and breakfast," he said, tickling the puppy under the chin. "Puppy needs encouragement to suck."

"Yes," his mother said, "rub his chin. He likes it. His sucking and swallowing reflexes are not well developed."

The puppy didn't want the food from Alice. He fussed and spat, so when Noah came back with the coffee, he showed her how to encourage him to open his mouth and where to put the teat so the puppy didn't spit it out. While she was engaged in the task, a little bird came to share her breakfast. No-one made any effort to shoo it away, even when two of its comrades flew down to join in the feast. Mealtimes here were even more liberal than at home, but Alice loved the harmony between humans and animals. Even the horses drew close to the family, grazing nearby. Fleet nudged Noah on the shoulder, gently at first, then less gently, until he gave her a morsel from the table.

The puppy dozed off with the bottle in his mouth, and Alice ended up drinking rather cold coffee before attempting the pecked pastry. The question of hygiene never came up.

"You like animals, Alice?" Selina smiled her approval.

"Yes, we have animals at home; dogs, a cat, horses, goats and chickens and a little cockatiel who is my special pet."

"Alice's home overlooks the ocean on one side and

pastures on the other," Noah said, tacitly letting his mother know he visited there. "It's glorious."

His mother noticed, pleased that it was not too early to rekindle hope.

"Do you live there alone?" Selina asked.

"Oh, no, not at all. I live with the aunties, Mary and her wife, Jane."

"In the Calamities, then?"

Alice wasn't sure how to answer. Segregation of a portion of society, but with complete acceptance, still filled her with a sense of injustice.

"I've met Alice's aunts, Mother," Noah smiled across at Alice, fueling his mother's hopes anew. "They are delightful—retired medical doctors."

"How wonderful to recover your health in the company of close family members, Alice. Family is everything to us. Now, let us put these animals down. Noah, please take Puppy from Alice and put him in his crate, the small one. We will take him with us so we can feed him. We will go now and enjoy our day."

Noah took the puppy from Alice, blowing her a secret kiss as he leaned over her. She smiled a secret smile back at him. Even being close to him made her feel flushed and breathless.

"Noah mentioned the crop formations interest you, Alice," Ben said. "There are two we can visit if you wish, and he tells us you have an interest in architecture, so Selina has suggested we go to the old city. We'll take your shuttle, Noah; I'll pilot."

Alice and Noah sat together in the back of the shuttle.

Noah's large frame took up most of the room and made it very snug. He discreetly linked his fingers with hers.

The first crop formation was close to the house and only took a few minutes to locate. The lack of design and blatant ordinariness disappointed Alice after her high expectations. The registry's images, showing intriguing and elaborate designs, drove her to expect much more than two simple interlinked circles with square protuberances at either end, all of which slightly underwhelmed her. They hovered above, and Ben piloted a full swing to see it from all angles.

"Noah told me some individuals believe aliens make these," Alice tried to see meaning in the shapes below.

"That's correct, Alice," Ben looked over his shoulder, "but we've never seen anything out of the ordinary around here."

"Aren't the A'khet aliens?" Alice thought they would qualify.

"Not anymore," Selina and Benjamin chorused together.

Alice stared down at the formation.

"I could make that pattern," she said, more to herself than the others, "and I have no artistic ability."

"A lot of the designs are primitive, Alice," Ben said. "A bit of fun by local children flying one-man shuttles or tubes, we hold that belief even if there is a complex mathematical element that confounds science," he laughed. "It makes living beside them more comfortable. Noah and his sisters made one once."

Alice was astonished. "You were a hoaxer?"

Noah grinned, "We didn't think so. We grew up with

the formations, and I suppose we didn't take them too seriously. It was just fun at the time."

"Surely wrecking a farmer's crop is vandalism? Did you get caught?"

"We did, and as punishment had to replant the part of the field we damaged using traditional methods. It was back-breaking work, but we learned a lot, and not only about respect."

"Do all these crop producers use the dome-field and drone methods to raise crops? Mary and Jane grow corn and vine vegetables like that."

"Yes, they do, Alice," Noah pointed out the housings that kept the field in place. "Apart from my experience with repairing the damage my sisters and I caused, you're the only person I've met who grows fruit and vegetables using the traditional method."

"I like getting my hands dirty. Wouldn't the dome-field alert the grower to a presence on the field? Alien or human? The dome-field at home goes red if we step inside."

"That's because it's detecting a life form and assessing what it needs to do to help it grow, does it clear after a while?"

"Yes, but couldn't they attach an alarm and catch aliens or people in the act?"

"It's been tried, Alice," Noah should have paid more attention to crop formation science. He'd never anticipated answering questions on the subject.

"That's right," Selina seemed to know more than her son. "They installed double annular-fields, like the bubble domes used on Mars. They reach below the surface for several hundred metres and above for the same distance. Nothing can penetrate; the atmosphere, life forms, nothing known to mankind, even so, the formations appeared, paying no attention to all our cleverness! This formation is simple, Alice, but we will show you the other one. It is new and more complex. Like other more intricate formations which have appeared overnight, it is under investigation."

"I don't understand how, with all the technology of this century, it's not possible to prove who makes them."

"Children," Noah said with certainty. "I can't imagine adults carrying out wanton destruction of crops on such a scale."

"The formations are a fraction of the size of those in the twentieth century, Alice," Ben joined in the conversation, "except for the one we are going to see next. It's unusually large."

"I don't see how crop circle architects get by twenty-sixth-century radar," The whole concept altogether stumped Alice.

"No-one has come up with any convincing argument, Alice," Ben replied, "the debate has raged for centuries."

Alice's response to the next formation was different. Struck by the geometrical patterns, she asked Ben to go higher so she could see it in one frame. For some reason she didn't understand, it made perfect sense.

Noah saw her expression and the question forming on her lips. He held up a finger to silence her. Not now, he mouthed. They could speak of it later. She nodded and returned her attention to the ground below.

Alice recognised the shape—the symbol for infinity.

As she watched, it appeared to rotate, she blinked, and the formation stilled. The other designs scattered around and within the structure had meaning, a meaning which escaped her, even though she'd seen such patterns before. And in colour. In frustration, she raked through her memory but couldn't recall where she'd seen them. The more she gazed at the formation, the more she felt she something was reminding her. But of what?

Like her sister, Principal Katya, Selina Ryan possessed limitless energy and enthusiasm. The entire day, spent looking over ruins and architectural treasures, included an ancient cathedral holding important historical relics. She felt as if she were time travelling, standing, awestruck in a building, constructed centuries before her own time, running her hand over the ancient supports and examining inscriptions that surprisingly, withstood the ravages of time.

Late into the evening, they arrived back at the house, and Selina decided not to impose on Alice's cooking skills after such a busy day, so the Providore was summoned. The exhilaration of everything she'd seen and done during the day filled Alice's head, and she found herself restless, interrogating Noah about the cathedral, the fascinating old city and the agricultural applications of growing barley. But not once did she mention the crop formation.

That night, Alice offered to take a turn in feeding Puppy. Selina, secretly desperate to make her feel welcome, gave her and Noah the first shift. This time the puppy took the feed greedily from Alice and deposited some formula back on Alice's shirt. She held the hot little body against her and kissed the tiny face.

"He's so sweet, Noah, and your parents so devoted to his care. Has your home always been like this?" Alice's mother wouldn't even let her have a goldfish.

"Always, and they are as kind to people as they are to animals. My sisters are the same; fortunately, they have tolerant husbands!"

"What will happen to Puppy?"

"If he survives, he'll probably stay here, and as he grows, be renamed Dog. The other dogs are old, and I couldn't imagine there not being canines around the house."

"I can't bear to think he might not live."

"If my parents have anything to do with it, he'll be fine, but in our home, the loss of a puppy or kitten was a sad fact of life. It's getting late, Alice. I don't know why you aren't exhausted." He kissed her forehead and took the pup from her, "I'll put him in his bed; he should sleep now until his next feed."

Noah tucked Puppy into his crate and then turned to her. She'd made no move to go to her room. Only two more nights before Noah was due at the Tabernacle, and both quietly knew how quickly time was passing, neither of them would voice the private agony they felt, knowing they must soon part. He stepped towards her and gathered her into his arms, and she held him tightly, burying her face in his chest.

"Alice," he breathed her name, and hearing the emotion in his voice, she felt an overwhelming desire to weep. She had been given so many beautiful gifts since waking to this new world, but her time with Noah was the most precious of all. How could she bear now to be parted from him?

"Noah, do we need to go to the Top of the World?" she said, her voice muffled against his shirt and stifling her desire to cry. "Can't we go somewhere, be alone? Just we two?"

"I already considered it, Alice. We'll arrange it so we barely see another person there." He reached down and kissed her neck, pushing his hand inside her blouse to caress her shoulder, his other hand circling her waist to pull her closer.

"I could, you know...here, right now."

She smiled. "In front of Puppy?"

"Not in front of Puppy." He scooped her up in his arms and carried her to his room.

———

Alice woke in the morning to find Noah sitting beside her on the bed. He kissed her and offered her a cup of coffee. She wriggled up and took it from him.

"Have I overslept?"

"No, the Providore just arrived, so there's plenty of time."

But there wasn't plenty of time. As he said it, he realised, as she did, they could measure the time left to them in hours rather than days. The first time they made love in the woods was the most profound and powerful experience of Noah's life. These last few nights, lying beside her, he already felt the pain of being without her, but to resign or withdraw from the mission would be catastrophic, even though the thought, with guilty indulgence, crossed his mind more than once. And more than once, he considered his father's suggestion of marrying her, but he knew, while she was still discovering her world, now was not the time.

"We should go to breakfast," he said, pulling her up to sit on the side of the bed. He would not spend this last too short a time lamenting his departure. "We can have breakfast again in Colombia Province if we leave here by lunch."

"I could get confused by such rapid changes in time, Noah," Alice disappeared naked into the washer, "I have visions of meeting myself on a return journey from somewhere!"

CHAPTER TWENTY-SEVEN

Noah's parents waved them off cheerfully, prompting Alice to ask him why they seemed so comfortable with him being gone for so long, from what was clearly, a close-knit family.

"We leave home at fifteen, Alice," he took an equally matter-of-fact attitude towards leaving them as well. "I haven't lived here full-time for twenty-five years. It's how this society works. Parents take a lot of comfort and pride in their children's successes, I know my parents do, and they have a busy life here. They've done their job, bringing us up. Besides, they usually come up to the ship to see me before I leave."

"Still, they must miss you."

"I hope so. I miss them too, but they explored their world, and now celebrate that I explore mine. That's the way of things. Different from the ways of your society, I expect."

"Very different, but I must ask, why did you shush me at the crop circle? I noticed you put a finger to your lips."

"I thought you saw something you recognised."

"And turn into my clever other self and not

remember a word I said?"

"Perhaps, and that might be too much for my parents. You were quite a shock, and they were just becoming used to you. Your scientific side might have pushed my mother over the edge," he laughed and squeezed her hand. "What did you see in the pattern?"

"Well, and this is not the other me talking; I've seen part of it before. I can't remember where."

"Can you remember when, a time frame, your old life or your new?"

There followed a strange silence. Alice wiped her hand over her cheek and looked down, as if expecting to find something in the palm. She held up her fingers, studying them, deep in contemplation. And then, he felt glad he'd silenced her. For all her intelligence, his mother would have found Alice's crossovers bewildering. Better for her, she only sees one side of Alice for now. Here, manifesting herself with confidence, was the other side.

"The mathematical component of the formation was to the base twenty, the vigesimal system. This society uses base ten. I'm not an expert, but I know the Mayans used the base twenty system. I say that because much of their art suggests extraterrestrial contact."

Answer her, he told himself. Say something to draw this other self out. "Did you deduce a vigesimal system from the geometry?"

He'd not paid enough attention to the circle, mainly because he knew it was possible to reproduce them, given enough skill.

"The symbol for infinity is overlaid at the upper pole

by a design, as we flew above and around, it retained its symmetry."

"A Fibonacci spiral? They're common in crop formations. Simple math and easy to reproduce."

She didn't hear him.

"The pattern over the lower half of the lemniscate is a geometrical sequence; cuboid at the far left, looking from the North, but from the East, another aspect emerged. I'm not sure about the snowflake design, depicting the end of time I think. I recognise the cubes, but for the rest of the geometry, the calculation escapes me." Then she laughed, "I'm sorry, Principal Ryan, I'm rambling. The sequences have their roots in ancient geometry, I recognise the Mayan influence, but some of it goes back further. You're interested in astronomical sequences; I'm surprised it didn't interest you more. My uncle Martin would know the technical argument. That's his forte, along with theoretical physics and a whole bunch of other stuff!" She glanced up at him, and just as he thought Alice would re-emerge, she offered what sounded like a simple, and loaded, throwaway line.

"I believe it's a message."

"A message?" That had been a popular theory over the years. "For you?"

"Maybe, definitely meant for someone."

"Do you have any idea who created it?"

"Yes, I do," she said brightly. "Nature."

Noah had no answer; he didn't even have a question. In a few moments, she would have no recollection of this conversation, so he tried to ask why she believed the circle was a natural phenomenon, but then Alice looked at him and shrugged, the moment gone.

The Top of the World, Alice worked out from the registry on the shuttle, was near the Equator. Noah told her Colombia was a province, along with most of the area once called South America. Alice checked the climate and geographical features. It looked interesting enough, but she didn't care; she would be with Noah.

He asked if she would like to go through the phenomenon, and though she knew that meant a natural or unnatural occurrence, thinking it an apt description of her situation, she wasn't sure she wanted to meet another.

"I don't know what it is, Noah."

"A ripple in space, some people see colours, claiming it balances their mood and relaxes and clears the mind. I saw colours when I went but nothing else. The military controls visitation, and permission is required; I sent word ahead just in case you chose to go. Otherwise, we can head straight to the lodge and enjoy the rivers and rainforest."

"It might be interesting. Is it safe?"

"Completely safe, it's been there since the dawn of time. Only man's limitations kept it hidden. As to its purpose, scientists can only guess."

Noah brought the shuttle down on a small landing platform. A woman in a grey military uniform greeted them formally. The officer led them to an enclosure, showing them to a clear glass, single-seat tube. The only control Alice could see was an autopilot console.

The officer saw Alice hesitate. "Would you like to go

to the anomaly now, Dr Langley, or would you prefer to leave it until later?"

Alice looked at Noah. The tube looked like her sarcophagus—maybe this wasn't a good idea.

"By myself?" It hadn't occurred to her she would be alone.

"You can't experience it in company, Dr Langley," the officer told her. "The wave will only respond to a single presence."

"It's okay, Alice," Noah squeezed her hand. He'd never heard of anyone having a negative experience, so he encouraged her, anticipating no problems and hoping it might give her clarity.

"I'll be here. You'll be fine."

The tube, small, snug, and claustrophobic, momentarily sent Alice into a panic, but by the time she turned to say she'd changed her mind, the tube was already speeding away. She glimpsed Noah's smiling face as the tube moved towards the blue sky at an angle before pointing vertically towards space. Alice didn't look behind her as the earth fell away in only a few seconds. She'd become accustomed to speed now, but in this small capsule, she was far more aware of the velocity. She felt vulnerable and could only pray this would all be over soon.

Above her, streaks of crimson and orange flashed across like a wave. It's crest, or its borders, indistinct. It was only visible for an instant. The tube halted, and although she searched, the wave had disappeared. She saw only reflected light from the planet. Well, what a waste of time, she thought, assuming the experience was over and that she would now return to Earth.

But it wasn't over. As Alice waited for the tube to begin its descent, the wave engulfed her, shimmering like silver sparkles all over her body, like being inside a shaken snow globe. Alice found herself enveloped in a cloud of colours as the wave flowed through the tube's interior, melting through the hull. Alice looked around her as she floated, weightless, drifting on a sea of swirling, sparkling colours.

The safety field the officer activated to keep her in her seat vanished, and she moved upwards, weightless, free from any constraint. Her hands lifted to the level of her eyes, and as she turned them over, many brilliant lights moved with them. She floated, buoyed by all the colours of the rainbow. A pressure on her back propelled her forwards, causing her head to fall back, pockets of light beamed from her body. Laughter gurgled in her throat as colours she'd never seen before and defied description, curled and touched her face, then vanished into the bright mist as she reached to touch them.

She rested, suspended as the wave stirred around her. The colours cleared briefly, and a man and woman appeared, a woman with red hair, like hers. The scene changed to the monastery in Tibet, then to a grand, opulent building surrounded by roofs, Chinese roofs. Turning her head, Alice saw the colours join, pass away. Mountains appeared, and in the distance, she heard piano music. When the colours united once more, they darkened, losing their joy. Pain coursed with fiery intensity through her body, and she thought she cried out, her voice freezing in her throat as she gazed into the kind, worried eyes of a man she knew but couldn't recall from where.

The colours mingled brighter and fell in on the vision like a child's kaleidoscope. Alice's body gently rotated to her left. A young woman formed from the mist—Alexis Langley. Alice looked down at her hands. The gold band Ted placed there at their wedding hung loosely on her finger, the skin on the hand wrinkled and aged. She reached up and felt hair on her chin. Slowly, she lifted her gaze to Alexis. The young woman smiled the saddest of smiles, gazing at Alice with her wide green eyes, a question or a plea hanging in the space between them, but Alice felt no power to understand nor answer.

Both Alice, and the Alexis vision, raised their eyes as colours formed into people, into men and women Alice didn't know, then softly scattered as quickly as they organised themselves, like leaves on a breeze. Alexis seemed to recognise them, she returned her sad smile to Alice, and in doing so, the edges of the vision blurred and coiled upwards as smoke, taking Alexis along in its wake. Alice glanced down at her hands; the hands to which she had so lately become accustomed were there, young and smooth.

The forms gave way to words, not solitary, random words, but a sentence, a phrase perhaps. Alice peered into the haze and colour, trying to make them out as they came to her, letter by letter, syllable by syllable, entering through her chest, each one searing and burning its way into her heart. She opened her mouth to cry out in her pain, but again, no sound came, and she endured the words, their searing message.

"The path you walk is not your own. This is not your time."

Then a voice, one she'd never before heard, murmured in her ear as the pain subsided. She moved her head to see who whispered.

"You must let her go."

But she was alone in all the colours.

Alice's breath was forced from her body as she slammed back into her seat in the tube. She sat for a moment, taking deep breaths to recover and compose herself. What did all this mean? Did it contain a message for her? She looked around the tube. She hadn't been prepared, even though Noah seemed comfortable with her going. One thing was sure; it wasn't a fairground ride!

The tube looked the same as when she boarded it; the forcefield restraint remained in place. The phenomenon twinkled at her and disappeared. Alice turned her face away and didn't look back as the tube made its return journey. The whole experience took less than two minutes.

Noah's welcome smile dissolved as soon as he saw her. Not waiting for the officer, he released the tube and swooped Alice up into his arms, his eyes full of concern.

"Are you alright? You're so pale."

"I think so," Alice felt in one piece. Noah set her on her feet but kept hold of her to make sure she wouldn't fall.

The officer also expressed concern.

"Principal Ryan, shall I call for a medic? I've never seen anyone return with this reaction."

Alice held up a hand and managed a shaky smile at Noah.

"Alice?" he waited for her agreement, perhaps calling

a medic might be in order.

"I'm alright, thank you," she told the officer, composing herself.

"I will have a cup of tea," she smiled at the young woman and glanced at Noah, "and discuss the experience with Principal Ryan. I'm sure I'll recover in no time."

The officer was still unsure. Most people came back from the phenomena laughing or looking relaxed; it was considered therapeutic. No-one returned from the wave with such an ashen face; she'd not even seen space sickness in her time here.

"Principal Ryan, may I alert the Infirmary that Dr Langley has returned a little…anxious?" She wasn't sure how she would explain this unexpected event, but Noah understood protocols.

"Of course, you must. Please assure them that if Dr Langley is still 'anxious' in a little while, she will avail herself of their services."

The woman stepped away, and Noah took Alice back to the shuttle. The journey to the Top of the World resort took only minutes, and Alice stayed quiet the entire time. Noah led her out to the proscenium at the lodge's front, an area well-equipped with tables and chairs, eateries and pasticiums. He sat her down away from the central area where they could speak privately. His concern had not lessened, and he sat close, not pressing her to answer questions but waiting until she recovered and was ready to speak. He desperately hoped his father's warning would not come back to haunt him.

"What was I supposed to see?" she asked, leaning

against his arm and looking into his eyes. He wasn't sure he would have any response that would be adequate.

"It's a feeling more than seeing, Alice, apart from the silver lights," he said simply. "It levels and soothes."

But Alice was disturbed, not soothed.

"Of course, my experience in the phenomenon wasn't remarkable," he admitted. "I guess I led a dull life till I met you." He smiled at her, hoping his attempt at humour would make a difference.

"I think your life would be beyond all expectations for people of my time," she returned with a weak smile, and he was glad of it, but she still hadn't hinted to him what happened.

"What did you see, Alice?"

"Lights and rainbows at first," she paused, trying to remember it in proper order. "I felt timeless, like getting caught up in an old story. I saw a couple, the woman's hair was red, like mine, but I only caught a brief glimpse. Then the A'khet monastery and buildings with roofs, decorated roofs, red and gold, Chinese houses maybe, I think. No," she shook her head, "not houses, a school. The buildings were important, relevant, but then sickness, spreading through my body and pain, suffering, Noah, it was awful. The pain was awful."

She looked out towards the waterfall, tears springing to her eyes at the memory. "There was a man, a kind man," she continued, struggling to control the wavering in her voice. "I thought I recognised him. He cradled me in his arms and smiled so sadly."

Noah wondered who the man might be, a man who

cradled her in his arms when she was in pain. It could only be Martin Watkins.

She suddenly sat up, all dreaminess gone. Her voice became deliberate. Strong.

"I believe I experienced Alexis Langley's memories, and the man was Martin Watkins, her uncle, but Noah, there's more, Alexis Langley appeared in the vision. Not like a mirror image of me," she placed her hand on her chest, "but somehow separate. She was desolate, so terribly sad."

Alice slipped her hands from his and held them out in front of her. "I looked down," she told him, "and I could see Alice Watkins's hands. We stood in that moment, Alexis and I, facing each other, then people formed through the colours, Alexis knew them, but I didn't."

"How do you know she knew them?"

"The recognition in her eyes, then she became smoke and wafted away ever so gently." Alice placed her hands back in his.

"Words came from the forms; they entered here," Alice again slid one hand from his and touched the area below her throat. "The words had no voice, Noah, no sound, but they carved up my heart, and although I tried, I couldn't cry out with the pain."

Noah wondered if the A'khet might be involved in this vision. Knowledge was given in this manner, but no-one reported ever experiencing pain. He'd received it himself this way the day he took Alice to the monastery. If the A'khet were involved, and she'd received Knowledge, she would be unable to speak of it or answer him if he asked her.

"What did the words say, Alice?"

" 'The path you walk is not your own'," she answered quickly, considering the words as they'd been delivered, emphasising each syllable to make sure the recounting was precise. She'd replied without hesitating, dispelling his theory the A'khet might be involved somehow. This was not A'khet's doing, and it left him with no explanation.

"A voice, from here," she continued, and patted her left shoulder. "told me, 'You must let her go'."

Noah knew of no-one who experienced a voice in the phenomenon, but Alice seemed better to have spoken of the experience. By the time tea arrived at their table, she seemed to brighten and revive.

"What do you think it all means, Noah?" she asked. "There was nothing about Alice Watkins, not her past, not her children."

"I don't know, Alice," he answered honestly, his only theory blown out of the water. "That you didn't experience the memories of Alice Watkins but had a vision of Alexis Langley's life suggests her memories are hidden inside you and will, one day, resurface."

"I think the same."

She'd been so adamant she was Alice Watkins, insisting to Dr Grossmith and Kelly, now, after the phenomenon, perhaps there was more room for doubt. Maybe they were right. She looked across at Noah.

"What is it?" he asked.

"What sorts of things do I say, things I can't remember. Tell me."

"Well, you have extensive knowledge of cellular

biology, amongst other things. One time, speaking on the registry, you described what appeared to be a forerunner of KELA technology. You also seemed to understand the crop formation, making quite a startling claim."

"What claim?"

"That nature itself is responsible for the formations."

"I have a vague memory of saying that, but you don't believe it."

"Only because I made one myself and countless others have made them too. I concede there are some we can't explain."

"The old Alice Watkins would have already entered a stupefied state at what you have just told me, Noah. She would have no idea."

"But this Alice Watkins does?"

"It doesn't seem like science fiction anymore. I feel if I researched, studied, it would make sense."

"You've always maintained Alice Watkins was uneducated."

"In all areas," she brushed his fingers gently. "You are very patient with me. Both of me."

"Both of you are very important to me, but you know, something interesting has happened."

"What's that?"

"You usually refer to Alice Watkins in the first person, saying 'I', now it is 'she'."

Alice had seen this herself. "Since Tibet, whenever I'm with you, I've found I'm not fearful of Alice's memories. They have no power to hurt me. Today's experience seems to have brought Alexis Langley closer. I can't see the path clearly yet; I only know she's part of my future." Alice sighed, "I wish I could remember her."

"Will we need to start calling you 'Alexis' with the 'x'?"

Alice grinned, her colour back in her cheeks and the pain gone from her eyes.

"Not yet. I may need a new name altogether. I've changed Noah. I'm neither Alice nor Alexis. Even the way I speak, it's not how Alice spoke. I'm a different person now, whether I favour one or the other, I can't tell, maybe in time..."

Noah didn't ask more questions; he respected her need for reflection and to enjoy the simple pleasure of looking out at the rainforest through the waterfall.

She stood with a suddenness that took Noah by surprise. "Enough about me. We're here together. I spend too much time reflecting on what Alice couldn't do, and now, I am at liberty to do as I wish. And I would like to see the wildlife your mother told us about, just you and me."

She didn't want to be maudlin or serious during these last few precious hours with Noah. She took his hand, and he got to his feet, drew her arm around his waist, and they walked together towards the shuttle bay.

CHAPTER TWENTY-EIGHT _

That night, in their room high above the waterfall, wrapped in Noah's arms and lying across the enormous bed, a sleepless Alice listened to the water splash as it bounced off the rocks and fell into the river below. They'd spent a perfect day exploring the rainforest on foot, skimming over the treetops in the shuttle and soaring behind majestic condors as they rose on the thermals. The birds and animals more than made up for the province not being an historic site. Alice loved being so close to exquisite wildlife, once considered too dangerous to approach. Noah explained the entire rainforest and surrounding country became a sanctuary centuries before, and as a result, the native flora and fauna flourished. All wild animal species now lived in their native environment, with many beautiful havens for wildlife worldwide.

Now, in the stillness, listening to the distant sounds of animals and insects, Alice went over the events of the phenomenon in her mind. She recognised none of the people in her vision, only Alexis Langley. Her true self. She must stop holding fast to Alice Watkins and her memories.

Isn't that what the voice said?

"You must let her go."

Would it be that simple just to let go? The memories of Ted no longer bothered her. He was easy to discard, but the children, Michelle and Steven, they'd seemed so real, and Michelle had been her first thought on Saturn Station. Somehow, the memory of her character must have bled through into this reality, perhaps someone Alice had read about or studied, making enough of an impression to stay with her. And Eliza, the granddaughter, must come from the same story. Were there other grandchildren too? She couldn't remember. They were fading, which is as it should be, she told herself because that is precisely what dreams do.

They were right, Dr Grossmith, Principal Hardy, Principal Katya; it was Alice's memories that were the dream. That would mean she was indeed Alexis Langley; she should have accepted their word. Alice Watkins could never have intellectual discussions with Noah, play the piano or ride a horse; she had no education, no ambition, no courage.

Alice lifted her left hand; the skin was smooth and young. What did it mean when the vision showed her the old woman's hand, with the loose wedding ring? Alice let her breath out with a sigh. It would be impossible to decipher the vision without giving it further thought. It will become clear. She was sure of it.

She sat up and looked down at the sleeping Noah. Soft moonbeams slanted through the window and fell onto the bed, lending a cool, golden light that showed up the hairs on his chest. She stroked them gently, causing him to stir and open his eyes. He rested his hand on her thigh.

"Can't sleep?" he murmured.

"No, I was watching you."

"I'm on display?"

"No—yes, it's just that, soon you will be so far away, and I wanted, for now, to be able to reach out and touch you, simply because I could."

He lifted his arm, and with a smile, she nestled back into his embrace.

In the morning, Alice employed a few delaying tactics, Noah was happy to play along, but eventually, he had to be sensible.

"We have to go, Alice," he said, pulling her out of bed. "I'm expected in Cloisters in a few hours. I don't want to have to explain to Principal Katya."

"It's just been...so wonderful, Noah. I don't want it to end."

"It's not ending, Alice, we won't see each other for a couple of years, that's all," it sounded like an eternity put like that. "When I come back, it will be as if I'd never been away." Then he paused, "I'm not presumptuous, am I?"

Alice pulled an 'as if' face at him. He didn't need to doubt, so laughing, he grabbed her around the bottom and lifted her against him, making her giggle. He set her back on her feet with a kiss to the tip of her nose, and she snuggled into his chest,

"I just wish we could have contact while you're away," she sighed.

"Well, we will for the first little while." He tried to sound upbeat, knowing full well communications from threshold space were unreliable at best and non-existent as the norm.

She locked her arms around his neck, and her eyes found his.

"We'll be fine," she said, reassuring herself, as much as him.

Leaving the Top of the World lodge brought the moment of their parting that bit closer, and Alice would have had the shuttle fly them anywhere but home. After Noah entered the coordinates, he switched controls to autopilot, then pulled her close.

"I have something to tell you. Something I did," he said quietly, making sure he was in a position where he couldn't make eye contact with her, not till after he'd confessed.

"What did you do?"

"I'm responsible for Patrick going to the Accessor."

"You? How?" Alice was happily tucked under his arm, enjoying his nearness, not expecting any revelations, so his next words came as a surprise.

"He wouldn't let Crewman Oakes loose on the Gravidarum. I knew he would follow him, so I signed the order for Crewman Oakes's temporary transfer. It was a concession on my part. He wasn't scheduled to go."

"Why would you do that?" Alice wriggled out of his embrace and sat up, looking him squarely in the eye. He reached for her hand, she let him lace his fingers through hers, but she was waiting for the rest of the story. He couldn't delay it.

"At the time, I believed I could justify what I was doing. Principal Hardy had second thoughts about his choice of Patrick as your escort on the ship and asked me to keep my eye on proceedings after you returned to Earth."

"Patrick is perfectly lovely…" then she thought about his relentlessness, "most of the time."

"I have no criticism of Patrick, but at the Cotillion Ball, I saw he'd developed an attachment to you."

"Do you doubt his sincerity?"

"No, he's always sincere."

"Always?" Alice recalled Principal Katya's comment about Patrick leaving a trail of broken hearts across the galaxy.

Noah knew, to give her the full story, he mustn't leave out essential details. "Yes, Alice, I'm afraid so, and until now, I've never taken an interest in what he does or with whom, and there are usually a couple at one time. I've seen him hurt countless women in the past, and at that point, I understood Principal Hardy's concerns. I told myself I was acting in your best interests. The truth is, I acted out of selfishness."

"You thought to separate us?"

"Yes."

"It didn't work very well, Noah," Alice shook her head, hardly able to believe what she was hearing. It seemed so juvenile. "He still visited, and he linked through on the registry."

"I know that. Patrick was fascinated when Hardy briefed us before you came to the Significator. You were part of historical science for so long, the subject of so much speculation and so many theories; I thought—possibly I didn't think," he admitted, "to Patrick, you would be what you were to everyone else. A scientific wonder. I was wrong."

"I don't have illusions about Patrick, Noah. I was flattered by the attention at first, but then I'm hardly a woman of the world, and he is incredibly handsome and charming."

Noah nodded; that was one way of describing his first officer.

"In the auditorium on the Significator, I felt…truthfully? I don't know," he smiled and lifted her hand, gently biting her finger.

She grinned, she'd forgive him for being underhanded, but not yet. She'd get the rest of the confession first.

"I only remember running away from you. I panicked."

"I didn't mean to frighten you. I can be overbearing, habit, I'm afraid. When I saw you with Patrick at the Cotillion Ball, in that amazing dress, I knew my life would never be the same."

"I've told you, I don't return Patrick's feelings, and now, you are telling me you got rid of competition, who wasn't competition?"

"You told me you thought of Patrick as a 'protector'".

Alice gave him a quizzical look.

"At the ball, you had one of your crossovers…" but that same look stopped him.

"We had a conversation; you were…different, then

you stumbled and didn't know how you came to be out on the terrace."

Alice remembered it, and she remembered wondering at the time what had passed between them.

"I didn't think it through, Alice. I thought to protect you from Patrick as Hardy suggested. Patrick likes the company of women; he seldom sleeps alone."

"Even while he professes his love for me?"

"He's never confided in me about his feelings, but yes, since he met you."

"I'm not sure you should be telling me about Patrick's private life. It's gossip; besides, is it your business as his principal?"

"I'm trying to explain why I did what I did, and I can't without giving up what I know. Patrick is dedicated to his role on the ship, and his personal choices have never interfered with his duties. Believe me, he's a first-rate officer. But now, I will admit my feelings after seeing you in the auditorium, and our conversation on the terrace influenced my decision to sign Crewman Oakes's orders more than anything Principal Hardy said. I thought you should know."

Alice heard the dejection in his voice and saw the guilt on his face. Like a naughty child. A very large, prominent, old-enough-to-know-better naughty child. And he was far too special for her to be angry with.

"But you took me to the A'khet and Peru because Principal Katya told you to, isn't that right?"

"Tibet, yes, but Machu Picchu—I took some license with that one, I didn't tell her outright, but she guessed," again, the guilty look.

"We may have got to this point anyway, Noah," Alice scolded gently, "without the white lies and you tricking poor Patrick into leaving."

"I know I've behaved badly, but he can be very persuasive."

"Well, he didn't persuade me. Noah, is this the secret you want to keep? Your parents almost certainly guessed about us, and probably Principal Katya as well. You'll have to tell Patrick what you did, or he'll put two and two together."

"I told my father. He's agreed not to tell Principal Katya that we visited them."

"Why?"

"I believe…" Noah wasn't even sure this would happen,; it was just a hunch "If Patrick learns we've been seeing each other, it might make our position as officers, on a two-year mission, untenable. I believe he would resign to stay close to you."

Alice thought back to the day Patrick visited her at the farm when she'd become angry at the idea of him giving up the Significator for her.

"He's considered that already. I told him in no uncertain terms what my views were."

"I guessed it, I don't even know how, but I guessed it," Noah said.

"So, you propose keeping our relationship a secret? From everyone, Noah?"

His expression told her that was exactly what he proposed.

"You've woven a rather tangled web, haven't you? It's

hard to live with a lie, and it might be worse if he finds out from someone else. I've told Patrick I don't love him," she made particular emphasis on the 'don't', "and that he's wasting his time. What I do and with whom isn't Patrick's concern. I appreciate his friendship, I like and admire him, but I've been honest with him," Alice shook her head, "and he's a grown man. Neither of us can make ourselves responsible for how he reacts."

"Patrick and I have two years together on the Significator," Noah said. "I was hoping to avoid any difficulties in our working relationship. Like I said, when I started all this with Oakes's assignment, I didn't consider where it would lead."

Noah knew his reasoning sounded lame and pathetic, but it was done, telling Patrick now might have no effect on the upcoming mission in a threshold or a disastrous one. Patrick was popular on the Significator, but his expertise was also needed elsewhere in the military. He could be assigned another ship with the snap of his fingers. That would mean, for the two years Ryan was away, Patrick would be close to Alice. The idea unsettled him.

"So, Principal Ryan," Alice did at least smile, which made him feel better, "you are telling me, two senior members of the military, in command of a principality ship, cannot show enough professionalism to overcome any personal difficulties? You're better than that, Noah. Patrick's not going to resign, and if he is the philanderer you say, he may just shrug and wish us good luck."

Noah shook his head. "You're wrong about him, Alice. I've known him for years, and I can tell you, he's not too keen on us spending time together. Has he told you he loves you?"

"Well," Alice saw no point in hedging, "yes, he has."

"Patrick doesn't need the Significator as much as it needs him, Alice. Median and proximal space assignments would keep him occupied if he chose to leave, and he would no doubt continue to pursue you." Noah realised after meeting Alice, his priorities had changed. However, he was still the commander assigned to the most important mission ever undertaken, and he'd made some self-serving decisions of late, "I need Patrick on the Significator," he admitted. "There is no-one with his expertise. He can't be substituted, and if he left, I don't care to think what the effect on crew morale would be."

Alice squeezed his hand, "I disagree with how you handled this, but you may have a point. I probably won't see him now before you leave, so I won't say anything to anyone; that way, there's no danger of him finding out."

Alice couldn't shake the sense of a burden descending over her, but she wouldn't let on. She was perhaps just oversensitive, finding this out hours before Noah left. Besides, a lot can happen in two years; Patrick may meet someone else. It wasn't beyond the bounds of possibility that even Noah might change his mind.

The cliff and the Aunties house came into view. They could see Jane, Mary and the dogs walking across the grass to greet them. He kissed Alice quickly, hating that he'd been too much of a coward to confess until now. Casting a cloud over their last few hours hadn't been his intention, but she needed to know.

"They won't mind if I stay for a while, will they?"

"They won't mind at all."

Alice would have plucked the moon from the sky if it delayed him leaving.

Pecky, the welcoming committee's first wave, flew onto Alice's shoulder with a squawk, rubbing his beak on her cheek in admonishment for leaving him and with love for returning. Mary and Jane expressed their delight Noah could stay for a while, with Jane happy for any opportunity to entertain with tea and cakes.

They didn't know Alice hadn't been at the Tabernacle all this time. Fortunately, it seemed not to be a social habit, keeping in constant contact as people did with mobile phones. Alice didn't mention the Top of the World and hoped the subject wouldn't come up, but thankfully, no mention was made, and after a while, Jane and Mary stopped asking questions about Alice's visit to the Tabernacle.

"It's so kind of you, Principal Ryan, to escort Alice home," Mary said, intrigued as to why neither Alice nor Principal Ryan appeared to have much to say other than they'd taken a trip to Stonehenge and seen crop circles. They had no idea both places were close to his home.

"It's no trouble, Dr Greer. We like to discuss history."

"Jorrocks has missed you, Alice. We heard him whinnying when the shuttle landed, so you may need to go and say hello to him."

"Of course, come with me, Principal Ryan?"

He smiled at the aunts and followed Alice out the door. Jane watched them leave. "Principal Ryan? That was purely for our benefit," she said.

Mary nodded and couldn't help her smile. She liked Principal Ryan, but they were hiding something, those two.

Jorrocks was pleased to see her. She stroked him and kissed his soft grey neck. Pecky allowed Alice to show affection to the animals, provided she also accepted he was to be her number one. Noah sat on the hay bale and pulled Alice down beside him. She wriggled around and leaned her back against him, pulling his arms over her shoulders. He placed his hand inside her blouse and caressed her shoulder, contented in one another's company. They stayed there, no need for words, while Jorrocks pulled at the hay around them. Pecky moved onto Noah's arm and, lulled by the peace, fell asleep.

Noah was so still, and Alice thought he might be dozing. Through the stable door, she saw clouds drifting across the blue sky and listened to the lazy sound of insects, each playing their part in these special, timeless and tender moments. Alice Watkins, whoever she was, probably never experienced this. She felt sorry for her, what a terrible life, she was glad it was only an echo from an old story. She moved her head a little and kissed Noah's arm, feeling his face against her hair.

"I love you, Alice," he said, ever so softly.

"I love you too, Noah," she sighed and closed her eyes.

They stayed there until the afternoon sunshine faded and early evening shadows hung from the stable walls

Noah took his leave. He was already hours overdue to

the Tabernacle, so he bid Jane and Mary goodbye at the house, and Alice walked to the shuttle with him. As soon as they were out of sight of the aunties, they wrapped their arms tightly around each other, and Alice wished they could just fuse, then she could go everywhere with him and never again endure a parting such as this.

"I'll try to contact you before I leave," Noah felt the same pain. "It's impossible to gauge Cloisters, and I don't want to promise to call and then not deliver. If I don't, we'll have to wait till I get back to the ship. Perhaps you should tell Mary and Jane we were together these last few days."

"If the need arises, I will, but for now, don't worry. I'll look forward to hearing from you when you can; promise me you'll be safe, pack a toothbrush and stay away from aliens with sticks!"

At that, he did smile. Alice was glad her last image of him would not be sad.

After holding each other in an embrace that felt as if it needed to last them an eternity, he let her go. She watched until the shuttle lights disappeared. As the tears fell, she walked away from the house, her path taking her across the cliff top, needing time to compose herself before facing the aunties.

CHAPTER TWENTY-NINE _

Jane and Mary were together in the kitchen when Alice returned to the house. The registry blinked a message with a military signature. It was Patrick to say he would visit the next afternoon unless he heard from her that he shouldn't.

Mary saw Alice reading the message. "He called this afternoon, Alice. We said we thought you might return today and agreed it would be fine for him to visit, but we would have to make sure it was okay with you too. He left a message anyway. Is it okay?"

Alice forced a smile, "I suppose so. I would like to spend time with you both now, but he is another friend who's going away, so, yes, I guess it's fine."

Mary felt a sudden urge to hold Alice and place her arms around her to let her know that she would always be there for her whatever sadness she may endure. Alice appreciated Mary's love and concern but had already decided that she would respect Noah's wish for secrecy no matter how difficult it might be.

Noah barely arrived back at the Tabernacle when he linked through to Alice.

"Patrick tells me he's seeing you tomorrow?"

"I didn't expect to hear from you so quickly," Alice could barely disguise her delight. Fortunately, the aunties had gone out to the storeroom.

"Principal Katya is late arriving, she went to the city, so I had a few minutes."

"Patrick's coming for afternoon tea. Auntie Jane can't believe her luck in being able to bake two days in a row."

"If you're sure. I can make up some excuse to stop him."

"I think you've done enough of that already."

He conceded the point. "I miss you."

"I miss you too, Noah."

"Have your aunts guessed, do you think?"

"They haven't said; I don't know. They just want me to have friends and be happy."

"They love you, Alice. We'll speak soon."

To say goodbye twice in one day pushed Alice to the limit. She closed her bedroom door, threw herself down on her bed and wept.

It was dark when Alice woke. She waved her hand at the responder—four am, she'd cried herself to sleep, and her clothes were just a crumpled mess. She rubbed her eyes; she was so tired, she and Noah, well, they'd slept little these last couple of days, so he was probably exhausted as well.

Alice got out of bed and wandered out to the kitchen to draw a cup of coffee from the dispenser. Pecky, sleeping on the rim of her hat, opened one eye at her unexpected presence, then decided it might still be a little early and shut it again.

Alice sat out on the verandah; the night lights emitted a soft glow over the steps, and moonlight lit up the lawn beyond. The coolness of the early morning settled around her, and she curled her hands around the coffee mug, enjoying its warmth and holding it close. Weary, she tilted her head back against the chair.

"Her eyes are open. She's awake!" A man's voice startled her, causing Alice to sit up in alarm, nothing stirred, and the only other sound besides the sudden, rapid beating of her heart was the whispering of the breeze through the gum trees.

"I'm imagining things," she muttered, leaning back and allowing her mind to drift off to nowhere.

Figures in masks and green robes surrounded her. Lying on her side, she felt a hard vibration against her head, and again she heard the man's voice, urgent, almost angry.

"What's happening? Her eyes are open. She's regaining consciousness!"

"According to my readings," a woman's voice now, "she's sleeping like a baby."

Through the throng of masked faces and noise, the white-haired youth she'd seen so often before stretched his arms towards her.

Alice woke, choking for air. Above her, the first streaks of dawn busily pushed away the remnants of night. She heard the horses moving in the stable and the cock crowing. She craned her neck to see the clock in the house, six-fifteen am. She'd been asleep for two hours, her hands still wrapped around her coffee cup. Strange, it was still piping hot.

Patrick arrived in the mid-afternoon. He brought flowers for Alice and flowers for the aunties too, but they weren't there.

"Just us, Patrick, I'm afraid."

He hugged her quickly before she could protest.

"I love just us. Where is everyone?"

"Belinda, our neighbour, is very elderly and frail. She's a hundred and four years old. She took a fall, and Mary and Jane have gone over to help. They'll be back later. Auntie Jane is very disappointed at not being here to make you tea and fuss over you."

Alice sat opposite Patrick, creating a tacit distance between them. Faced with lemon meringue pie, he seemed not to notice, but after a while, moved closer, thankfully making no move to touch or embrace her again.

"Are you looking forward to going back into space?" she asked, keeping her tone very conversational and appreciating Pecky giving Patrick the evil eye whenever he leaned too close.

"I've enjoyed the Accessor refit. I'm not as keen on long assignments as Ryan. He's champing at the bit to get back out. I would have liked more time to convince you of my feelings."

She smiled and groaned a silent, *Oh, dear.* "What's Statesman Hennessey's replacement like?"

"Junnot? Brilliant. Ryan requested her because she's a communications expert, not just linguistics either. She's made modifications to our current communications array that shows real potential. She was the first officer on the

307

Inquisitor for years, but it's a small ship, so this is a promotion. She's new to the Significator."

"How old is she?"

"Fifty-ish, from memory, she loves mountaineering and diving and all sorts of extreme sports. She's quite the risk-taker, and with her track record on the principality ships, she should have been a principal by now, but she always refused advancement."

"Wasn't Principal Ryan young when he became principal?"

"Yes, but in years only. He was born old. With Ryan, everything is by the book. He's incapable of surprising me."

Oh, dear, Alice thought again. "He speaks well of you, Patrick."

"He does? When?"

"When we went to Tibet. We talked about you mainly."

"Did you?" Patrick seemed pleased. "Well, I've known him for a long time. I'm probably the most exciting thing that ever happened to him." He grinned. "I'm only joking, but, well, you've spent time with him; he doesn't exactly ooze charm."

"Like you, you mean?"

"Of course, like me."

"He said you made go-carts. Great ones."

"My goodness, yes, I did. I'd forgotten, how odd he remembered."

"Perhaps those times meant something to him."

"He was a good friend, that's for sure. I led a pretty isolated life at the Tabernacle. My mother wouldn't let me play with engines for quite a while after my father's accident, so I made carts with wheels, like the ones in history. They flew like the wind down that hill from the house," he gave a little laugh. "Ryan and his sisters used to go to the Tabernacle for two weeks at each recess to visit their aunt. They spent time with me even though they were all a few years older."

"Didn't you go to school?"

"Oh yes, locally, but Ryan, and Zoe and Mel, his sisters, did their aptitudes at the same time. Once they all started their space year, they didn't visit so often, I did get a bit lonely."

The conversation convinced Alice, Noah was right. They shouldn't tell Patrick; listening to him now, Alice believed when they did, their friendship could conceivably end.

"Ryan asked for me when he was made Principal," Patrick said. "I was dividing my time between being the second officer on the Inquisitor and space dock. I'd only just received Knowledge, I was happily working on the scaffolding and containment fields and the Gravidarums, just testing and refining. I've never regretted accepting the Significator, but the missions are longer than I would like."

"Did the Accessor exceed your expectations?"

"She's a great ship. I did my space year on her, and now, she's faster and more capable. The size of the ship and the resources it can hold limits what they can do. The Accessor can't explore planets further out; it can only chart systems, send probes, check weather patterns and the like. The Significator can do all those things and more and go far beyond where the Accessor and the Inquisitor can go, both those ships only travel to the far edge of median space. They operate there, perhaps for two months and then return to Saturn or Septimus for crew, maintenance, supplies, etc. Since the refit, the Accessor can go not only to the far rim of median space but also venture into threshold. And she can stay out longer. It will effectively widen median space. Ryan was wise not to let it delay any further."

"Will the Tabernacle build new ships? I can't imagine a single ship is capable of gathering much information on its own," Alice kept the questions coming, keeping the conversation in neutral territory.

"There is one under construction," Patrick was always happy to talk engines, "the Magellan. She'll be finished by the time we return. She's the same size as the Significator but has four Substance chambers. Theoretically, she could stay out for years. Perfect for Ryan, but I expect her maiden voyage will only be two. I'll be overseeing the Gravidarum and engineering systems when I get back. I'm reassigned from the Significator as Chief Engineer and First Officer until she's up and running."

"Will the Magellan be as fast?"

Patrick seemed unaware Alice was more interested in keeping him at arms-length than she was in the construction of starships.

"Yes, but you're right; two ships will double what we can accomplish, the speed capabilities of the deep space vessels aren't an issue. Do you remember those people at the assembly on the Significator, studying the effects of space travel?"

She remembered. It seemed like a hundred years ago.

"They believe a mission that exceeds two years is harmful to mental health. In the submissions to the Tabernacle, their findings were taken under advisement and discussed in Cloisters—today as a matter-of-fact, and so it seems, two years will be our maximum until we prove there are no ill-effects. I don't know where they got their information. I think it's nonsense personally, so does Ryan, but he never wants to come back, anyway."

Alice felt a knot forming in her stomach and resolved then and there, she would never try to keep Noah from doing what he loved most.

"They used to think," she forced a brightness she didn't feel into her voice, "in the early days of trains, speeds above thirty miles an hour would make a person's face implode," Alice remembered reading that piece of trivia somewhere.

"Is that a fact?"

They were interrupted by Jane and Mary returning. Alice was pleased she kept the conversation steered away from Patrick's romantic inclinations.

He jumped to his feet, all charm. "Auntie Jane. Auntie Mary."

They smiled graciously at his familiarity and breach of protocol, though he did remember to bow. On their walk home, the aunties had discussed Alice's relationships and decided they would be formal with Patrick, not sure if her interests lay with the handsome statesman or the somewhat enigmatic Principal Ryan.

"Statesman Patrick, "Jane smiled, "it's very nice to see

you again. I'm sure Alice has kept you entertained," She did rather carry a few hopes Alice might end up with him.

He acknowledged her with a smile that assured her, Alice had indeed kept him entertained.

"How is Belinda?" Alice enquired.

"Not good. They've taken her to the City Infirmary. Thomas is with her."

"That's terrible. Will she be alright?"

"I doubt it," Jane shook her head sadly. "I think it may be the beginning of the end."

Jane and Mary had known Thomas and Belinda for many years. Alice met them a few times, both sweet and funny and devoted to one another. A mixed-race couple, Alice felt sad they had no children. Losing Belinda would mean a lonely existence for Thomas.

Patrick, seeing the aunties might be upset, courteously made his excuses.

"Alice, I must go. I have the observers coming on board briefly this evening, and they are my responsibility. We leave in thirty-six hours. Ryan is in Cloisters for most of that time, so it's all left to me. Statesman Junnot is heading to the Tabernacle, so I am both command and welcoming committee."

This time, he took Alice's hand to ensure she accompanied him to the shuttle. She didn't want to make a fuss in front of Mary and Jane, but she slipped her hand out of his once they were away from the house. He grinned down at her.

"Still resisting? It's inevitable, Alice. Why fight it? You'll miss me during these two years. Wait and see."

Now she knew the stories about him, Alice wondered just how much he would miss her on the mission, with all those lovely young crew members on board.

"I *will* miss you, Patrick," she told him truthfully, "but not in the way you hope. Anyway, you might meet a nice alien girl!"

"I doubt it. No woman has ever spurned me the way you do."

"That's an old-fashioned term, Patrick. Now stay safe."

"I will. I can stay in contact until we get to threshold. With some luck, we'll get good communications going on this trip now we have Junnot."

He climbed into the automatrans and looked down at her; it was incomprehensible to him he wouldn't see her for two years. Her face, upturned towards him, smiling, radiant in the late afternoon sun, so beautiful, he desperately wanted to hold her, convince her of his feelings, but he knew he could only steal kisses from her and catch her unaware with an embrace, otherwise, she kept herself from him.

"Alice, I'll miss you. I mean what I say, I love you."

"Just stay safe."

She waved to him as he closed the door, he smiled brightly, but when she was out of sight, he shook his head.

"Damn!" he hissed as he thumped his fist on the arm of the seat. "Damn!"

Alice walked along the cliff top with the dogs bounding along beside her for company. She waited until the dying sun cast orange ripples across the sea, then shivering against the coolness of the evening, she walked back to the house.

Alice was up and about early next morning, seeing to the horses and helping Jane and Mary. Another restless night robbed her of her energy. Still, moping would not help her mood, the memory of the nightmare stayed with her, so when she woke in the small hours of the night, she didn't venture out to the verandah,and she'd dismissed the still-hot coffee incident as a coincidence.

"We're a little worried you might be sad with your friends leaving," Mary said when they met up at the stable where Alice was keeping herself busy.

"I am sad, Mary, but I can't change the way things are. Perhaps I should have made friends with people who don't live in space."

"Well, that's very philosophical. But things seldom work out as we expect, besides, we love having you to ourselves, and you'll see Amelia."

A tearful Jane appeared at the stable door. "Thomas is home. Belinda died. He's asking for us."

"Poor Thomas, let him know we're on our way," Mary turned to Alice, "will you be alright?"

"Of course, shall I come?"

"No, we've been friends with him for many years. He might want to be private. Is that okay?"

"Of course," Alice understood completely.

"I'm not sure how long we'll be. He has a brother in the Loyalties. I expect he'll come."

Later in the morning, Alice was sitting alone out on the verandah when she heard the registry in her room beep an incoming call, a general link from the Tabernacle. Alice thought it might be Principal Katya, but it was late in the evening at the Tabernacle, and Principal Katya only ever called her on the aunties' registry. She accepted the link. Noah's face appeared. He was in uniform, leaning close to the console and whispering urgently.

"Alice, I've despatched a high altitude automatrans. It'll be there in a few minutes. Can you get away?"

"Yes. Jane and Mary aren't here."

"I'll be through here in about thirty minutes. Alice, I must see you just once more before I leave, but we'll only have a few hours," he said, glancing away. "I have to go. I'll meet you when you arrive."

Alice's heart beat fast with excitement. Calming herself, she left a message on the registry to let the aunties know she'd popped out for a few hours. Then she quickly showered and changed into slacks and a shirt, forgetting her panties in her hurry, and dashed out to the front of the house in time to see the automatrans descending.

Mary and Jane walked across the field that divided their property from Thomas's house. His family had arrived, and Mary and Jane felt it best to leave them to grieve in private. They watched from a distance as Alice ran from the house and jumped into the automatrans. It rose vertically at speed.

"She's in a hurry," Mary said.

"That's a military automatrans," Jane stopped and shielded her eyes from the sun. "Didn't Statesman Patrick return to the ship? I wonder who she's going to see?"

Mary nodded. "He did. But if we were playing that

wagering game Alice showed us, my money would be on Principal Ryan."

CHAPTER THIRTY _

Cloisters, with its deliberating about this and cogitating about that, was usually a drawn-out affair. Late in the evening, a worn-out Principal Katya headed off to the great hall, her thoughts dwelling on the idea she might be getting too old for all this. These last few days discussions involved the Significator, and she questioned the wisdom of spending often up to eighteen hours cloistered with plans and protocols. Noah looked tired, not an ideal start to the mission. Cloisters business made her tired too. In fact, it made the entire council tired, and she didn't like important decisions to be made by people with tiredness-fogged brains.

She walked through the great hall to Statesman Mellor's favourite seat near the library, where he liked to sit in quiet contemplation and muted light at the end of the evening, usually in the company of a bottle of single malt. He had the right idea. She'd said goodbye to her nephew before he retired to his suite in the courtyard. He would leave for the ship before daylight.

Statesman Mellor's usual spot near the library was empty.

"Principal Katya!"

He called to her from much further down the hall, a bottle of whisky in hand and already pouring her a glass. The Tabernacle staff believed Statesman Mellor sat in the Great Hall for solitude, but seldom did he drink alone. Someone always strayed in.

"Not your usual spot, Statesman?"

"I've relocated," he laughed. "As I age, Principal Katya, I confess I find even these late summer evenings a little cool. It's less chilly here, and the view of the lake is restful at night."

"I agree, Mellor, my bones feel a chill these evenings also. Summer will be over soon enough, and we will be into fall. The next summit and Cotillion is not even six weeks away." She took the glass from him and sat down with a sigh of relaxation. Lifting her legs onto one of the low stools, she allowed her sandals to slip from her feet and wiggled her toes.

"A long day, Principal Katya," Statesman Mellor sympathised. "I anticipate this expedition into threshold will be the most successful so far. Evesham is disappointed the last one ended with a quarantined sector."

"I personally do not see how we manage to debate so much about something of which we know so little, Mellor. Perhaps the debate needs to start after the Significator returns, and we have a clearer picture of what it is we deliberate on."

"We have to debate, Principal Katya. There are guidelines, conventions."

"You sound like my nephew," she flicked him a

weary glance. "Just let them go, I say, chart the space, explore, contact, anything they need to do with no restrictions. This convention, that convention, it gives me a headache. Let Principal Ryan decide, let his statesmen decide, and between them, they will do what is necessary; they are not fools. We are here on our bottoms and in no place to direct and insist."

"You can veto, Principal Katya."

She laughed. "If you think that, Mellor, you are not ready to take over my job."

Statesman Mellor grinned into his whisky; he suspected he would be very old before her job became available, thank goodness.

"But this time," he pointed out, "they are travelling without any help from the A'khet."

"The information from A'khet before was of no assistance if we go by the accounts of the last contact. This area of threshold space is unknown even to them. The A'khet's abilities set them apart, but humankind also has many attributes,, and the Significators crew will employ those attributes if they encounter life forms. I do not believe as a species, we will be found wanting."

He agreed but didn't answer. They were both exhausted from such debates and wanted no more, preferring to sit in companionable silence, musing privately on the day's events, gazing at the nighttime view across the lawns, and watching, in quiet and individual contemplation, as a military automatrans descend silently onto the grass.

This time of night, visitors to the Tabernacle were rare, even rarer arriving in a principality ship vehicle. The lights from the Great Hall cast a dim light across the garden, but Principal Katya recognised her nephew as he ran across the lawn. Alice climbed down from the transport and ran towards him, jumping into his arms. He caught her and lifted her, her legs curling around him, her arms around his neck and his hands under her buttocks. Noah swung her around before setting her down, and the two walked off together, towards the courtyard, arms about each other, secure in the belief that the use of a quiet ship and the lateness of the hour guaranteed their privacy. They'd reckoned without Statesman Mellor's decision to change his long-held position in the great hall from where previously, he would not have had a view of the garden.

Neither Principal nor Statesman spoke as the scene unfolded. Principal Katya sensed Statesman's Mellor's disbelief as he slowly turned his head towards her.

"Don't say anything. Ever," she said.

Alice lay under Noah's arm, close to his heart, their legs intertwined and her arm across his chest, watching the moon on its slow voyage past the window. She sighed. They'd been granted these few precious last hours. Bitterly sweet and bitterly sad, but she wouldn't have missed them for the world.

"Are you cold?" he asked suddenly, reaching for the sheet.

"No, you are a cuddly warm bear," she said, wriggling in closer, giggling.

"I don't suppose anyone on the ship would think that about me."

"They don't know you. What's it like? Being the principal of a starship?"

He didn't answer right away. He'd never considered it, just took it as another opportunity to ensure he remained in space.

"It can be very solitary," he said after a moment, placing one arm behind his head and gently stroking her shoulder with his other hand. "I don't mind, though. Once we get into deep space, I spend most of my time on the bridge or in celestial mapping. With this mission, we have no information as to what we might find. We'll enter threshold space at the same point we left it on our last mission and travel the edge of the quarantined sector. The planets on that grid are charted, but after we move from the grid, we're on our own."

"Are you afraid?"

"Afraid?" he looked down at her. "Afraid of what?"

"Of what or who you might meet?" she went back to resting on his chest. "You might meet someone hostile, I mean really hostile." She'd thought about the possibility a great deal.

"I'm not afraid, Alice, but I do think it's wise to proceed with caution, and I won't take chances. The ship has incredible speed and manoeuvrability, and it has a defence capability."

"Weapons?" It hadn't occurred to her.

"Not weapons of aggression. If we got fired on, and it would have to be a substantial attack, the hull has an armour generator that sets up a harmonic rate equal to the blast. If the attack is repeated, it deflects. Of course, we don't know what weapons are out there, possibly far superior to our defence shield, and though we doubt it, a hostile species might have a way of disabling Substance, so all systems are affected. It's all assumption. We hope anyone we meet will have good intentions. Humans have been exploring since time immemorial and lived to tell the tale."

"Do you get on with the crew?"

"You are full of questions, aren't you? I have little to do with the crew apart from the bridge officers and those I need to work with directly. I make it a point to meet with team leaders, and I have a knack for putting names to faces. I familiarise myself with the crew manifest, so even if I never speak directly to a crew member, I know who they are, but it's really Patrick who's the true leader. Everyone gravitates toward him. Any problems, any issues, he's their first choice, and he always finds a resolution. The crew respect and admire him."

"Don't compare yourself to Patrick. Everyone has something special, some spark that sets them apart from other people."

She twisted up into a kneeling position, and his eyes wandered over her body. He gently stroked the front of her thigh. She looked pale and golden in the moonlight and his breath caught in his throat. She asked if he was afraid. Yes, he was—afraid of being without her.

She stroked his chest and waited for him to respond to her statement.

"I didn't mean to compare," he understood what she meant. "I'm a specialist in my field, and Patrick, a specialist in his. I take my role seriously and expect the same dedication of the crew. My standards are high, and that makes me seem unapproachable."

"I used to think that," she could smile about it now, even though she'd just called him a teddy bear.

"I assume you didn't tell Patrick about us when he came to visit?" he said.

"No. He talked a lot about the mission; he seems to be very positive. I expect by the time the two years are over, he will have forgotten all about me. Either way, I'm not going to be one of his floozies. He believes I'll change my mind."

"A floozie! Alice, what on earth is a floozie?"

"Never mind, but I won't be one. Patrick is dear to me, but as friends only."

"I wasn't too worried. I knew your aunts would be there."

"They weren't there, Noah. A neighbour had a crisis, so I was alone with him, but it's fine, he is just a friend, and he only stayed a few hours." She knew he knew but wanted to reassure him, anyway. There could be no doubts between them.

"I'm glad to hear it."

"Anyway," she said, her voice becoming lower, seductive, "someone who is just a friend wouldn't do this…" she bent forward and kissed his mouth, holding his hands away from her body.

"or this…" she continued with a saucy grin, kissing his chest,

"or this…" her mouth trailed teasing kisses as she slid down his body, her hair stroking his flesh. She looked up under her eyelashes as he groaned and covered his eyes with his arm.

"Oh, Alice, I'm so glad we aren't just friends!"

Just before dawn, in the courtyard, the two stood wrapped one final time in each other's arms.

"I love you so much, Alice," he said, trying to put two years of breathing in her perfume, feeling the warmth and softness of her skin into this one last embrace. "I hate to leave you."

"I hate it too, Noah, but…" she looked up at him, her lip trembling, willing the tears not to fall, but despite her best efforts, one or two escaped and dribbled down her cheek. "We had these few unexpected hours together, and I know you have an important job to do. I love you, Noah, I really do, and I'll be here when you get back, I promise."

Reluctantly, he let her go. "I've programmed a Tabernacle shuttle to take you home. I have to leave, Patrick's taken the Significator out, and it's right above us."

Alice looked up.

"You can't see it."

She shook her head.

"No, it already seems a long way away."

He kissed her again and lifted her into the shuttle. As it rose, she watched him stride towards the high altitude automatrans she arrived in last night. When he was out of sight, she looked ahead through the forward viewport, at the dawn, at what remained of the night sky and already, she missed him desperately.

CHAPTER THIRTY-ONE _

Principal Ryan's command chair on the Significator's bridge didn't feel like it fitted now. The contours felt strange, unfamiliar and unwelcome. Only a few hours had passed since he left Alice and the weight of separation lay heavily on him. He thought about their whispered words of love that morning and how she clung to him, determined not to cry. He was confident she knew how much he loved her and that he would be counting the months and hours until he held her again.

The institution of reliable communications would be a priority on this mission; without them, it would be difficult to contact Alice privately. He wanted to hear her voice rather than rely on the military channels usually employed at the entry into threshold, where so often, voice communication converted to text, followed by an inevitable delay. Ryan often thought it a pity the telepathic A'khet didn't need a communications array. He would have rather liked some Knowledge about decent comm. systems. Communication from within Threshold was the Achilles heel of deep space travel.

He opened the crew manifest on the registry. Besides Junnot, most of the crew were returning engineers and crewman. He skipped the Tyros as he had nothing to do with them; they would be Junnot's responsibility. The manifest appeared to be in order, but one name stopped him as he flicked through, Dr Rosa Quintock. He knew that name. Rosa Quintock? He opened her profile. Yes, her face was unmistakable. Dark hair, large eyes, from the Americas Province, very beautiful. He remembered when she came on board the Inquisitor, most of the male crew went gaga. She was also very provocative. He thought of Alice's word—floozie—and understood its meaning. He smiled. Yes, Quintock might be called that. She once bailed him up in an elevator on the Inquisitor. She liked rank, but he'd been cool towards her, and she didn't find that appealing. In his opinion, where physical charms were concerned, she was a female version of Patrick, and now, she was here on the Significator, on the medical team. He opened the orders:

'Dr Rosa Quintock, assigned 63rd day/3rd quarter/2513 - Principality ship Significator, transfer—Accessor.

Accessor? He checked the transfer entry, signed by Principal Anil Ahmed on request from Statesman Carmichael Patrick. Patrick? What was he playing at?

It was common enough to request transfers if the requesting officer considers a specialist suited to a mission and if the commanding officer is agreeable, but this was for the medical team. She wasn't a mission specialist.

Principal Ahmed's call signature flicked up at him. The Accessor would be accompanying them to threshold space.

"Ryan, we're just about ready to get underway. You'll see that three of my crew have transferred under the request of Statesman Patrick. I've approved it. Have you seen the orders?"

"Yes, Ahmed, they're fine. Why have you released Dr Quintock? She isn't a specialist."

"Patrick requested her and the two design engineers who will be working on your communications array. You need them more than I do, and after you let me have Oakes, I thought I would return the favour. I realise Dr Quintock isn't a statesman, but she is keen to work in frontier medicine. She is also an outstanding pilot, quite matches you and Patrick. I think she'll complement your crew. I believe she's wasted here, and Patrick was keen to give her a chance. You can reject her if you wish."

"Crew assignments are Patrick's area. I trust his judgement. All decks have reported in. Civilians are back on dock. We're ready."

Ryan watched the Earth drawing away. Statesman Patrick and Statesman Junnot joined him on the bridge, the three standing silently as the ship turned to starboard and the expanse of space slowly filled the viewports. Before meeting Alice, Principal Ryan considered the world held little to interest him, little to explore or satisfy and until now, his world, his life of exploration held everything. In the seconds before the ship turned and the blue Earth drifted from view, he understood fully what his heart had told him these last few days, there was only one place in the universe he wanted to be, and that was with Alice. But he had a responsibility to this ship and this crew, and for now, he had to choose the galaxy over her. He allowed himself only a moment to reflect on the recent weeks, then taking a deep breath, he tuned out of his private thoughts and tuned back into his role as Principal of the Significator.

Alice arrived back home to find the aunties enjoying a glass of wine out on the verandah. They didn't ask where she had been, and after enquiring after Thomas, smiled in understanding when she said she might miss dinner and go straight to bed. After discussion, they had a fair idea where she'd spent the last few hours.

The next morning, breakfast passed without a mention of the evening before, and Alice spent the rest of the day with the aunties, looking after animals, fishing, cooking, and talking, but not once did they question her. She didn't know they'd seen the automatrans, and they didn't tell her. They would wait until she came to them with whatever she wanted to share.

With Principality 19's winter almost behind them and Spring just around the corner, Alice made sure she filled her days. She had no real need or desire to leave the homestead, save to go to the beach with Mary and Jane. She spent long hours at the registry, determined to learn as much as possible about her new world over the next two years, although she often found herself drifting into the history and architectural areas.

There were a few visits to Dr Grossmith's home, where she met his brother. Principal Katya and Statesman Mellor came to the homestead once, allowing Alice to show off her garden. Principal Katya reminded Alice about the bi-annual ball at the Tabernacle, assuming she would be attending? Alice agreed, but only from duty and love for Principal Katya, for herself, she couldn't garner any enthusiasm at the prospect.

And almost every day, she heard from Noah. She longed for those times when she heard his voice and saw his face. The day-night cycle on the ship was the same as for the Northern Hemisphere, so though there was a time difference, he'd leave a message to say when she could contact him if she was sleeping or not at home. Both Noah and Alice tried to make those brief messages cheerful and bright, but one time, she cried, and Noah, in gentle understanding, lifted his hand to the registry panel, encouraging her to do the same, and they touched each other across the vastness of space.

She also heard from Patrick, chatty and lively and full of enthusiasm. He made occasional comments about his feelings for her, but she only ever just smiled at him and changed the subject.

As the ship moved through the borders of proximal and median space, visual contact became less distinct. Noah said this was an issue to be worked on during the mission, and Alice hoped with all her heart they might discover how to make it work efficiently in deep space. As it stood, once the ship passed into threshold space, they would lose visual communication, and as they ventured further, most likely audio as well. The region they headed for was uncharted and unexplored, and it bothered Alice that Noah would be in a sector of space where all manner of dangers could lurk.

Without effective communications, anything could happen, but then, she supposed, even if something happened, no other ships had the capability of effecting a rescue. She had to trust he would make it back safely and not fill her head with such thoughts, or it could be a gloomy two years.

Six weeks after Noah left and not wishing to disappoint Principal Katya, Alice reluctantly attended the Tabernacle's biannual ball. She wore a green gown not too dissimilar in style to the one she wore in Spring, not caring to design anything different and allowing the aunties to select the colour. She avoided dancing and spoke dutifully with curious principals she hadn't previously met, skillfully deflecting questions of a more personal nature. As soon as she was able, and hoping no-one would see her leave, she walked alone to the courtyard and stood in the spot where she and Noah had said goodbye. She looked up at the window of Noah's quarters. Alice knew she was only torturing herself, but she couldn't help it. The stars above twinkled their indifference that they had taken him from her, and she felt desperately alone. Hot tears fell onto her cheeks as she looked to the heavens and whispered,

"I miss you, Noah, I really, really do," and she felt as if her heart would break.

The night after the ball, Principal Katya went in search of Statesman Mellor to join him in a late-night scotch. He was seated in his new comfortable seat. She sat beside him, knowing he expected her. He handed her a glass. It had become quite a regular late-night ritual, not a time for speaking too much, just keeping company and unwinding. The sound of piano music, mournful and sad, came from the library. Principal Katya nodded towards the door.

"It's Alice," Statesman Mellor said, looking over.

"I have never heard her play before," Principal Katya said. "But I know of these nocturnal wanderings." She studied her glass and thought about the night she'd seen Alice and Noah in front of the Tabernacle. Alice must miss him, but in all these weeks, neither she nor Noah spoke of it. If they wished to keep their romance a secret, so be it, as World Principal, she would not pry, and as Noah's aunt, no doubt she would learn of it in due time.

"She plays at least once every time she's here," Statesman Mellor said. "She never remembers."

Principal Katya rose, handed Mellor her glass and headed for the library. The red-haired woman at the piano wore only a nightgown. Her feet were bare and her hair messy, as if she'd just lately risen from her bed.

Principal Katya walked towards her and stood in the well of the grand piano. The woman looked up and stopped playing. There was an impression of something other-worldly, oddly bright and out-of-place surrounding the woman.

"Hello," the woman said.

"Hello," Principal Katya smiled back. "It's Alexis, isn't it?"

The woman nodded.

"You play well. Where did you learn?"

Alexis stopped for a moment, a small frown

shadowing her eyes, then she tinkered with a few keys.

"At school, I think. I was a boarder."

Principal Katya was unsure what 'boarder' meant and resolved to check on the registry later. Now was not the time to have a lesson in vernacular.

"Do you know where you are, Alexis?"

Alexis looked up to the high ceilings and around the library.

"A place of governance, this is the library. I've been here before, but I'm not entirely sure why."

"Do you know who I am?"

"You are familiar, but I find it difficult to hold onto new memories when I'm like this, in this state. Other times, I seem to be somewhere else, a different dream place. The only thing that stays with me throughout is music, and sometimes, I find my way to this piano. I don't even know where I find my way from. I played another piano one time, but I can't remember where. And here," she looked down and pulled out the skirt of her nightgown, "I wear these funny nightclothes and have bare feet," she smiled at Principal Katya. Not Alice's smile, but a beautiful smile.

"Do you have other memories, Alexis?"

Alexis tilted her head in thought, "I remember not having any hair and being very sick and my..." she raised her hands a little helplessly, "my poor Uncle Martin was so worried, he said he would do anything to save me, but we all knew it was hopeless. And now, I find my hair has grown back, so I wonder if I'm dreaming, or in a coma, or dead."

"You are not dead, Alexis. You have been asleep for a long time."

"Uncle Martin asked A'khet to help. At first, they said they couldn't, but then, I don't know what they did. It's vague. I was ill, too late to make any difference, I would have thought."

Principal Katya was aware Alexis had been desperately ill when she was preserved, but this woman seemed resigned to death. It appeared to hold no fear for her. And the A'khet, they'd known her uncle? Principal Katya saw the pieces of the puzzle fitting together. Alexis spoke again.

"Do you know where I am? How can I be in two places?"

"I am afraid I don't know that other place, Alexis, but part of you is here, and we love you. We are hoping you will be restored to us fully."

Alexis appeared not to have heard. "There's a woman," she placed her hand over her heart. "Here, and I have a voice when I'm with her. I don't know who she is, but people call her Alice, and she tells them, 'Alexis without the x'."

Alexis stood suddenly, her face losing all expression. "It is because the love of the A'khet transcended all others," she announced. Then with neither glance nor hint of recognition towards Principal Katya, she turned and left the room.

Principal Katya followed and watched her as she ascended the stairs. She would return to her suite and, in the morning, would be Alice again. Principal Katya now understood what A'khet meant at that first meeting. Alice and Alexis were not one and the same.

She returned to Statesman Mellor and her whisky.

"She spoke to you?" he enquired.

Principal Katya nodded. "She spoke."

"Why do you seem troubled, Principal Katya?"

"I am sad for the girl I met tonight."

"Sad? For Alice? Why are you sad for her? Surely this is her amnesia?"

"I am not sad for Alice. Alice is very dear to me. I am sad for Alexis Langley."

CHAPTER THIRTY-TWO _

Alice and Principal Katya spent an enjoyable morning together before Alice was due to leave for home, taking tea and talking about Principal Katya's favourite subjects, food and crochet.

Principal Katya elected not to tell her about the exchange of the previous night, concerned it might be a complication to her life, but today, she had other unpleasant and worrying news for Alice.

"Alice, do you recall, Dr Clere proposed further debate and study regarding your preservation?"

"Yes, I understood he had support, at least from his team."

"They have withdrawn this support since you successfully began living your life as a normal citizen. They knew and liked you on Saturn Station and want you to continue your life undisturbed."

"So, he's on his own?"

"Regrettably, no. He has converted several, much younger and less experienced scientists from several disciplines, eager to blaze similar paths of glory as Clere, to join his cause."

"Can he force me to submit to these studies?"

"No," Principal Katya reassured her. "But he has put forward a demand that you return to Saturn Station. He intends to analyse tissue and blood samples, undertake psychological assessment and the use of 'techniques' to uncover your real memories."

"What techniques?"

Principal Katya was not an expert in medical matters but knew the outdated methods Clere proposed as fundamental to his research were deficient in most areas. If supplemented by present-day technology, he argued, he could quickly bring Alice to a state of recognition. These methods were not without considerable risk and long abandoned as potentially harmful. Alice could lose all the memories she'd made since waking, or her amnesia could become total. The areas of the brain Clere planned to stimulate might not be repairable if his team made a miscalculation. Clere reasoned it mattered little if Alice lost her Alice Watkins memories, they were false anyway. The risk needed weighing against the possibility of the memories of Alexis Langley being recovered and the offering up of the preserving fluid formula. He insisted the benefits outweighed the risk. Those words, 'what do we have to lose?' was mentioned only once in his proposal, but to Principal Katya, they crawled over every sentence.

Principal Katya had seen the timid Alice Watkins persona diminish significantly over the months. She had blossomed, matured. Now, having met Alexis Langley, she realised no amount of scientific study would unravel this great mystery. Even for the A'khet, the answer would undoubtedly prove beyond their mystical abilities.

"Clere believes you have condensed memories," she said, "one false, one true. He proposes to conduct a procedure whereby your memories are completely isolated and returned to you, one by one, eliminating those he believes are superfluous, which could be all of them. This procedure, called psychobiographism, involves inserting a probe into your spine; a technique developed at the end of the twenty-first century to rehabilitate criminals. It was not without its merits in that application. Clere has managed to replicate a probe from an example in the Bell Institute. He means to use it to lift any censorship your subconscious is employing to fill in the gaps in your knowledge. It has serious side effects. Any memories you value will be lost. Do you understand these implications, Alice?"

To Principal Katya's amazement, instead of answering, Alice's usually sweet mouth fixed into a straight, angry line and her hands clenched into fists.

"I know exactly what the implications are, Principal Katya. How dare he! He's a barbarian! And he asked the Tabernacle for permission? It didn't occur to him to approach me? What am I? Does he not recognise my freedom as an individual?" Alice stood, her voice raised and angry.

Principal Katya saw the anger but couldn't discern if she observed Alice or Alexis. Either way, she liked the fight in the girl's eyes!

"Yes, therein is the great dichotomy" Principal Katya looked up at Alice. "He agrees you are a living breathing being, capable of taking your place in society with freedom to choose, but argues you truly belong to science. He believes you may hold the key to the evolution of medical breakthroughs, and your life, your choices, are mere molecules in the grand scheme of things. He plans to return you here after he has conducted his research, and you resume your life with whatever memories remain intact."

"What did the Tabernacle say, Principal Katya? How did you respond?"

"I haven't responded, dear girl. If I had, it would be to issue a reprimand for asking the Tabernacle to violate the personal liberties of one of its most beloved subjects. He is here, now, with his confederates, to speak to us in person."

"To you or me?"

"To me, Alice. He has not considered your thoughts on the matter. That is why I bring it to you."

"It's time I spoke with Dr Clere." Alice's tone turned icy, incensed by his treachery. She was going to war!

Principal Katya knew Clere reckoned without Alice moving on from her earlier convictions about her origins, arrogantly believing that he could manipulate her unhindered away from Grossmith and Hardy. She smiled her approval as Alice turned on her heel and headed towards Cloisters. Principal Katya pushed back her chair and hurried after her, although she doubted Alice would need support judging by her reaction. Principal Katya wouldn't miss this for the world.

The councilman who stood at the Cloisters door made to stop Alice but caught sight of Principal Katya following behind, waving to let Alice pass.

Alice came upon Dr Clere seated with several men and women at the council table, deep in discussion. On the opposite side sat Statesman Mellor, very pleased and most gratified to see an outraged Alice storm in, accompanied by a smiling Principal Katya.

Dr Clere was so surprised and astonished to see Alice; he almost knocked his chair over in his haste to stand. He'd anticipated these discussions would take place without her. His colleagues watched and waited for introductions that did not come.

"Dr Clere." Alice's voice, low, quiet, cold, offered no greeting. She positioned herself, making sure each person in the room had a clear view of her.

Dr Clere didn't speak. He didn't even bow. She'd changed, gone the frail and forlorn figure he remembered from Saturn Station, in her place stood a defiant, startlingly independent young woman.

This must be Dr Alexis Langley, one or two murmured, for such a small woman, her fury bore down on them all, making those who would study her swallow hard and shift in their seats. They saw the truth of it now, a human being, not a potential subject for study, revealed as a woman with thoughts and emotions Clere insisted she did not possess, and she was livid! And worryingly close to the World Principal. Perhaps lending support to Clere wasn't such a good move.

"You've submitted a proposal to the Tabernacle detailing your desire to use me as a subject for study?" Alice said, the tone of her voice so cold, Principal Katya swore she felt the temperature in the room drop a few degrees.

Alice planted her hands on the table and looked Clere in the eye, challenging him to answer.

He remained silent. Statesman Mellor smiled under his hand. A gentle person by nature, he would have liked to throw Clere through the window for daring to sully Cloisters with this proposal.

With Clere steadfast in his silence, trying to recover from his surprise at seeing his former patient so changed, Alice spoke instead.

"Nothing to say, Dr Clere? Then let me! I can't permit what you and these...", she gestured at Clere's supporters, scornfully refusing to make eye contact with any of them, "others like you propose. I am unable to provide you with any more information about my preservation than you already know."

Clere cleared his throat and tried to defend himself, but his voice didn't match the strength of hers. She'd caught him off balance and her anger deflected his zeal, but he would not back down. He would not give in, not now, with so much at stake. He could see the others were hesitating, but he would redeem himself, and they would see this one opportunity could not be lost simply because the subject had worked herself into a sweat.

"Dr Langley, I do not believe that is the case. Left to your own devices, with those..." he wasn't mentioning names, but he meant Principal Hardy and Dr Grossmith and all her friends, "around you who encourage your fantasies, you will continue in your delusion you are Alice Watkins. We know you are Alexis Langley. We have proof you are Alexis Langley."

"What proof? A microchip? From an age where technology was easily tampered with? And does it matter? If I'm Alexis Langley, who has no memory of her preservation, what good would further study do? You have all the tissue samples, blood samples, hair samples, and god knows what other samples. And now you propose using ancient and risky techniques to help me recover memories. Dr Clere, would you violate the rights of any other member of society in this manner to satisfy your curiosity?"

"Dr Langley, I would not, but you are not just any other member of society. Your invented memories are obliterating the truth. A truth that belongs to you as much as it belongs to science. As a scientist, can't you see the potential? The preservation technique begs further study. It reversed the course of a terminal disease; there is evidence of this process in your own body. How can that be? We must learn how. Once the study is complete, you can return to your life." If Clere thought to appeal to the scientist in her, his calculation didn't work.

"I will never surrender to any form of testing, Dr Clere," Alice spat and slapped her hand so hard on the table, Clere's cronies jumped in their seats. "Because I do not possess the information you require. It is as beyond my knowledge and comprehension as it is yours."

"Are you certain? Or do you simply choose to keep it from us?"

"The fluid vanished from under your noses, Dr Clere," Alice lifted her arms in a gesture towards the heavens and then folded them in defiance, her face red with anger. "It was never meant to be discovered. Not by you," she jabbed a finger towards him, then to herself, "not by me."

Clere looked at Principal Katya, "You have friends in high places, Dr Langley."

Alice remembered her misplaced fear of Noah and how she'd reformed her opinion. A big reform. She smiled a little. This would end here. Her anger dissipated somewhat; in this arena, Dr Clere seemed small and insignificant to her and he had no power.

"Something amuses you, Dr Langley?" Clere made the mistake of sounding self-righteous, and Alice eyed him up and down.

"I don't find this amusing at all, Dr Clere. I'm merely recalling how I made mistakes in appraising people when I first awoke. I assumed all doctors would have my best interests at heart. But not you, Dr Clere, not you."

He shook his head. "You are one person. I have the best interests of the whole world at heart. The preservation technique is beyond anything available today. If your uncle could see what has become of you now, wouldn't he want the whole world to know the secret? It might have been his intention to share this success?

"I was preserved so I might live, Dr Clere. My uncle loved me. I doubt he saw beyond saving my life."

"I believe you are mistaken."

"I don't think so." She paused, "Perhaps when you grew a heart for me, you should have grown one for yourself."

Clere's colleagues sat open-mouthed throughout the entire exchange, and now, they watched as the proposed subject turned and stalked from the room. Alice didn't stop until she reached the garden, where she bent over and took a few deep breaths, her rage subsiding. What a pig of a man! She would love to have slapped that sanctimonious face! Statesman Mellor and Principal Katya caught up with her moments later.

"That told him!" Principal Katya laughed, clasping Alice's hands.

Statesman Mellor enveloped Alice in a hug of victory. "Well done, Alice! He's a pompous ass. I thought you very measured under the circumstances!"

"What will happen now?" Alice asked, her breathing returning to normal. She'd never confronted anyone in her entire life, and her life was worth defending. Dr Clere had no rights over it.

Principal Katya linked arms with her and pointed to a table. Statesman Mellor withdrew, still grinning, maybe an early glass of scotch.

Principal Katya sat Alice down, her earlier mirth subsiding, her voice serious. "Alice, even in our enlightened society, there are those who seek personal glory. When a subject as fascinating and challenging as you presents itself and provides no answers to the centuries of speculation, the hunger for gaining all knowledge outweighs judgement. Clere would blow out your candle to make his burn brighter." She sighed, "He will hand over the reins to his team, retire and be bitter in defeat the rest of his life. He will not defy the Tabernacle."

Alice closed her eyes and nodded, calm returning. Principal Katya, unaccustomed as she was to seeing the ordinarily gentle and sweet Alice roused to anger, wondered if she'd witnessed Alice or Alexis just now, so ably confronting Clere.

"Clere called you 'Dr Langley'," she said, "you didn't correct him. Does this mean anything?"

Strange thing, Alice remembered everything that took place since Principal Katya told her of Dr Clere's presence here. Herself or Alexis? Alice didn't know, but she sure as hell got courage from somewhere. She shook her head.

"I'm not sure, Principal Katya. But I know the memories I held so dearly when I first woke are not the memories that bind me to this life. Clere did not consider the possibility I've changed, he said I think of myself as Alice Watkins, but in truth, I'm not so sure I do now."

Principal Katya didn't answer. Whoever manifested today, Alice showed strength and presence of mind in defending herself against a tyrant. She announced to the world; her life was hers and hers alone.

CHAPTER THIRTY-THREE _

The day Alice returned home to the aunties, all visual contact with the Significator ceased, meaning the ship had, at last, entered far side median and would soon cross into threshold space, with all the dangers the region might hold. Alice and Noah continued to communicate as much as possible, but she missed seeing his dear face. She told him of her exchange with Dr Clere, and he congratulated her on standing up to him and that she must now put the question of any study firmly out of her life. She also told Patrick, who, in his reply, wondered if there might not always be someone who considered Alice a mystery worth solving. His words unnerved her, but she determined not to give in to those fears and would cross any bridges as she came to them.

Her aunts now knew for sure which man she cried for at night, for all she tried to hide it but didn't understand why she never spoke of him.

Mary and Jane let her quietness go for a week or two after she returned from the Tabernacle, but when her low spirits continued, they stepped in, knowing just the person to cheer her up.

Alice came up from the stable late in the afternoon. Jorrocks and the other horses were clean and settled, the other animals were fed, and the plants tended. Pecky fluttered up to the verandah, chasing a moth. Alice looked forward to a shower and change of clothes before Mary and Jane came back from Thomas's house but stopped as a one-person shuttle, showing city markings came to rest near the gum trees. To her delight, Amelia jumped out and bounded over to Alice, catching her in an affectionate hug.

"What, no Aunties?" Amelia looked around.

"They're visiting Thomas," Alice laughed. "I didn't expect you! What a lovely surprise!"

"Well, I haven't seen you since the theatre, and that was weeks ago. Your aunties called me and said you need cheering up."

Alice nodded.

"They're right, but you're busy with work, and John, of course. I didn't want to bother you. I've been pottering about and enjoying the peace, but I feel out of sorts."

Amelia linked arms with her while they walked the rest of the way to the house.

"Well, your aunties tell me you're sad. You know what I think?"

Amelia grinned and didn't wait for Alice to reply.

"I think you miss Patrick."

Seeing her friend's smiling face and understanding her willingness to help, Alice decided to tell Amelia her terrible secret. She stopped walking and looked up at her. Amelia seemed very tall today, out of uniform, blonde hair a mass of messy curls. She would be shocked, but Alice couldn't keep this hidden. Amelia also stopped as Alice turned to her, her smile changing to a puzzled frown as Alice's pale, anxious expression confronted her.

"What is it, Alice?"

"Amelia, I missed my period," she whispered, almost not daring to give the secret a voice because if she did, it would confirm what she already suspected.

"What?"

"I missed my period. In fact, I've missed two."

"Alice, you goose," Amelia took her by the shoulders. "You don't have periods; menstruation only happens when the biochemical component of your chip is disabled after you marry and want a baby."

"I've had periods for *months*."

"Didn't they replace your original chip on Saturn Station?"

"No-one said anything, and I didn't know enough to ask. Maybe the old one is still there."

"This is a huge oversight by Dr Grossmith and Principal Hardy. Alice," Amelia's brown eyes grew wide in disbelief and shock as the truth dawned, "are you telling me you're *pregnant?*"

Amelia looked towards the house, towards the cliff, towards the shuttle and then back to Alice before recovering herself with a sharp exhalation of breath.

"Wow, Alice. Does Statesman Patrick know?"

Alice's pale expression gave way to bewilderment. What would Statesman Patrick have to do with it? But of course, the other secret had been kept so well; now she would have to come clean about Noah.

"No, Amelia, not Patrick."

Amelia's curls bobbed about as she shook her head in her confusion. "I don't understand, Alice. If it isn't Patrick? Who?" Amelia was in the throes of processing the information when the answer hit her like a tonne of bricks. She put her hands to her face.

"Oh, my lord, not Principal *Ryan?*"

Alice bowed her head and crumpled to her knees, weeping into her hands with sorrow and relief. Amelia quickly dropped to the ground beside her, cringing at her own insensitivity. She'd made it sound as if Principal Ryan had all the characteristics of a bad smell. But Alice didn't care what Amelia thought of Noah. The emotion of these last few weeks overwhelmed her, and she was glad this part of the truth, at least, was out.

"Alice, I'm so sorry," Amelia held her close and stroked her hair, "I never suspected, even for a moment. Have you told your aunties?" She cupped Alice's face to wipe away her tears, but a sudden, sneaking suspicion came upon her, "Alice, you *have* told Principal Ryan?"

Alice shook her head, gulping against sobs as she tried to explain why she couldn't.

"I'm not telling him, Amelia, at least not yet. All his life, he dreamed of going into space, of doing what he does. With a child, he must stay here, and he would have to marry me. It would ruin his career, his life. Besides, I can't tell him, he's out of visual range, and he would want to come back. It would be all my fault if his life is ruined," she finished, sobbing against Amelia's shoulder.

"Oh, sweetie, shh, it'll be alright," Amelia soothed, holding Alice close, rocking her, and stroking her hair until her crying ceased.

Amelia helped Alice to her feet, wiping away her tears with her thumb.

"Well, he might prefer to be with you and his child," Amelia said reasonably. "Put to him, Alice, I bet he'd say you are more important than his career."

But though Alice insisted informing Noah was out of the question, the next step must be to tell the aunties.

"I don't know what to say, Alice. This must be your decision, but I can't see any way of not telling Jane and Mary. They love you and will want to support you."

"I know," Alice said, forlorn and resigned. "I'll tell them when they get home."

"I'm going to stay with you until I'm sure you're okay. But for now, we're going to the city, to the studios and entertainment levels. Go shower and change your clothes, Alice. You smell of horse shit!"

Alice tried to wipe away her tears with the heel of her hand but only succeeded in rearranging the dirt from her hands all over her face. She looked a sorry sight, with her dirt-streaked, tear-stained face and Amelia smiled one of her silly smiles to reassure her best friend things would turn out just fine.

"Thank you, Amelia," Alice managed a small grin. "I'm grateful you're here."

Later in the evening, after abandoning the trip to the city due to Alice not cheering up to the level Amelia hoped, they sat together on the clifftop, looking out to sea.

"I'm sorry about earlier, Alice," Amelia said. "I confess learning Principal Ryan is the baby's father rather floored me. It's hard for me to imagine him stopping his arrogance long enough to…" Amelia pulled a face, "I'm making it worse."

Alice grinned sideways at her. She'd pulled up her knees and folded her arms to use as a chin rest to watch the moon.

"I know you think he's arrogant, Amelia, so did I at first. He terrified me."

"What happened to change your mind?"

"He's Principal Katya's nephew. After the Cotillion Ball, she asked him to take me to see the A'khet, we spent the whole day together then a few days later, he came here, and we went to Machu Picchu. He's nothing like he seems on the ship."

"You're in love with him?"

Alice answered with a small smile.

Well, Amelia was doubly flabbergasted. He must have redeeming features not apparent to anyone but his mother, and Alice.

"He grows flowers, Amelia, roses, beautiful roses, and he weaves baskets and hand rears puppies."

"He does not!"

"Yes, he does, and he's endlessly patient and understanding." Alice couldn't help but grin at Amelia's disbelief.

"I can't believe we're talking about the same man. Sorry, Alice, I'm just trying to get my head around the fact you passed up the most gorgeous man in the universe—apart from John, of course—and went for the total opposite!"

"Amelia, I didn't pass up on the most gorgeous man in the universe—not to me, anyway. It was never Patrick."

Amelia put her arm around Alice. "I'll get used to it, sweetie. Don't mind me!"

Mary and Jane didn't get home till late, well after Alice went to bed and Amelia, still in a state of amazement, lay awake all night in the guest room rather than leave her alone.

Mary and Jane were delighted to see Amelia in the morning, but Alice, nervous about the coming revelation, hovered about, anxious and fearful. As it happened, she didn't need to say anything. One look at a chocolate pastry sent Alice out into the bushes, retching violently. She'd only suffered mild nausea up till that morning, but now it looked as if the symptoms were going to settle in with a vengeance. The three women at the table looked at each other as they listened to Alice. Jane rose and went inside, returning with a diagnostic kit. When Alice came back, white and shaking, Jane held the Diaprime panel up to her body and checked the readings. Without a word, she handed it to Mary, who glanced at the results, then looked at Alice.

"A little girl, Alice, seven weeks and three days," Mary placed the diagnostic tool on the table for Alice to see, but she kept her eyes cast down and didn't look. Noah had left her with something precious. If only she didn't feel so sick. Once again, the bushes beckoned as another wave of nausea washed over her.

When she finally returned to the table, Mary brought damp fibrelettes and gently wiped Alice's face. Alice didn't resist.

"Why didn't you tell us, sweetheart," Mary asked.

"I didn't believe it myself." Alice felt ashamed to have thrust all this on them.

"And Principal Ryan?"

"He doesn't know. I only really realised these last few days."

"Amelia told us while you were out at the bushes that they didn't replace your chip. That is indeed an oversight."

"I never gave it a thought. I can't tell Noah, Mary; he'd come back. He has to stay on Earth if he has a child. It's why Statesman Hennessey left the ship; because his wife had a baby. He loved his work in space."

"Principal Ryan wouldn't come back, Alice," Mary looked at Jane for confirmation, she nodded her agreement. "He would remain with the ship."

"Did you know Alice was involved with Principal Ryan rather than Statesman Patrick?" Amelia asked, still finding this turn of events astonishing and not having much success in accepting Principal Ryan possessed any worthy attributes.

"Yes, it was apparent when they were together, but we only saw them a couple of times," Mary said. She turned to Alice.

"When did you get the opportunity for this to happen? You've seen so little of him, and this obviously happened after Peru?"

"The last time I went to the Tabernacle, he was there," Alice explained. Under the circumstances, there was no point in trying to hide it anymore. "We'd been speaking on the registry before that. I'd planned to spend time with Principal Katya, but she had urgent business, so I thought I'd cut short my visit. Noah invited me to spend a few days at his home and then go to the Top of the World."

"Did you say anything to Principal Katya?"

Alice shook her head. "There was nothing to tell at the time.".

"Well, clearly, that's not the case. In fact, why didn't you tell any of us?" Alice had hurt Mary's feelings, that much was obvious, and Alice knew she'd made an unforgivable error in judgement in not telling the aunties the truth.

"Because of Patrick. He told me he loved me but refused to believe I don't return his feelings, and it's just…well, Noah has to spend two years with him, and we felt—we felt it would be…awkward."

"When the truth is hidden, misunderstandings occur, Alice," Jane said, pragmatic as always, and though she shared Mary's disappointment, her tone held no reproach.

"You're right, Auntie Jane, we thought we were just keeping a little secret, one we could sort out when they returned."

"He is a Principal, Alice. It's his job to resolve issues," Jane continued, privately resentful someone in Principal Ryan's position had not shown more foresight.

"We let it go too far. It appears Patrick still has relationships, even while professing his love for me. Noah thought he might simply get over it in the two years and would accept the situation when they got back." She looked at them all, tears of shame and sadness spilling over her cheeks. "I know we mishandled it, but we couldn't have predicted this."

"It'll be a lot harder when Patrick finds out you've had Principal Ryan's baby, surely you should tell Principal Ryan now, and then he can tell Statesman Patrick?" Amelia suggested, not at all sure what course of action would be for the best.

But Alice remained firm, despite her distress. "There's another mission planned, and Noah is hoping for three years in threshold space. I'm not going to tie him down. We aren't married. He hasn't asked me to marry him, and he can't take me with him, so there's the end to it."

"I think wives do go on starships," Amelia said, an expression of thought-wrangling lining her face.

Alice shook her head. No, not the case. "I met up with Statesman Hennessey at the Cotillion Ball. I was just making conversation and asked if he was enjoying being home. He looked happy, a bit wistful, and I said how nice it would be if he could go back to the Significator and take his wife too. He just laughed and said he couldn't imagine a more unwise career move. It reminded me of what you said, Amelia, about parents needing to be on hand to raise their child."

"I was generalising, Alice. It didn't occur to me you'd put it to the test."

"Anyway, I can't do that to Noah. We were only together a few days, and he's dreamed of this all his life."

"I don't know much about military law," Mary said, "but he loves you...doesn't he?"

Alice trembled and clasped her hands together, almost in a gesture of supplication, her voice pleading.

"I beg you not to tell anyone, any of you. Noah's ship has left median space, and we don't have visual contact, only unreliable audio-text communications. You say he wouldn't abandon the mission, but it would make it much more difficult for him to continue, even if he concealed it from Patrick. I'll tell him on our first link when he returns."

"What about Principal Katya?"

"Please don't tell her! She'd probably send a ship after him," she cried. "I started all this secrecy, and now I must beg others to keep the secret. Auntie Jane, Auntie Mary, I don't want to disrupt Noah's life, and I've brought you nothing but problems. I'm so sorry." Alice folded her arms on the table and buried her face in her sleeves. Amelia stroked her back to ease her distress.

"You haven't brought us problems, Alice," Mary knew she spoke for Jane. She went over to Alice, and kneeling beside her, lifted her tear-stained face. She took a fibrelette and wiped the tears away.

"Alice, you bring us so much joy," Mary's voice faltered. "You are like the daughter we could never have, seeing you grow in your new life, learning, having friends and now...a baby! Alice, you've brought happiness beyond our wildest dreams! We won't tell anyone for now, but soon, the truth is going to come out. We will face all this together. Alice, we love you."

Alice threw her arms around Mary and held her tight.

Jane and Amelia sat quietly, watching on, each tearfully considering the potential consequences this situation might yield.

CHAPTER THIRTY-FOUR _

That afternoon, the aunties thanked Amelia for her support and sent a still overwrought Alice for a nap. Jane brought coffee out to where Mary sat at the registry.

"I tried to check the military guidelines regarding marriage," Mary said, pointing to her research. "There's not much at all, at least for public viewing."

"Nevertheless," Jane said, "I'm sure Alice is wrong about this. On the Argos, years ago, Principal Stanley's wife was a science officer." She perused the scant information Mary found, "True, they were childless, and she was military and qualified, but they were assigned together."

"Alice has no current skills, and now it would appear she isn't properly chipped either," Mary sat back; the events of the day had wearied her.

"Principal Katya could sort that out in an instant," Jane waved her hand and turned to the registry to check for further information, "and she could settle the question of whether Alice is correct in her assumptions."

"Jane, Principal Katya needs to be told; it would sort it all out."

"Yes, but we can't unless Alice agrees, and I don't see much chance of that happening at the moment. The problem is…" Jane searched through a list of felonies. Of the very few, one was a failure to report the birth of a child. She showed it to Mary.

Mary was horrified and read the list for herself. "Oh, my goodness, don't tell Alice. It says nothing about concealing a pregnancy, so it isn't unlawful yet."

"She spends a lot of time on the registry, Mary; she might find out herself."

"Let's give ourselves some breathing space, and Alice time to settle down, we can tell her—just not right away."

"Well, if she isn't chipped, then she isn't registered, so there can be no consequences, for her at least, but for us…"

"I know," Mary said, her face grim. "I don't fancy going back to work, particularly as penance."

"That's what'll happen," Jane was equally disinclined to make any changes to her happy life.

Alice eventually came to her senses and decided to tell Principal Katya, but every time they spoke on the registry, and Alice steeled herself to come clean, each time, her nerve failed her. She knew the Accessor, out in far side median space, still had some sporadic and unreliable communication with the Significator; however, none filtered through to her, only to the Tabernacle, and Alice was still fearful Principal Katya would tell Noah.

Alice remembered her bravery in confronting Dr Clere, but in this, what did she feel? Shame? She shuddered at the idea any remnants of Alice Watkins's old guilt complexes remained. After four months of grappling with her conscience, avoiding visiting the Tabernacle and ensuring Dr Grossmith on his regular links didn't notice her growing tummy, Statesman Mellor contacted Alice, and the matter was taken out of her hands.

"Statesman Mellor, what a surprise."

"Alice—Dr Langley."

"Is everything alright?" Alice felt a rush of concern, he hadn't addressed her by her title for a long time, and he'd never called her at home.

"Principal Katya is suffering from syncope and has been prescribed complete rest."

"Syncope?"

Principal Katya hadn't mentioned feeling faint. Alice spent considerable time on the registry, reading and learning and knew about syncope. Amelia even teased her that the Eduction chip must still work for her to absorb so much knowledge.

"Yes, it's happened on several occasions. Principal Katya refuses to take time away from the Tabernacle and hasn't done so in twenty years, save for one or two visits with you. Her physician believes her body is insisting that she do it now. She has dictated a text, and I'm transmitting it to you. Alice, I understand there is no need for concern." He inclined his head with a smile, and the transmission ended. The letter appeared directly; Alice smiled; even the text sounded like Principal Katya's voice.

'My dear Alice,

No doubt Statesman Mellor has advised you by now of my infirmity. I can trust him not to inject too much drama into the situation. I am tired and have felt so for a little while. The specialists proposed stasis to ensure my body rested, but I could imagine nothing worse! Instead, I persuaded the physician to allow me to come to Tibet for complete rest with the A'khet and the monks. The physician will attend me regularly until I am declared fit to return. It occurred to me to suggest I came to stay with you and your aunties but then thought better of asking you to care for a decrepit old lady, although I know you would be kindness itself. I do not know how long I will be away, dear girl. There is no registry at the monastery. You may communicate via the Tabernacle, and it will be delivered by my physician when he visits. I am sorry we will not see each other for a while, but I have no wish to retire completely yet; this rest will ensure my continuation. As soon as I leave the monastery, I will contact you, and we will enjoy a visit.

My respect to your aunties and my deep love to you.

Katya.'

Katya. Not Principal Katya. Alice went to find the aunties to tell them the news. Despite reassurances, she was anxious for her friend and felt no gratitude in the reprieve she'd been handed in not telling her about the baby. Alice sent a note to Principal Katya, thanking her for letting her know and reiterating everyone's insistence she takes things easy.

Flowers were delivered to Alice with astonishing regularity, Patrick had put in an order before he left, but one day, a shuttle arrived with a gift from Noah. Alice, Mary, and Jane stood and watched it being unloaded.

"A piano," Mary exclaimed. "What an extraordinary gift! Alice, I didn't know you played."

In all this time, it never occurred to Alice to mention her nocturnal musical excursions.

"I do, apparently, Auntie Mary, but only when I sleepwalk. It's beautiful, though. I love it. What an incredibly thoughtful gift."

The piano, a replica of the one on the Significator, was installed in the parlour, below Alice's portrait. She ran her fingers over the cabinet and caught a memory, the smoothness of the wood, the lights of the auditorium, and Noah. Mary saw her small, sad smile.

"Do you think you could play something for us?"

"I can only play when I forget who I am, Auntie Mary. Statesman Mellor, Statesman Patrick and Noah, all say I play well. I just can't remember. It must be a subconscious skill; maybe if I practice, it'll come back."

Mary turned on the piano registry and requested the tutorial. The tutorial came up, and Mary lifted the lid, inviting Alice to sit down, but the keys meant nothing to her. She shook her head.

"I can't remember a thing."

"The tutorial will help; go on; it'll be fun."

And as the days and weeks past, practice she did, incorporating the discovery of music into her world, along with history and architecture and an interest in the stars, the latter so she could see where Noah might be. She stubbornly refused to give any thought to what might happen when he got back or if anyone found out about the baby.

Seven months into the mission, all communication

with the Significator ceased. The Tabernacle sent the Accessor back out to the edge of threshold space, but they only encountered silence. Principal Katya, still on retreat, sent Alice a message via the Tabernacle to assure her this happened on their previous mission and not to worry unduly.

The southern hemisphere summer turned to Autumn and the nights became cool. A restless Alice sat in front of the general registry, wrapped in a blanket, Pecky asleep on her shoulder. Jane came out of the bedroom and saw her sitting there, staring at a blank panel.

"What is it, Alice?"

Alice didn't look up, "I don't know who I am, Auntie Jane."

"Well, you are our precious girl," Jane smiled, sitting down next to her. "Other than that, I don't need to know anything else."

Alice smiled.

"I know you love me, but sometimes, I question where I come from. I'm still officially Alexis Langley, and since the baby," she placed her hand on her swollen tummy, "those memories of Alice Watkins have become very vague. I don't even know if she's relevant, but not so long ago, I'd convinced myself I was her. If I could honestly remember Alexis Langley, it might be okay, but tonight, I couldn't sleep for thinking about Alice Watkins's children. I haven't thought about them in ages. Two children, a boy and a girl, grandchildren too and a life that's fading away every day."

"Maybe it's because you're pregnant."

"I had these memories right from the start. I don't accept them now as true, but they often creep in, and I have this urge to find out if somehow, they were ever true for someone in my distant past."

"My people believed the spirits of our ancestors walk with us, give us courage and guidance," Jane said.

"What a lovely tradition."

"Well, it *was* a lovely tradition, lost with all the others now, we weren't so lucky in preserving our culture as others. Mary will help you with this, Alice; it's between you and her."

Jane kissed her on the forehead and went back to her bedroom.

Alice sighed and put the still sleeping Pecky on her hat. Returning to her room, she flicked onto Noah's signature. The panel remained blank and quiet, but that simple act made her feel close to him and reminded her of the last time they were together, when she lay under his arm, close to his heart, the night she conceived their child.

CHAPTER THIRTY-FIVE _

The next morning, Mary sat with Alice in front of the registry. Jane had told her about Alice's thoughts from the night before.

"Where do you want to start?" she asked, bringing the registry to life.

"I'd like to see how we're related."

"Well, we would need to give the registry a time frame. Many records were lost, and few were kept during the plague cycles, so it might be sketchy. They're not terribly reliable until you get into modern times."

"Okay. Let's try the twentieth century."

"Decade?" she asked Alice.

"1940s."

"Registry, common ancestor, Alexis Langley and Mary Greer, twentieth century, fourth decade," Mary commanded the responder, but the registry couldn't comply. It believed the Alexis Langley mentioned was dead due to her birth being several hundred years before.

"We'll have to get your status updated at the Principality House, Alice. You can't go around being dead."

Alice agreed.

"Common ancestor, Alexis Langley deceased, Mary Greer, living."

A whole list of people flashed up, but the registry homed in on one line. To Alice's amazement, an image appeared.

"Albert and Mary Hallett," Mary read.

Alice stared in amazement. Two elderly people in a bar, seated with glasses of stout and cigarettes in their hands. Her grandparents, her mother's father and mother.

"They're my grandparents."

"Your grandparents?"

"Well, Alice Watkins knew these people."

"They're possibly your grandparents many times removed. And mine. Let's see if we can trace any posterity or establish a link."

"Here we are. Issue: Joyce Hallett, born, twelfth of December 1934 and David Hallet born eleventh of May 1936, dates are recorded using an old-style calendar, but I can read it, you can help if I get stuck."

Alice nodded. She looked at her mother's name but stayed silent. Joyce Hallet, seeing it now, Alice felt removed from her.

"One or other of these might give us a clue," Mary said, then commanded, "Joyce Hallett."

The registry moved with eerie slowness, almost like the glass pointer on a Ouija board as it highlighted Joyce's name and brought up her details, it reminded Alice of the day she saw her sarcophagus on the registry, but this time, she had no urge to run.

"Well," Mary read the entry, "Joyce Hallett, date of death is May 18, 1975. She had issue, Alice Hallett born on fourth November 1951. So, Joyce was only sixteen when she had a baby, and unmarried."

Alice's father was unknown, so Alice was probably the result of the triggered hormones her mother so often warned her about. He wasn't dead. Her mother had lied.

"Are there any images, Mary?"

"No, it seems not. What about Alice Hallett? We might both be descended from her."

Alice nodded, but she already knew what happened to Alice Hallett.

"Here we are," Mary pointed to the name. "Alice, this is interesting! Alice Hallett, born fourth November 1951, married Edward Watkins. Alice Hallett became Alice Watkins!" she looked up at Alice. "That's extraordinary. Let's see when they married. 25 October 1967." Mary continued to study the information for a moment until she saw Alice was sitting utterly still. She sat back.

"This is *the* Alice Watkins, isn't it?"

Alice didn't answer at first, just stared at her name on the registry.

"Check the date of death, please, Auntie Mary."

Mary had already seen the entry.

"Date of death not recorded."

"Why would that be?" Alice searched the entry herself for a clue. Mary wasn't an expert in genealogy and could only hazard a guess.

"Well, the plague started around 2026; she may have died then. We can't be sure. If she did, few records survive because of the scale and suddenness of fatalities and the ensuing chaos. It says here Alice and Edward had two children, Michelle and Steven," but Alice's gaze drifted somewhere beyond the registry, to a time long gone.

"Shall I tell you their birthdates?" Mary spoke quietly, not understanding where Alice had gone but sensed Alice already knew the answer, and when it came, it sent a chill through her body.

"There's no need. I know."

A feeling of disquiet crept into Mary's heart as if she'd suddenly become part of something far larger than she ever imagined. Alice's response to the entries suggested prior knowledge, and her memory of dates, uncanny. She must have undertaken very serious research, enough to feel a kinship to these people, but when Alice briefly spoke of them before, Mary dismissed her memories as fantasy.

"I accept Alice," Mary said after a moment, "that somehow, you know all this already. I can only assume you researched this branch of your family at some point and connected to these people in some way. I don't want you to be upset."

Alice turned her head slowly, still with distance in her eyes.

"I'm not upset, Mary. Are you happy to continue?" Then she smiled, back in the present, and Mary let out a mighty sigh of relief.

"Yes, I'm happy, but stop me if you find it's too much. You seemed quite lost there for a moment."

"Sorry, Mary. Nothing we've seen so far is strange to me. You must be right; I've researched it and retained accurate memories."

Mary allowed herself to be reassured, but her sense of disquiet lingered. She pulled herself together; she'd consider it later.

"It seems Michelle went on to have a family," she continued, "but Steven seems to have dropped off the face of the earth like his mother—like Alice Watkins. Michelle—no death date, had six children but going by this, not all of them had children. This one," Mary displayed a poor-quality image of a child, "Eliza, didn't marry, but her death date is recorded as second of December 2203. She lived for one hundred and three years."

Eliza. Her darling granddaughter. Alice didn't flinch.

"Only two of the other five have marriages and death dates recorded. They all die out before the end of the twenty-third century. Alice, we aren't descended from Alice Hallett, so I'm not sure why you identify with Alice Watkins. I think we should try David Hallett."

Alice believed her memories were stray, random pieces of information she'd picked up, even though it was evident Alice and Alexis were related somehow, but seeing it on the registry and knowing all the details even before the dates were revealed, unnerved and confused her. Perhaps a further examination of the records would bring clarity. Mary turned her attention to Uncle David.

"Here, David Hallett married Glenys Simpson third of September 1960, died, twenty-second September 1990. Issue: Peter born tenth of February 1961, and Imogen born, the fifteenth of August 1963. (SB)."

"What's SB?"

"Stillborn."

Alice never knew that about Uncle David. How awful for him.

"So, Peter it is then. Peter Hallett married Ellen Norris on August 10, 1982."

Alice thought about Ellen Norris, with tattoos and foul language, a girl from a rough family. Her mother would not have approved, but the girl had always been kind to Alice despite her roughness. She said nothing of this to Mary.

"There's an image," Mary smiled, delighted. "My goodness, they look old in this."

The image was of a much older Peter and Ellen and marked December 2030. They looked happy. Mary followed their line with optimism, hoping it would reveal the connection between her and Alice.

"Their issue, Lily, born on fourteenth of May 1984, Stuart born fourteenth of November 1985 and Elaine born on the twenty-second of November 1987. No death dates for either Peter or Ellen. We should try the children."

For Mary, these people were mere ghosts, but to Alice, she believed she'd once known them. Elaine died in 2007 in a car crash. Alice attended her funeral, it was terribly sad. Stuart never married, preferring the company of males, and so it only left Lily, who Alice remembered as being blonde and pretty. She pointed to Lily.

"Let's try the oldest, Lily," she said.

"Might as well. Here, married young."

Yes, Alice thought, she was young and had a beautiful wedding, she looked like a little doll. Michelle was her matron of honour.

"Married Michael Bell," Mary was saying. "There's an image of him; he looks pleasant."

Alice didn't recognise the man, he was far too short to be Michael Bell, but she didn't say so.

"And their issue, Thomas Michael born second of December 2003, Siena born second of November 2005 and no death dates recorded for either Michael or Lily."

"Is this the only source of records"? Alice asked, frustrated at the slowness of the process. She would have preferred to view a proper family tree. "It's quite incomplete".

"Yes, pulled from every source ever available, remember, many records were lost in the panic and confusion after the second wave of plague. So, will we try Thomas or Siena?"

Alice knew both of Lily's children. Siena wanted to travel the world. Thomas was a homebody and liked school.

"Let's try Thomas," Mary didn't wait for Alice to choose. "Here we are, married, firstly, Sharon Smith October 10, 2023, then married again, Abigail Pink January 29, 2030. I can't find any children, though. Date of death for him was second of December 2060."

"His birthday."

"So, it was. Perhaps we try Siena."

"Sen-sen," Alice drifted again, remembering aloud Siena's pet name. A sweet child. Mary looked up.

"Sen-sen," Alice repeated, "it's her nickname."

"Perhaps this isn't a good idea, Alice," Mary turned off the registry, but Alice just smiled, gave a gentle nod to the screen and urged her to continue.

It felt odd to Alice, seeing her nieces and nephews' deaths on record as if she was eavesdropping on future events, even though these events were now in the distant past.

Mary returned to the registry with some trepidation. She took a deep breath, hoping against hope this wasn't a mistake.

"Registry. Siena Anne Bell born second of November 2005. There's no marriage date, Alice, but she had a child, no, wait, two children, but the birth dates aren't recorded. Samuel and Isadora. Isadora? What sort of name is that? Anyway, the line seems to end there. There's an image of Siena, though; it's poor quality."

Alice peered for a moment at the image, but it certainly looked like Siena. Probably around forty years old, maybe less, and wearing a Red Cross uniform, holding a small, dark-skinned baby.

"I wonder what she's doing?" Alice said. "That uniform was worn by aid workers."

"I'll check. It only mentions her last recorded whereabouts as Central Africa around 2042, the information was taken from a photograph, but it doesn't say why she was there."

"Does her line end?"

"Well, we may pick it up if we try the twenty-first century. It might list some of those we've already seen and linked them elsewhere."

"I don't understand why we can't just follow the leads. How did Principal Katya find out we're related?"

"It's a different process, Alice. Principal Katya wouldn't look at our family history because there's no need; she only needed to know we had a genetic connection, how we got to that wouldn't have been of interest."

"I'm not clear why so many historical records have been lost."

"The devastation of the plague left many historical and other records unattended and in disarray. Who knows what happened? And names change. While a line may end in one place, it can appear in others. These records are not comprehensive and could be inaccurate. Let's try; common ancestor, Mary Greer living, Alexis Langley deceased, twenty-first century, sixth-decade overlap."

Several records appeared. Mary directed the registry to one area.

"There's an Isadora Daniels in Sydney in 2059, born January 1, 2020. If that's the same Isadora, then Siena had her at fifteen, my goodness! Isadora's husband was Dominic Daniels. Their children were Elise Siena, born on the twenty-second of May 2044, Simon Dominic, born on the twenty-fourth of September 2045 and Stuart Anthony, born on the third of July 2050. Isadora Daniels, Dominic Daniels, Elise Daniels deceased 2068—plague resurgence."

"Oh, they all died of plague." Alice felt sad for them; almost an entire family lost.

"Yes, and usually, if it's recorded, that's all the information they give. It leaves Simon and Stuart to follow. Which one?"

"Can the registry give a pedigree chart? We can see in one glance then. We should have tried that before."

"It wouldn't have worked, Alice, only if we can confirm the links. But we can try it if you like. Pedigree; Simon Dominic Daniels born September 24, 2045."

The registry searched and came up with similar names but no exact matches. A Simon Dominic Daniels worked for NASA in 2076, but no pedigree was available.

Mary tried the brother. "Pedigree; Stuart Anthony Daniels born third of July 2050."

And this time, a few lines emerged with the two brothers listed. Mary couldn't explain why it hadn't shown up before, but the page gave useful information.

"See," Mary displayed the chart. "It shows his mother as Isadora Daniels, born Isadora Bell. So, we're on the right track. We can follow this line, and it might lead us to where we want to go."

"It's a long way to here," Alice said, pointing to them both and glum about the gaps in the information.

"Yes, but we have a name now. Progeny previous subject," Mary commanded.

Stuart's progeny appeared. Some even had images, and Alice believed she saw a family resemblance, but harder to believe, all these people had university degrees and high positions in government and commerce. All descended from her dear Uncle David, who couldn't even spell.

Mary displayed new records, picking out the ones she believed connected them. "As we go down the list, it's clear none of them were prolific breeders. In fact, they appeared to be academics for the most part. It looks like some fell victim to the plague between 2103 and 2109, but for others, no death date is recorded. We know now the plague came in three surges, but at the time, they didn't know that. It took the A'khet to tell them."

"Did people know about the A'khet then?"

"Not until the twenty-second century. No-one even knew how long they'd been here, hidden away."

Alice returned to the pedigree, a line merged. A recent addition. She showed Mary, who grinned broadly.

"This is where the line meets with the Greer family. Only a hundred or so years ago."

"But I still don't know how I got to be here. I remember Alice Watkins and all her details but not Alexis Langley. You came down through David Hallett's line, but whose line did I come down through. And why would I have researched his sister, Joyce Hallett?"

"I can't explain it, Alice. Principal Katya told me in the beginning your memories were muddled. It's possible when you researched your family history, you found a link to Joyce Hallett. Shall we try again?"

"Yes, please."

"Ancestry, Twentieth century, Alexis Langley, prior entry."

The picture of Gran and Grandpa Hallett came up with the information they had seen earlier.

"The registry can't link a direct line here, Alice, there must be gaps, so we have to do it generation by generation."

"Try one of Alice Watkins's children. Michelle," Alice suggested.

"Of course, Michelle Watkins married Peter Campbell on the thirteenth of July 1998; then it lists the children and their birth dates. We know Eliza didn't have children. This one, Marianne, one child, no date of marriage. Her child was called Alice-Ann and has only a date of birth. Let's search Alice-Ann Campbell. No, nothing. Oh wait, date of death, this is sad. Marianne Campbell died, twentieth of April 2033 and Alice-Ann Campbell the same day, mother and daughter," Mary turned to Alice.

Marianne. Outspoken and opinionated, even for a thirteen-year-old. Dead at thirty. Michelle must have been devastated. Alice wasn't sure how she felt or even if she should feel. Was this tragic event something she would witness if she were still Alice Watkins? Marianne was a lovely girl. This should hurt, but Alice felt strangely disconnected. And Marianne had called her little girl "Alice".

"Does it say how they died?" Alice asked quietly, scanning the display.

"It often doesn't. As I said, records from the twentieth and twenty-first century are often incomplete. We're lucky to find the information we have so far. When we get to the twenty-third century, and chips get their biomechanical subroutines, records are more accurate because of the DNA."

Alice nodded. "Shall we try these, the twins?"

"This symbol," Mary pointed to a diamond shape, "is an acknowledgement of having lived, gleaned from some long-forgotten government record or another source, but no other records."

"Does it mean they died young?"

"Not at all. It just means their records were lost. We can try to pick them up in a search later in the century when we have more clues."

"What about Toby?"

Toby had told her about her chin hairs. Instinctively, her hand went to her chin.

"Toby Campbell, here, a date of birth."

But Alice remembered it. Fifteenth of March 2009.

"Twelfth of April 2009," Mary said.

Alice thought for a moment, yes, that's right, April, not March. Which one was March? No—the memory escaped her.

"He married Heather Evans on the twenty-second of January 2034. No death date recorded and no children by the look of it."

"Who was Michelle's last child?"

"Let's see. That's an Alice as well. A popular name in this family. There are several Alice's."

Michelle's new baby was a girl, and she'd named her for her grandma. Alice put her hands on her tummy; the baby had been quiet the last couple of days.

"Did that Alice have a family?"

"No records. You may be descended from the twins or Alice Campbell. It will be hard to say looking that far back. We can try directly before you were born in 2098 and head backwards."

"Okay," Alice agreed, even though this would be as emotionally fraught as researching Alice.

"Alexis Langley, deceased, parentage."

At first, Alice thought it would return no results. Then it flicked up. With images. Alexis Langley's parents. A portrait photograph, Mary turned to her, openmouthed.

"Alice, you look exactly like her!"

Alice had seen this woman in her vision at the Top of the World. The mother of Alexis Langley. All of them were right. It was reaffirmed. She could not possibly be Alice Watkins. Regardless of her memories, her uncanny knowledge of birth dates, she was an almost exact likeness of the woman in the photograph. The same green eyes, the same hair, the freckles, her build, even the style of clothes. These people were her parents, why, oh, why didn't she know them?

"Caroline and John Langley. Do you remember anything about them?"

Alice shook her head. "No, but I do look like her. I've seen her before, in a vision at the Top of the World."

"Right, let's try this; Two-generation pedigree; previous subject."

The pedigree, though incomplete, gave a vital clue. Caroline Langley's maiden name was Watkins, born on the first of April 2078. She had a brother, Martin, born eighteen years before his sister. Date of death was the same for both Caroline and John, ninth of August 2103. Alexis would have been five.

Alice wanted to get a clear picture of the events in her mind. "What happened to me then?"

"I don't know, Alice," Mary said. "I don't think anyone knows your history for certain. You were educated, that's for sure, at a time when education was difficult to obtain due to the end of the plague's final wave and the rebuilding. Principal Katya told me there's a record of your attendance at the University of New South Wales in 2116, enrolled by Martin Watkins, but you didn't graduate from there, and no-one knows what happened then until they found you in the cave."

"I knew about the university, Dr Grossmith told me. It isn't just that I was in the capsule for four hundred years; there's a whole gap in my life before then. Dr Grossmith, Dr Clere, Principal Hardy all believe Martin Watkins put me in the stasis chamber, but they aren't sure what type of research he was conducting. He seemed to have several degrees by all accounts."

"I honestly don't know, Alice, but from this, I can't find any records of Caroline Langley's parents. John Langley appears to be an only child born to a Sarah and John Langley, but after his birth, their record also stops. It could be a result of plague resurgence in 2068. At least we saw a common link between us, and you are somehow related to the Watkins family. It might explain your cryptomnesia."

"Yes, I'm okay with what we learned today. It's helped me come to terms with who I am, or rather, who I'm not. I hope in time my true memories do come back."

"We like who you are, Alice. You don't have to worry; now, there may be more images. Here's one. I'm not sure…"

Alice turned deathly pale.

"What is it?" Mary stood quickly, alarmed, and gripped Alice's shoulder, fearing she might topple from her chair. "Do you know them? You look like you've seen a ghost!"

Alice wasn't looking at the registry. She was looking up at Mary.

"My water just broke."

CHAPTER THIRTY-SIX _

No pain, no exertion, no exhaustion accompanied giving birth in the twenty-sixth century. Having delivered hundreds of babies in their careers, Jane and Mary guided the wide-eyed little girl with wispy red hair into the world. Auntie Jane placed her in Alice's arms.

"Eliza," Alice whispered as she tenderly cradled the baby's tiny body against her. "My own sweet Eliza."

"She's beautiful, Alice," Auntie Mary sat beside her. "Do you feel alright, any pain?"

Alice shook her head. "I only wish Noah were here to share in all this."

"He'll be back and thrilled and astonished all at once."

"I think he might be shocked and unprepared."

"He'll get over it, Alice," Mary kissed the baby's tiny feet and smiled, "he's out in deep space searching for new life forms. Imagine his delight when he finds out he's made one of his own back here!"

"I hope he sees the irony, Auntie Mary, but what will happen now?" Alice fidgeted nervously, and Eliza began to cry. "I should have told Principal Katya."

"It might have been a good thing you didn't while she was unwell, but Eliza needs to be chipped and immunised. You can't put it off."

"What if I decide against it?"

"You can't decide against it, Alice. Eliza wouldn't exist," Mary said. "She would have no rights and would have to hide out here in the Calamities with a pair of elderly great aunts. No laws were broken by you becoming pregnant outside of marriage, but there are specific rules now she's born."

Alice nodded. She knew she had to report the birth, she'd checked that information on the registry, but she didn't realise the immediacy in which the authorities needed that notification.

"As soon as Principal Katya contacts me, I'll tell her," Alice said.

"It can't wait, Alice," Mary could not spare Alice's feelings on this matter. "It's a felony for Jane and me to keep Eliza's birth a secret. We have to inform our principal here in Principality 19 now, today."

The information Alice read on reporting a birth never mentioned that *not* reporting was illegal.

"The registry said the parents have seven days. It said nothing about felonies."

"The attending physician notifies the principal's office, Alice. Then the parents have seven days to attend for immunisation and chipping. Jane and I are the attending physicians. We have to inform our principal."

"Will the Principal tell Noah?"

"He'll ask about the father, but the real problem arises in seven days when Noah isn't here to attend the Principality House. Both parents are required to attend, except in rare circumstances. They will almost certainly ask Principal Katya for her advice."

Alice looked down at the little bundle in her arms. All this secrecy she'd been born into.

"What if I send a message to Statesman Mellor and ask he visits us urgently?" Alice suggested. "I believe he will help us."

Mary thought for a moment, notifying a senior statesman such as Mellor would most likely be acceptable, just for today.

But it didn't happen that way. Statesman Mellor replied to the message saying that unless they required his immediate attendance, he was delighted to inform them that Principal Katya was returning the following day. He will advise her that her beloved Alice has made an urgent request for a visit. He was confident that if the problem could wait, then Principal Katya would prefer it be left to her.

And so, only a day after giving birth, Alice sat propped up in bed. Eliza, bathed and fed, slept peacefully in her arms. Alice loved that here, she could sleep with her baby, cuddle her whenever she wanted, and suffer none of the old wives' tales about teaching a baby it had to learn to settle itself, and not feed it when it was hungry because four hours hadn't passed. Such nonsense.

Mary appeared in the doorway.

"Principal Katya's shuttle has arrived, Alice." Mary knew this would be difficult, and for a fleeting moment, regretted being complicit in the secrecy surrounding Alice's relationship with the World Principal's nephew. She had to trust it would all turn out as Alice hoped. "Do you want me to take the baby while you speak to her?"

Alice tucked Eliza into her blanket and got out of bed, cradling the infant close to her.

"No, thank you, Auntie Mary. It'll be alright. This rests with me."

Alice heard Principal Katya, chirpy and restored to health, greeting Jane and enquiring what matter compelled her immediate attention. Alice went out to the parlour, hearing her footsteps, Principal Katya turned, smiling broadly, and stretched out her arms for an embrace, but her smile changed to an expression of puzzlement when she saw the bundle Alice carried, and she slowly lowered her arms to her sides.

Mary and Jane retreated wordlessly to the verandah, leaving Alice and Principal Katya alone. Principal Katya looked in silence from Alice to the baby, then reached out and took the sleeping Eliza into her arms, holding the soft little head against her cheek and closing her eyes, breathing in the sweet new baby smell. She stood in absolute wonderment, rocking the baby and examining her tiny fingers.

"A beautiful child, Alice. A girl?" she breathed, a small smile on her lips.

Alice nodded, "Eliza."

"Eliza," Principal Katya smiled down at the baby. "Eliza? I am your Great Aunt, Katya. I am very pleased to meet you," she looked up. "Alice, did you tell Noah he was to be a father?"

"No, Principal Katya."

"Don't you think he deserves to know?"

"I couldn't tell him. He was already in far side median space when I found out, and I thought he would come back, or at the very least, this would make his two years in space seem a dreadfully long time. I'm sorry I didn't tell you, Principal Katya, I kept telling myself I would, and then you became ill."

Principal Katya understood; this must have been very confusing for Alice, who herself was only recently born into this time and into this society.

"I saw you both the night before Noah left," she said. "It was no surprise, although I am not sure why it was such a secret. My nephew is dear to me, Alice, the child of my heart. His happiness is my happiness. Perhaps you can help an old lady understand why you couldn't share such joy."

She laid Eliza back in Alice's arms and drew her to the sofa. As she always did, Principal Katya took Alice's hand in hers, careful not to disturb Eliza, who dozed off again following the introductions.

"After Peru," Alice said, looking down, ashamed at not inviting her dear friend into her confidence. "I realised, for me at least, it wasn't just friendship. Noah told me later it started for him the night he saw me in the auditorium on the Significator, but I only remember running away from him."

"Did he tell you about his little act of sabotage concerning Patrick?"

"Yes, he did. Apparently, at the ball, and I don't

remember this, I told him I had no interest in Patrick, that he would never commit to a relationship and said he liked the ladies too much or something. Noah thought he was protecting me from Patrick's philandering."

Principal Katya thought back to that night when she saw her nephew follow Alice out onto the terrace. She told herself then; it would all unfold as the universe dictated.

"I saw Noah's reaction as you came down the stairs on Patrick's arm, Alice. In all these years, I never saw a glow about my nephew like the one I saw that day! Oh, there were girls here and there during aptitudes and in his university years, but he never told us of them, such things came to our ears as gossip from his sisters! His mother had quite given up hope," she laughed. "Even as a child, he always looked to space and sought what was beyond our solar system, perhaps something magnificent and splendid to discover just beyond the next star or hidden in the next nebula. I believe this time, he will find it wanting because you are here. And now, his child is here also."

"Principal Katya, I didn't want to ruin his career. When he comes back, he won't be able to pursue what I know is his lifelong passion."

"Alice, if he had learned of the baby, he would not have abandoned the mission. I accept it would have been a long two years, and he would be desperate to see you and his child, but it is his duty to stay and complete his work. I do not understand why you think having a family would ruin his career?"

"Because he must stay here, Principal Katya. I know that when a couple has a baby, the requirement is that both parents are available and only given assignments that allow them to care jointly for the child until it reaches fifteen and goes to aptitudes."

"Who told you this?" Principal Katya smiled. Alice had been misinformed.

"In my first lessons with Educator Sebel and from what I learned from the registry. There's so little on military rules, but Statesman Hennessey told me it would be a bad career move to remain on board the Significator with a wife and child."

"Alice, he was right. It would have been a bad career move—for her. Sylvia Hennessey breeds dairy cattle. Space exploration does not require dairy cattle. He continues in his profession, and he is well-matched to it. And you are wrong. There is provision for Military Principals to take their families with them. It seldom happens—and I cannot think of one instance where a child is involved, it is usually only married couples, but there is no reason to deny a principal his family. We would need to assign you, but Noah can take you with him. His career will not be affected at all. In all honesty, I believe it will be enhanced now."

"I don't understand." What a blunder! The aunties and Amelia had tried to tell her, but in her shame and panic, she'd refused to listen and now, Alice had made a difficult situation a dozen times worse.

"Military conventions are separate to public policies and not available on general registers," Principal Katya explained further. "Educator Sebel would have taught you only civilian rule. Principal Best from the Argos has his wife, a botanist, on board. They do not have children, and she is also in the military, but they are together and not the first married couple assigned to the Argos."

"But I'm not in the military, and I'm not a scientist."

"You are designated as Dr Alexis Langley. A scientist. You need not be in the military."

Tears streaked down Alice's face, "What have I done, Principal Katya?" she gulped, "Mary and Jane tried to tell me I was wrong. Even Educator Sebel said she thought wives do go on starships. I wouldn't listen. I was so frightened and ashamed. In the end, they stopped speaking of it because I got so upset." Her weeping disturbed the sleeping Eliza, who joined in with a few yells. "I've put Jane and Mary and my dear friend Amelia through all this because of my stubbornness and ignorance. I'm such a fool!"

"There, there, you are new to our ways. We will permit a few errors in judgement," Principal Katya soothed, tucking Alice's hair behind her ear and kissing her forehead. She clucked and cooed at Eliza until the baby stopped crying and turned new eyes on a few stray sunbeams.

"Your aunties appear to have forgiven any stubbornness; Principal Katya lifted a hand in the direction of the verandah, "I suspect they are delighted with the addition to their family. But I would like you to tell me the reason behind your secretive relationship with Noah. Was it to protect Patrick somehow?"

"Patrick claims he is in love with me."

Principal Katya roared with laughter, slapping her hands on her knees. "Of course, he is, my dear! Along with most of the single males at the Tabernacle!"

Alice's mouth dropped open, "Oh—I didn't know,"

this was news to Alice; she had no idea. "Noah and I didn't realise our decision to keep our relationship private would take on such gargantuan proportions. Can you forgive me, Principal Katya? Us?"

"There is nothing to forgive, Alice. Patrick is dear to us all at the Tabernacle. He was the only child brought up amongst us and believe me, he may indeed love you, but he loves all women and tires of them easily. I can't say he isn't genuine in his feelings for you; he may well be sincere. I did once wonder if he might capture your heart." She laughed and patted Alice's hand, "I believe he is capable of deep love, but you haven't responded so, he is still chasing you. I can see why Noah hesitated to tell him; Patrick would not be gracious in defeat. He was jealous when he knew you and Noah had spent time together."

"I still feel like a fool." Then Alice remembered a vital issue. "The original chip I had, Dr Grossmith didn't replace it. That's how Eliza happened. Presumably, it didn't occur to him I might start a relationship."

"Well, keeping an affair secret is one thing, but keeping a baby secret is another. I find myself mostly saddened for the two grandparents who would love to meet their new grandchild."

Ben and Selina! Alice covered her face with her hand, how stupid she had been. How selfish.

Principal Katya understood and reassured her, all the while making sure Alice was aware she disapproved of all the secrecy but forgiving her because she knew Alice had, in her innocence, did what she did to protect Noah. But now, Principal Katya took matters into her own hands. There was business to attend to, emotions must be put aside now, and her voice took on a no-nonsense, stop being self-indulgent tone that made Alice sit up straight and cease her tears.

"Our protocols naturally expect the father to be the first to know. I am vexed with Noah he didn't marry you when he realised his feelings, but I will allow him to explain himself when he returns. Now, you have both involved the World Principal in your scheming, and Eliza must receive a chip and Moses Pathogen immunisation. Both parents are required to attend for DNA sampling..." she hesitated; that couldn't happen right now, but there was a way... "Alice, may I use this registry?"

Alice had only ever seen Principal Katya taking charge in matters of food and handicraft. In matters of law and government, a different quality emerged, one of brisk efficiency and a sharp mind.

Principal Katya was no stranger to technology. She took a few seconds to bypass all privacy protocols on the home registry and tapped through to Principality 19 government administration using Tabernacle codes. A surprised, smiling face appeared.

"Councilman Sanchez," Principal Katya acknowledged the young woman.

"Principal Katya! What an unexpected pleasure, and on a coded carrier. Are you still away from the Tabernacle?"

"I am returning there soon. Councilman Sanchez, I need your help—and your discretion."

Moments later, Principal Katya turned from the registry, "Job done, Alice, it is arranged. You will attend the government building on the mainland this evening at 7. I have arranged a city shuttle and preset the coordinates. Councilman Sanchez will perform the chipping on both you and Eliza, and Eliza will receive immunisations. Now, Alice, this matter will not wait until Noah returns. Immunisation against the Moses Pathogens is important. I could give dispensation for the chipping, but two years is far too long in the absence of a marriage covenant, and questions we wish to avoid for now might be raised. I have explained to Councilman Sanchez, the father cannot attend, and this circumstance is restricted. She will encrypt the record to my personal files at the Tabernacle and embed them at the Principality once Noah is informed; barring a catastrophe, he will not find out from anyone else."

"Yes, Principal Katya. I'm sorry."

Principal Katya leaned forward and smiled, her earlier officialdom now giving way to the Principal Katya Alice was more familiar with.

"The sky isn't going to fall in, Alice, but little lies have a habit of becoming big lies, as I am sure you are now painfully aware. Jane and Mary risked a good deal on your account. Now, I will take tea with your aunties, and then I am going home to crochet the most splendid blanket for my new great-niece!"

Alice smiled her relief, then suddenly remembered, "I didn't even ask if you are feeling better!"

"I recovered, my dear, within a month of being at the monastery and then enjoyed not having to leave until it was necessary. But I did miss you and looked forward to your text links. It seems I missed all the fun! But there were no pressing matters, well, none of which I was aware, anyway, and I took advantage. Statesman Mellor coped admirably, and it was good practice for him. I need more holidays! Now I have the perfect excuse to visit you often," she bent and kissed Eliza's sleeping face.

Auntie Jane poked her head around the door to signal tea was laid out and ready for them.

"Lamingtons, I hope, or lemon meringue pie?" Principal Katya said to Alice, her eyes lighting up, "food at the retreat tastes of grass and manure. I hope Chef at the Tabernacle has prepared hamburgers for dinner!"

CHAPTER THIRTY-SEVEN _

Eliza's arrival brought Alice and the aunties indescribable joy. Principal Katya visited often, but she secretly longed for the day when Noah would learn of his child. Not telling her sister was the most difficult to endure, but Noah should know of Eliza first. She wished Ben and Selina could be part of the little girl's babyhood; it was not right she was growing up without their knowledge and their love. She prayed the Significator would return safe and sound and on time.

Meanwhile, unaware of all the fuss her arrival caused, Eliza thrived. As she learned to crawl, the dogs became accustomed to having their fur combed and preened, and the cat often slept with objects attached to his half-tail. Pecky took on the role of guardian to his new little friend, usually falling asleep on the job while Eliza napped.

By the time she turned eighteen months old, Eliza could swim, ride with Alice on Jorrocks's back and hold babbling conversations with the registry. Her hair, lighter than when she was born, was now a mix of Alice's red and Noah's fair, resulting in strawberry blonde curls. She'd inherited Noah's blue eyes and sported a determination to have her own way, a trait Alice at first couldn't pinpoint, but eventually recognised a compelling argument that this organising side of her child's nature might just come from Noah's aunt and mother.

Alice waited for news of the Significator, but the days and weeks stretched endlessly. The date the Significator was due back in median space brought hope, but it came and went, with no communication received from them in over fourteen months. The Accessor was again dispatched to patrol the border of threshold space. The Inquisitor positioned itself as close to the Significators entry to Threshold as possible to maintain open registry communication. The Argos diverted from its usual duties to be used as a supply ship, allowing the larger ships to focus on their task.

The night she heard the news an alert was issued for the Significator, Alice put Eliza to bed and walked alone on the clifftop. Above her, the stars were hidden by rainclouds; no moon skipped over the ocean, nothing to illuminate, nothing to reassure her Noah was safe and would return to her.

Summer was almost over when the Significator entered a remote area of far side median space, four months overdue. Principal Ahmed's communications team on the Accessor picked up the signal on long-range sensors several days earlier, but so far, the ship failed to answer any hails.

When the Accessor came alongside, the external damage was visible. The Significators new communications array was destroyed, which accounted for the lack of contact, and a generated field was protecting most of the aft tower. Ahmed shuttled across, fearing what awaited him.

To his relief, Principal Ryan and Statesman Patrick met him at the airlock, both men looking weary and Patrick's usual enthusiasm, notably absent.

"I'm glad to find you both alive and well," he dispensed with any formalities in finding them unharmed. He looked around. The damage to the tower extended to the bulkhead. "What happened here? We couldn't get a lock on the Significator, echoes only, it was like trying to throw a dart at a moving object."

"We'll give you a run down, Ahmed," Ryan said. "We're just glad to be back in one piece."

"We'll link the data manually, Ryan, and upload it to the Accessor," Ahmed suggested when they reached the bridge. "I doubt you'll have much in the way of communications until proximal. The Inquisitor stayed close to the mouth of Threshold where you first entered, but obviously, it can't remain there too long. I sent word to the Inquisitor and the Tabernacle when we confirmed the Significator was intact. The Inquisitor is coming across to assist, but I will also leave a few extra hands here. Ryan, we didn't know what to expect, if there were casualties or worse, and I certainly didn't expect to find you in this area of median space. It's pretty barren."

"Evesham's plan was too ambitious," Ryan said. "You're aware of the mission parameters, Ahmed, so I won't bore you. I—we," he acknowledged Patrick, "advised the Tabernacle moving away from the grid principle in an unknown region was inadvisable. Evesham disagreed, so we followed orders."

"You encountered something; that much is evident."

"It had the appearance of a cirrus dust cloud," Ryan said, "almost four billion km across. It didn't show up on any sensors until it blocked our path. We realised then; it wasn't like any stellar dust we'd encountered before." Ryan opened the registry to give Ahmed more detail; it looked like fine dust to him as well.

"It blocked our way," Ryan continued, "initial analysis proved inconclusive, so we didn't take the chance of flying through it. We came to all stop while we investigated."

"What's the source of the light emission?" Ahmed asked, pointing to a dense area in the centre of the cloud.

"We have no idea," Patrick joined in. "We launched a probe but received no telemetry, so Quintock and Junnot took a tube and flew along the perimeter. They located the probe and picked it up, dead in space, almost half a light-year away as if something spat it out."

"When did this happen? You're months' overdue."

"About nine months in," Ryan said. "After encountering the anomaly and sustaining damage, we changed course and didn't engage magnitude until we cleared the anomaly at its furthermost edge."

"We plotted a course away from the anomaly," Patrick commanded the registry to display the scale and detail of the cloud. "In following Evesham's directive, it would appear we already, and unknowingly, travelled along this edge, here," he outlined their trajectory along the longitudinal edge. "When we started moving again, we were hit with a projectile."

"A projectile? From another ship? A weapon? An asteroid from a cloud that fine wouldn't have caused this amount of damage." Ahmed studied the cloud for a clue; it looked like any cloud except for the dense nucleus.

Principal Ryan held up his hand, indicating to Ahmed he should wait for a moment before speculating further.

"Asteroids would have made sense, but this was targeted; too well placed. Another ship, hidden within the cloud was our initial thought, but our sensor readings after the attack came back garbled. Junnot's sweep of the anomaly gave up little. She said that even visually, there didn't appear to be anything concealed within it, apart from the dense area, but she reported stars being visible on the other side, so she wasn't convinced it harboured anything resembling a ship." Ryan changed the registry to a view of the aft tower.

"That single projectile caused this amount of damage. We evacuated the tower and implemented the field."

"Were you able to analyse the composition of the missile?"

"Yes." Principal Ryan sat down. "A rock."

"A rock?" Ahmed echoed.

"Yes, silicates, carbon…a simple rock."

"I suppose not unexpected in stellar dust, but how could it cause so much damage, particularly if you hadn't entered the cloud?"

"It could only be the force with which it was propelled," Patrick shrugged, but a little of his inherent good nature showed through his weariness, and he grinned. "It didn't like us spying on it."

That's better. Ahmed felt relieved. Even after all this,

it was good to see Patrick still had his sense of humour intact.

"I'm convinced the dense interior holds the key," Ryan said, "evidently there is intelligence involved, only we don't know how to communicate with it. The rock might not even have been a hostile act because, despite the force, our defences didn't respond. It makes me wonder if the attack was measured, designed to discourage our interest. Another rock came our way as a warning when we tried to reverse to go back the way we came. We had to go ahead and negotiate the opposite end of the anomaly; we decided against attempting magnitude until we cleared, but it took us light-years out of our way."

"The outcome could have been worse, Ryan. In the scheme of things, the damage isn't too bad," Ahmed pointed out as Ryan closed the registry. "Did you encounter anything else of interest?"

"We were out there to learn, Ahmed," Principal Ryan said, smiling to himself a little at the idea of anyone, particularly a man who spent his life in space, asking if there was anything interesting out there. "I suppose you might say the anomaly alone made it interesting."

"I mean other life forms?"

"No, no life forms, well not humanoid, unfortunately," Patrick spoke up. "But Ahmed, what we did find, including the anomaly, was amazing and marvellous and terrifying."

"Very poetic, Patrick."

"Until we reached the anomaly, Ahmed," Patrick said, rapidly regaining his old enthusiasm now they were in familiar territory, "it was pretty mundane, but once we were able to back away and leave, what we found on the other side was incredible. Junnot and I took a tube to a planet with oxygen-nitrogen atmosphere after our communications were knocked out. Risky, but so worth it."

"He's right, Ahmed," Ryan agreed. "That system had several planets capable of supporting life without the domes used on Mars and Kepler."

"I'll pretend you didn't tell me that, Ryan. It might put people out of work."

"Well, let's adjourn this discussion until after the official briefing at the Tabernacle."

Patrick took advantage of the change of subject. "What's the news from Earth. I feel like I've been away forever."

"Not many changes there, I'm afraid. Principal Katya finally had a holiday. A long one, a few months, the first year you were away," Ahmed momentarily forgot Principal Katya was Ryan's aunt, reminded only by the slight change in Ryan's usually impassive expression.

"She's fine, Ryan," Ahmed hastened to add. "Don't worry, she's a tough old bird and back at the Tabernacle. Other news is Lawrence Clere has been retired. Apparently, he made a fuss about Dr Langley, you know, the Sleeping Beauty, and not being able to study her. As soon as she was declassified, he petitioned the Tabernacle that he might study her; I understand Principal Katya stepped in and retired him. That stopped him. He wouldn't get any support from the wider community, anyway."

Noah knew it was Alice, not his aunt, who stopped

Clere.

"Oh, any news of her?" Patrick tried not to sound too eager.

"Who?"

"Dr Langley."

"She got married and had a baby, extraordinary in itself," Ahmed shrugged. "I don't know anything else."

Noah's heart pounded so hard he thought it might lift him from his chair. The veins in his temples throbbed, and his throat tightened, but he forced himself to appear calm and detached. Not so Patrick, who could barely stammer out the single word,

"Married?"

"So, I overheard," Ahmed continued, not noticing Patrick's shocked expression. "She was at Principality 19 with a new baby for chipping, Statesman Carr saw her. I don't know if they spoke."

"When?

"I don't know, Patrick. Recently, I suppose. I pay little attention to gossip. Didn't you have a thing with her?"

"It appears not," Patrick excused himself with his short answer, his earlier lack of humour returning. Ryan let him go, wishing he could do the same, but instead, he leaned back in his seat and lifted his left ankle onto his right knee, folding his hands across his chest, pretending disinterest and changing the subject.

"Is there other news, Ahmed?" he asked, hoping there wasn't enough to keep Ahmed here for too long, but it was several hours before he made it back to his quarters to be alone.

Married? Noah paced the room. He ran his hands through his hair, went to the washer to throw water on his face, anything to clear away the shock of Ahmed's news, but the words kept playing over in his head.

"She got married and had a baby."

He should have listened to his father and married Alice and brought her with him. How foolish to expect her to wait—she was spreading her wings, trying out her new emotions, it was only natural someone would come along and sweep her off her feet, she was beautiful and warm and sweet—but married? And not to him. And a baby?

Noah lay fully dressed on his bed, his emotions switching between disbelief and anger, then back to disbelief and dismay, but he disguised his feelings behind a wall of composure when a link came through from Ahmed.

"Ryan, I received a communication from Principal Katya. She asks you to return with us. Patrick can remain on the Significator."

Ryan could cheerfully have taken a shuttle and gone back the way he came. Anomaly or no, but instead, he just nodded.

"I'll be across in an hour, Ryan out."

At least on the Accessor, he told himself, he could speak to his aunt and casually discover what happened.

In a jolly mood, having found the Significator and having got over his initial astonishment at the news of the anomaly, Principal Ahmed was greatly looking forward to the official debriefing.

"So, Ryan, last time you got chased by aliens with

sticks, this time, they threw stones at you. What next, eh? Name-calling and face pulling? Strikes me we should send ten-year-olds up with you; they might handle it better!" Ahmed clapped Ryan on the shoulder and laughed at his joke. Ryan didn't even smile, but then, he seldom did, and Ahmed wasn't disappointed

"Ahmed, I might take an automatrans and leave now."

"You're kidding, Ryan?" Ahmed's laughter ceased abruptly. "That'll be bloody uncomfortable."

"I'll wear a support suit. I can manage forty-eight hours; I don't want to delay any further."

Ahmed didn't understand why the hurry, why he would take an automatrans from median space to Earth, but there would be no point in asking.

"Okay," he said, resigned. "Go to the mess and get some protein and then report to Dr Lascelles to check your hydration. I'll organise a suit."

"I'd prefer to get going, Ahmed. I'll be fine."

"Do you want my arse kicked out into space on the toe of a very angry World Principal's boot, Ryan? Do it, or I say no, I'm still Principal on this ship."

Ryan held his gaze for a long moment, but Ahmed didn't waver. He was in the right, and Ryan knew it.

"Very well, thanks, Ahmed."

Principal Ahmed watched him walk away. Whatever happened out in threshold space must have been very profound because he swore he heard Ryan say "thanks".

Principal Katya was delighted when she saw her nephew's

face on visual.

"Noah, we were so worried. Once the Accessor called in that you were safe, we all rejoiced."

"We're all safe, Aunt. The communications array got destroyed though, and our course, as I suspected, couldn't be controlled in the way Evesham insisted."

"Perhaps he should have listened to you."

"Perhaps, but in the end, we encountered much worthy of further study. All reports were transmitted to the Accessor. You can see for yourself in a few hours."

"I've informed your parents you are safe. What about this anomaly you encountered? Ahmed made it sound most intriguing."

Noah only wanted to ask one question, but he made himself answer hers first.

"It was intelligent, Aunt, I believe protecting something, but it wouldn't let us get close. We had to back away, slowly."

"My goodness! Well, I look forward to reading your reports. We were so long without communication and…" in her happiness to see him; she hadn't noticed. "Why are you in an automatrans, wearing a support suit and not on board the Accessor?"

"Aunt. Alice got married. You must have known."

Principal Katya hesitated. How could he know? And to have got it so wrong.

"I think it best you speak to Alice."

"We've got nothing to say to each other."

"Are you so sure?"

"You knew, didn't you?"

"If you are speaking of the secrecy you and Alice created about your relationship, yes I do. That there even *was* a relationship, well, I suspected. As no-one here has ever seen you with a woman, no-one else suspected anything between you."

"Then you know how hurt and let down I feel."

"You need to go to her, Noah."

"I'd have to think about it."

"No, Noah, I am determined. You are to go and see her. If necessary, I will have the controls on that automatrans rerouted or disabled by central command and reassigned to her aunt's home."

"I can't. What if her husband is there?"

"I know she is there with her aunties. You are to go. It is an order. You will not disobey an order from your principal."

"You don't give orders, aunt."

"I am giving one now. You *will* go."

"It will be difficult."

"More difficult than a stone-throwing alien? Noah, you have spent over two years in unknown and uncharted space, with all manner of dangers, and you are afraid to face one slip of a girl?"

"I'm not afraid of Alice, aunt. I'm disappointed and betrayed, but…" it was no use arguing. She would get her way. "Very well, I will go, then come directly to the Tabernacle."

It was difficult to see someone she loved on the bitter edge of disappointment, but all would be well, of that his aunt was sure. He had just spent two days in a cramped space suit in an automatrans faster than light speed, negotiating treacherous A-waves. If he had no intention of seeing Alice, he would have stayed on board the Accessor. Principal Katya doubted she would see him too soon after he saw Alice.

CHAPTER THIRTY-EIGHT _

On the brief, reflective journey to Alice's home, Noah deliberately dawdled, distracting himself by thinking about his time away from her. Patrick and Quintock had a short-lived affair, both quickly moving onto various others. Still, she became a valuable member of the crew, earning commendations from both the Chief Medical Officer and Statesman Junnot, who scouted the anomaly and surveyed several planets alongside her, citing her as "observant and innovative."

In private conversation, Patrick often spoke of Alice, even once telling Noah of his love for her, that the two years apart would only prove to her how much she cared for him, despite her earlier rejections.

Noah asked him casually about fidelity and met with the expected reply.

"Fidelity, Ryan? There's no requirement for me to be faithful to Alice! She rejected me. Anyway, it's just sex, a bit of fun to while away the hours. You should try it, loosen up," he'd grinned at Ryan before becoming serious. "If Alice changes her mind, I'll marry her, and it will be a whole different story. She will be my princess."

Noah listened to him making plans, regretting now he'd not taken Patrick seriously. He planned to ask Alice to marry him as soon as they were in communications range, but now—she wouldn't be marrying either of them, so no point in owning up to their relationship.

And if the news of her marriage and motherhood saddened him, he felt worse when the aunties house, perched on the cliff, came into view, a place that held so many precious memories. He brought the automatrans down silently, as far from the house as possible to avoid immediate detection and giving him time to think and plan for the hundredth time what he would say to her. Conventional words and phrases like "congratulations" or "you look well, Alice" just sounded trite and redundant. He sat for a moment, looking at the house through the forward viewport. With her, he'd been truly happy, so secure in her love for him, even with the prospect of two years apart. Now, with all his hopes dashed, the next mission couldn't come quick enough for him.

Near the stables, three figures walked toward the house. Noah peeled off his deep space support suit and climbed from the automatrans. This would have to be the most challenging walk of his life, and he kept his focus on the figures. Alice was one of them, Mary and Jane arm in arm beside her.

Alice's hair had grown so long, loose and shining in the sunlight, even from here, he saw it lifting and blowing freely in the breeze. How could she do this to him? To them? Alice's head was turned and bent towards the little figure whose hand she held.

Puzzled, he stopped. Realisation dawning, with a tiny spark of understanding as he peered across the field. That wasn't a new baby! What was Ahmed talking about? That was a toddler! Most likely born in the few months after he left. His heart hammered against his chest, and he broke into a run. The aunties saw him first and drew Alice's attention. She looked at them, then at Noah dashing across the grass.

Alice lifted Eliza into her arms and waited for him to reach her. Noah slowed as he drew close, breathing heavily from exertion, astonishment, relief. Alice had no idea about the misinformation, and his dear face looked so troubled and confused. He lifted his hands in question to her, to the child in her arms, he would have spoken, but he couldn't find the words. Eliza threw her teddy at him and giggled. In his bewilderment, he didn't catch it as it got him squarely in the chest, falling to the ground at his feet. Looking down, he bent and picked up the toy and turned it over in his hands. For all his education, for his exploring, his deep space travels, and his knowledge of far-flung planets, Principal Ryan was now faced with the most critical question the universe ever placed before him.

"How?"

But Alice had prepared herself for this moment. "The chip," she said. "It was old technology."

Of course! The chip! The chip? He didn't care; there would be time for explanations later.

He stretched out his arms. This baby, this tiny version of Alice, she was his. They were both his, these beautiful girls. Alice lifted Eliza across to him with a smile.

"Eliza, meet your daddy," Alice said and slipped herself under Noah's other arm. He held her gently at first, then pulled her against him with such force, she was lifted off the ground, and they both laughed out loud in their happiness. He kissed the top of her head, kissed the top of Eliza's head and swung them both around, his heart so full he could have wept. Space could stay where it was. He was right where he wanted to be.

That night they lay in Alice's bed, arms and legs intertwined and making up for all the time they lost over the last two years or more. Together again, they felt no awkwardness, no getting to know each other, almost as if there had been no separation. She remained faithful to her love for him, as he had for her, and he was utterly and blissfully happy. But Noah couldn't sleep because nothing he'd seen or experienced in the past two years compared with the events of the past day. He looked down at Alice, her face against his shoulder. She opened her eyes.

"You want to talk, don't you?" she murmured.

"I'm sorry, Alice, I didn't mean to wake you. I do have questions."

"I know. Ask them." Alice turned on her tummy to face him and then rested herself against his chest. He stroked her hair.

"When did you find out you were pregnant?"

"Seven weeks and a few days after you left. I had a suspicion before that, but I was just in denial."

"We were only just out of median space. Why didn't you tell me?"

"It would have made it a long two years, Noah. I remember what you said about Hennessey being desperate to get back when his baby was born. Then I was frightened to tell Principal Katya in case she told you and the secret about Patrick would come out. It was a huge mess."

"I would have resigned and come home."

"No, you wouldn't. You're more responsible than that. But I believed, wrongly, this would ruin your career."

"Why did you think that?"

"Hennessey. He told me taking his wife with him was a bad career move. Amelia told me once that parents stay with their children until they are fifteen and don't go back to full-time service until their child is in aptitudes. We tried to access military rules without success. I just continued in stubborn ignorance."

"Hennessey is a civilian married to a farmer. They barely made scale, and that was with interventions. Military rulings are different from civilian rulings; Amelia wouldn't know about military rules."

"But the Hennessey's *were* on the scale, weren't they? Otherwise, they would live in the Calamities."

"Well, yes. His wife is an agricultural scientist, but at a basic level I believe. He likes space, but he's happy to do what he's doing. He's with his wife and son."

"Yes, I've seen the baby. Lester."

"Lester? Did they call him Lester? He hates that name!" Noah laughed, fancy that. Lester.

"Noah, I have to ask. When I saw you coming across the paddock, I thought you might be angry. Did you know about Eliza?"

"Ahmed told us you'd married and had a child. Someone saw you at the Principality House here in the principality. You can imagine my disbelief, my dismay. I took an automatrans from the Accessor because I had to know for myself. Aunt Katya told me nothing and insisted I come here before I went to the Tabernacle."

"Principal Katya didn't know about Eliza until after she was born. I'm afraid I handled it all rather badly."

"It's my fault starting the whole secrecy thing in the first place. Besides, I suspect you're forgiven, although I will have some explaining to do to my parents tomorrow and, no doubt, my aunt."

"Oh, dear, yes, of course. How did Patrick react when he heard I'd married?"

"Shocked. He was sure you'd change your mind and planned to ask you to marry him. The fact that we were together before the Significator left and that Eliza is mine, well, that might be harder to explain to Patrick than my parents. The Significator isn't due for three weeks, but I'll have to contact him before that."

"Did he meet anyone on board to take his mind off me?"

"Patrick was his usual self. I thought he'd brought one of the new doctors on board because they had a history. It turns out I was wrong, but he found other companions. Sex and love mean different things to Patrick. But I believe now he was sincere in his feelings for you."

"I told him he couldn't fall in love in such a short time; then I did exactly that with you. I believed Patrick was sincere too but had I given in, I'm not sure I wouldn't eventually become one in a galaxy full of discarded floozies."

"Patrick will be okay. He's going over to the Magellan as Chief Engineer on secondment for two years. Perhaps it might be good for him and me to have time apart after all this."

"Noah, what happens now, to us. We need to consider Eliza. You're going back to space in a few months..."

"...and you are both coming with me, right?"

"We will go anywhere you go," she said, snuggling back into her favourite place, under his arm, near to his heart.

They married at Alice's home. Noah's parents attended the ceremony and fell in love with Eliza at first sight, offering no reproach to Alice about not being told of her birth. Noah's somewhat bemused sisters, Mel and Zoe, also attended, surprised that Noah had not only met someone who could put up with him, but they'd also had a child before marrying. Such a stickler for protocols all his life, they told Alice, they now viewed their brother through new eyes. Amelia and John came to help celebrate along with Dr Grossmith and Principal Hardy, who, when they learned of Eliza, good-naturedly blamed each other for the oversight regarding Alice's chip but were both glad it turned out so wonderfully.

Statesman Mellor and Principal Katya officiated, and to Alice's surprise, Patrick turned up, covering his hurt, but as always, gracious and charming. Noah made a special journey to the Significator to speak to him as they travelled home.

"I'm happy for you, Alice," he told her when they had a moment alone. "But I wish I'd known. I made an ass of myself."

"No, you didn't, Patrick, that's nonsense. Besides, there was nothing to tell until a few days before you left." She laid her hand on his arm; she hadn't set out to hurt him. "I said many times, I didn't return your feelings, that you were a dear friend to me. I hope we are still friends?"

He hesitated before hugging her, then stepped back, his gorgeous smile lighting his face.

"Yes, Alice. I should have taken you at your word or punched Ryan on the nose. Who would have thought it? That you would choose Ryan over me!"

She laughed. Patrick would be fine.

Eliza, overcome by being the centre of attention all afternoon, was exhausted by the time everyone left, and the aunties took her with them so Alice and Noah could spend time alone.

They walked along the cliff in the evening, Alice shivered and cuddled into Noah for warmth and gratitude they were finally together. But she had a favour to ask.

"Is it alright if we stay here until the next mission, Noah? Mary and Jane are so attached to Eliza."

"I already anticipated that," he said. "We don't need to be assigned accommodation. We can stay here for as long as you wish. Most of our time will be spent in space anyway if that's okay with you."

"I don't want us to be apart again, but sometimes, I

feel like I only just got here! So much has happened in the last couple of years."

CHAPTER THIRTY-NINE _

Over the next months, the Tabernacle assigned Noah command of the Magellan, and plans began for the next mission. Patrick stayed with Noah as his first officer. Junnot continued as the second officer, and a delighted Ahmed took over the Significator.

The Tabernacle agreed they would attempt the three years' mission. The Significator would explore the anomaly charted in Sector 932, and the Magellan would chart and explore Sector 933.

The time to leave Earth was upon them, and Noah was due to depart for the Magellan, with Alice and Eliza following in two days. That morning, a beautiful morning at the beginning of the Southern Hemisphere Summer, Noah and two-and-a-half-year-old Eliza, perched on her father's lap, busily explored the merits of peeled apples. Alice walked out onto the verandah, touching Noah's shoulder as she passed the back of his chair. He looked up and smiled. She walked over to the balustrade and perched herself on the rail, looking out over the paddock, lending half an ear to the goings-on at the table.

"Look, here's mummy, washed and dressed," Noah said, pointing out Alice to Eliza. "Daddy and Eliza are having breakfast, mummy. We're having apple."

Eliza didn't look up at Alice, instead gave a piece of apple skin to Pecky before trying to force another piece between Noah's lips.

Alice watched them for a moment, then looked out over the gardens. The aunties were down near the stables; Mary looked over and waved. Alice breathed in deeply and leaned her head back against the support. When had she ever felt such peace? She rolled her head ever so slightly to look at her family and sighed.

Somewhere, she remembered other children she'd loved, in a dream, ghosts of people she once thought she knew. Letting the thought go, she closed her eyes and felt the beauty of the day, the beauty of her life. A voice stole quietly across her mind, stepping on her peace.

"These are only moments in time. You must let her go."

Alice's eyes snapped open, her heart fluttering wildly. She'd heard that voice at the Top of the World, but what did it mean? She stood, startled.

Noah saw it. Settling Eliza safely on her seat, he quickly came to where Alice stood. He'd seen this before, at the Cotillion Ball, and now he held her arm, fearing she might fall.

"Are you alright, Alice?"

"I'm fine," she managed a smile but held onto his arm anyway. "I'm thinking about us leaving," she lied, not wanting to worry him. "I'll miss the aunties."

"Well, I know you would take them with you if you

could," he smiled, relieved, "and Pecky and Jorrocks…"

"Yes, I would!" she poked him in the chest, recovered. "Noah, you need to get going. Change your shirt; you've got Eliza's apple spit all over the front."

Noah looked down and frowned. "That'll teach me. Clean shirts and children don't go together."

Alice slid her arms around him and smiled at Eliza dressing Pecky in apple peel. Noah held her tightly and kissed her head. No more long separations.

"Noah," she murmured against his chest, "as we're not joining you for another two days. I would like to take a little trip."

He held her away from him.

"A trip? To where?"

"I thought to go and visit the A'khet."

Somehow, he expected this.

"Did you receive an invitation?"

"No, but they'll welcome me."

Noah thought back to their meeting with the A'khet; it seemed so long ago now, so long since Alice spoke so poetically of the effects of Knowledge. They would welcome her. Those possessed of Knowledge needed no invitation.

"Of course, sweetheart. Are you taking Eliza?" he turned to look at his daughter, now eating the much played with apple.

"I think she'll enjoy it." Alice felt it essential Eliza accompany her.

Noah changed his shirt and hugged the aunties, who tearfully kissed him goodbye, then let Eliza and Alice walk down to the shuttle alone with him.

"Are you excited about being a space wife," he grinned as Alice put her arm around his waist.

"I can't wait. It's nice there will be another family on board, though."

"I think we've ushered in a new era in space travel. Military families."

"Not before time."

He kissed Alice, then swooped Eliza up and blew raspberries on her neck until she squealed, helpless with laughter.

"See you soon. Call me when you get back and enjoy your visit with the A'khet. I'll send an automatrans to take you to Tibet."

As always, Alice waited and watched until Noah's shuttle was out of sight.

"Daddy skoy," Eliza said, pointing upwards.

"Yes, Daddy's going up in the sky, and we're going to see him there soon."

"On 'is spayship," Eliza wrinkled up her nose.

"That's right. A new spaceship," Alice still used her old-fashioned words, and Eliza was picking them up.

"I'm going to visit A'khet," Alice announced to the aunties. "Noah is organising a high altitude automatrans."

The sudden decision surprised them.

"Oh, did you get an invitation?"

"Of sorts, Auntie Mary. I think they're expecting me."

"Would you like us to keep Eliza with us?" The aunties knew it was unusual for anyone without Knowledge to turn up at the monastery, but they didn't know the full story. Alice herself didn't remember the events of her last visit fully, and Noah never spoke of it.

"I'll take her; she likes flying."

The Tabernacle automatrans arrived within a few hours, and Alice settled Eliza inside with toys for the trip, even though Eliza would most likely treat her to non-stop chatter.

"We're going to Tibet, Eliza. The first place your daddy took me," Alice told her.

"Tibbit," Eliza echoed, but as she always did, paid little attention to Alice as she became fascinated by the Earth disappearing beneath them. Alice was glad she hadn't asked for a regular shuttle. She wanted to do this quickly, finish her business with the A'khet, whatever it was, and go home. Despite all the wonderful things and events of the past three years, joining Noah on the Magellan would be the first day of the rest of her life. Everything else was just a lead-up, a preparation. She had a place now, a place she loved, as Noah's wife and Eliza's mother.

CHAPTER FORTY _

Alice lifted Eliza from the automatrans and held the wriggling child tightly in her arms, remembering the sheer drop near the landing site. Not geared for child visitors, she thought. Alice didn't take time to marvel at the scenery this time, just headed for the steps, Eliza in her arms. A female monk waited on the terrace and held out her arms to take Eliza from Alice.

"Welcome, A'khet are expecting you. We will look after the little one. I'm sure she will love the little lambies in the meadow, won't you, dear?"

"Eliza loves lambs," Alice handed over the curious child. "She loves any animals."

"There, we have lambs and lemonade. Shall we have those? Eliza, you say?" the woman took Eliza with a smile.

"Yes—Eliza." She would be safe with these lovely people, and she gave Eliza a little wave, a wave the child ignored in anticipation of lambs and lemonade.

Alice walked along the terrace, unescorted. At the far end, a lone A'khet greeted her, speaking aloud and holding the door to the small stone room where they last met.

"Alice, you brought your child. A'khet is honoured."

"I'm expected?"

"A'khet are happy you are here. Please, sit, and we will bring tea."

"Thank you. I'm sure you know why I've come?"

On cue, a monk brought in the fragrant tea she had on her last visit. This time, Alice considered it without interest.

"Your child is beautiful, Alice, and a credit to you and Principal Ryan."

"Aunt Katya told you we had a child?"

A'khet took the seat opposite her, not answering immediately. A'khet never hurried, and Alice felt no impatience, no urgency. It would unfold as surely it should.

"When you visited with our brother, Noah, A'khet sensed such a course of events would follow. But A'khet rejoices with you."

"Thank you. A'khet, who am I?" she asked simply.

"In physical form, Alexis Langley is before us."

"Why then, do you acknowledge me as Alice?"

"Alexis Langley never fully returned to us. Within her dwells the essence of another. It is this other who denies her the memories of who she truly is."

"You mean Alice Watkins?" A'khet did not respond. They didn't need to.

"It's strange, A'khet, I identified with Alice Watkins, but those feelings faded over time. I still don't remember my life as Alexis Langley or have any connection to her."

"How can you understand that which is not yours to know? A'khet sees the shadow within you, our dear sister, but it is a matter for greater powers than ours."

"Greater powers?"

Again, the question went unanswered. A'khet instead asked one of her.

"You have seen the source, the Substance, on the Significator, that which you call engines."

"I seem to remember something, yes, is it important?"

"To hear Substance sing, to see its light, requires Knowledge. You have Knowledge."

As A'khet uttered the word 'Knowledge', a memory hit her like a sledgehammer.

"I did hear them!" she cried. "I remember! They chime, like bells, or like notes on a stave, with a music of their own, or the whisper of a breeze lifting leaves as it passes through trees, and the light, A'khet, I saw it as blue, but it came to me as purple. I have never spoken of it to anyone."

A'khet smiled in understanding.

"All those who possess Knowledge receive the paralysis; they cannot share their Knowledge, other than that there is light and that there is sound. Those with other kinds of Knowledge also cannot communicate if they attempt to speak of it or make explanation. Knowledge may also be given in areas other than those which Patrick possesses."

"What I heard and saw, is it the same as Patrick hears and sees?"

"It is the same, and Substance links the communication between two people with this Knowledge. They can have no discourse on Knowledge unless Substance is present. But it will speak to them singly."

"I can't use Knowledge. I have no abilities with engineering as Patrick does."

"Because it is not necessary. Patrick combines his abilities with Knowledge. You have Knowledge of all A'khet. You are A'khet Umru."

Before Alice could ask the meaning of A'khet Umru, two other A'khet entered the room. Inclining their heads and smiling in greeting, they each placed one hand on the nape of her neck, holding their outstretched arms towards the first A'khet. A hushed reverence fell over them, even calmer and quieter than Alice felt in their presence on her previous two encounters.

A vision appeared, covering the table in front of her. A small red-haired child, a child who looked remarkably like Eliza and an old woman, someone familiar, stood in a doorway. Alice felt herself lifted high and saw a vehicle that looked like a small aeroplane, but she didn't recognise its design. A man held her, kind and funny, with patchy hair, he seemed very tall. Alice looked down at the top of his head. He smelt of unusual spices. Alice inhaled. She could smell them now.

A journey followed; he showed her pictures in a book, then he carried her up those same steps where only minutes before she'd carried Eliza. From the safety of his arms, she watched as the monks in their orange and brown robes gathered around with smiling faces. They were greeted and welcomed, and she felt the shyness of a child.

The vision fell in on itself and reappeared where the little girl ran and played, laughing as the tall man chased her and played hide and seek games with her. The monks made toys for the child and patiently taught her to read and write. Alice basked in indescribable happiness, the perfection of a happy childhood.

But then the girl, perhaps ten years old, was crying and waving goodbye to the monks and the A'khet who stood on the terrace. She was sad because they were sad, and she clung to the tall man's coat.

There was a school where the child found it hard to relate to the other schoolchildren. Her friends in her home in the mountains were secret, and no-one could ever learn of them, but once, trying to be accepted and join in with the other children, she tried to speak of them, only to find words deserted her. She cried as the other children laughed.

At first, each day after school, she went home to the tall man, Uncle Martin. They had a beautiful home. A bridge spanned the harbour close to her bedroom window. Uncle Martin liked numbers. He wrote on whiteboards and explained formulae to her. She tried to make sense of it, but it was too hard, so he would tickle her to make her laugh.

One day, he got tired and ill, and he left her. She had to live at the school, only staying at the house each school holiday with a lady Uncle Martin employed. She hated it and wondered why he didn't come for her even when she cried for him.

But one day, after many years, Uncle Martin did come, recovered. Smiling, he took her away. The girl, now a young woman, had made friends, become involved in her music, and started university. Her old life had faded, and she made up a story to protect where she came so it wouldn't ever be exposed. But Uncle Martin made her go back. She was angry and wouldn't speak to him. Her defiance reached into Alice's heart.

Alice saw roofs in the vision, like the ones she saw at the Top of the World, Chinese roofs, ornate, red and gold, and a vast building, a university. The young woman studied the sciences, learned the language, continued her music and grew to love her new life, eventually forgiving Uncle Martin. She lived at the university and remained there after she graduated, returning quietly, as often as time permitted, to the monastery, where Uncle Martin became reclusive and eccentric and struggled to keep his mind still.

For a moment, Alice found herself back in the room with A'khet but immediately sensed pain through her body, a pain which grew in intensity until she doubled over, her head touching the table. Her fingernails dug deep into the palms of her hands, her mouth opening to scream a scream which never left her lips. A'khet's hands stayed on her neck throughout her suffering.

Her head snapped up. Uncle Martin was sad. An undeniable, unbearable sadness. His face close to hers, he looked old and weary. She reached up to touch him, to comfort him, but her arm didn't move. He was carrying her up the steps, just as he had when she was a child. The monks stood about, weeping. She caught sight of her reflection in a terrace window. She had no hair, her face drawn and thin, and she saw the frailness of her body in the glass. Pain tore through the length of her spine, and she couldn't feel her legs. Joy had turned to sadness.

Although Alice had never seen any other room in the

monastery, the vision cleared to show her the room Alexis Langley stayed in throughout her years there. Uncle Martin knelt beside the bed, crying and holding her hand. He often rose to pace the floor and once, punched the wall in his anguish, then came back to hold her hands in his, blood seeping from his grazed knuckles. He held her hands against his face, begging her, willing her not to die. She felt the wetness of his tears and the weakness of her smile. He'd been so good to her.

"Dear Uncle Martin", she heard herself whisper, his sadness crushing her heart. "Don't cry. We were so happy."

As she tried again to lift her arm to comfort him, an intense peace filled her. Not like the peace of earlier in the day with Noah and Eliza, or even the peace of the A'khet. This was different. Complete and beautiful surrender to serenity. No need to breathe, no need for a heartbeat. Thoughts strayed in, her life, such a precious gift, and now, it was to end. Martin picked her up, and she rested a weary head against his shoulder.

Then the vision stopped. A'khet removed their hands from her neck and, with graceful bows, withdrew a short distance. Without their touch, their support in the vision, Alice faced the appalling grief at the sadness she witnessed.

"What happened to her?" she said, her voice barely above a whisper, unable to stop the tears slipping over her cheeks. She wiped them away with her hand.

The lone A'khet responded with gentleness, knowing this vision would bring sorrow.

"Your people give many names to the disease that would take Alexis from us. A'khet does not know disease

425

and could not help our brother Martin nor our dear daughter, whom we loved beyond our existence. A'khet could offer no cure. Our despair so great, A'khet mourned."

"How did her uncle gain knowledge in the preservation technique?" Alice knew this was leading somewhere.

"A'khet have both physical and non-physical existence. A'khet before you now is corporeal. When the time comes for renewal, our Umru renews us. We never die, we never experience sickness nor disease, and so, we never experience childhood, nor birth or the joy that is a child. As Alexis, you were to us, the dearest and loveliest being to enter our world, our existence enhanced by your presence, and our spirituality edified as we watched you grow. When the disease struck, only death would be the outcome. We could not carry the burden. A'khet had only one sacred gift to offer."

The A'khet once again solemnly placed their fingers on Alice's neck, and the vision returned.

Her body lay in a shell-like dish, hard and cold against her thin flesh and protruding bones, but she rested now, waiting for the end. She didn't have to fight to breathe anymore. Her chest rose and fell gently, the effort of past days now gone. She heard Uncle Martin sobbing as A'khet led him away. Peace descended on her, and she felt herself washed clean, the pure water of the end of life trickling into her. She heard the slow beat of her heart and imagined the blood flowing ever slower. Soon, her heart would stop its struggle; there would be no more pain—only peace, perfect peace.

Again, the vision folded in as Alice was pulled up and away. She watched as A'khet formed a semicircle around where Alexis Langley lay unmoving, many A'khet stood, each with one hand on another's shoulders, Alexis's body bathed in a glistening sac. Below her, the still body of a single A'khet. A sacrifice of Umru. From their mouths, A'khet pulled a gossamer-like thread. As the thread left their mouths, it lifted to weave itself around the capsule and Umru, forming a dome above. Alice saw the colours of Knowledge and heard its chimes. Within the sarcophagus, Alexis Langley changed from blue to purple to blue. Alice felt Alexis smile as she listened to the chiming, comforting her, speaking to her as she entered her long sleep.

A'khet saw her expression, and the vision ended.

"It spoke to you."

"Yes, more than just a light and a sound. And the peace. The serenity. No wonder science failed."

"Umru joined with your body," A'khet continued, "to protect and nourish until humankind found a cure. We are artisans; we do not cure disease, but never has A'khet Umru—renewal—joined with another species, nor has our own renewal continued for so long. The one who nourished your body never returned to us."

Alice knew A'khet would read her thoughts.

"Umru didn't return, A'khet," she said, the words never reaching her lips, "because Alexis Langley didn't return to you."

"A'khet joined with you, joyously, that your life be preserved."

She shook her head. "I'm not Alexis Langley. I'm not

the one for whom you made such a terrible sacrifice."

"A'khet made the sacrifice willingly. There is no regret."

"Can this be undone? Can Alexis return here, to her body, to her rightful place?"

Alice spoke the words aloud, more as an affirmation to herself that for so long, she had believed herself to be Alice Watkins, but then, as those memories faded, convinced herself she was truly Alexis Langley. She knew now, her first instincts were correct.

"You never truly believed you were Alexis, you are the custodian of her body, and A'khet must respect and honour this mystery."

"I thought I believed, for a while. Why didn't science suspect A'khet were involved?"

"It is a spiritual joining to the physical; there is no science. That is why Alice Watkins recognises Knowledge; she can learn its power if she chooses. When one of our chosen lays down in death, the human spirit is released from A'khet Knowledge. Within the chamber, as with your body, A'khet is bathed by the non-corporeal Umru until our bodies renew. When renewal is complete, the union dissolves, no trace is left. It is beyond human science."

"Did Uncle Martin know this?"

"Our brother Martin saw you after the renewal ritual when you were safely and peacefully sleeping. In his grief and anger, he believed the chamber would be breached, and all A'khet secrets revealed to the world. He would not be consoled. In his madness, he placed tissue samples you worked on during your visits here, and even heads of recently departed monks. He made written statements and recordings, believing this would encourage any future scientific investigation to consider more conservative techniques of his time. A'khet could not soothe his distress. He believed you had died."

"What about the capsule? I understand it was analysed?"

"Simple material from your time. Resin. Our brothers, the monks, used such vessels for growing tomatoes."

"My goodness!" Alice almost laughed. A'khet also saw the humour.

"The plague ravages other worlds," A'khet told her. "This world will never suffer the effects again, but it leaves such devastation. Your species struggled to rebuild after the final wave. Your people's spirits became low, apathy and pointlessness came over humanity, and despair clouded the world. A'khet was saddened, so we revealed ourselves to humankind. They accepted us because we offered a solution. A'khet had a purpose. On our world, long since gone, we are artisans, builders, architects. We gave Knowledge and techniques to help rebuild cities and utilities that would have taken humankind decades, possibly centuries, to restore. We removed this Knowledge, for fear of abuse, choosing only those subjects worthy of receiving it."

"And was it abused?"

"In the decades following the final wave of plague, this world formed a tolerant and accepting society. We have lived in peace and tranquillity."

"And how did I get to China after the preservation?"

"A'khet's transport lay hidden beneath the monastery. That is where A'khet placed our beloved daughter. After many decades, A'khet learned a cure for your disease was developed, but you needed to be where your people would discover you. A'khet took the transport many miles across the border to an area designated as part of a road-building project. We constructed a chamber within the rock and kept watch until you were discovered. In honour of Martin's concerns, A'khet placed the tissue samples in the chamber."

"It frightens me to think of being in that chamber alone for all those years."

"Only days. Those who found the chamber summoned the authorities and transported the capsule to their facilities with all reverence and care. But Umru did not release our beloved daughter as expected. Umru was wise and knew the cure was not the one we sought and remained bound to her. When A'khet were questioned about the preservation, we remained silent. A'khet are not gods; we could not know if Umru would save our daughter or if she might still be lost. And A'khet could not foretell how long Umru would remain with her."

"What happened to Martin Watkins?"

"He stayed with us until his death and watched over his niece. He is buried in the earth here; his resting place is behind the monastery. You visited there the first day you came back to us."

Alice remembered the rock in a meadow behind the monastery the time Noah brought her here. She'd lost time between viewing the scenery and lying on the grass near the rock but remembered gravitating towards that place.

Alice stood. There remained nothing more for her to learn here. Whatever else might still be revealed in the future, whatever explanation may come from her presence in a different time, no more would be offered by the A'khet.

"Thank you, A'khet, for all I've learned today and for your kindness and care of Martin Watkins and Alexis Langley. I hope somehow; she understands as well," Alice reached out and touched the spokesman A'khet, a gesture each A'khet received with a smile. "It saddens me," she said, "that my being here caused you to lose one of your own."

The three other A'khet stepped back for her to leave the room.

"The child, Eliza."

Alice turned. "What about her?"

"There will be a time when she will bring to humankind the knowledge to preserve those whom they cannot cure, as our dear daughter was preserved."

"But not by Umru?"

"Not by Umru, she will gain A'khet Knowledge and bring science to the world using the tools of humankind. A'khet has found a way to make this so."

"And your secret will remain safe." Alice instinctively understood. The A'khet could not offer a cure, but they could provide an opportunity for humanity to wait while it found one.

A'khet nodded. "A'khet suffer no grief now."

The monks brought a very happy Eliza back to Alice with a small shank of lamb's wool she'd woven into a ball. She showed it to everyone, enjoying being the centre of attention. Alice picked her up and made her way along the terrace as her little girl, the great scientist of the future, waved and called "bye-bye" to A'khet and the monks as they went.

CHAPTER FORTY-ONE _

As she walked along the terrace, Alice felt a quiet instinct that what passed between her and A'khet today was not the end of her search for the truth; something more would come. Soon she would learn why she'd been placed on this path, why she led a life of beauty and happiness that rightfully belonged to another. To Alexis Langley. Alice Watkins was trespassing. She looked up at the sky; it seemed bluer today. The grass greener. The air sweeter.

As she reached the top of the steps, she once again felt drawn to the meadow behind the monastery, to the resting place of Martin Watkins. Alice went through the archway and put Eliza down to play on the grass. The cluster of rocks where Martin was buried was unmarked, so she sat on the smallest, hoping Martin's grave wasn't beneath her and watched as Eliza ran off some of her boundless energy, chasing insects.

A movement in the distance caught her eye. She watched as the white-haired young man walked towards her. She'd seen him before, countless times, in dreams, on Saturn Station, at the Tabernacle, reflected in a picture at Patrick's home. She shielded her eyes from the sun to watch his approach. Each step he took sent shafts of colour swirling up from the ground, geometric shapes of many hues surrounded and moved with him. As he neared, the colours and patterns fell away. In form, he seemed little more than a child, but his eyes held wisdom, his face ageless, and now, she knew he'd stepped through dimensions to stand before her. His appearance exuded pure gentleness and light. He smiled down at her where she sat.

"Alice. I am Ariel. I have come to correct a grave error. I am here to return you."

His voice, perfect in both pitch and timbre, was a voice Alice heard before, at the Top of the World.

"You are out of time, Alice," he said as he knelt beside her. His eyes, a colour not yet known to man, held her reflection. He touched the earth, and a wheel-like structure rose. In the centre, encompassed by a shallow cup, hung a droplet of fluid-like brilliance, breathtaking in its beauty, brighter than any diamond, more glorious than any sun. Stretching outwards from the cup, shining strands, linked like a chain, reached towards a glowing outer rim.

They watched it together, and he smiled.

"The most unique of creations, Alice. Life."

Alice gazed at the hovering droplet in the centre of the wheel, drawn into its depths. When she looked at Ariel, instead of her reflection, the droplet reflected in his eyes as if it stood in her place. This symbol, this wheel, was to help her understand her place in the universe.

"The essence of life," he said, "brighter than any star, any moon or any sun, existing within the fabric of time.

Each of the links is a soul covenant, reaching from your life essence to the continuity of time at the edge of eternity."

He touched the earth, and another wheel appeared. The outer rim glowed, but the links were dull, the central life essence dim.

"Alexis," she whispered, understanding.

"A'khet spoke of the union between their corporeal and non-corporeal selves. In humankind, such a union also takes place between the spirit and the body. This union is the soul. Each spirit forms countless soul covenants on its journey to eternity. The physical body, subject to its mortality, eventually dies, severing the soul bond. It is then the spirit is released to link with a new body within the same soul group. At the time of your death, Alice, the union between your spirit and your body, ceased to exist."

"I'm dead?" Alice whispered.

He didn't answer her, only continued. "The preservation of Alexis Langley was achieved by a melding of human and A'khet. The soul union of Alexis Langley was present, but the mantle of the non-corporeal A'khet, itself a spirit form, created a quiescence, a temporary death, concealing the spirit from natural universal forces and Time. Alice Watkins died, the soul bond dissolved, and her spirit withdrew, entering another of her soul family who Time believed was near to a quickening, a birth. Alexis Langley woke, possessed of a new, unnatural soul covenant formed between Alice Watkins's spirit and the body of Alexis Langley."

"How can such an error be made? How can anyone possess two souls?" Alice shook her head.

"The life essence of the one you call Alexis Langley is now part of the ethereal canopy, A'khet is with her, and they must be released. While her life essence remains in a soul union, she cannot attain eternity nor return while her body is host to another covenant. Death is the only force that can dissolve a covenant already made, but your covenant with this body has no foundation, no veil drawn between lives, there could be no forgetting."

"That's why I remembered being Alice."

Ariel smiled. The wheel that represented Alice revolved slowly. As it did, the chains blurred, and a golden light exploded towards the heavens. As it spun, so Alexis's wheel became darker.

"Each decision made," Ariel said, "each path chosen during a lifetime changes destiny. Only one constant remains, unchangeable and eternal, and that is the destiny of the human spirit to inhabit these physical temples. Each temple is reborn countless times, and many life essences make covenants with each physicality. Your life essence has distilled many times into the physicality you now occupy; it is another of your life essence's temples, so upon release from Alice Watkins, it became drawn back to its family. It is the natural order of the universe. The soul union of Alexis Langley never dissolved because she continued to live under a mantle of concealment of A'khet Umru. The body now inhabited by Alice Watkins's spirit belongs to the soul union of Alexis Langley, although many times has your spirit been born to this existence, and yet more in worlds to come. I am here to tell you this timeline has no place in eternity and must cease."

"So, I *am* dead?" Alice knew she was thinking in primitive terms; it was impossible to comprehend the vision of eternity Ariel presented. She remembered the feeling of peace during her vision of Alexis Langley's descent towards her passing, so beautiful and profound, but now, she had so much to live for.

"Are you God?"

Ariel smiled. "No, Alice, I am a sentinel. I stand at the gate of time and eternity. I am the beginning and the end."

"And you are going to take me away from Noah and Eliza, where I have been so happy?"

Alice saw the inevitability. How could she remain? To continue walking Alexis Langley's path, imprinting her footsteps where another's should be? It would be too cruel. She'd been here long enough, borrowing joy and happiness for only a brief point in time.

Alice buried her face in her hands. "I can't bear it. Eliza is a baby. This will break Noah's heart!"

"Time will be forfeit," Ariel spoke so gently, "and they are not lost to you; they are waiting for you, but not here, not now."

"Time will be forfeit? Then none of this will have happened?"

"This error set in motion a thread never meant to be, not in accord with the universe."

"These are only moments in time," Alice spoke her thoughts aloud, and though she felt tears, she also smiled.

"We tried many times to bring an end to this. Now, you are ready to allow the life essence of Alexis Langley to return from the ethereal canopy. She must be released. You said, when you defended her rights, she was preserved so she may live.

"Will Alexis meet Noah and love him as I do?"

In answer, Alexis's wheel vanished, and Ariel once more touched the earth. Alice's wheel continued to spin, and another wheel came to life. The wheels rotated in perfect balance. Together, they formed the symbol of infinity, across the centre where the rims overlapped, geometric shapes danced and moved in glorious harmony.

"This time is forfeit. It will cease to be, but as the universe blinks, so another time is born." He smiled tranquilly, "Across the reach of eternity; you will find each other; you are forever linked."

"What happens in other timelines when A'khet Umru covers Alexis's spirit? Will this happen again? When will I come back to this body and live this life?"

Ariel didn't answer, just rose from his kneeling position. "When the veil is drawn, Alice. A'khet understood this timeline must end but time continues as it should, for you, and Alexis, within its folds."

How could she fight it? The universe and Time set these laws. Alice knew then what happened was unique. Because of her, this timeline was changed. She looked over to where Eliza laughed and played in the grass. Alice was stealing time, stealing life, and stealing from someone now straddled between worlds.

"Many choices and many paths, Alice. You will remember nothing," Ariel said as he took her hand. "Not even in dreams."

As he touched her, the coolness she so often felt back

on Saturn Station swept along her body. The brightness and the beauty of her new life faded as she called out to Eliza.

CHAPTER FORTY-TWO _

"I'm here, Grandma, it's alright," Eliza's voice drifted through the fog. She held tightly onto her grandmother's hand and called to her mother, "Mum, Grandma's awake!"

Michelle's frightened face appeared over Eliza's shoulder.

"Mum! Oh, Mum, we were so scared. Nurse! Mum's awake!" Alice heard distant hurried footsteps and urgent voices.

Gasping for breath, she tried to sit up, but her body felt heavy and weighted down, her legs straight out in front of her. What happened? She'd been sitting in the chair with Sammy on her lap, waiting for Michelle, and now she was in bed? A doctor and a nurse took Michelle and Eliza's place beside her, checking her pulse, shining lights into her eyes, adjusting tubes. She must try to smile and reassure Eliza whatever happened; her grandma is okay now, and she mustn't worry.

The doctor finished his examination and sat on the side of the bed, an older man with greying hair and a kind voice.

"Mrs Watkins? Welcome back. Can you hear me?"

Alice felt very weak; she tried to nod her head. Yes, she could hear him.

"You are in St Mary's, and you are quite safe. You've had a massive stroke," the doctor explained. "caused by an artery in your brain giving way. We call this event an aneurysm, and one such as yours carries a very high fatality rate. However…" the doctor smiled towards the side of the bed where Alice could just see Michelle and Eliza from the corner of her eye, but she didn't have the strength to turn her head. "Your son and daughter and granddaughter insisted we give you every chance after we operated and repaired the artery."

Alice tried to speak, but her mouth was too dry, and her voice hoarse, so she only managed a whisper.

"Am I—will I be alright?"

"We are hopeful. You didn't wake after the surgery, Mrs Watkins, and at times, we needed to help you breathe. At times, your heart needed some assistance. Your family," he smiled again at Michelle and Eliza, "barely left your bedside, even when we felt they should not hope."

"You started to breathe on your own two weeks ago, Grandma," Eliza said through her tears. Alice made a supreme effort to turn her head and smile at her granddaughter.

"Yes, you did," the doctor agreed, patting her hand. "Now, we are tiring you with all these explanations. You've been here a long time, and you still have some way to go."

"How long?" Alice mustered up the strength to ask.

"Nine weeks, Mrs Watkins."

Alice tried to say, 'thank you'. Nine weeks? The doctor stood and smiled broadly at Michelle and Eliza, then left the three alone.

"Nine weeks, Mum," Michelle's eyes were red from crying. "At first, if it wasn't for the occasional brain wave patterns or whatever they called them, I think they were going to give up."

"I would never let them, Grandma," Eliza said fiercely.

"The baby?" Alice remembered. Yes, there was to be a new baby.

"A little girl. We were so worried about you, Mum, we called her Alice, just in case...you know...just in case. Michelle dissolved into tears, speaking through her sobs. "Steven is here; he came straight away. He comes to sit with you in the mornings and Eliza and I come in the afternoon. We didn't want you to wake up and be alone."

Alice lifted her hand weakly, reaching out to her daughter, and Michelle collapsed forward in tears onto the bed, Alice's hand smoothing down her hair. Her hand looked withered and thin; the wedding ring Ted placed there hung loosely on her finger.

Another little granddaughter. She must get well and finish that crochet jacket before the baby grew out of it.

Five weeks after she woke, Alice gazed into her hall mirror. Her hair, cropped short from the brain surgery, had grown back into a soft bob. She liked it. It was pure white; she liked that too. She checked herself for chin hairs. Still there. Nothing a razor won't fix. Then she removed her wedding ring and placed it in the hall table drawer.

Eliza and Michelle were making up the spare bed, talking and laughing. Eliza would stay here until the family were sure Alice could manage alone. Sammy wandered around the living room, yowling, then found his favourite spot where the sun came in through the window. He looked sleek and slim from his time with Michelle, who didn't spoil him like Alice, and his new diet, which Michelle found under the sink, obviously agreed with him.

Alice sat in her chair. The branch had been cut back and wasn't tapping on the window. She reached down for her crochet; the yarn felt strange and coarse on her fingers, and she placed her work in her lap. The new baby, little Alice, had grown too big for the jacket now, anyway. She listened to Eliza and Michelle's happy laughter and sighed. So lovely to be home and to be so loved.

CHAPTER FORTY-THREE _

Added by Eliza Campbell, 23rd August 2103

I stayed with Grandma after her stroke, never living at my parent's home again. I went to university to study law and stayed with Grandma during the holidays. In 2019, my uncle Steven married a girl from Scotland, and their little boy came along in the same year. Grandma's dearest wish was to visit Scotland to see them, I agreed to go, but we didn't finally get there until the end of 2025. Grandma adored Uncle Steven's red-haired, green-eyed wife, Margaret, and when our planned three months were up, she stayed on a little longer. I knew she would be safe with Uncle Steven, but I made her promise to come home in a few months.

On the night before I was due to fly back to Australia, Grandma asked me to walk with her. I'll never forget that walk. Grandma changed so much after she woke from her coma. She learned to use a computer, threw out her entire wardrobe of old-fashioned clothes, and mum and I went with her to choose everything new. Grandma even learned to drive and bought a car, which surprised me, but not as much as the story she related that last night. I couldn't even guess where she dreamed up such an extraordinary tale.

On a freezing cold evening in a Scottish Northern Highlands park, we sat on a bench, and she took my hands in hers. I never saw Grandma so in earnest. Our breaths puffed out like steam in the light from the streetlamp, but she wouldn't go back to the house until she told me everything she needed me to hear. She said I would find what she had to say unbelievable, but I had to listen. I mustn't interrupt. She spoke of a plague soon to strike the Earth. She told me the names of family members, some not yet born, but who I would come to know and to watch for the little red-haired Alexis Langley who would be born in 2098. When I protested that I would be dead long before then, she stopped me.

"No, Eliza, you *will* see Alexis Langley."

Grandma told me I would find the complete story on her computer in her apartment, along with information about events involving family members. This information would corroborate everything she said, and to help me understand her story was not a mere flight of fancy. She begged me to promise I would not dismiss her words as imaginings, not to share them with anyone until after Alexis was born. Faced with her urgent plea, I agreed.

I returned to Australia the next day. I never saw her again.

When the plague decimated the UK in 2026, the borders were closed. Europe and Australia were affected, and only America and Asia, and parts of Africa escaped this first onslaught. Grandma and Margaret had gone to London on a weekend away at the beginning of the wave. Steven and his little boy remained in Scotland. As they lived in a remote area, they were relatively safe from the effects, but people collapsed and died in the streets in populated areas.

That's what happened to Margaret. Days passed before Uncle Steven learned of her death, and though he tried every channel available, he never received news of Grandma. There were so many deaths in London over those weeks; when he received no word from her, he had to assume that she'd become a victim. Five more years passed before Steven and his son were able to make their way to Australia.

I didn't look for the story until we gave up all hope of finding Grandma, and because I promised, I read the account. A fascinating and imaginative account, but at first, I considered it a work of fiction, notwithstanding her uncannily accurate prediction of the plague. In the story, she also mentioned my cousins, some of whom were alive when Grandma died. As years went by, their fates unfolded as she predicted with eerie accuracy, right down to the dates, including the tragedy of my sister and her daughter, who both died in a house fire.

Ariel, the messenger, told her Time made an error. But he made another. That she would not remember, but she did, all of it, and her last words to me would echo through the years.

"I couldn't take Alexis's life from her, Eliza, or the promise of future lives," Grandma said. "Time gave me a beautiful gift, and it was too brief, but it needed to be forfeit to allow her to return. That timeline was removed. The universe blinked, and it ceased to be." She smiled a faraway, wistful smile and clasped my hands to her bosom, holding them there as if in so doing, she could impart her deepest emotions, the beauty of her life with Noah Ryan. She looked young and happy that night as if she knew something was about to change, her voice clear and expressive.

"I loved him, Eliza," she closed her eyes and breathed a sigh. "With all my heart, I loved him, and now," she pressed my hand against her heart, "he is here with my other sweet Eliza, the aunties, Principal Katya, Amelia, and those wonderful people who love me. One day, at another time, I will be with them again. Write the story, even if no-one ever reads it."

So, I did, but not until after I retired as a high court judge and after a long career in politics. Before then, the story was always in my mind. Despite the "coincidences", I so often consigned it to fantasy, to Grandma's newfound fertile imagination. That scepticism continued even after Marianne's death, my logical brain telling me there was no way Grandma could have known.

But after the birth of Martin Watkins in 2060, I put pen to paper and listed the people and events as they became relevant. On the day she was born, I held Alexis Langley in my arms and stopped questioning. When Uncle Steven's great-granddaughter Caroline and her husband John died in an accident, the authorities brought Alexis to me because I was the only relative they could locate. There was an uncle, they said, who'd vanished and couldn't be found. Perhaps I knew where he was? They had no time to search, the plague was spreading, and many other little orphans needed help.

I remembered when Martin disappeared years before, a genius IQ with PhDs in physics and mathematical sciences, his brilliant, ever thinking and creative mind craved peace and quiet. Thanks to Grandma's story, I knew where to find him, so I sent for him. He would come because he was part of Alexis's story, just as much as she was part of his.

Alexis has been with me these last two weeks, but I'm too old to care for a child. Martin Watkins arrived, looking older, more peaceful. I hadn't seen him in many years. He's a gentle and kindly soul who responded to my message within two days. Even with the distress of losing his younger sister, he and Alexis bonded instantly.

As he lifted her from my arms this morning to take her to the transport, I thought I saw something in her eyes, something familiar. I thought of Ariel's words, that we live many lives repeatedly, that Grandma would be born again as Alexis Langley, part of the same soul family, that each choice determines a new path. Alexis looked at me over Martin's shoulder; I couldn't shake the sense of familiarity in her eyes.

"Grandma?" I said softly, not wanting Martin to hear and knowing that if it was her, the veil had already been drawn.

Alexis smiled her sweet smile and tilted her head to one side, studying me, her ginger curls falling in a little cascade over her uncle's shoulder. He was distracted by the pilot of the transport and didn't hear.

"I not your grandma, Auntie 'liza," she said with fierce wisdom. "I only five," and she opened and closed her little hand in farewell.

I'll never see them again. The plague is on its last rise, and I am one hundred and three years old. But it comforts me to believe Grandma has gone home, that the time was now right for her to be born as Alexis Langley, and there, in that far distant future where before she was history, Noah will be waiting.

EPILOGUE _

Eliza Ryan–80th day/2nd quarter/y2529

Registry, Eliza Ryan, diary. I cannot believe it! I'm fifteen! Are you listening registry? Blooming thing, what on earth is that rattling? Okay, I know I'm shouting. It's just that I'm so excited! I start my aptitudes in two days! I am doing agriculture first, lots of animals, I hope. We've been to see Granny and Grandad and the aunties, and now we're here with Auntie Katya. I have mummy's old room, and I can see all the way to the lake. Mother and Daddy and Matteo are feeding the ducks. Matteo still has five years before aptitudes. He is so jealous!

I thought I might do veterinary science like Granny and Grandad, but then I think I may like education or science. Educator Ryan sounds good, but so does Dr Ryan. Principal Patrick says I should go to the Galileo and be a science officer (but I think that is because he is secretly in love with mummy and knows she will come and visit). I don't know yet. I've spent most of my life in space. And now, I can do anything! Oh, my gosh! I must settle down, but I feel like jumping off the roof of the Tabernacle!

(Voice command standing by)

Okay, diary, I'm sitting quietly. Breathe, Eliza, you goose, be sensible.

I'm going to feed the ducks for the last time. Who knows when I'll get the chance again? I'll miss everyone so much, even Matteo, as much as anyone can miss a little brother! I don't expect Mother and Daddy ever had an adventure like this!

Eliza Ryan out!

END

ACKNOWLEDGEMENTS _

Thank you so much for reading The Afterlife of Alice Watkins: Book Two. If you enjoyed Alice's story, I'd love for you to pop back to your orders page and leave a review. Good reviews are the lifeblood of Indie Authors and we thank you for your support.

I would like to thank, as always, my wonderful editors, Amy and Jo, for their help and enthusiasm. I am so lucky to have them on the team!

If you would like to contact me or subscribe to my (occasional) emails for updates on new releases, please go to my webpage at https://matildascotneybooks.com/

Or connect with me on Facebook https://www.facebook.com/Offtheplanetbooks/

OTHER BOOKS BY MATILDA SCOTNEY

When my mind is not off on a quest of imaginings somewhere out in the galaxy with my trusty chihuahua sidekick, Oggie, I can be found in Australia, collecting teapots and nerding about all things Star Wars.

Printed in Great Britain
by Amazon